浙江省大学英语三级考试指南

浙江省大学外语等级考试办公室　组编

浙江大學出版社

图书在版编目（CIP）数据

浙江省大学英语三级考试指南 / 浙江省大学外语等级
考试办公室组编. —杭州：浙江大学出版社，2003.3
ISBN 7-308-03277-9

Ⅰ.浙...　Ⅱ.浙...　Ⅲ.英语—高等学校—水平考
试—自学参考资料　Ⅳ.H310.42

中国版本图书馆 CIP 数据核字（2003）第 017757 号

责任编辑　田　华
出版发行　浙江大学出版社
　　　　　（杭州天目山路 148 号　邮政编码 310028）
　　　　　（网址：http://www.zjupress.com）
　　　　　（E-mail：zupress@mail.hz.zj.cn）
排　　版　浙江大学出版社电脑排版中心
印　　刷　德清县第二印刷厂
开　　本　787mm×1092mm　1/16
印　　张　15
字　　数　403 千
版 印 次　2005 年 3 月第 2 版　2006 年 12 月第 8 次印刷
印　　数　134001—144000
书　　号　ISBN 7-308-03277-9/H・216
定　　价　22.00 元

前　言

随着我国经济和社会发展步伐的加快,特别是 2001 年正式加入 WTO 之后,社会各界对掌握宽厚扎实的知识和技能、具备国际交往能力的复合型人才的需求大大增加,这对承担人才培养任务的高等教育提出了更高的要求。因此,高校的英语教学也应在内容及方法等方面进行相应的改革,以适应时代发展的需求。

英语是高校教学中一门十分重要的课程。多年以来,浙江省广大英语教师共同努力,积极开展教改实践,认真施教,取得了良好的教学效果。在省大学英语教学研究会的大力支持下,本省开展的大学英语三级考试,也已成为检验大学英语教学效果、衡量大学专科学生掌握和运用英语知识和技能的尺度,成为促进教师改进教学方法,促进学生努力学习、提高英语能力的有效手段。本省参加大学英语三级考试的学生人数,从 1994 年的不足万人,到 2004 年的 20 万人。这从一方面充分证明了大学英语三级考试是符合本省大学专科英语教学实际的,也是符合大学专科英语教学规律的。

为适应本省高等教育发展的需要,在更大层面上满足不同类型的大学专科层次学校的英语教学需要,加强大学专科学生语用能力的培养,进一步提高大学英语三级考试的信度和效度,我们编写了《浙江省大学英语三级考试指南》一书。本书收录了浙江省高等专科英语课程教学基本要求和大学英语三级考试大纲,以及 2002 年以来浙江省大学英语三级考试试卷及试题解析。参加本书编写的有万昌盛、祝鸿平、张坚欣、蒋联海、郑亚非、朱晓蓉、沈雷燕等。

希望本书能对提高学生的英语水平有所帮助。书中若有疏漏之处,敬请广大教师学生批评指正,以便进一步修改完善。

编　者
2005 年 3 月

目　　录

浙江省普通高等专科英语课程
教学基本要求

一、教学对象

　　本教学基本要求根据教育部组织制订的普通高等专科英语课程教学基本要求,结合我省具体情况编写,适用于我省普通高等专科各专业学生。他们入学时一般应掌握英语基本语音和语法知识及 1600 个以上英语单词,并在读、听、写、说等方面受过基本的训练。

二、教学目的

　　普通高等专科英语的教学目的是:培养学生掌握必需的、实用的英语知识和应用能力,具有阅读和翻译有关专业英文资料的初步能力以及简单的英语听说和写作能力,并为进一步提高英语水平和应用能力打下一定的基础。

三、教学要求

　　根据普通高等专科教育的培养目标和特点,本课程必须在整个教学过程中突出实际应用,加强语言实践能力的培养。通过本课程的学习,应使学生达到以下几方面的要求:

1. 词汇

要求掌握 3500 个单词(包括中学掌握的 1600 个单词)以及由这些单词构成的常用词组。对其中 2000 个左右的常用词要求能正确拼写,并掌握其主要词义和用法。

2. 语法

进一步加深和扩大中学学过的语法知识,侧重其在阅读和翻译中的应用。

3. 阅读能力

掌握基本阅读技能,能看懂语言难度中等的一般题材文章、科普读物及与本专业有关的英语资料,阅读速度达到每分钟 50 个单词。

4. 翻译能力

掌握英译汉的基本方法和技巧,能借助词典将与本专业有关的英语资料译成汉语,译文达意,笔译速度达到每小时 250 个单词。

5. 听、说、写的能力

能听懂简单的对话,能进行简单的会话,能写简单的信函和应用文。

四、教学安排

普通高等专科英语课程教学应至少安排3个学期,180~220个学时,分为两个阶段。

第一阶段

第1~2学期或第1~3学期,约150个学时,侧重培养学生阅读和翻译的基本能力,重视语言共核教学,重视中英文对比,打好必需的语言知识和语言能力的基础。

第二阶段

第3学期或第4学期,约60个学时,侧重培养学生阅读和翻译与本专业有关的英语资料的能力,培养学生简单会话和写作的能力。

五、教学中需要注意的几个问题

1. 英语课应是普通高等专科教育的必修课,应保证必要的学时数,有条件的学校应做到英语课三年不断线,保持英语教学的连续性。基础阶段结束后安排一定的专业阅读课。

2. 在整个教学过程中突出实际应用,加强语言应用能力的培养。第二阶段应结合实际应用逐步过渡到专业阅读。

3. 重视语言学习规律,正确处理听、说、写与阅读、翻译之间的关系。在重点培养阅读和翻译技能的同时也应进行必要的听、说、写训练,并达到教学基本要求。

4. 积极开展高等专科英语教学研究,努力探索专科英语教学规律,不断改进教学方法,充分调动学生的积极性,提高课堂教学效果。要充分利用现代化教学手段,开展第二课堂活动,营造良好的英语学习环境。

5. 注意因材施教,对英语水平低于入学要求的学生,各校要采取措施,使他们毕业时达到本课程的教学基本要求。对入学水平较高的学生可提出较高的要求,进一步提高他们的英语水平和语言应用能力。

六、测 试

语言测试应侧重考核学生的英语实际应用能力。浙江省教育厅每年举行两次大学英语三级考试。考试要求和题型由大学英语三级考试大纲规定。

浙江省高等学校英语三级考试大纲

（高等学校专科适用）

本大纲根据教育部批转的大学英语教学大纲三级(CE-3)的要求及浙江省普通高等专科英语课程教学基本要求编写,包括大纲正文、语法结构表、词汇表和考试样卷。

一、考试对象

浙江省高等学校专科学生修完 180 学时以上的英语课程后均可报名参加按本大纲要求组织的统一考试。

二、考试标准和成绩证书

英语三级考试系标准化水平考试,考试标准相当于全日制大学英语教学大纲的三级要求。试卷成绩采用百分制,60 分为及格标准,85 分为优秀标准。成绩合格或优秀者由浙江省教育厅发给英语三级考试合格证书或优秀证书。

三、考试要求

1. 词汇

掌握 3500 个单词(包括中学掌握的 1600 个单词)以及由这些单词构成的常用词组。对其中 2000 个左右的常用词要求能正确拼写,并掌握其主要词义和用法。

2. 语法

掌握基本语法规则、结构和句型。对其中常用的规则和结构,要求能熟练应用。

3. 阅读能力

能比较顺利地阅读并正确理解语言难度为中等的文章。阅读速度达到每分钟 50 个单词,理解准确率以 70% 为合格。

4. 翻译能力

能将语言难度为中等的文章译成汉语,理解基本正确,译文达意。笔译速度达到每小时 250 个单词。

5. 听力

能听懂题材熟悉,基本上无生词的对话和短文。语速为每分钟 120 个单词,对话听一遍,短文听两遍,理解准确率以 70% 为合格。

6. 写作能力

能应用所学的词汇、词组和语法结构写出或译出简单的应用文或信函。

四、考试内容和形式

本考试包括六个部分,考试时间为 120 分钟。试卷分客观性试题和主观性试题两大类。客观性试题采用多项选择法,要求考生从每题四个选择项中选出最佳答案。主观性试题为翻译,包括英译汉和汉译英。

第一部分:听力理解(Part Ⅰ　Listening Comprehension)

共 20 题,考试时间为 20 分钟。这一部分包括两节:A 节(Section A)和 B 节(SectionB)。A 节有 10 道题,每题含一组对话,共两句,对话后有一个问句,听一遍。B 节有三篇听力材料,听两遍。每篇听力材料后有 3~4 个问题。

听力部分每个问题后都有约 15 秒的间隙,要求考生从所给的四个选择项中选出一个最佳答案。选材的原则是:

1.对话部分为日常生活中的一般对话,句子结构和内容不复杂。

2.短文部分为题材熟悉、情节不复杂的故事、对话、新闻报道等。

3.所用词语不超过本大纲所附的词汇表范围。听力理解部分主要测试学生获取口头信息和理解信息的能力。

第二部分:词汇(Part Ⅱ　Vocabulary)

共 20 题,考试时间为 15 分钟。每题有一空白,要求考生从四个选择项中选出一个最佳答案填空。词汇部分主要测试学生认识和掌握词汇及常用词组的能力。考试范围为本大纲所附词汇表的内容。

第三部分:语法结构(Part Ⅲ　Structure)

共 20 题,考试时间为 15 分钟。每题有一空白,要求考生从四个选择项中选出一个最佳答案填空。语法部分主要测试学生理解和运用语法结构的能力。考试范围为本大纲所附语法结构表的内容。

第四部分:阅读理解(Part Ⅳ　Reading Comprehension)

共 15 题,考试时间为 30 分钟。共三篇短文,每篇短文约 300 个词左右。每篇短文后有 5 个问题,考生根据短文内容从每题四个选择项中选出一个最佳答案。选材的原则是:

1.题材熟悉,包括社会文化知识、科普知识等。

2.体裁多样,包括叙述文、说明文、议论文等。

3.语言难度中等,如有超出本大纲词汇表的生词而又无法根据上下文揣测词义时,用汉语注明词义。

阅读理解部分主要测试以下能力:

1.掌握所给材料的中心大意。

2.了解说明中心大意的事实和细节。

3.既能理解字面意思,也能根据所给材料进行一定的推论和判断。

4.既能理解个别句子的意义,也能理解上下文的逻辑关系。

阅读理解部分主要测试学生通过阅读获取信息的能力,既要求准确,也要求有一定的速度。

第五部分:英译汉(Part Ⅴ　Translation from English into Chinese)

考试时间为 20 分钟。要求考生将一篇实用性短文中划线的 5 个英语句子译成汉语。主要测试学生理解、表达和实际应用能力。

第六部分：汉译英(Part Ⅵ Translation from Chinese into English)

考试时间为20分钟。要求考生将5个汉语句子译成英语。主要测试学生英语理解能力和应用能力。

试卷六个部分的题目数、计分和考试时间列表如下：

序　号	题　号	项　目	题　数	计　分	考试时间
Ⅰ	1～20	听力理解	20	20分	20分钟
Ⅱ	21～40	词　汇	20	10分	15分钟
Ⅲ	41～60	语法结构	20	10分	15分钟
Ⅳ	61～75	阅读理解	15	30分	30分钟
Ⅴ	76～80	英译汉	5	15分	20分钟
Ⅵ	81～85	汉译英	5	15分	20分钟
		合　计	85	100分	120分钟

语 法 结 构 表

13. 句子成分

主语、谓语、宾语、定语和状语及其一致关系

14. 句子种类

简单句、并列句和复合句

15. 句子类型

陈述句、疑问句(一般和特殊)、祈使句和感
叹句

16. 主语、表语和宾语从句

16.1 主语从句　16.2 表语从句

16.3 宾语从句　16.4 连接手段

16.5 It 在主语从句和宾语从句中的应用

17. 定语从句

17.1 限制性定语从句和非限制性定语从句

17.2 连接手段

17.3 the same/such . . . as

17.4 关系代词 that 的省略

17.5 特种定语从句:which/as 指代句子

17.6 定语从句的分割现象

18. 同位结构

18.1 同位语

18.2 同位语从句

19. 状语从句

19.1 表示时间

when,while,as,after,before,since,until(till),
once,as soon as,whenever

19.2 表示地点

where,wherever

19.3 表示条件

if,unless,as long as

19.4 表示让步

though, although, whether, as, even though,
even if, no matter how (what, which), whatever, while

19.5 表示原因

because,as,since

19.6 表示目的

so that,that,in order that

19.7 表示结果

so that,that,so(such) . . . that

19.8 表示方式

as,just as,as if,as though

19.9 表示比较

than,as . . . ,not so(as) . . . as,
the . . . the . . .

20. 强调句型

21. 省略

21.1 并列句中的省略

21.2 由 when,while,if,unless 等引导的从句中的
省略

21.3 as 和 than 从句中的省略

22. 倒装

22.1 neither,nor 和 so 位于句首的句子

22.2 only + 状语或状语从句位于句首的句子

22.3 here,there 等地点状语位于句首的句子

22.4 否定状语位于句首的句子

23. 构词法

23.1 词缀法:加前缀,加后缀,加前后缀

23.2 合词法

23.3 缩略法

24. 标点

词　汇　表

【说　明】

一、本词汇表收集单词 3346 个,常用词组 536 个。

二、本词汇表主要依据高等学校理工科本科用和高等学校文理科本科用两份全日制《大学英语教学大纲》的词汇表,按高等专科教育的实际需要筛选而成。

三、拼法相同的同形异义词,列在同一条下,不分立。一个单词有不同拼写形式时若拼写形式接近,列在同一词条下。如:favo(u)r＝favour,favor;centre(-ter)＝centre,center。

四、在注动词词类时,v.表示该动词既可作及物动词,也可作不及物动词;vi.表示只能作不及物动词或本词汇表中只收作不及物动词;vt.表示只能作及物动词或本词汇表中只收作及物动词。

五、词汇注有国际音标;有多种发音的,取其最常见的发音。

六、词汇表后附有词组表,供检索。词组表中的词组不注释义,可根据表中用黑体标出的词,从词汇表相应词条中找到词组释义。

※　　　　　※　　　　　※

A

a [ei], **an** [æn, ən]
art. 一,任一,每一

abandon [əˈbændən]
v. 1. 放弃
2. 离弃,抛弃

ability [əˈbiliti]
n. 1. 能力
2. 才能,才干

able [ˈeibl]
a. 1. 有能力的,有才干的
2. 显示出才华的
be ～＋to V. 能,会

aboard [əˈbɔːd]
ad. 在船(飞机,车)上,
上船(飞机,车)
prep. 在(船,飞机,车)上,上船
(飞机,车)

about [əˈbaut]

prep. 1. 在……周围
2. 关于,对于
ad. 1. 周围,附近,到处
2. 大约
be ～＋to V. 即将

above [əˈbʌv]
prep. 高于,在……之上
a. 上面的,上述的
ad. 以上,在上面

abroad [əˈbrɔːd]
ad. 到国外,在国外

absence [ˈæbsəns]
n. 1. 不在,缺席
2. 缺乏,没有

absent [ˈæbsənt]
a. (from)不在的,缺席的

absolute [ˈæbsəluːt]
a. 完全的,绝对的

absorb [əbˈsɔːb]
vt. 吸收

be ～ed in 专心于
abstract [ˈæbstrækt]
a. 抽象的
n. 摘(提)要
vt. 提(抽)取

abuse [əˈbjuːz]
n. & *v*. 1. 滥用
2. 辱骂

academic [ˌækəˈdemik]
a. 1. 学院的
2. 学术的

accent [ˈæksənt]
n. 1. 口音,腔调
2. 重音

accept [əkˈsept]
vt. 1. 接受,领受
2. 同意,承认

acceptable [əkˈseptəbl]
a. 可接受的

access [ˈækses]

n. 1. 接近,进入
　　2. 接近(或进入)的方法
have/gain ～ to 可以获得

accident [ˈæksidənt]
n. 事故,意外的事
by ～ 偶然

accompany [əˈkʌmpəni]
vt. 1. 伴随,陪同
　　 2. 为……伴奏

accomplish [əˈkɔmpliʃ]
vt. 完成

according [əˈkɔːdiŋ]
～ to 按照,根据

account [əˈkaunt]
n. 1. 账,账户
　　2. 叙述,说明
vi. 说明
～ for 说明(原因等)
on ～ of 因为
take into ～ 考虑

accuracy [ˈækjurəsi]
n. 准确(性),精确(性)

accurate [ˈækjurit]
a. 准确的,精确的

accuse [əˈkjuːz]
vt. (of)控告,谴责

ache [eik]
vi. 痛
n. 痛,疼痛

achieve [əˈtʃiːv]
vt. 1. 完成
　　 2. 达到,得到

achievement [əˈtʃiːvmənt]
n. 1. 完成,达到
　　 2. 成就,成绩

acid [ˈæsid]
n. 酸
a. 酸的

acquire [əˈkwaiə]
vt. 1. 取得,获得
　　 2. 学到

across [əˈkrɔs]
prep. 1. 横过,穿过
　　　 2. 在……对面,
　　　　 与……交叉
ad. 1. 横过,穿过

　　　 2. 宽,阔

act [ækt]
vi. 1. 行动,做事
　　 2. (on)作用
n. 行为,动作

action [ˈækʃən]
n. 1. 行动,行为,活动
　　2. (on)作用于

active [ˈæktiv]
a. 1. 有活动力的,积极的,
　　　 活跃的
　　2. 在活动中的

activity [ækˈtiviti]
n. 1. 活动
　　2. 活性,活力

actor [ˈæktə]
n. 男演员

actress [ˈæktris]
n. 女演员

actual [ˈæktjuəl]
a. 实际的,现实的

A.D. (*Anno Domini*)
公元

adapt [əˈdæpt]
vi. (to)适应
vt. 1. 使适应,使适合
　　 2. 修改,改编

add [æd]
vi. (to)加,增加
vt. 补充说,又说
～ up to 合计,总计

addition [əˈdiʃən]
n. 1. 加,加法
　　2. 附加,附加物
in ～ 另外
in ～ to 除……之外

additional [əˈdiʃənl]
a. 附加的,另外的

address [əˈdres]
n. 地址
vt. 1. 写姓名、地址
　　 2. 向……讲话

adequate [ˈædikwit]
a. 足够的,充分的

adjective [ˈædʒiktiv]
n. 形容词

adjust [əˈdʒʌst]
vt. 调整,调节,校正

administration
[ədminisˈtreiʃən]
n. 1. 管理,经营
　　2. 行政部门
　　3. [A-](美国的)政府

admire [ədˈmaiə]
vt. 钦佩,赞美

admission [ədˈmiʃən]
n. 1. 准许进入,准许加入
　　2. 承认,供认

admit [ədˈmit]
vt. 1. 让……进入
　　 2. 承认

adopt [əˈdɔpt]
vt. 1. 采用,采纳
　　 2. 收养

adult [ˈædʌlt]
a. 成年人的,已成熟的
n. 成年人

advance [ədˈvɑːns]
vi. 前进,进展
vt. 1. 推进
　　 2. 提出(建议等)
　　 3. 提前

advanced [ədˈvɑːnst]
a. 高级的,先进的

advantage [ədˈvɑːntidʒ]
n. 1. 优点,长处
　　2. 利益
gain/have an ～ over 胜过,优于
take ～ of 利用,趁……之机

adventure [ədˈventʃə]
n. 1. 冒险
　　2. 奇遇

adverb [ˈædvəːb]
n. 副词

advertisement [ədˈvəːtismənt]
n. 广告

advice [ədˈvais]
n. 劝告,(医生等的)意见

advise [ədˈvaiz]
vt. 劝告,建议

affair [əˈfεə]
n. 事情,事件

affect [əˈfekt]

vt. 1. 影响

2. 感动

afford [əˈfɔːd]

vt. 担负得起

afraid [əˈfreid]

a. 1. (of)怕,害怕

2. 恐怕,担忧

Africa [ˈæfrikə]

n. 非洲

African [ˈæfrikən]

a. 非洲的,非洲人的

n. 非洲人

after [ˈɑːftə]

prep. 在……以后,在……后面

ad. 以后,后来

afternoon [ˈɑːftəˈnuːn]

n. 下午,午后

afterward(s) [ˈɑːftəwəd(z)]

ad. 后来,以后

again [əˈgen, əˈgein]

ad. 又,再

against [əˈgenst, əˈgeinst]

prep. 1. 逆,对着,反对

2. 倚在,紧靠

3. 对比

age [eidʒ]

n. 1. 年龄

2. 时期,时代

vi. 变老,老化

agency [ˈeidʒənsi]

n. 1. 代理行,经销处

2. (政府等的)专业行政部门

agent [ˈeidʒənt]

n. 代理(人/商),经纪人

ago [əˈgəu]

ad. 以前

agree [əˈgriː]

vi. (to, with)同意,赞成

agreement [əˈgriːmənt]

n. 1. 同意,一致

2. 协定,协议

agriculture [ˈægrikʌltʃə]

n. 农业

ahead [əˈhed]

ad. 在前,向前,提前

~ of 在……前面

aid [eid]

vt. 援助,帮助

n. 1. 援助,帮助

2. 助手,辅助设备

AIDS [eidz]

n. 艾滋病

aim [eim]

vi. (at, for) 1. 瞄准,对准

2. 致力,旨在

vt. 1. 把……瞄准,把……对准

2. 使针对,使旨在

n. 目标,目的

air [ɛə]

n. 空气,大气

vt. 通风

aircraft [ˈɛəkrɑːft]

n. 航空器,飞机

airline [ˈɛəlain]

n. 航空公司

airplane [ˈɛəˌplein]

n. 飞机

airport [ˈɛəpɔːt]

n. 机场,航空港

alarm [əˈlɑːm]

n. 警报

vt. 1. 使惊恐

2. 向……报警

alike [əˈlaik]

a. 相同的,相像的

alive [əˈlaiv]

a. 活着的

all [ɔːl]

a. 所有的,全部的

pron. 一切,全部

ad. 完全地,十分

above ~ 首先,首要

after ~ 终于,毕竟

~ but 1. 几乎,差一点

2. 除……之外,其余都是

~ over 遍及,到处

in ~ 总共

not at ~ 一点也不

allow [əˈlau]

vt. 1. 允许,准许

2. 让……得到

vi. (for)考虑到

almost [ˈɔːlməust]

ad. 几乎,差不多

alone [əˈləun]

ad. 1. 单独地,独自

2. 只,只有,仅仅

a. 单独,独一无二

along [əˈlɒŋ]

prep. 沿着

ad. 向前

~ with 与……一起

aloud [əˈlaud]

ad. 高声地,大声地

alphabet [ˈælfəbit]

n. 字母表

already [ɔːlˈredi]

ad. 已经

also [ˈɔːlsəu]

ad. 1. 也,同样

2. 而且,还

alter [ˈɔːltə]

v. 变更,改变

although [ɔːlˈðəu]

conj. 尽管,虽然

altogether [ˌɔːltəˈgeðə]

ad. 1. 完全,全部地

2. 总共

3. 总而言之

alumin(i)um [əˈljuːminəm]

n. 铝

always [ˈɔːlweiz]

ad. 1. 永远,始终

2. 一直,总是

a.m. (*ante meridiem*)

上午,午前

amaze [əˈmeiz]

vt. 使惊奇,使惊愕

ambulance [ˈæmbjuləns]

n. 救护车

America [əˈmerikə]

n. 1. 美洲

2. 美国

American [əˈmerikn]

a. 美洲的,美国的,美洲人的,美国人的

n. 美洲人,美国人

among [ə'mʌŋ]
prep. 在……中间,在……之中

amount [ə'maunt]
n. 数量,总额
vi. (to)合计,总计

amuse [ə'mju:z]
vt. 逗……笑,娱乐

analysis [ə'næləsis]
n. 分析,分解

analyze(-yse) ['ænəlaiz]
vt. 分析,分解

ancient ['einʃənt]
a. 古代的,古老的

and [ænd]
conj. 1. 和,与
　　2. 那么
　　3. 连接,又

anger ['æŋɡə]
n. 怒,愤怒

angle ['æŋɡl]
n. 1. 角
　　2. 角度,方面

angry ['æŋɡri]
a. 1. 发怒的,愤怒的
　　2. (风雨等)狂暴的

animal ['æniməl]
n. 动物,牲畜

ankle ['æŋkl]
n. 踝

announce [ə'nauns]
vt. 宣布,发表

annoy [ə'nɔi]
vt. 使烦恼,打搅

annual ['ænjuəl]
a. 每年的,年度的
n. 年刊,年鉴

another [ə'nʌðə]
a. 1. 再一,另一
　　2. 别的,不同的
pron. 另一个,类似的一个

answer ['ɑ:nsə]
vt. 回答,答复
vi. (for)负责,保证
n. 回答,答案

ant [ænt]
n. 蚁

anxious ['æŋkʃəs]
a. 1. (about)忧虑的,焦急的
　　2. 渴望的

any ['eni]
a. 1. 什么,一些
　　2. 任何的,任一的
pron. 无论哪个,无论哪些,一个,一些
ad. 稍微,丝毫

anybody ['eni,bɔdi]
pron. 1. 任何人
　　2. 无论什么人

anyhow ['enihau]
ad. 1. 不管怎样,无论如何
　　2. 不论用何种方法

anyone ['eniwʌn]
pron. = anybody

anything ['eniθiŋ]
pron. 1. 什么事(物),任何事(物)
　　2. 无论什么事(物),一切
~ but 除……以外任何事(物),并不,决不

anyway ['eniwei]
ad. = anyhow

anywhere ['eniwɛə]
ad. 任何地方,无论哪里

apart [ə'pɑ:t]
ad. 1. (from)除去,撇开
　　2. 分开,分离
　　3. 相隔,相距

apartment [ə'pɑ:tmənt]
n. 房间,套间

apologize(-ise) [ə'pɔlədʒaiz]
vi. 道歉,认错,谢罪

apology [ə'pɔlədʒi]
n. 道歉,认错

apparent [ə'pærənt]
a. (to)明显的,显而易见的

appeal [ə'pi:l]
vi. (to) 1. 呼吁,要求
　　2. (对……)有吸引力
　　3. 上诉,申诉
n. (to) 1. 呼吁,要求
　　2. 吸引力
　　3. 上诉,申诉

appear [ə'piə]
vi. 1. 出现,显露
　　2. 露面,来到
　　3. 看似,好像

appearance [ə'piərəns]
n. 1. 出现,显露
　　2. 外貌,外观

appetite ['æpitait]
n. 1. 食欲,胃口
　　2. 欲望,爱好

apple ['æpl]
n. 苹果

application [,æpli'keiʃən]
n. 1. 请求,申请,申请表
　　2. 应用,运用
　　3. 施用,敷用

apply [ə'plai]
vi. 1. (for)申请,请求
　　2. (to)适用
vt. (to)应用,运用

appoint [ə'pɔint]
vt. 1. 任命,委派
　　2. 约定,确定,指定(时间,地点)

appointment [ə'pɔintmənt]
n. 1. 约会,预约
　　2. 任命

appreciate [ə'pri:ʃieit]
vt. 1. 感谢,感激
　　2. 正确评价,欣赏

approach [ə'prəutʃ]
v. 靠近,接近,临近
n. 方法,途径

appropriate [ə'prəupriit]
a. (to)适当的,恰如其分的

approve [ə'pru:v]
vi. (of)赞成,满意
vt. 批准,通过

approximately [ə'prɔksimətli]
ad. 近似地,大约

April ['eiprəl]
n. 四月

area ['ɛəriə]
n. 1. 面积
　　2. 地区,区域
　　3. 范围,领域

argue [ˈɑːgjuː]

　　vi. 争论,辩论

　　vt. 说服

argument [ˈɑːgjumənt]

　　n. 1. 争论,辩论

　　　　2. 论据,论点

arise [əˈraiz]

　　vi. 出现,发生

arithmetic [əˈriθmətik]

　　n. 算术

arm [ɑːm]

　　n. 1. 臂

　　　　2. [pl.]武器,军火

army [ˈɑːmi]

　　n. 1. 军队,陆军

　　　　2. 大群,大批

around [əˈraund]

　　ad. 1. 各处

　　　　2. 在周围,在附近

　　　　3. 大约

　　prep. 在……周围,在……附近

arrange [əˈreindʒ]

　　vt. 整理,排列,布置

　　vi. 作安排,准备

arrest [əˈrest]

　　vt. & *n*. 逮捕,拘留

arrival [əˈraivəl]

　　n. 1. 到来,到达

　　　　2. 到达者

arrive [əˈraiv]

　　vi. 到,来到

　　～ at 达到,得出

arrow [ˈærəu]

　　n. 1. 箭

　　　　2. 箭头符号

art [ɑːt]

　　n. 1. 艺术,美术

　　　　2. 技术,技艺

　　　　3. [pl.]人文学科

article [ˈɑːtikl]

　　n. 1. 文章,论文

　　　　2. 物品,商品

　　　　3. 项目,条款

　　　　4. 冠词

artist [ˈɑːtist]

　　n. 艺术家,美术家

as [æs]

　　prep. 作为,如同

　　conj. 1. 像……一样

　　　　　2. 由于,鉴于

　　　　　3. 当……的时候

　　　　　4. 虽然,尽管

　　pron. 1. 像……样的人(物),凡

　　　　　　是……人(物)

　　　　　2. 这一点

　　ad. 一样,同样

　　～…～ 像……一样

　　～ for 至于,就……方面说

　　～ if 好像,仿佛

　　～ to 至于,关于

　　～ well 也,又

　　～ well ～ (除……之外)也,

　　　　既……又

ash [æʃ]

　　n. 灰,灰烬

ashamed [əˈʃeimd]

　　a. (of)羞耻的,惭愧的

Asia [ˈeiʃə]

　　n. 亚洲

Asian [ˈeiʃən]

　　a. 亚洲的,亚洲人的

　　n. 亚洲人

aside [əˈsaid]

　　ad. 在旁边,到旁边

　　～ from 除……以外

ask [ɑːsk]

　　vi. 1. 问,询问

　　　　2. 要求,请求

　　vt. 邀请,请

asleep [əˈsliːp]

　　a. 睡着的,睡熟的

aspect [ˈæspekt]

　　n. 1. 样子,外表,面貌

　　　　2. (问题等的)方面

assembly [əˈsembli]

　　n. 1. 集合

　　　　2. 装配

　　　　3. 集会

assist [əˈsist]

　　v. 援助,帮助

assistance [əˈsistəns]

　　n. 援助,帮助

assistant [əˈsistənt]

　　n. 助手,助教

　　a. 辅助的,助理的

associate [əˈsəuʃieit]

　　vt. (with)使发生联系,使联合

　　vi. (with)交往,结交

　　n. 合作人,同事

　　a. 副的

association [əˌsəusiˈeiʃən]

　　n. 1. 协会,社团

　　　　2. 联合,联系,交往

assume [əˈsjuːm]

　　vt. 1. 假定,设想

　　　　2. 采取,呈现

assure [əˈʃuə]

　　vt. 1. 使确信,使放心

　　　　2. 保证,担保

astonish [əsˈtɔniʃ]

　　vt. 使惊讶

astronaut [ˈæstrənɔːt]

　　n. 宇航员

at [æt, ət]

　　prep. 1. 在……时

　　　　2. 在,到……处

　　　　3. 对着,向

　　　　4. 在……方面

　　　　5. [表示速度,价格等]以

athlete [ˈæθliːt]

　　n. 运动员,体育家

Atlantic [ətˈlæntik]

　　a. 大西洋的

　　n. [the ～]大西洋

atmosphere [ˈætməsfiə]

　　n. 1. 大气,大气层

　　　　2. 空气

　　　　3. 气氛,环境

　　　　4. 大气压(压力单位)

atom [ˈætəm]

　　n. 原子

attach [əˈtætʃ]

　　vt. (to)缚上,系上,贴上

　　be ～ed to 附属于,隶属于

attack [əˈtæk]

　　vt. & *n*. 1. 攻击,进攻

　　　　　　2. 着手,开始

attain [əˈtein]

vt. 达到,获得

attempt [ə'tempt]

 vt. 尝试,试图

 n. (at)企图,努力

attend [ə'tend]

 vt. 出席,参加

 v. 照顾,护理

 vi. (to)专心,留意

attention [ə'tenʃən]

 n. 注意,留心

attitude ['ætitjuːd]

 n. (to, towards)态度,看法

attract [ə'trækt]

 vt. 吸引,引起(注意等)

 vi. 有吸引力

attractive [ə'træktiv]

 a. 有吸引力的,引起兴趣的

audience ['ɔːdjəns]

 n. 听众,观众,读者

August ['ɔːgəst]

 n. 八月

aunt [ɑːnt]

 n. 姨母,姑母,伯母,婶母,舅母

Australia [ɒs'treiljə]

 n. 澳洲,澳大利亚

author ['ɔːθə]

 n. 作者

authority [ɔː'θɔriti]

 n. 1. 权威,权力

  2. [pl.]当局,官方

  3. 权威者,有权威性的典籍

automatic [ˌɔːtə'mætik]

 n. 自动机械

 a. 1. 自动的

  2. 无意识的,机械的

automobile (auto)

 ['ɔːtəməbiːl](['ɔːtəu])

 n. 汽车

autumn ['ɔːtəm]

 n. 秋,秋季

available [ə'veiləbl]

 a. 1. 可用的,可得到的

  2. 可以见到的,随时可来的

avenue ['ævinjuː]

 n. 林阴道,大街

average ['ævəridʒ]

n. 平均数

 a. 1. 平均的

  2. 平常的

 vt. 平均

on (the / an) ~ 平均,一般说来

avoid [ə'vɔid]

 vt. 避免,回避

awake [ə'weik]

 vi. 醒,觉醒

 vt. 唤醒

 a. 警觉的,醒的

award [ə'wɔːd]

 vt. 1. 授予,给予

  2. 判给,裁定

 n. 奖,奖品,奖金

aware [ə'wɛə]

 a. (of)意识到的,知道的

away [ə'wei]

 ad. 1. 离,离开

  2. ……去,……掉

  3. 不断……下去

right ~ 立即,马上

awful ['ɔːful]

 a. 1. 可怕的,令人敬畏的

  2. 极度的,极坏的

awfully ['ɔːfuli]

 ad. 非常,很

ax(e) [æks]

 n. 斧

B

baby ['beibi]

 n. 婴儿

back [bæk]

 n. 背,背面,后面

 a. 后面的

 ad. 1. 在后,向后

  2. 回,回原处,回原状

  3. 以前

 v. (使)后退,倒退

 vt. 支持

~ and forth 来来往往地,来回

background ['bækgraund]

 n. 背景

backward ['bækwəd]

 ad. 向后

a. 向后的

bacteria [bæk'tiəriə]

 n. (bacterium 的复数)细菌

bad [bæd]

 a. 1. 坏的,恶的

  2. 低劣的,拙劣的

  3. 不舒服的

  4. 腐败的

badly ['bædli]

 ad. 1. 坏,恶劣地

  2. 严重地,非常

bag [bæg]

 n. 袋,包

baggage ['bægidʒ]

 n. 行李

bake [beik]

 v. 1. 烤,烘,焙

  2. 烧硬,焙干

balance ['bæləns]

 v. (使)平衡

 n. 1. 天平,秤

  2. 平衡,均衡

ball [bɔːl]

 n. 1. 球,球状物

  2. 舞会

~ point pen 圆珠笔

balloon [bə'luːn]

 n. 气球

ban [bæn]

 vt. 1. 取缔,查禁

  2. 禁止

 n. 禁止,禁令

banana [bə'nɑːnə]

 n. 香蕉

band [bænd]

 n. 1. 带,箍带

  2. (管)乐队

  3. 波段

bank [bæŋk]

 n. 1. 岸,堤

  2. 银行,库

bar [bɑː(r)]

 n. 1. 酒吧间,餐柜

  2. 条,杆,棒

  3. 栅栏,障碍物

 vt. 阻挡,拦住

barber [ˈbɑːbə]

n. 理发师

bare [bɛə]

n. 1. 赤裸的,无遮蔽的
　 2. 稀少的

vt. 露出,暴露

bargain [ˈbɑːgin]

n. 1. 廉价货
　 2. 交易

vi. 议价,成交

barrel [ˈbærəl]

n. 桶

barrier [ˈbæriə]

n. 1. 栅栏,屏障
　 2. 障碍,障碍物

base [beis]

n. 1. 基础,底部
　 2. 根据地,基地

vt. (on)把……基于,
　　 以……为根据

basic [ˈbeisik]

a. 基本的,基础的

basin [ˈbeisn]

n. 1. 盆,脸盆
　 2. 盆地

basis [ˈbeisis]

n. 基础,根据

on the ~ of 根据,
　　 在……的基础上

basket [ˈbɑːskit]

n. 篮,篓

basketball [ˈbɑːskitbɔːl]

n. 篮球

bat [bæt]

n. 1. 短棒,球棒,球拍
　 2. 蝙蝠

bath [bɑːθ]

n. 1. 浴,洗澡
　 2. 浴缸

v. [英](给)……洗澡

bathe [beið]

vt. [美](给)……洗澡

vi. (在河、海里)游泳,洗澡

bathroom [ˈbɑːθruːm]

n. 1. 浴室
　 2. 盥洗室

battery [ˈbætəri]

n. 电池(组)

battle [ˈbætl]

n. 战役,战斗,斗争

v. 斗争,搏斗

bay [bei]

n. 海湾,湾

be [biː, bi]

vi. 1. 是
　 2. 在,存在
　 3. 到达,来到
　 4. 发生

aux. v. 1. [与动词的现在分词连
　　　　 用,构成各种进行时
　　　　 态]
　　　 2. [与及物动词的过去分
　　　　 词连用,构成被动语
　　　　 态]

beach [biːtʃ]

n. 海滩,湖滩,河滩

beam [biːm]

n. 1. 梁,桁条
　 2. (光线的)束,柱

bean [biːn]

n. 豆,蚕豆

bear [bɛə]

vt. 1. 负担,负荷,承担
　 2. 忍受,容忍
　 3. 结(果实),生(孩子)

n. 熊

beard [biəd]

n. 胡须

beast [biːst]

n. 1. 兽,家畜
　 2. 凶残的人,举止粗鲁的人

beat [biːt]

v. 打,敲

vt. 打败,战胜

vi. (心脏等)跳动

n. 1. 敲打,敲击声
　 2. (心脏等)跳动

beautiful [ˈbjuːtəful]

a. 美的,美好的

beauty [ˈbjuːti]

n. 1. 美,美丽
　 2. 美人,美的东西

because [biˈkɔz]

conj. 因为

~ of 由于

become [biˈkʌm]

vi. 成为,变得

bed [bed]

n. 1. 床
　 2. 苗床,花圃,河床,矿床

bee [biː]

n. 蜂

beef [biːf]

n. 牛肉

beer [biə]

n. 啤酒

before [biˈfɔː]

prep. 1. 在……以前
　　 2. 在……前面,
　　　 当着……的面

conj. 在……以前

ad. 以前,前面

beg [beg]

v. 1. 乞求,乞讨
　 2. 请求,恳求

begin [biˈgin]

vi. (with)从……开始

vt. 开始,着手

beginning [biˈginiŋ]

n. 开始,开端

behave [biˈheiv]

vi. 1. 举动,举止
　 2. 运转

behavio(u)r [biˈheivjə]

n. 1. 举止,行为
　 2. (机器的)特性

behind [biˈhaind]

prep. 在……后面

ad. 在后,向后

being [ˈbiːiŋ]

n. 1. 生物,人
　 2. 存在,生存

belief [biˈliːf]

n. 1. 相信,信心
　 2. 信仰,信条

believe [biˈliːv]

vt. 1. 相信
　 2. 认为

vi. (in)相信,信仰

bell [bel]

n. 钟,铃

belong [bi'lɔŋ]

vi. (to) 1. 属于,附属

2 应归入(类别,范畴等)

below [bi'ləu]

prep. 在……下面,在……以下

ad. 在下面,向下

belt [belt]

n. 1. 带,皮带

2. 地带

bench [bentʃ]

n. 长凳

bend [bend]

v. (使)弯曲

n. 弯曲,弯曲处

beneath [bi'ni:θ]

prep. 在下边

benefit ['benifit]

n. 利益,好处

vt. 有益于

vi. (from, by)受益

beside [bi'said]

prep. 1. 在……旁边,

在……附近

2. 与……相比

besides [bi'saidz]

prep. 除……之外

ad. 而且,还有

best [best]

a. 最好的

ad. 1. 最好地

2. 最

at ~ 充其量,至多

do /try one's ~ (+ to V.) 尽力

get the ~ of 胜过

make the ~ of 充分利用

bet [bet]

v. 1. 打赌

2. 敢说,肯定

better ['betə]

a. 较好的,更好的

ad. 更好地

for the ~ 好转,改善

get the ~ of 打败,智胜

had ~ 最好还是

between [bi'twi:n]

prep. 在(两者)之间

beyond [bi'jɔnd]

prep. 1. 在(或向)……的那边,

远于

2. 迟于

3. 超出

bible ['baibl]

n. 1. [B-]圣经

2. 有权威的书

bicycle (**bike**) ['baisikl] ([baik])

n. 自行车

big [big]

a. 1. 大的,巨大的

2. 重要的,重大的

bill [bil]

n. 1. 账单

2. 纸币

3. 议案,法案

billion ['biljən]

num. 十亿

bind [baind]

vt. 捆,绑

biology [bai'ɔlədʒi]

n. 生物学

bird [bə:d]

n. 鸟,禽

birth [bə:θ]

n. 1. 出生,分娩

2. 出身,血统

birthday ['bə:θdei]

n. 生日

biscuit ['biskit]

n. 饼干,点心

bit [bit]

n. 一点,一些,小片

bite [bait]

v. & *n*. 咬,叮

bitter ['bitə]

a. 1. 有苦味的

2. 痛苦的,厉害的

black [blæk]

a. 1. 黑的,黑色的

2. 黑暗的

n. 1. 黑人

2. 黑色

blackboard ['blækbɔ:d]

n. 黑板

blame [bleim]

v. 1. 指责,责备,责怪

2. (on, onto)归咎于,

把……归咎于

n. 1. (过错,事故等的)责任

2. 责备,指责

blank [blæŋk]

a. 1. 空白的,空着的

2. 失色的,没有表情的

n. 1. 空白

2. 表格

blanket ['blæŋkit]

n. 毛毯,毯子

blast [blɑ:st]

n. 1. 一阵(风),一股(气流)

2. 爆炸,冲击波

vt. 爆炸,爆破

bless [bles]

vt. 1. 祈求上帝赐福于,祝福

2. (with)赐福,降福

3. 保佑

blind [blaind]

a. 1. 瞎的

2. 盲目的

vt. 使失明

block [blɔk]

n. 1. 大块,大块木料(石料,金

属)

2. 一排房屋,街区

3. 阻塞,障碍物

vt. 阻塞,拦阻

blood [blʌd]

n. 1. 血,血液

2. 血统,家庭,门第

blow [bləu]

v. 1. 吹,充气

2. 吹响(乐器,号角等),吹风

n. 打,一击,打击

blue [blu:]

a. 1. 蓝色的,天蓝色的

2. 沮丧的,忧郁的

n. 蓝色

board [bɔ:d]

n. 1. 木板,板

    2. 全体委员,委员会,部门

    3. 伙食

    4. 船舷

vt. 上(船,车,飞机)

on ~ 在船(车,飞机)上

boat [bəut]

n. 小船,艇

body ['bɔdi]

n. 1. 身体,躯体,本体

    2. 尸体

    3. 物体

boil [bɔil]

v. (使)沸腾,煮

bold [bəuld]

a. 1. 大胆的,勇敢的

    2. 黑体的,粗体的

bolt [bəult]

n. 1. 螺栓

    2. (门窗的)插销

v. 闩(门),拴住

bomb [bɔm]

n. 炸弹

vt. 投弹于,轰炸

bond [bɔnd]

n. 1. 结合(物),粘结(剂),联结

    2. 公债,债券

bone [bəun]

n. 骨

book [buk]

n. 1. 书,书籍

    2. 卷,篇,册

vt. 预订,订(戏票,车票,房间等)

boot [buːt]

n. (长统)靴

border ['bɔːdə]

n. 1. 边界,国界

    2. 边,边沿

vt. 1. 与……接壤

    2. 接近

bore [bɔː]

v. 钻(孔),挖(洞)

vt. 使厌烦

n. 惹人厌烦的人(物)

boring ['bɔːriŋ]

a. 令人厌烦的,乏味的,无聊的

born [bɔːn]

a. 出身于……的

borrow ['bɔrəu]

v. 借,借入

boss [bɔs]

n. 工头,老板,上司

both [bəuθ]

pron. 两者,双方

a. 两,双

~ ... and 既……又,两个都

bother ['bɔðə]

vt. 烦扰,打扰

vi. 烦恼,操心

n. 麻烦

bottle ['bɔtl]

n. 瓶

bottom ['bɔtəm]

n. 1. 基础,根基

    2. 底部,底

    3. 海底,湖底,河床

boundary ['baundəri]

n. 分界线,边界

bow [bau]

v. 鞠躬,点头

n. 弓

bowl [bəul]

n. 1. 碗,钵

    2. 碗状物

box [bɔks]

n. 箱,盒

v. 拳击

boy [bɔi]

n. 男孩

brain [brein]

n. 1. 脑

    2. [常 pl.]脑力,智能

branch [brɑːntʃ]

n. 1. 枝,分枝

    2. (机构的)分部,分支

    3. 支流,支脉,支线

brand [brænd]

n. 商标,(商品的)牌子

brass [brɑːs]

n. 1. 黄铜

    2. 铜管乐器

brave [breiv]

a. 勇敢的

bread [bred]

n. 面包

breadth [bredθ]

n. 宽度

break [breik]

v. 打破,打断,破碎

vt. 1. 使中止,打断

    2. 破坏,破除

n. 休息时间

~ down 损坏

~ off 断绝,结束

~ out 逃出

~ up 1. 中止,结束

    2. 打碎,分解

breakfast ['brekfəst]

n. 早餐

breath [breθ]

n. 气息,呼吸

breathe [briːð]

v. 呼吸

breed [briːd]

vt. (使)繁殖

vi. 教养,抚养

n. 品种,种类

brick [brik]

n. 砖

bride [braid]

n. 新娘

bridge [bridʒ]

n. 桥,桥梁

brief [briːf]

a. 简短的,简洁的

vt. 简短介绍,简要汇报

in ~ 简单地说,简言之

bright [brait]

a. 1. 明亮的,辉煌的

    2. 欢快的

    3. 聪明的,伶俐的

brilliant ['briljənt]

a. 1. 光辉的,辉煌的

    2. 卓越的,才华横溢的

bring [briŋ]

vt. 1. 带来,拿来

    2. 引起,导致

~ about 带来,造成

~ down 1. 打倒,挫伤
　　　　2. 降低

~ forth 产生,提出

~ forward 提出

~ up 教育,培养,使成长

broad [brɔːd]

　　a. 1. 宽的,广阔的
　　　　2. 广大的,广泛的

broadcast ['brɔːdkɑːst]

　　v. 广播
　　n. 广播,广播节目

brother ['brʌðə]

　　n. 兄弟

brow [brau]

　　n. 眉,眉毛

brown [braun]

　　a. 褐色的,棕色的
　　n. 褐色,棕色

brush [brʌʃ]

　　n. 1. 刷子,毛刷
　　　　2. 画笔
　　vt. 刷,掸,拂

bubble ['bʌbl]

　　n. 泡,水泡,气泡
　　vi. 冒泡,沸腾

bucket ['bʌkit]

　　n. 水桶,吊桶

budget ['bʌdʒit]

　　n. 预算,(专项)经费
　　vt. 1. 计划(资金、时间的分配等)
　　　　2. 按预算安排(某项资金)

build [bild]

　　vt. 建造,建筑,建设
　　~ up 1. 积累,堵塞
　　　　2. 树立,逐步建立
　　　　3. 增进,锻炼

building ['bildiŋ]

　　n. 1. 建筑物,房屋
　　　　2. 建筑

bullet ['bulit]

　　n. 子弹

bunch [bʌntʃ]

　　n. 束,捆,串

bundle ['bʌndl]

　　n. 捆,束,包

burden ['bəːdn]

　　n. 担子,负担

burn [bəːn]

　　vt. 燃烧,烧伤,灼伤
　　n. 烧伤,灼伤
　　~ up 1. 烧起来,旺起来
　　　　2. 烧完,烧尽

burst [bəːst]

　　v. 爆裂,炸破
　　n. 突然破裂,爆发

bury ['beri]

　　vt. 1. 埋葬
　　　　2. 埋藏,遮盖

bus [bʌs]

　　n. 公共汽车

bush [buʃ]

　　n. 灌木,灌木丛

business ['biznis]

　　n. 1. 商业,生意
　　　　2. 事务
　　on ~ 因事,因公

busy ['bizi]

　　a. 1. 忙的,繁忙的
　　　　2. (with)忙于……的
　　vt. 使忙于

but [bət, bʌt]

　　conj. 但是,可是,而
　　prep. 除了
　　ad. 只,仅仅
　　~ for 如果没有,若非

butter ['bʌtə]

　　n. 黄油
　　vt. 涂油于……上

button ['bʌtn]

　　n. 1. 钮扣
　　　　2. 按钮(开关)
　　v. 扣紧,扣上钮扣

buy [bai]

　　v. 买
　　n. 购买,买卖

by [bai]

　　prep. 1. 在……旁边,靠近
　　　　2. 被,由
　　　　3. 经过……旁边
　　　　4. 不迟于,到……时(为止)

　　　　5. 根据,按
　　ad. 在近旁,经过

C

cabbage ['kæbidʒ]

　　n. 卷心菜

cabin ['kæbin]

　　n. 1. 客舱,机舱
　　　　2. 小屋

cable ['keibl]

　　n. 1. 电报
　　　　2. 缆,索,钢丝绳
　　　　3. 电缆

café ['kæfei, kæ'fei]

　　n. 咖啡馆,小餐厅

cage [keidʒ]

　　n. 笼

cake [keik]

　　n. 饼,糕,蛋糕

calculate ['kælkjuleit]

　　v. 计算
　　vt. 计划,打算

call [kɔːl]

　　v. 1. 叫,喊
　　　　2. 打电话(给……)
　　vt. 把……叫做,称呼
　　vi. (on, at)访问,拜访
　　n. 1. 叫,喊
　　　　2. 打电话,通话
　　　　3. 访问
　　~ for 1. 邀约
　　　　2. 要求,需要
　　~ forth 1. 唤起,引起
　　　　2. 振作起,鼓起
　　~ off 放弃,取消

calm [kɑːm]

　　a. 1. (天气,海洋等)静的,平静的
　　　　2. 镇静的,沉着的
　　v. (使)平静,(使)镇定

camel ['kæməl]

　　n. 骆驼

camera ['kæmərə]

　　n. 照相机

camp [kæmp]

　　n. 野营,阵营

vi. 设营,宿营

campaign [kæm'pein]

　　n. 战役,运动

campus ['kæmpəs]

　　n. (大学)校园

can [kæn, kən]

　　aux. *v*. 1. 能,会

　　　　　　2. 可以

　　　　　　3. 可能

　　n. 罐头

canal [kə'næl]

　　n. 运河,沟渠

cancel ['kænsəl]

　　vt. 1. 取消,把……作废

　　　　　2. 删去,划掉

cancer ['kænsə]

　　n. 癌

candle ['kændl]

　　n. 蜡烛

candy ['kændi]

　　n. 糖果

cap [kæp]

　　n. 1. 便帽,军帽

　　　　2. 盖,罩,套

　　vt. 覆盖于……顶端

capable ['keipəbl]

　　a. 1. 有能力的,有才能的

　　　　2. (of) 可以……的,

　　　　　能……的

capacity [kə'pæsiti]

　　n. 1. 容量,容积

　　　　2. 能力

capital ['kæpitəl]

　　n. 1. 首都,首府

　　　　2. 大写字母

　　　　3. 资本

　　a. 首位的,最重要的,基本的

captain ['kæptin]

　　n. 1. 首领,队长

　　　　2. 船长

　　vt. 做……的首领,指挥

capture ['kæptʃə]

　　vt. & *n*. 捕获,俘获

car [kɑ:]

　　n. 1. 车,汽车

　　　　2. (火车)车厢

carbon ['kɑ:bən]

　　n. 碳

card [kɑ:d]

　　n. 1. 卡片

　　　　2. 纸牌

care [kɛə]

　　n. 1. 小心,谨慎,注意

　　　　2. 关怀,照料

　　vi. 1. (for, about)关心,介意

　　　　2. (for)喜欢,愿意

　　　　3. (for)关怀,照料

　　take ～ 小心,当心

　　take ～ of 照料,照顾

career [kə'riə]

　　n. 生涯,职业

careful ['kɛəful]

　　a. 1. 仔细的,小心的

　　　　2. 细致的,精心的

careless ['kɛəlis]

　　a. 粗心的,疏忽的

cargo ['kɑ:gəu]

　　n. 船货,货物

carpenter ['kɑ:pintə]

　　n. 木工,木匠

carpet ['kɑ:pit]

　　n. 地毯

carriage ['kæridʒ]

　　n. 1. (四轮)马车

　　　　2. (火车)客车厢

carry ['kæri]

　　vt. 1. 提,抱,背,挑,扛

　　　　2. 运送,运载

　　　　3. 传送,刊登

　　～ off 夺去

　　～ on 继续下去

　　～ out 贯彻,执行,实现

cart [kɑ:t]

　　n. (二轮运货)马车,手推车

case [keis]

　　n. 1. 箱,盒,容器

　　　　2. 情况,事实

　　　　3. 病例

　　　　4. 案件

　　in any ～ 无论如何,总之

　　in ～ 免得,以防(万一)

　　in ～ of 假使,万一

in no ～ 决不

cash [kæʃ]

　　n. 钱,现款

　　vt. 把……兑现

cassette [kə'set]

　　n. 1. 盒子

　　　　2. 盒式磁带

cast [kɑ:st]

　　vt. 1. 投,扔,抛

　　　　2. 铸造

castle ['kɑ:sl]

　　n. 城堡

casual ['kæʒuəl]

　　a. 1. 漠不关心的,冷淡的

　　　　2. 随便的,非正式的

cat [kæt]

　　n. 猫

catch [kætʃ]

　　vt. 1. 捕捉,捕获

　　　　2. 赶上

　　　　3. 感染

　　　　4. 理解,听到

　　～ up with 赶上

cattle ['kætl]

　　n. 牛

cause [kɔ:z]

　　vt. 使产生,引起

　　n. 1. 原因,理由

　　　　2. 事业,事件

cave [keiv]

　　n. 洞穴

cease [si:s]

　　v. 停止,中止

ceiling ['si:liŋ]

　　n. 天花板

celebrate ['selibreit]

　　vt. 庆祝

cell [sel]

　　n. 1. 细胞

　　　　2. 小室

　　　　3. 电池

cement [si'ment]

　　n. 1. 水泥

　　　　2. 胶泥,胶结剂

　　vt. 1. 胶合

　　　　2. 巩固,加强

cent [sent]

  n. 1. 分(货币单位)

    2. 百

  per ～ 百分之……

centigrade ['sentigreid]

  a. 1. 摄氏温度计的

    2. 百分度的

centimetre(-ter) ['senti,mi:tə(r)]

  n. 厘米

central ['sentrəl]

  a. 1. 中心的,中央的

    2. 主要的

centre(-ter) ['sentə]

  n. 1. 中心,中央

    2. 中心区

  v. 集中

century ['sentʃuri]

  n. 世纪,(一)百年

ceremony ['seriməni]

  n. 1. 典礼,仪式

    2. 礼节,礼仪

certain ['sə:tən]

  a. 1. 某,某一,某种

    2. (of)一定的,确信的

certainly ['sə:tənli]

  ad. 一定,必定

certificate [sə'tifikit]

  n. 证书,执照

chain [tʃein]

  n. 1. 链(条)

    2. [常 pl.]镣铐

    3. 一连串,一系列

    4. 联号,连锁店

  vt. 用链条拴住

chair [tʃɛə]

  n. 1. 椅子

    2. 主席

chairman ['tʃɛəmən]

  n. 主席

chalk [tʃɔ:k]

  n. 粉笔

challenge ['tʃælindʒ]

  n. 挑战

  vt. 向……挑战

champion ['tʃæmpjən]

  n. 胜利者,冠军

chance [tʃɑ:ns]

  n. 1. 机会

    2. 可能性

    3. 偶然性,运气

  vi. 碰巧,偶然发生

  by ～ 偶然,意外地

change [tʃeindʒ]

  n. 1. 改变,变化

    2. 零钱,找头

  v. 1. 改变,变化

    2. 兑换

    3. 更换,调换

channel ['tʃænl]

  n. 1. 海峡

    2. 频道

    3. 路线,途径

chapter ['tʃæptə]

  n. 章,章节

character ['kæriktə]

  n. 1. 性格,品质

    2. 特性,特征

    3. 人物,角色

    4. 字符,(汉)字

characteristic [,kæriktə'ristik]

  a. (of)特有的,表示特性的

  n. 特性,特征

charge [tʃɑ:dʒ]

  vt. 1. 索(价),要(人)支付

    2. 控告,指控

    3. 充电

  n. 1. [常 pl.]费用,代价

    2. 电荷

  in ～ of 负责,主管

  take ～ of 担任,负责

chart [tʃɑ:t]

  n. 图,图表

chase [tʃeis]

  v. & n. 追逐

chat [tʃæt]

  vi. & n. 聊天,闲聊

cheap [tʃi:p]

  a. 1. 便宜的

    2. 低劣的

cheat [tʃi:t]

  vt. 欺骗

  vi. 作弊

check [tʃek]

  vt. 1. 检查,核对

    2. 制止

  n. 1. 方格图案,格子织物

    2. = cheque 支票,账单

  ～ in (在旅馆/机场等)登记,

    报到

  ～ out 结账离去,办妥手续离去

cheek [tʃi:k]

  n. 面颊,脸

cheer [tʃiə]

  vt. (使)振奋,(使)高兴

  v. 喝彩,欢呼

cheerful ['tʃiəful]

  a. 愉快的,高兴的

cheese [tʃi:z]

  n. 乳酪,干酪

chemical ['kemikəl]

  a. 化学的

  n. [常 pl.] 化学制品,化学药品

chemist ['kemist]

  n. 1. 化学家

    2. 药剂师

chemistry ['kemistri]

  n. 化学

cheque [tʃek]

  n. 支票,账单

chest [tʃest]

  n. 1. 胸腔,胸膛

    2. 箱,柜

chew [tʃu:]

  vi. 咀嚼,咬

chicken ['tʃikin]

  n. 1. 小鸡

    2. 鸡(肉)

chief [tʃi:f]

  a. 主要的,首席的

  n. 首领,领袖

child [tʃaild]

  n. 小孩,儿童

childhood ['tʃaildhud]

  n. 童年

chill [tʃil]

  n. 寒冷,寒气

chimney ['tʃimni]

  n. 烟囱

chin [tʃin]

n. 颏，下巴

China ['tʃainə]

n. 1. 中国

2. [c-]瓷器

Chinese ['tʃai'niːz]

a. 1. 中国的，中国人的

2. 中国话的，汉语的

n. 1. 中国人

2. 中国话，汉语

chocolate ['tʃɔkəlit]

n. 1. 巧克力，巧克力糖

2. 赭色

choice [tʃɔis]

n. 1. 选择，抉择

2. 供选择的种类，选择项

a. 精选的，上等的

choose [tʃuːz]

v. 选择，挑选

Christmas ['krisməs]

n. 圣诞节

church [tʃəːtʃ]

n. 1. 教堂

2. 教会(组织)

cigaret(te) [ˌsigə'ret, 'sigəˌret]

n. 纸烟，烟卷

cinema ['sinimə]

n. 1. 电影院

2. 电影，影片

circle ['səːkl]

n. 1. 圆，圆周

2. 圈子，集团

v. 环绕，旋转

circumstance ['səːkəmstəns]

n. 1. [pl.]情况，形势，环境

2. [pl.]境况，境遇

citizen ['sitizn]

n. 1. 公民

2. 市民，(城市)居民

city ['siti]

n. 城市，都市

civil ['sivl]

a. 1. 公民的，市民的

2. 文职的

3. 民用的

civilization(-isation)

[ˌsivilai'zeiʃən]

n. 文明，文化

claim [kleim]

vt. 1. 要求

2. 声称，主张

n. 1. 要求

2. 主张，断言

clap [klæp]

vi. 拍手

vt. 拍，轻拍

n. 拍(手)

clash [klæʃ]

vi. 发生冲突

n. 冲突

class [klɑːs]

n. 1. 班级，年级

2. (一节)课

3. 阶级，阶层

4. 等级，类别

vt. 把……分类，把……分等级

classical ['klæsikəl]

a. 古典的，经典的，古典文学的

classify ['klæsifai]

vt. 分类，分等级

classmate ['klɑːsmeit]

n. 同班同学

classroom ['klɑːsrum]

n. 教室，课堂

clay [klei]

n. 粘土，泥土

clean [kliːn]

a. 1. 清洁的，干净的

2. 清白的

v. 打扫，使干净

clear [kliə]

a. 1. 清晰的，明白的

2. 晴朗的

3. 清澈的，明亮的

4. 畅通的，无阻的

vt. 1. 扫清，清除

2. 使清澈，使清楚

~ away 扫除，收拾

~ up 1. 整理，收拾

2. 消除，解除

clerk [klɑːk, kləːk]

n. 1. 职员，办事员

2. 店员

clever ['klevə]

a. 聪明的，机敏的

cliff [klif]

n. 悬崖，峭壁

climate ['klaimit]

n. 气候

climb [klaim]

v. & n. 攀登，爬

clinic ['klinik]

n. 门诊部，诊所

clock [klɔk]

n. 钟

close [kləuz]

v. 关，闭

a. 1. (to)近的，接近的

2. 不公开的，秘密的

3. 紧密的，严密的

4. 关闭着的

cloth [klɔ(ː)θ]

n. 布，织物，衣料

clothes [kləuðz]

n. 衣服

clothing ['kləuðiŋ]

n. [总称]服装，衣着

cloud [klaud]

n. 1. 云

2. 遮暗物，阴影

cloudy ['klaudi]

a. 多云的，阴天的

club [klʌb]

n. 1. 俱乐部，夜总会

2. 棍棒

clue [kluː]

n. 线索，提示

coach [kəutʃ]

n. 1. (铁路)客车，长途公共
汽车，大客车

2. 辅导员，教练

v. 教练，指导，辅导

coal [kəul]

n. 煤，煤块

coarse [kɔːs]

a. 粗糙的，粗劣的

coast [kəust]

n. 海岸，海滨

coat [kəut]

　n. 1. 外套,上装

　　　 2. 皮毛,表皮,涂层

　vt. 涂上,盖上,包上

cock [kɔk]

　n. 1. 公鸡

　　　 2. 龙头,开关

code [kəud]

　n. 1. 准则,法规

　　　 2. 密码,代码

coffee [ˈkɔfi]

　n. 1. 咖啡

　　　 2. 咖啡色

coin [kɔin]

　n. 硬币

　vt. 铸造(硬币)

cold [kəuld]

　a. 1. 寒冷的

　　　 2. 冷淡的

　n. 1. 感冒

　　　 2. 寒冷

collar [ˈkɔlə]

　n. 1. 衣领

　　　 2. 环状物

colleague [ˈkɔliːg]

　n. 同事,同僚

collect [kəˈlekt]

　vt. 收集,搜集

　vi. 聚集,堆积

collection [kəˈlekʃən]

　n. 收藏(品),收集(物)

college [ˈkɔlidʒ]

　n. 学院,高等专科学校

colo(u)r [ˈkʌlə]

　n. 1. 颜色,彩色

　　　 2. 颜料

　　　 3. 肤色

　vt. 给……着色,染

column [ˈkɔləm]

　n. 1. 圆柱

　　　 2. 列

　　　 3. (报刊中)的专栏

comb [kəum]

　n. 镜子

　vt. 梳

combination [ˌkɔmbiˈneiʃən]

　n. 1. 结合,联合,合并

　　　 2. 化合,化合物

combine [kəmˈbain]

　v. (with) 1. (使)结合,

　　　　　　　　(使)联合

　　　　　　 2. (使)化合

come [kʌm]

　vi. 1. 来,来到

　　　 2. 出现于

　　　 3. 是,成为

　　　 4. 开始,终于

　~ off 1. 实现,成功

　　　　 2. 脱离,脱落

　~ on 1. 跟着来

　　　　 2. 进展,发展

　~ out 1. 出现,显露

　　　　 2. 被解出

　~ to 总计,达到

　~ up 1. 走近,上来

　　　　 2. 发生,被提出

　~ up to 达到,符合

　~ up with 提出,提供

comfort [ˈkʌmfət]

　n. 1. 舒适,安逸

　　　 2. 安慰

　vt. 安慰,使舒适

comfortable [ˈkʌmfətəbl]

　a. 舒适的

command [kəˈmɑːnd]

　n. 1. 命令,指令

　　　 2. 统帅,指挥(权)

　v. 1. 命令

　　　 2. 指挥,统帅

commander [kəˈmɑːndə]

　n. 司令员,指挥员

comment [ˈkɔment]

　n. 注释,评论

　vi. (on) 注释,评论

commercial [kəˈməːʃəl]

　a. 商业的,贸易的

　n. 商业广告

commission [kəˈmiʃən]

　n. 1. 委员会

　　　 2. 委任,委托

　　　 3. 佣金

commit [kəˈmit]

　vt. 1. 把……交托给,提交

　　　 2. 犯(错误),干(坏事)

committee [kəˈmiti]

　n. 委员会

common [ˈkɔmən]

　a. 1. 普通的,平常的

　　　 2. (to) 共同的

　in ~ 共同

communicate [kəˈmjuːnikeit]

　vt. 传达,传送

　vi. 1. 交流,交际,沟通

　　　 2. 通讯,通话

communication [kəˌmjuːniˈkeiʃn]

　n. 1. 通讯,传达,传送

　　　 2. 交流,交际,沟通

　　　 3. [pl.] 通讯系统

communism [ˈkɔmjunizəm]

　n. 共产主义

communist [ˈkɔmjunist]

　n. 共产主义者,共产党员

　a. 共产主义的,共产党员的

community [kəˈmjuːniti]

　n. 1. 同一地区的全体居民,

　　　　 社区

　　　 2. 共同体

companion [kəmˈpænjən]

　n. 同伴,共事者

company [ˈkʌmpəni]

　n. 1. 公司

　　　 2. 陪伴

　　　 3. (一)群,(一)队,(一)伙

　　　 4. 连,连队

compare [kəmˈpeə]

　vt. 1. (with, to) 比较,对比

　　　 2. 比作

comparison [kəmˈpærisn]

　n. 比较,对比,比拟

　by ~ 比较起来

compass [ˈkʌmpəs]

　n. 1. 罗盘,指南针

　　　 2. [pl.] 圆规

compete [kəmˈpiːt]

　vi. 1. 竞争

　　　 2. 比赛

competition [ˌkɔmpiˈtiʃən]

　n. 1. 比赛

2. 竞争

complain [kəm'plein]

v. 1. (about, of)抱怨

2. 投诉

complete [kəm'pliːt]

a. 完全的,圆满的

vt. 完成,使完满

complex ['kɔmpleks]

a. 1. 复杂的

2. 合成的,综合的

n. 联合体

complicated ['kɔmplikeitid]

a. 复杂的,难解的

compose [kəm'pəuz]

vt. 组成,构成

v. 创作(乐曲,诗歌等)

composition [kɔmpə'ziʃən]

n. 1. 作品,作文,乐曲

2. 写作,作曲

3. 构成,组成,成分

compound ['kɔmpaund]

n. 混合物,化合物

a. 混合的,化合的,复合的

comprehension [ˌkɔmpri'henʃən]

n. 理解(力)

computer [kəm'pjuːtə]

n. 计算机,电脑

comrade ['kɔmrid]

n. 同志,同伴,同事

concentrate ['kɔnsntreit]

v. 1. (on)集中,专心

2. 浓缩

concept ['kɔnsept]

n. 概念,观念,思想

concern [kən'səːn]

vt. 涉及,关系到

n. 1. (利害)关系

2. 关心

as /so far as...be ~ed

就……来说

be ~ed with 有关,从事于

concerning [kən'səːniŋ]

prep. 关于

concert ['kɔnsət]

v. 音乐会,演奏会

conclude [kən'kluːd]

v. 结束,终止

vt. 1. 推断,断定,下结论

2. 缔结,议定

conclusion [kən'kluːʒən]

n. 1. 结束,终结

2. 结论,推论

in ~ 最后,总之

concrete ['kɔnkriːt]

a. 具体的,有形的

n. 混凝土

v. 用混凝土修筑,浇混凝土

condition [kən'diʃən]

n. 1. 状况,状态

2. [pl.]环境,形势

3. 条件

on ~ that 如果

conduct [*n*. 'kɔndʌkt, *v*. kən'dʌkt]

n. 行为,举动,品行

vt. 1. 引导,带领

2. 处理,管理

v. 1. 指挥(乐队)

2. 传导,传(热,电等)

conductor [kən'dʌktə]

n. 1. (乐队的)指挥

2. (电车等的)售票员,

列车员

3. 导体,导线

conference ['kɔnfərəns]

n. 会议

confess [kən'fes]

v. 供认,承认,坦白

confidence ['kɔnfidəns]

n. 1. (in)信任

2. 信心,自信

confident ['kɔnfidənt]

a. (of, in)确信的,自信的

confine [kən'fain]

vt. (to, within)限制

confirm [kən'fəːm]

vt. 1. 证实,肯定

2. 进一步,确认

3. 批准

conflict ['kɔnflikt]

n. & *v*. 冲突,抵触,战斗

confuse [kən'fjuːz]

vt. 使混乱,混淆

congratulate [kən'grætjuleit]

vt. (on)祝贺,向……致祝贺词

congress ['kɔŋgress]

n. 1. (代表)大会

2. [C-] (美国等国的)国会,

议会

connect [kə'nekt]

v. (with)连接,联结

connection [kə'nekʃən]

n. 连接,联结,关系

conquer ['kɔŋkə]

vt. 1. 征服,战胜,占领

2. 克服,破除(坏习惯等)

conscious ['kɔnʃəs]

a. 1. (of)意识到的,自觉的

2. 有意识的,神志清醒的

consequence ['kɔnsikwəns]

n. 结果,后果

in ~ 因此,结果

in ~ of 由于……的缘故

consequently ['kɔnsikwəntli]

ad. 因而,所以

consider [kən'sidə]

vt. 1. 认为,把……看做

2. 考虑,细想

3. 体谅,照顾

considerable [kən'sidərəbl]

a. 1. 相当大(或多)的

2. 值得考虑的

consist [kən'sist]

vi. 1. (of)由……组成,由……

构成

2. (in)在于,存在于

constant ['kɔnstənt]

a. 1. 经常的,不断的

2. 坚定的,永恒的

n. 常数,恒量

construct [kən'strʌkt]

vt. 1. 建造,构造

2. 创立

construction [kən'strʌkʃən]

n. 1. 建造,建筑,建设

2. 建筑物,建造物

consult [kən'sʌlt]

v. 1. 请教,向……咨询,

找……商量

2. 查阅,查看

consume [kən'sjuːm]

vt. 消耗,耗尽,消费

consumer [kən'sjuːmə]

n. 消费者,用户

contact ['kɔntækt]

v. (使)接触,联系

n. 接触,联系

contain [kən'tein]

vt. 1. 包含,容纳

2. 等于,相当于

container [kən'teinə]

n. 容器

content [kən'tent]

a. (with)满足的,愿意的

n. 1. 容量,含量

2. [pl.]内容,(书刊的)目录

continent ['kɔntinənt]

n. 大陆,陆地

continual [kən'tinjuəl]

a. 不断的,连续的

continue [kən'tinjuː]

v. 继续,连续,延伸

continuous [kən'tinjuəs]

v. 连续的,持续的

contract ['kɔntrækt]

n. 契约,合同

v. 1. 缩小,缩短

2. 订(约)

contrary ['kɔntrəri]

a. (to)相反的,矛盾的,对抗的

n. 1. 反对,矛盾

2. [pl.]对立物

on the ～ 反之,正相反

contrast [*v.* kən'trɑːst, *n.* 'kɔntrɑːst]

vt. (with)使与……对比,
使与……对照

vi. (with)和……形成对照

n. 对比,对照,差异

in ～ with/to 与……成反比

contribute [kən'tribjuːt]

v. (to) 1. 贡献,有助于

2. 捐献,捐(款)

control [kən'trəul]

n. (over)控制,支配

vt. 控制,支配

convenience [kən'viːnjəns]

n. 便利,方便

convenient [kən'viːnjənt]

a. (to)便利的,方便的

conversation [kɔnvə'seiʃn]

n. 会话,谈话

conversely ['kɔnvəːsli]

ad. 相反地

convert [kən'vəːt]

v. (使)转变,(使)转化

convey [kən'vei]

vt. 1. 表达,传达,传递

2. 运送,输送

convince [kən'vins]

vt. (of)使确信,使信服

cook [kuk]

n. 炊事员,厨师

vt. 烹调,煮,烧

cool [kuːl]

a. 1. 凉的,凉快的

2. 冷淡的

v. (使)变凉,(使)冷却

cooperate [kəu'ɔpəreit]

vi. 合作,协作,配合

cooperation [kəuˌɔpə'reiʃən]

n. 合作,协作

copper ['kɔpə]

n. 铜

copy ['kɔpi]

n. 1. 抄本,副本,复制品,拷贝

2. (一)本,(一)册

vt. 誊写,复制

core [kɔː]

n. 1. 果核

2. 中心,核心

corn [kɔːn]

n. 谷物,玉米

corner ['kɔːnə]

n. 角,(街道)拐角

correct [kə'rekt]

a. 1. 正确的

2. 恰当的,端正的

vt. 改正,纠正

correspond [kɔris'pɔnd]

vi. 1. 通信

2. (with)符合,一致

3. (to)相当,相应

cost [kɔst]

v. 价值为,花费

n. 成本,费用,代价

at all ～s 不惜任何代价,无论
如何

at the ～ of 以……为代价

costly ['kɔstli]

a. 昂贵的,价值高的

cottage ['kɔtidʒ]

n. 村舍,小屋

cotton ['kɔtn]

n. 1. 棉花

2. 棉线

cough [kɔf]

n. & vi. 咳嗽

could [kud]

aux. v. 1. [can 的过去式]

2. [用于语气婉转的请
求]能

3. [用于虚拟语气]能,
可以

council ['kaunsil]

n. 理事会,委员会

count [kaunt]

v. 1. 数,计数

2. 算入,计进

n. 计数,计算,数(目)

～ on 依靠,期待

counter ['kauntə]

n. 1. 柜台

2. 计数器

v. 对抗,反驳

country ['kʌntri]

n. 1. 国家

2. 乡下,农村

countryside ['kʌntrisaid]

n. 乡下,农村

county ['kaunti]

n. (英国的)郡,(美国的)县

couple ['kʌpl]

n. 1. (一)对,(一)双

2. 夫妇

vt. 连接,结合

courage ['kʌridʒ]

n. 勇气,胆量

course [kɔːs]

  n. 1. 课程,教程

    2. 过程,进程

    3. 路程,路线

in the ～ of 在……过程中,

  在……期间

of ～ 当然,自然

court [kɔːt]

  n. 1. 法院,法官

    2. (网球等的)球场,庭院

cousin [ˈkʌzn]

  n. 堂(表)兄弟,堂(表)姐妹

cover [ˈkʌvə]

  vt. 1. 覆盖,遮蔽

    2. 涉及,包含

  n. 1. 盖子,套子

    2. (书)的封面

cow [kau]

  n. 母牛,奶牛

crack [kræk]

  n. 1. 裂缝,缝隙

    2. 破裂声,爆裂声

  v. 1. (使)破裂,(使)爆裂

    2. (使)发出爆裂声

crash [kræʃ]

  n. 1. 碰撞,坠落,坠毁

    2. 撞击声,爆裂声

  v. 碰撞,坠落,坠毁

crawl [krɔːl]

  vi. 1. 爬行,蠕动

    2. 徐徐行进

  n. 1. 爬行,蠕动

    2. 缓慢行进

crazy [ˈkreizi]

  a. 1. 疯狂的,古怪的

    2. (about)狂热的,热衷的

cream [kriːm]

  n. 1. 乳脂,(鲜)奶油

    2. 奶油色

create [kriˈeit]

  vt. 1. 创造,创作

    2. 引起,造成

creature [ˈkriːtʃə]

  n. 生物

credit [ˈkredit]

  n. 1. 信用贷款,赊欠

    2. 赞扬,荣誉,功劳

    3. 学分

    4. 信任,相信

  vt. 1. 信任,相信

    2. 把……记入贷方

    3. (to)把……归于

crew [kruː]

  n. 全体船员,全体乘务员

crime [kraim]

  n. 罪行,犯罪

criminal [ˈkriminl]

  n. 罪犯,犯人

  a. 犯罪的

critical [ˈkritikəl]

  a. 1. 批评的,评论的

    2. 危急的,紧要的

    3. 临界的

criticism [ˈkritisiz(ə)m]

  n. 批评,批判

crop [krɔp]

  n. 1. 作物,庄稼

    2. (谷类等的)一熟,收成

cross [krɔs]

  n. 十字形

  v. 1. 越过,穿过

    2. (使)交叉,(使)相交

crowd [kraud]

  n. 1. 人群

    2. 一群,一伙

  vi. 聚集,群集

crown [kraun]

  n. 王冠,冕

crude [kruːd]

  a. 1. 天然的,未加工的

    2. 粗鲁的,粗野的

    3. 生的,未煮熟的

cruel [ˈkruəl]

  a. 残忍的,残酷的

cry [krai]

  vi. 哭,流泪

  v. 叫,喊

  n. 1. 哭泣,哭声

    2. 叫喊,喊声

crystal [ˈkristl]

  n. 1. 水晶,水晶饰品

    2. 结晶,晶体

cube [kjuːb]

  n. 1. 立方形,立方体

    2. 立方,三次幂

cultivate [ˈkʌltiveit]

  vt. 1. 耕,耕作

    2. 培养,磨炼

culture [ˈkʌltʃə]

  n. 文化,文明

cup [kʌp]

  n. 1. 杯子

    2. (一)杯,一杯的容量

    3. 优胜杯,奖杯

cupboard [ˈkʌbəd]

  n. 碗碟橱

cure [kjuə]

  v. (of)治愈,治疗

  n. 治愈,痊愈

curiosity [ˌkjuəriˈɔsiti]

  n. 好奇心

curious [ˈkjuəriəs]

  a. 好奇的

currency [ˈkʌrənsi]

  n. 通货,货币

current [ˈkʌrənt]

  n. 电流,水流,气流

  a. 1. 流行的

    2. 当前的,现在的

curtain [ˈkəːtən]

  n. 窗帘,门帘

curse [kəːs]

  v. & *n*. 咒骂,诅咒

curve [kəːv]

  n. 1. 曲线

    2. 弯曲,弯曲物

  v. 弄弯,成曲形

custom [ˈkʌstəm]

  n. 1. 习惯,风俗,惯例

    2. [pl.]海关,关税

customer [ˈkʌstəmə]

  n. 顾客,主顾

cut [kʌt]

  n. 1. 切,割,剪,吹

    2. 伤口,切口

  v. 切,割,剪,吹

  vt. 削减,删节

  ～ down 削减

~ off 切断,使隔绝

~ out 删掉

cycle ['saikl]

  n. 1. 自行车

    2. 周期,循环,一转

  v. 1. 骑自行车

    2. 循环

D

daily ['deili]

  a. 每日的

  ad. 每日,天天

  n. 日报

dam [dæm]

  n. 水坝,水闸

damage ['dæmidʒ]

  vt. 损害,毁坏

  n. 损害,毁坏

damp [dæmp]

  a. 潮湿的, 微湿的

  n. 潮湿, 湿气

dance ['dɑːns]

  vi. 跳舞

  n. 1. 跳舞,舞蹈

    2. 舞会

danger ['deindʒə]

  n. 1. 危险,威胁

    2. 危险物

dangerous ['deindʒrəs]

  a. 危险的

dare [dɛə]

  aux. v. 敢,竟敢

  vt. 冒险,敢于承当

dark [dɑːk]

  a. 1. 黑暗的

    2. (颜色)深的

    3. 隐秘的

  n. 黑暗,暗处

darling ['dɑːliŋ]

  n. 心爱的人

dash [dæʃ]

  vi. 猛冲,突进

  v. (使)冲撞,(使)碰撞

  n. 1. 猛冲,突进

    2. 破折号

data ['deitə]

n. 数据,资料

date [deit]

  n. 1. 日期,日子

    2. 约会,约会的对象

  vt. 1. 注明日期

    2. 与……约会

out of ~ 废弃的,过时的

up to ~ 直到最近的,最新式的

daughter ['dɔːtə]

  n. 女儿

dawn [dɔːn]

  n. 黎明,拂晓

  vi. 破晓

day [dei]

  n. 1. (一)天,(一)日

    2. 白昼,白天

daylight ['deilait]

  n. 日光,白昼

dead [ded]

  a. 1. 死的

    2. 无感觉的

deaf [def]

  a. 1. 聋的

    2. 不愿听的

deal [diːl]

  vt. 给予,分给

  n. 交易

  ~ with 1. 处理,对付

    2. 与……交易,做买卖

    3. 论述,涉及

a great/good ~ (of) 大量(的),许多(的)

dear [diə]

  a. 1. 昂贵的

    2. 亲爱的

    3. (to)宝贵的,珍贵的

  int. [表示惊讶,怜悯等]啊,哎呀

death [deθ]

  n. 1. 死亡

    2. 毁灭

debt [det]

  n. 债,债务,欠款

decade ['dekeid]

  n. 十年,十年期

December [di'sembə]

  n. 十二月

decide [di'said]

  v. 1. 决定,决心

    2. 解决,裁决

decision [di'siʒən]

  n. 1. 决定,决心

    2. 决议,决策

deck [dek]

  n. 甲板

declare [di'klɛə]

  vt. 1. 断言,宣称

    2. 宣布,宣告,声明

decorate ['dekəreit]

  v. 装饰,装潢

decrease [di'kriːs]

  v. & n. 减少,减小

deed [diːd]

  n. 1. 行为,行动

    2. 事迹

deep [diːp]

  a. 1. 深的

    2. 深切的,深厚的

deer [diə]

  n. 鹿

defeat [di'fiːt]

  n. 1. 击败,战胜

    2. 失败

  vt. 1. 击败,战胜

    2. 使失败,挫折

defence(-se) [di'fens]

  n. 1. 防御,保卫,防护

    2. 防务,防御物

    3. 辩护,答辩

defend [di'fend]

  vt. 1. 防守,保卫

    2. 为……辩护,为……答辩

define [di'fain]

  vt. 1. 给……下定义

    2. 限定,规定

definite ['definit]

  a. 明确的,肯定的

degree [di'griː]

  n. 1. 度,度数

    2. 学位

    3. 程度,等级

delay [di'lei]

  v. & n. 耽搁,延迟

delicate ['delikət]

　　a. 1. 精巧的,精致的

　　　　2. 病弱的,脆弱的

　　　　3. 微妙的,棘手的

delicious [di'liʃəs]

　　a. 美味的

delight [di'lait]

　　n. 快乐,高兴

　　v. (使)高兴,(使)欣赏

deliver [di'livə]

　　vt. 1. 递,送

　　　　2. 发表,表达

　　　　3. 移交,交付

delivery [di'livəri]

　　n. 投递,传送

demand [di'mɑːnd]

　　vt. 1. 要求,请求

　　　　2. 需要知道,查问

　　　　3. 需要

　　n. 1. 要求,请求

　　　　2. 需要,需求(量)

democracy [di'mɔkrəsi]

　　n. 民主

demonstrate ['demənstreit]

　　vt. 1. 论证,证实

　　　　2. 演示,说明

dense [dens]

　　a. 1. (烟、雾等)浓厚的

　　　　2. 密集的,稠密的

department [di'pɑːtmənt]

　　n. 1. 部,局,处,科,部门

　　　　2. 系,学部

depend [di'pend]

　　vi. (on) 1. 依……而定,取决于

　　　　　　2. 依靠,依赖

　　　　　　3. 相信,信赖

dependent [di'pendənt]

　　a. (on) 1. 依靠的,依赖的

　　　　　　2. 由……决定的,

　　　　　　　随……而定的

deposit [di'pɔzit]

　　vt. 1. 储蓄,付(保证金)

　　　　2. 使沉淀,使淤积

　　n. 1. 存款,保证金

　　　　2. 沉积物,矿床

depth [depθ]

n. 1. 深,深度

　　2. 深奥,深刻

describe [dis'kraib]

　　vt. 描写,记述,形容

description [dis'kripʃən]

　　n. 1. 描写,记述,形容

　　　　2. 种类

desert [*n*. 'dezət, *v*. di'zəːt]

　　n. 沙漠,不毛之地

　　vt. 抛弃,遗弃

deserve [di'zəːv]

　　vt. 应收,值得,应得

design [di'zain]

　　vt. 设计,构思,绘制

　　n. 设计,图样

desirable [di'zaiərəbl]

　　a. 称心的,期望得到的

desire [di'zaiə]

　　vt. 欲望,期望,希望

　　n. 愿望,心愿

desk [desk]

　　n. 书桌,办公桌

despair [dis'pɛə]

　　n. 绝望

　　vi. (of) 对……绝望

despite [dis'pait]

　　prep. 不管,尽管

destroy [dis'trɔi]

　　vt. 1. 破坏,毁坏

　　　　2. 消灭

detail ['diːteil]

　　n. 细节,详情

　　vt. 详述,细说

　　in ~ 详细地

detect [di'tekt]

　　vt. 1. 觉察,发觉

　　　　2. 侦察,探测

determination [ditəːmi'neiʃən]

　　n. 1. 决心

　　　　2. 决定,确定,限定

determine [di'təːmin]

　　vt. 1. 决定,决心

　　　　2. 确定,限定

develop [di'veləp]

　　vt. 1. 发展,开发,研制

　　　　2. 使成长(生长)

vi. 生长,发育

development [di'veləpmənt]

　　n. 1. 生长,成长,进化

　　　　2. 发展,开发,研制

devil ['devl]

　　n. 魔鬼,恶棍

devise [di'vaiz]

　　vt. 设计,发明

devote [di'vəut]

　　vt. (to) 把……奉献给,把……专
用于

diagram ['daiəgræm]

　　n. 图解,图表,简图

dial ['daiəl]

　　v. 拨(电话号码),
打电话(给……)

　　n. 钟(表)面,刻度盘,拨号盘

dialog(ue) ['daiəlɔg]

　　n. 对话

diameter [dai'æmitə]

　　n. 直径

diamond ['daiəmənd]

　　n. 1. 金刚石,钻石

　　　　2. 菱形

diary ['daiəri]

　　n. 日记,日记簿

dictation [dik'teiʃən]

　　n. 听写,口述

dictionary ['dikʃənəri]

　　n. 词典,字典

die [dai]

　　vi. 死

differ ['difə]

　　vi. 1. (from) 不同,相异

　　　　2. (with) 与……意见不同

difference ['difərəns]

　　n. 1. 差异,差别

　　　　2. 差,差额

different ['difərənt]

　　a. 1. (from) 差异的,不同的

　　　　2. 各种的

difficult ['difikəlt]

　　a. 困难的,艰难的

difficulty ['difikəlti]

　　n. 困难,艰难

dig [dig]

v. 掘,挖

digest [di'dʒest]

  v. 1. 消化

    2. 吸收,领悟

  n. 文摘

dim [dim]

  a. 1. 不明亮的,暗淡的

    2. 朦胧的,模糊不清的

dimension [di'menʃən]

  n. 1. 尺寸,尺度

    2. 维(数),度(数),元

dinner ['dinə]

  n. 正餐

dip [dip]

  v. 浸,蘸

direct [di'rekt]

  a. 直接的

  v. 管理,指导,指挥

  vi. (to, at)把……对准

direction [di'rekʃən]

  n. 1. 方向,方位

    2. [常 pl.]用法说明,说明书

directly [di'rektli]

  ad. 1. 径直地,直接地

    2. 马上,立即

director [di'rektə]

  n. 指导者,主任,导演

dirt [dət]

  n. 污物,污垢

dirty ['dəti]

  a. 1. 脏的,肮脏的

    2. 下流的,黄色的

  vt. 弄脏,玷污

disadvantage [ˌdisəd'vɑːntidʒ]

  n. 不利,不利条件,缺点

disagree [ˌdisə'griː]

  vi. (with)意见不同,不同意

disappear [ˌdisə'piə]

  vi. 不见,消失

disappoint [ˌdisə'point]

  vt. 使失望,使受挫折

discharge [dis'tʃɑːdʒ]

  v. 1. 卸(货)

    2. 流出,排出,放(电)

  n. 1. 卸货

    2. 流出,排出,放电

discipline ['disəplin]

  n. 1. 纪律

    2. 学科

discourage [dis'kʌridʒ]

  vt. 使泄气,使沮丧

discover [dis'kʌvə]

  vt. 发现

discovery [dis'kʌvəri]

  n. 1. 发现

    2. 被发现的事物

discuss [dis'kʌs]

  vt. 讨论,商议

discussion [dis'kʌʃən]

  n. 讨论,商议

disease [di'ziːz]

  n. 病,疾病,病害

disgust [dis'gʌst]

  n. 厌恶

  vt. 使厌恶

dish [diʃ]

  n. 1. 盘,碟

    2. 盘装菜

dislike [dis'laik]

  vt. & *n*. 不喜爱,讨厌

dismiss [dis'mis]

  vt. 1. 免……的职,解雇,开除

    2. 遣散,解散

disorder [dis'ɔːdə]

  n. 1. 杂乱,凌乱

    2. 骚乱,混乱

    3. (身心,机能的)失调,病

display [di'splei]

  vt. & *n*. 1. 陈列,展览

    2. 显示,展示

dissolve [di'zɔlv]

  v. (使)溶解,(使)融化

distance ['distəns]

  n. 距离,间隔

in the ～ 在远处

distinct [dis'tiŋkt]

  a. 1. 清楚的,明显的

    2. (from)截然不同的,独特的

distinguish [dis'tiŋgwiʃ]

  vt. 1. (from)区别,辨别,识别

    2. 辨认出

distribute [dis'tribju(ː)t]

  vt. 1. 分发,分配

    2. (over)散布,分布

    3. 配(电)

district ['distrikt]

  n. 1. 地区,区域

    2. 区,行政区

disturb [dis'təːb]

  vt. 1. 弄乱,打乱

    2. 打扰,扰乱

ditch [ditʃ]

  n. 沟,沟渠

dive [daiv]

  vi. & *n*. 潜水,跳水,下潜,俯冲

divide [di'vaid]

  v. 1. 分,划分

    2. 分开,隔开

    3. (by)除

division [di'viʒən]

  n. 1. 部分,部门,科,处

    2. 分,分开

    3. 除(法)

divorce [di'vɔːs]

  v. & *n*. 离婚,分离

do [dəu]

  aux. v. [构成疑问句和否定句]

  vt. 1. 做,干

    2. 制作,产生

    3. 学习,研究

    4. 算出,解答

  vi. 行,适合

～ away with 废除,去掉

～ without 没有……也行

have nothing to ～ with

  和……毫无关系

have something to ～ with

  和……有点关系

doctor ['dɔktə]

  n: 1. [Dr.]博士

    2. 医生

document ['dɔkjumənt]

  n. 公文,文件,文献

dog [dɔg]

  n. 狗

dollar ['dɔlə]

  n. 元(美、加等国货币单位)

domestic [də'mestik]

a. 1. 家里的，家庭的
    2. 本国的，国内的

donkey [ˈdɔŋki]
n. 驴

door [dɔː, dɔə]
n. 1. 门
    2. 家，户

dot [dɔt]
n. 点，圆点
vt. 在……上打点

double [ˈdʌbl]
a. 1. 双的，双重的
    2. 两倍的
v. (使)加倍

doubt [daut]
n. 怀疑，疑问
v. 怀疑
no ~ 无疑地

doubtful [ˈdautful]
a. (of, about)怀疑的，可疑的

down [daun]
ad. 1. 向下，在下面
    2. (to)直到
    3. 由大到小，由多到少
    4. 减退下去，平息下去
    5. 往下游，往南，往农村
    6. 处于低落状态
prep. 沿着……往下

downstairs [daunˈsteəz]
ad. 在楼下，往楼下
a. 楼下的

downtown [ˈdaunˈtaun]
ad. 往(在)商业区(闹市区)
a. 商业区的，闹市区的

dozen [ˈdʌzn]
n. (一)打，十二个

draft [drɑːft]
n. 草稿，草案，草图
vt. 起草，为……打样，设计

drag [dræg]
v. 拖，拖曳

drain [drein]
n. 1. 排水沟，阴沟
    2. 消耗，负担
vt. 排去，放干

dramatic [drəˈmætik]

a. 1. 戏剧的，剧本的
    2. 戏剧性的

draw [drɔː]
v. 1. 拉，曳，牵
    2. 画，绘制
vt. 1. 汲取，领取，提取
    2. 引起，吸引
vi. (to, towards)向……移动，挨近
n. 平局，和局

drawer [ˈdrɔːə]
n. 抽屉

drawing [ˈdrɔːiŋ]
n. 绘图，图画，图样

dream [driːm]
v. (of) 1. 做梦，梦见
    2. 梦想，想到
n. 梦，梦想

dress [dres]
n. 1. 女服，童装
    2. 服装
v. (给……)穿衣

drift [drift]
v. (使)漂流
n. 漂流

drill [dril]
n. 1. 操练
    2. 钻头，钻床
v. 1. 操练
    2. 钻(孔)

drink [driŋk]
v. 饮，喝
n. 饮料

drive [draiv]
v. 开(车)，驾驶
vt. 1. 驱，赶
    2. 把(钉、桩等)打入
    3. 驱动，推动
n. 驾驶，驱车旅行

driver [ˈdraivə]
n. 驾驶员，司机

drop [drɔp]
v. 1. 滴下，落下
    2. 变弱，下降
n. 1. 落下，下降
    2. 滴

3. [pl.]滴剂
    4. 点滴，微量
~ in 顺访
~ off 减弱，减少
~ out 退出，离队，退学

drown [draun]
v. 溺死，淹死
vt. 淹没

drug [drʌg]
n. 1. 药物，药材
    2. 麻醉药品，成瘾性毒品
vt. 使服麻醉药，使麻醉

drum [drʌm]
n. 1. 鼓
    2. 圆桶

dry [drai]
a. 1. 干的，干燥的
    2. 口渴的
vt. 使干燥，使变干

duck [dʌk]
n. 鸭

due [djuː]
a. 1. (to)应支付的
    2. (车，船等)预定应到达的，预期的
    3. 应有的，正当的
~ to 由于，因为

dull [dʌl]
a. 1. 单调的，枯燥的
    2. 迟钝的
    3. 钝的，不锋利的

dumb [dʌm]
a. 1. 哑的
    2. 无言的，沉默的

during [ˈdjuəriŋ]
prep. 在……期间

dusk [dʌsk]
n. 薄暮，黄昏

dust [dʌst]
n. 灰尘，尘土
vt. 掸掉……上的灰尘

duty [ˈdjuːti]
n. 1. 义务，责任
    2. 职务
    3. 税
off ~ 下班

on ～ 值班,上班

dye [dai]

   n. 染料

   vt. 染

E

each [i:tʃ]

   a. 各,各自的,每

   pron. 各,各自,每个

   ～ other 相互

eager ['i:gə]

   a. (for)渴望的,热切的

eagle ['i:gl]

   n. 鹰

ear [iə]

   n. 耳朵

early ['ə:li]

   ad. 早,在初期

   a. 早的,早期的,及早的

earn [ə:n]

   vt. 1. 赚,挣得

     2. 获得,赢得

earth [ə:θ]

   n. 1. 地球

     2. 土,泥

     3. 陆地,地上

earthquake ['ə:θkweik]

   n. 地震

ease [i:z]

   vt. 减轻,使舒适,使安心

   n. 1. 容易

     2. 舒适

easily ['i:zili]

   ad. 容易地,不费力地

east [i:st]

   n. 东,东方,东部

   a. 东方的,东部的

eastern ['i:stən]

   a. 东方的,东部的

easy ['i:zi]

   a. 1. 容易的,不费力的

     2. 安逸的,宽裕的

eat [i:t]

   v. 吃,吃饭

echo ['ekəu]

   n. 回声,反响

   vi. 发出回声

economic [ˌi:kə'nɔmik]

   a. 经济(上)的,经济学的

economical [ˌi:kə'nɔmikəl]

   a. 节约的,经济的

economy [i(:)'kɔnəmi]

   n. 1. 节约

     2. 经济

edge [edʒ]

   n. 1. 边,棱,边缘

     2. 刀口,刃

edition [i'diʃən]

   n. 版,版本

editor ['editə]

   n. 编辑,编者

educate ['edju(:)keit]

   vt. 1. 教育

     2. 训练,培养

education [ˌedju(:)'keiʃən]

   n. 1. 教育

     2. 训练,培养

effect [i'fekt]

   n. 1. (on)作用,影响

     2. 结果

     3. 效果,效力

   vt. 产生,招致

   carry/bring into ～ 使生效,使起

    作用

   come/go into ～ 生效,实施

   in ～ 实际上,实质上

   take ～ 生效,起作用

effective [i'fektiv]

   a. 有效的,生效的

efficiency [i'fiʃənsi]

   n. 1. 效率

     2. 功效

efficient [i'fiʃənt]

   a. 1. 有效率的,效率高的

     2. 有能力的,能胜任的

effort ['efət]

   n. 努力,艰难的尝试

egg [eg]

   n. 蛋,鸡蛋,卵

eight [eit]

   num. 八,八个

eighteen ['ei'ti:n]

   num. 十八,十八个

eighth [eitθ]

   num. 第八

eighty ['eiti]

   num. 八十,八十个

either ['aiðə(r)]

   a. (两者之中)任一的

   pron. (两者之中)任何一个

   ad. [用于否定句]也

   ～ ...or... 或者……还是,

    不论……还是

elder ['eldə(r)]

   a. 年龄较大的,年长的

elect [i'lekt]

   vt. 选举,推选

   v. 选择,作出选择

election [i'lekʃ(ə)n]

   n. 选举

electric [i'lektrik]

   a. 电的,导电的,电动的

electrical [i'lektrik(ə)l]

   n. 电的,电学的

electricity [ilek'trisiti]

   n. 1. 电流

     2. 电,电学

electronic [ilek'trɔnik]

   a. 电子的

element ['elimənt]

   n. 1. 元素

     2. 组成部分,成分

elementary [ˌeli'mentəri]

   a. 1. 基本的

     2. 初级的,基础的

elephant ['elifənt]

   n. 象

elevator ['eliveitə]

   n. 电梯,升降机

eleven [i'levən]

   num. 十一,十一个

else [els]

   a. 其他的,别的

   ad. 另外,其他

   or ～ 否则,要不然

elsewhere ['els'hwɛə]

   ad. 在别处,向别处

email (E-mail) [i:'meil]

n. 电子邮件

v. 给……发电子邮件

emergency [i'məːdʒnsi]

  n. 紧急情况,突然事件,非常时刻

emotion [i'məuʃən]

  n. 情绪,情感

emphasis ['emfəsis]

  n. 强调,重点

emphasize(-ise) ['emfəsaiz]

  vt. 强调,着重

employ [im'plɔi]

  vt. 1. 雇用

    2. 用,使用

employee [ˌemplɔi'iː]

  n. 雇工,雇员

employment [im'plɔimənt]

  n. 1. 雇用

    2. 使用,利用

    3. 工作,职业

empty ['empti]

  a. 1. 空的

    2. 空洞的,空虚的

  vt. 使成为空的,倒空

enable [i'neibl]

  vt. 使能够,使成为可能

enclose [in'kləuz]

  vt. 1. 围住,圈起

    2. 把……封入

encourage [in'kʌridʒ]

  vt. 鼓励,怂恿

end [end]

  n. 末端,尽头,梢

  v. 终止,结束

endure [in'djuə]

  v. 忍受,忍耐

  vi. 持久,持续

enemy ['enimi]

  n. 敌人,敌军

energy ['enədʒi]

  n. 1. 活力,精力

    2. 能,能量

engage [in'geidʒ]

  v. (in) (使)从事于,(使)忙着

  vt. 1. 使订婚

    2. 雇用,聘

engine ['endʒin]

  n. 1. 发动机

    2. 机车,火车

engineer [ˌendʒi'niə]

  n. 1. 工程师,技师

    2. 火车司机,轮机员

English ['iŋgliʃ]

  a. 1. 英格兰的,英国的,英国人的

    2. 英语的

  n. 英语

enjoy [in'dʒɔi]

  vt. 享受……的乐趣,欣赏,喜爱

enormous [i'nɔːməs]

  a. 巨大的,庞大的

enough [i'nʌf]

  a. (for)足够的,充足的

  n. 足够,充分

  ad. 足够地,充分地

enter ['entə]

  v. 1. 进入

    2. 加入,参加

entertain [ˌentə'tein]

  vt. 1. 招待,款待

    2. 使欢乐,使娱乐

enthusiasm [in'θjuːziæzəm]

  n. 热情,热心

entire [in'taiə]

  a. 全部的,完整的

entrance ['entrəns]

  n. 1. 进入

    2. 入口

entry ['entri]

  n. 1. 进口

    2. 入口

envelope ['enviləup]

  n. 1. 信封

    2. 包裹物,封皮,封套

environment [in'vaiərənmənt]

  n. 环境,外界

envy ['envi]

  vt. & *n*. 羡慕,忌妒

equal ['iːkwəl]

  a. 1. (to)相等的,均等的

    2. (to)胜任的,经得起的

  n. 地位相等的人,对等的事物

  vt. 等于

equip [i'kwip]

  vt. (with)装备,配备

equipment [i'kwipmənt]

  n. 设备,器材,装置

era ['iərə]

  n. 时代,纪元

erect [i'rekt]

  vt. 1. 树立,建立

    2. 使竖立,使竖直

  a. 直立的,垂直的

error ['erə]

  n. 1. 错误

    2. 误差

escape [is'keip]

  vi. & *n*. 逃跑,逃脱

  v. 避开,避免

especially [is'peʃəli]

  ad. 特别,尤其

essential [i'senʃəl]

  a. 1. (to)必要的,必不可少的

    2. 本质的,基本的

establish [is'tæbliʃ]

  vt. 1. 建立,设立

    2. 建立的机构(或组织)

estimate ['estimeit]

  v. & *n*. 估计,估价

etc (*et cetera*) 等等

Europe ['juərəp]

  n. 欧洲

European [ˌjuərə'pi(ː)ən]

  a. 欧洲的,欧洲人的

  n. 欧洲人

eve [iːv]

  n. (节日等的)前夜,前夕

even ['iːvən]

  ad. 甚至(……也),连(……都)

  a. 1. 平的,平坦的

    2. 双数的,偶数的

    3. 均匀的

  ~ if/though 即使,虽然

  ~ then 即使那样,连……都

evening ['iːvniŋ]

  n. 1. 傍晚,晚上

    2. 晚会

event [i'vent]

n. 事件,事情

at all ~s 无论如何

in any ~ 无论如何

in the ~ of 万一,如果发生

eventually [i'ventjuəli]

ad. 终于,最后

ever ['evə]

ad. 在任何时候

for ~ 永远

every ['evri]

a. 1. 每一的,每个的

2. 一切的,所有的

everybody ['evribɔdi]

pron. 每个,人人

everyday ['evridei]

a. 1. 每日的

2. 日常的

everyone ['evriwʌn]

pron. = everybody

everything ['evriθiŋ]

pron. 每件事,事事

everywhere ['evrihwɛə]

ad. 处处,到处

evidence ['evidəns]

n. 1. 根据,证据

2. 形迹,迹象

evident ['evidənt]

a. 明显的,明白的

evil ['iːvl]

a. 邪恶的,罪恶的

n. 邪恶,罪恶

exact [ig'zækt]

a. 1. 确切的,正确的

2. 准确的,精密的

exactly [ig'zæktli]

ad. 1. 确切地,精确地

2. 恰恰正是

examination（exam）

[igˌzæmi'neiʃən]

n. 1. 考试

2. 检查,细查

examine [ig'zæmin]

vt. 1. 检查,细查

2. 对……进行考试

example [ig'zɑːmpl]

n. 1. 例子,实例

2. 模范,榜样

for ~ 例如

exceed [ik'siːd]

vt. 1. 超出,胜过

2. 越出

excellent ['eksələnt]

a. 卓越的,极好的

except [ik'sept]

prep. 除……之外

~ for 除……之外

exception [ik'sepʃən]

n. 例外,除外

with the ~ of 除……之外

exchange [iks'tʃeindʒ]

vt. & *n*. 1. (for)交换,调换,

兑换

2. 交流,交易

excite [ik'sait]

vt. 1. 刺激,使激动

2. 激发,激励

exclaim [iks'kleim]

v. 呼喊,惊叫,大声说

excuse [iks'kjuːz]

vt. 1. 原谅,宽恕

2. 免除

n. 借口,辩解

execute ['eksikjuːt]

vt. 实施,执行

exercise ['eksəsaiz]

n. 1. 练习,习题

2. 训练,锻炼

v. 训练,锻炼

vt. 行使

exhaust [ig'zɔːst]

vt. 1. 使筋疲力尽,耗尽

2. 抽完,汲干

exhibit [ig'zibit]

vt. 展出,陈列

n. 展览品,陈列

exhibition [ˌeksi'biʃən]

n. 1. 展览会

2. 陈列,展览

exist [ig'zist]

vi. 1. 存在

2. 生存,生活

existence [ig'zistəns]

n. 1. 存在,实在

2. 生存,生活(方式)

expand [iks'pænd]

v. 1. (使)膨胀,(使)扩张

2. 张开,展开

expect [iks'pekt]

vt. 1. 预期

2. 期望,指望

expense [ik'spens]

n. 花费,消费,消耗

expensive [iks'pensiv]

a. 花费的,昂贵的

experience [iks'piəriəns]

n. & *vt*. 1. 经验,经历

2. 感受,体验

experiment [iks'perimənt]

n. 实验,试验

vi. (on)进行实验,做试验

expert ['ekspəːt]

n. 专家,能手

a. 1. 熟练的,有经验的

2. 专门的

explain [iks'plein]

vt. 解释,说明

explanation [ˌeksplə'neiʃən]

n. 解释,说明

explode [iks'pləud]

v. (使)爆炸,(使)爆发

explore [iks'plɔː]

vt. 1. 勘探,探测

2. 探究,探索

explosion [iks'pləuʒən]

n. 爆炸,爆发

explosive [iks'pləusiv]

a. 爆炸(性)的,爆发(性)的

n. 爆炸物,炸药

export ['ekspɔːt]

vt. 输出

n. 1. 出口货

2. 输出,出口

expose [iks'pəuz]

vt. (to) 1. 使暴露,使处于……

作用/影响之下

2. 使曝光,揭露

express [iks'pres]

vt. 表达,表示

n. 快车

expression [iks'preʃən]

n. 1. 表达，表示

    2. 词句，措词

    3. 式，符号

extend [iks'tend]

v. 1. 延长，延伸

    2. 扩大，扩充

extensive [iks'tensiv]

a. 广大的，广阔的

extent [iks'tent]

n. 1. 广度，宽度，长度

    2. 程度，限度

external [eks'tə:nl]

a. 外部的，外面的

extra ['ekstrə]

a. 额外的，外加的

extraordinary [iks'trɔːdnri]

a. 非常的，特别的

extreme [iks'triːm]

a. 1. 末端的，尽头的

    2. 极度的，极端的

n. 极度(状态)，最大程度

extremely [iks'triːmli]

ad. 极端，非常

eye [ai]

n. 1. 眼睛

    2. 眼状物

vt. 看，注视

eyesight ['aisait]

n. 视力，视野

F

face [feis]

n. 1. 脸，面貌

    2. 面容，表情

    3. 正面，表面

vt. 1. 面对

    2. 朝，面向

in (the) ~ of...

    1. 面对，在……面前

    2. 不顾，即使

facility [fə'siliti]

n. 1. [常 pl.]设施，工具

    2. 容易，便利

fact [fækt]

n. 事实，实际

in ~ 其实，实际上

factor ['fæktə]

n. 因素，要素

factory ['fæktəri]

n. 工厂

fade [feid]

vi. 1. 褪色

    2. 衰减，消失

Fahrenheit ['færənhait]

n. 华氏温度计

fail [feil]

vi. 1. (in)失败，不及格

    2. 衰退，减弱，衰弱

    3. 不，未能，忘记

vt. 评(考生)为不及格

failure ['feiljə]

n. 1. 失败，不及格

    2. 失败者，失败的事

    3. 失灵，故障

faint [feint]

a. 减弱的，不明显的

vi. 昏厥，晕倒

fair [fɛə]

a. 1. 公平的，合理的

    2. 尚好的，中等的

    3. 晴朗的

    4. (肤色)白皙的，

      (头发)金色的

n. 1. 集市

    2. 交易会

fairly ['fɛəli]

ad. 1. 公正地，正当地

    2. 相当，还算

faith [feiθ]

n. 1. 信任，信用

    2. 信仰，信条

faithful ['feiθful]

a. 1. 守信的，忠实的

    2. 如实的，可靠的

fall [fɔːl]

vi. 1. 跌倒，倒塌

    2. 下降，减弱

    3. 落下，降落

    4. 变成，成为

n. 秋，秋季

~ in with 1. 符合，与……一致

        2. 碰见

false [fɔːls]

a. 1. 谬误的，不正确的

    2. 伪造的，假的

familiar [fə'miljə]

a. 1. (with, to)熟悉的，通晓的

    2. 亲近的

family ['fæmili]

n. 1. 家庭，家庭成员

    2. 氏族，家庭

    3. 族，科

famous ['feiməs]

a. 著名的，出名的

fan [fæn]

n. 1. 扇子，风扇

    2. (影、球等)迷

vt. 扇

far [fɑː]

ad. 远，久远地

a. 远的，不久的

as ~ as 1. 远至

      2. 到……程度

by ~ ……得多，最

~ from 1. 远非

      2. 远离

so ~ 迄今为止

fare [fɛə]

n. (车、船，飞机等的)费，票价

farewell ['fɛə'wel]

int. 再会

n. 告别辞，告别

a. 告别的

farm [fɑːm]

n. 农场，饲养场

v. 种田，经营农牧业

farmer ['fɑːmə]

n. 农民，农场主

farther ['fɑːðə]

ad. 更远地，再往前地

a. 更远的

fashion ['fæʃən]

n. 1. 流行式样(货品)，风尚，

     风气

    2. 样子，方式

fast [fɑːst]

a. 1. 快的,迅速的
　　2. (钟表)快的
　　3. 紧的,牢的
ad. 1. 快,迅速地
　　2. 紧紧地,牢固地

fasten ['fɑːsn]
vt. 扎牢,使固定

fat [fæt]
a. 肥胖的,丰满的
n. 肥肉,脂肪

fate [feit]
n. 命运

father ['fɑːðə]
n. 父亲

fault [fɔːlt]
n. 1. 过失,过错
　　2. 缺点,毛病

favo(u)r [feivə(r)]
n. 1. 恩惠,善意的行为
　　2. 好感,喜爱
vt. 1. 赞成,有利于
　　2. 偏爱,偏袒
in ~ of 1. 有利于,便于
　　2. 赞成,支持

favo(u)rite ['feivərit]
a. 特别喜爱的,中意的
n. 特别喜爱的人(物)

fear [fiə]
n. & *vt*. 害怕,畏惧

feather ['feðə]
n. 羽毛

feature ['fiːtʃə]
n. 1. 特征,特色
　　2. 特写

February ['februəri]
n. 二月

federal ['fedərəl]
a. 联邦的

fee [fiː]
n. 费,酬金

feed [fiːd]
vt. 1. (on, with)喂(养),饲(养)
　　2. (with)向……供给,加进
　　　(原料)等

feel [fiːl]
vi. 有知觉,有感觉

vt. 1. 感觉,觉得
　　2. 以为,认为
~ like 欲,想要

feeling ['fiːliŋ]
n. 1. 感情,心情
　　2. 同情,体谅

fellow ['feləu]
n. 1. 人,家伙
　　2. 伙伴,同事
a. 同伴的,同事的

female ['fiːmeil]
a. 女的,雌的

fence [fens]
n. 栅栏,篱笆

fertilizer ['fəːtiˌlaizə]
n. 肥料

festival ['festəvəl]
n. 1. 节日
　　2. 音乐节,戏剧节

fetch [fetʃ]
v. 取来,接来

fever ['fiːvə]
n. 1. 发热,发烧
　　2. 狂热

few [fjuː]
a. 少的,不多的
a ~ 有些,几个

fibre(-ber) ['faibə]
n. 纤维

field [fiːld]
n. 1. 田,田野
　　2. 运动场
　　3. 领域,方面
　　4. (电、磁等)场

fierce [fiəs]
a. 1. 凶猛的,残忍的
　　2. 狂热的,强烈的

fifteen ['fif'tiːn]
num. 十五,十五个

fifth [fifθ]
num. 第五

fifty ['fifti]
num. 五十,五十个

fight [fait]
v. 打(仗),搏斗,斗争
n. 战斗,搏斗

figure ['figə]
n. 1. 体形,外形
　　2. 数字
　　3. 图形,插图
　　4. 人物
v. 猜想,认为
~ out 计算出,理解,明白

file [fail]
n. 1. 档案,卷宗
　　2. (计算机数据等的)文件
v. 1. 把……归档
　　2. 提出(申请等)

fill [fil]
v. (with)填满,充满
~ in/out 填充,填写

film [film]
n. 1. 影片,电影
　　2. 胶卷
　　3. 薄膜
v. (把……)摄成电影

filter ['filtə]
n. 滤器,滤纸

final ['fainəl]
a. 最终的,决定性的

financial [fai'nænʃəl, ˌfi-]
a. 财政的,金融的

find [faind]
vt. 1. 找到,发现
　　2. 发觉,感到
~ out 查明,弄清

fine [fain]
a. 1. 晴朗的
　　2. 美好的,漂亮的
　　3. 细致的,精致的
n. 罚金,罚款
v. (对……)处以罚金

finger ['fiŋgə]
n. 手指

finish ['finiʃ]
v. 结束,完成
n. 结束,最后阶段

fire ['faiə]
n. 1. 火
　　2. 热情,激情
v. 1. 开(枪,炮等),射出(子弹)
　　2. 点火,着火

3. 解雇

firm [fə:m]

　a. 1. 结实的,坚固的

　　2. 坚定的,坚决的

　n. 商行,公司

first [fə:st]

　num. 第一

　a. 首先的,最初的

　at ～ 最初,起先

　～ of all 首先,第一

fish [fiʃ]

　n. 鱼

　v. 钓鱼,捕鱼

fist [fist]

　n. 拳,拳头

fit [fit]

　v. 1. (使)适合,(使)配合

　　2. (使)合身

　vt. 安装,装置

　a. 1. (for, to)适合的,恰当的

　　2. 健康的,结实的

five [faiv]

　num. 五,五个

fix [fiks]

　v. 1. 修理,校准

　　2. (使)固定,安装

　　3. 确定,安排

　　4. 整理,收拾

flag [flæg]

　n. 旗

flame [fleim]

　n. 1. 火焰

　　2. 光辉,光芒

　　3. 热情,激情

flash [flæʃ]

　n. 闪光

　vt. 1. 闪亮,闪光

　　2. 闪现

　　3. 飞驰,掠过

flat [flæt]

　a. 1. 平的,平坦的

　　2. 平伸的,平展的

　　3. 单调的

　n. 1. 一套房间

　　2. 平面,平坦部分

flavo(u)r [ˈfleivə]

n. 味,风味

　vt. 给……调味

flexible [ˈfleksəbl]

　a. 1. 柔韧的,易弯曲的

　　2. 灵活的

flight [flait]

　n. 1. 飞翔,飞行

　　2. 航班,航程

float [fləut]

　v. (使)漂浮,(使)浮动

flood [flʌd]

　n. 洪水,水灾

　vt. 淹没

　vi. 发大水,溢出

floor [flɔ:, fləə]

　n. 1. 地板

　　2. (楼房的)层

flour [ˈflauə]

　n. 面粉

flow [fləu]

　vi. 流动

　n. 流动,流量

flower [ˈflauə]

　n. 花

　vi. 开花

fluent [ˈflu(:)ənt]

　a. 流利的,流畅的

fluid [ˈflu(:)id]

　n. 流体,液体

　a. 流动的,流体的

fly [flai]

　vi. 1. 飞,飞行

　　2. 飞奔,飞逝

　vt. 驾驶(飞机),空运

　n. 蝇

focus [ˈfəukəs]

　n. 1. 焦点

　　2. (活动,兴趣等的)中心

　v. (on)(使)聚焦

fog [fɔg]

　n. 雾

fold [fəuld]

　vt. 折叠

　n. 褶,褶痕

folk [fəuk]

　n. 人们

a. 民间的

follow [ˈfɔləu]

　v. 1. 跟随,接着

　　2. 领会,听得懂

　vt. 1. 沿着……前进

　　2. 遵循,仿效

　vi. 结果是

　as ～s 如下

following [ˈfɔləuiŋ]

　a. 接着的,下列的

fond [fɔnd]

　a. (of)喜爱的,爱好的

food [fu:d]

　n. 食物,食品

fool [fu:l]

　n. 蠢人

　vt. 愚弄,欺骗

foolish [ˈfu:liʃ]

　a. 愚蠢的

foot [fut]

　n. 1. 脚,足

　　2. 英尺

　　3. 最下部,底部

football [ˈfutbɔ:l]

　n. 足球

footstep [ˈfutstep]

　n. 1. 脚步,脚步声

　　2. 足迹

for [fɔ:, fə]

　prep. 1. 往,向

　　2. 对于,供

　　3. 为了

　　4. [引出动词不定式的逻辑主语]

　　5. 达,计

　　6. 代,替,代表

　　7. 赞成,拥护

　　8. 由于,因为

　　9. 至于,就……而言

　conj. 因为

forbid [fəˈbid]

　vt. 禁止,不许

force [fɔ:s]

　n. 1. 力,力量

　　2. [pl.]军队,部队

　　3. 势力

vt. 强迫,迫使

in ～ 有效,实施中

come/go into ～ 生效,实施

forecast [ˈfɔːkɑːst]

vt. & *n*.预测,预报

forehead [ˈfɔrid]

n. 额,前额

foreign [ˈfɔrin]

a. 1. 外国的

　　2. 外来的,异质的

foreigner [ˈfɔrinə]

n. 外国人

forest [ˈfɔrist]

n. 森林

forever [fəˈrevə]

ad. 永远,常有

forget [fəˈget]

v. 忘记,遗忘

forgive [fəˈgiv]

vt. 原谅,饶恕

fork [fɔːk]

n. 1. 叉,耙,叉形物

　　2. 餐叉

form [fɔːm]

n. 1. 形状,形式

　　2. 表格

vt. 组成,构成

v. 形成

formal [ˈfɔːməl]

a. 1. 正式的

　　2. 形式的

format [ˈfɔːmæt]

n. 1. 设计,安排

　　2. 格式,样式,版式

v. (使)格式化

former [ˈfɔːmə]

a. 以前的,在前的

pron. 前者

formula [ˈfɔːmjulə]

n. 公式

forth [fɔːθ]

ad. 向前方,向前

fortunate [ˈfɔːtʃinit]

a. 幸运的, 侥幸的

fortunately [ˈfɔːtʃinətli]

ad. 幸运地,幸而

fortune [ˈfɔːtʃən]

n. 1. (大量的)财产, 大笔的钱

　　2. 运气, 时运, 命运

forty [ˈfɔːti]

num. 四十,四十个

forward [ˈfɔːwəd]

ad. 向前,前进

a. 向前的

found [faund]

vt. 建立,创立

foundation [faunˈdeiʃən]

n. 1. 基础,根本

　　2. 建立,创立

　　3. 地基

　　4. 基金,基金会

fountain [ˈfauntin]

n. 1. 泉水,喷泉

　　2. 源泉

four [fɔː]

num. 四,四个

fourteen [ˈfɔːˈtiːn]

num. 十四,十四个

fourth [fɔːθ]

num. 第四

fraction [ˈfrækʃən]

n. 1. 小部分,片断

　　2. 分数

frame [freim]

n. 1. 框架,框子

　　2. 架,骨架

vt. (给)装框架,构造

framework [ˈfreimwəːk]

n. 构架,框架,结构

frank [fræŋk]

a. 坦白的,直率的

free [friː]

a. 1. 自由的,无约束的

　　2. 免费的,免税的

　　3. 空闲的,空余的

　　4. (from, of)没有……的,

　　　免去……的

vt. (from, of)使自由,免除

freedom [ˈfriːdəm]

n. 自由,自主

freeze [friːz]

v. (使)结冰,(使)冷冻

freight [freit]

n. 1. (运输的)货物

　　2. 运费

French [frentʃ]

a. 1. 法国的,法国人的

　　2. 法语的

n. 法语

frequency [ˈfriːkwənsi]

n. 频率,周率

frequent [ˈfriːkwənt]

a. 常常发生的,频繁的

frequently [ˈfriːkwəntli]

ad. 常常,频繁地

fresh [freʃ]

a. 1. 新的,新近的

　　2. 新鲜的,(水)淡的

　　3. 清新的,凉爽的

　　4. 鲜艳的

Friday [ˈfraidi]

n. 星期五

friend [frend]

n. 朋友

friendly [ˈfrendli]

a. 友好的,友谊的

friendship [ˈfrendʃip]

n. 友谊,友好

frighten [ˈfraitn]

v. (使)惊恐

frog [frɔg]

n. 蛙

from [frɔm]

prep. 1. 从,自,从……来

　　　2. [表示去除、免掉、阻止

　　　　等]

　　　3. [表示识别、区别]

　　　4. 由于,出于

front [frʌnt]

a. 前面的,前部的

n. 1. 前面,正面

　　2. 前线,战线

v. 面对,朝向

in ～ of 在……前面

frontier [ˈfrʌntjə]

n. 国境,边境

frost [frɔst, frɔːst]

n. 1. 霜

2. 霜冻,严寒

frown [fraun]

vi. 皱眉,蹙额

fruit [fruːt]

n. 1. 水果,果实

2. 成果,效果

fry [frai]

v. 油煎,油炸

fuel [fjuəl]

n. 燃料

v. 加燃料,加油

fulfil(l) [ful'fil]

vt. 1. 履行,实现

2. 完成

full [ful]

a. 1. (of)满的,充满的

2. 完全的,十足的

fun [fʌn]

n. 1. 玩笑,娱乐

2. 有趣的人(事情)

function ['fʌŋkʃən]

n. 1. 功能,作用

2. [常 pl.]职务,职责

3. 函数

vi. 起作用

fund [fʌnd]

n. 资金,基金

fundamental [ˌfʌndə'mentl]

a. 基础的,基本的

n. [pl.]基本原则,基本原理

funny ['fʌni]

a. 滑稽的,可笑的

fur [fəː]

n. 毛皮,毛

furnace ['fəːnis]

n. 炉子,熔炉

furniture ['fəːnitʃə]

n. 家具

further ['fəːðə]

ad. 1. 更远地,再往前地

2. 而且,此外

a. 更多的,进一步的

future ['fjuːtʃə]

a. 将来的,未来的

n. 将来,未来

in (the) ~ 今后,将来

· 36 ·

G

gain [gein]

v. 1. 获得,博得

2. 增加,(钟,表)走快

n. 收益,得益

gallon ['gælən]

n. 加仑

game [geim]

n. 1. 游戏,娱乐

2. 比赛

3. [pl.]运动会

gap [gæp]

n. 1. 缺口,裂口,间隙

2. 差距,隔阂

garage ['gærɑː(d)ʒ]

n. 1. 汽车间

2. 修车厂

garden ['gɑːdn]

n. 花园,菜园

gas [gæs]

n. 气体,煤气,汽油,毒气

gasoline ['gæsəliːn]

n. 汽油

gate [geit]

n. 大门

gather ['gæðə]

v. 聚集,聚拢

gay [gei]

a. 1. 同性恋(者)的

2. 色彩鲜艳的

3. 愉快的

n. (尤指男)同性恋者

gene [dʒiːn]

n. 基因

general ['dʒenərəl]

a. 1. 一般的,普通的

2. 总的,大体的

n. 将军

in ~ 通常,大体上

generally ['dʒenərəli]

ad. 一般,通常

generate ['dʒenəˌreit]

vt. 1. 产生,发生

2. 发电

generation [ˌdʒenə'reiʃən]

n. 1. 产生,发生

2. 一代,一代人

generator ['dʒenəreitə]

n. 发电机,发生器

generous ['dʒenərəs]

a. 宽宏大量的,慷慨的

genius ['dʒiːnjəs]

n. 1. 天才,天赋

2. 天才人物

gentle ['dʒentl]

a. 1. 有礼貌的,文雅的

2. 柔和的

gentleman ['dʒentlmən]

n. 1. 阁下,先生

2. 有身份的人,绅士

3. [pl.]男厕所,男盥洗室

gently ['dʒentli]

ad. 1. 有礼貌地,文雅地

2. 柔和地

genuine ['dʒenjuin]

a. 真正的,名副其实的

geography [dʒi'ɔgrəfi, 'dʒiɔg-]

n. 地理(学)

geometry [dʒi'ɔmitri]

n. 几何(学)

German ['dʒəːmən]

a. 1. 德国的,德国人的

2. 德语的

n. 1. 德国人

2. 德语

gesture ['dʒestʃə]

n. 姿势,手势

get [get]

vt. 1. 获得,得到

2. 使得,把……弄得

vi. 1. 变得,成为

2. (to)到达

~ along/on 1. 有进展,有进步

2. 生活,过活

~ along/on with 1. 进展

2. 和……相处

~ at 1. 达到,够着

2. 意思是

~ by 通过,勉强混过

~ down 1. 从……下来

2. 写下

~ in 1. 进入

    2. 收获,收集

~ into 1. 进入

    2. 陷入

~ off 1. 从……下来

    2. 脱离,离开

~ over 1. 从……中恢复过来

    2. 克服

    3. 度过,结束

~ through 1. 通过

      2. 办完,结束

~ up 1. 起床

    2. 增强,增加

have got 有

have got + to V. 必须

ghost [gəust]

  n. 鬼魂,幽灵

giant ['dʒaiənt]

  a. 巨大的

  n. 巨人

gift [gift]

  n. 1. 赠品,礼物

    2. 天赋,才能

girl [gəːl]

  n. 女孩子,姑娘

give [giv]

  vt. 1. 送给,给

    2. 授予,赐予

    3. 交付,委托

    4. 献出,献给

~ away 1. 泄露

     2. 分送

~ in 1. 交上,交来

    2. 投降,屈服

~ off 放出,释放

~ out 1. 分发

    2. 放出

~ up 1. 停止

    2. 放弃

glad [glæd]

  a. 高兴的,乐意的

glance [glɑːns]

  v. (at, over)扫视,匆匆一看

  n. 一瞥,眼光

glass [glɑːs]

  n. 1. 玻璃

    2. 玻璃杯

    3. [pl.]眼镜

glimpse [glimps]

  n. 一瞥,一看

globe [gləub]

  n. 1. 球体,地球仪

    2. 地球,世界

glorious ['glɔːriəs]

  a. 1. 辉煌的,灿烂的

    2. 光荣的

glory ['glɔːri]

  n. 荣誉,光荣

glove [glʌv]

  n. 手套

glow [gləu]

  vi. 发光,发热

glue [gluː]

  n. 胶,胶水

  vt. 胶合,粘贴

go [gəu]

  vi. 1. 去,走

    2. 放置,装入

    3. 运转,运行

    4. 变为,成为

    5. 消失,离去

~ after 追求

~ back on 违背

~ by 过去

~ down 1. 下降,降低

      2. 被载入,传下去

~ in for 参加

~ into 1. 进入

    2. 研究,调查

~ off 1. 爆炸,发射

    2. 动身,离开

~ on 1. 继续

    2. 发生

~ out 1. 外出

    2. 熄灭

~ over 1. 检查,审查

    2. 复习,重温

~ through 1. 经历,经受

      2. 详细检查

~ up 1. 上升,增加

    2. 建起

~ with 1. 伴随

    2. 与……协调

~ without 没有……也行

goal [gəul]

  n. 1. 目的,目标

    2. 球门

    3. (球赛等的)得分

goat [gəut]

  n. 山羊

god [gɔd]

  n. 1. [G-]上帝

    2. 神

gold [gəuld]

  n. 黄金,金币

  a. 金的,金制的

golden ['gəuldən]

  a. 1. 金色的,金黄色的

    2. 贵重的,极好的

good [gud]

  a. 1. 好的

    2. (for)适合的,有益的

as ~ as 和……几乎一样,实际上

    等于

for ~ 永久地

goodbye [ˌgudˈbai]

  int. 再见

goodness ['gudnis]

  n. 善良,仁慈

goods [gudz]

  n. 商品,货物

goose [guːs]

  n. 鹅

government ['gʌvənmənt]

  n. 政府,政体

governor ['gʌvənə]

  n. 1. 统治者,管辖者

    2. 地方长官, 州长, 省长

grace [greis]

  n. 优美,雅致

graceful ['greisful]

  a. 优美的,雅致的

grade [greid]

  n. 等级,级别

  vt. 评分,评级

gradual ['grædjuəl]

  a. 逐渐的,逐步的

graduate

[n . 'grædjuət, v. 'grædjueit]

n . 1. (大学)毕业生

    2. 研究生

v . (使)(大学)毕业

grain [grein]

n . 1. 谷物,谷类

    2. 谷粒

    3. 细粒,颗粒

gram(me) [græm]

n . 克

grammar ['græmə]

n . 语法

grand [grænd]

a . 1. 盛大的,豪华的

    2. 重大的,主要的

grandfather ['grænd‚fɑ:ðə]

n . (外)祖父

grandmother ['grænd‚mʌðə]

n . (外)祖母

grant [grɑ:nt]

vt . 同意,准予

take for ～ed 想当然,认为理所

    当然

grape [greip]

n . 葡萄

graph [grɑ:f]

n . 图表,曲线图

grasp [grɑ:sp]

vt . & n . 1. 抓住,抓紧

    2. 掌握,领会

grass [grɑ:s]

n . 草

grateful ['greitful]

a . (to, for)感激的,感谢的

grave [greiv]

n . 坟墓

gravity ['græviti]

n . 重力,地心引力

great [greit]

a . 1. 伟大的,大的

    2. 美好的,绝妙的

greatly ['greitli]

ad . 大大地,非常

greedy ['gri:di]

a . 1. 贪吃的

    2. (for)贪婪的,渴望的

Greek [gri:k]

a . 1. 希腊的,希腊人的

    2. 希腊语的

n . 1. 希腊人

    2. 希腊语

green [gri:n]

a . 1. 绿的,青的

    2. 未熟的,嫩的

n . 1. 绿色

    2. [pl.]蔬菜,植物

greet [gri:t]

vt . 问候,向……致意

greeting ['gri:tiŋ]

n . 问候,致敬

grey (gray) [grei]

a . 灰色的,灰白的

n . 灰色

grind [graind]

v . 磨(碎),碾(碎)

grip [grip]

vt . 紧握,紧夹

n . 掌握,控制

grocery ['grəusəri]

n . 食品杂货(店)

ground [graund]

n . 1. 地,地面

    2. 场所,场

    3. 根据,理由

on the ～(s) of 由于,以……为

    理由

group [gru:p]

n . 群,组

vt . 把……分组

grow [grəu]

vi . 1. 生长,成长

    2. 渐渐变得

vt . 种植,栽培

growth [grəuθ]

n . 1. 增长,增大

    2. 生长,发育

guard [gɑ:d]

n . 1. 卫兵,警卫员

    2. 守卫,看守

vt . 保卫,守卫

vi . (against)防止,防范

guess [ges]

vt . & n .猜测,推测

guest [gest]

n . 客人

guide [gaid]

n . 1. 领路人,导游

    2. 指南

vt . 为……领路,指导

guilty ['gilti]

a . (of) 1. 有罪的

    2. 内疚的

gulf [gʌlf]

n . 海湾

gum [gʌm]

n . 1. 树胶,树脂

    2. 口香糖

gun [gʌn]

n . 炮,枪

H

habit ['hæbit]

n . 习惯,习性

hair [hɛə]

n . 头发,毛发

half [hɑ:f]

n . 半,一半

a . 一半的,半个的

ad . 一半

hall [hɔ:l]

n . 1. 礼堂,会堂

    2. 门厅, 走廊

ham [hæm]

n . 火腿

hammer ['hæmə]

n . 铁锤,槌

v . 锤击,锤打

hand [hænd]

n . 1. 手

    2. 指针

vt . 交给

at ～ 在手边,附近

～ down 留传下来

～ in 交上,递交

～ in ～ 1. 携手,手拉手

    2. 结合起来

～ out 分发,散发

～ over 发出,转交

in ～ 在掌握中,在控制中
on ～ 在手边
on (the) one ～ , on the other ～
　　一方面……,另一方面……
handkerchief [ˈhæŋkətʃiːf]
　n. 手帕
handle [ˈhændl]
　n. 柄,把手
　vt. 处理,对待
handsome [ˈhænsəm]
　a. 1. 漂亮的,英俊的
　　2. 慷慨的,数量可观的
handwriting [ˈhændˌraitiŋ]
　n. 笔迹,书法
hang [hæŋ]
　v. 1. 悬挂,垂吊
　　2. 绞死,吊死
　～ on 1. 抓紧不放
　　2. 继续下去
　　3. 等一下
happen [ˈhæpən]
　vi. 1. 发生
　　2. (＋to V.) 碰巧,偶然
happiness [ˈhæpinis]
　n. 1. 幸福
　　2. 快乐
happy [ˈhæpi]
　a. 1. 幸福的
　　2. 快乐的
harbo(u)r [ˈhɑːbə]
　n. 海港,港口
hard [hɑːd]
　a. 1. 硬的,坚固的
　　2. 困难的,艰难的
　　3. 冷酷无情的
　ad. 1. 努力地
　　2. 困难地
harden [ˈhɑːdn]
　v. (使)变硬
hardly [ˈhɑːdli]
　ad. 几乎不,简直不
　～ any 几乎没有,几乎什么也不
　～ ...before/when 刚一……就
hardware [ˈhɑːdwɛə]
　n. 1. 五金器具
　　2. 硬件

harm [hɑːm]
　vt. & *n*. 伤害,损害
harvest [ˈhɑːvist]
　n. 1. 收获,收成
　　2. 结果,成果
　v. 收获,收割
haste [heist]
　n. 匆忙,草率
hat [hæt]
　n. 帽子
hate [heit]
　vt. 1. 憎恨,恨
　　2. 不愿,不喜欢
　n. 憎恶,憎恨
have [hæv]
　aux. v. [加过去分词,构成完成
　　时态]已经,曾经
　v. 1. 有
　　2. (＋to V.) 必须,不得不
　　3. 吃,喝
　　4. 经历,遭受
　　5. 使,让
　　6. [与名词连用,表示该名词
　　相应的动词意义]
hay [hei]
　n. 干草
he [hi]
　pron. 他
head [hed]
　n. 1. 头,头部
　　2. 首脑,首长
　　3. 头脑,才智
　vt. 率领,站在……前头
　～ for 朝、向……走去
　keep one's ～ 保持镇静
　lose one's ～ 不知所措
headache [ˈhedeik]
　n. 头痛
health [helθ]
　n. 健康,健康状况
healthy [ˈhelθi]
　a. 1. 健康的,健壮的
　　2. 有益于健康的
heap [hiːp]
　n. 1. 堆
　　2. 大量,许多

　vt. (up)堆,堆起
hear [hiə]
　v. 1. 听,听见
　　2. 听说,得知
heart [hɑːt]
　n. 1. 心(脏)
　　2. 内心,心肠
　　3. 中心,要点
　learn/get by ～ 记住,背诵
heat [hiːt]
　n. 1. 热,热度
　　2. 激烈,热烈
　v. 给(加热),(使)变热
heaven [ˈhevən]
　n. 1. 天,天空
　　2. 天堂
heavy [ˈhevi]
　a. 1. 重的,重型的
　　2. 猛烈的,狂暴的
　　3. 沉重的
height [hait]
　n. 1. 高度,高
　　2. [常 pl.]高处,高地
helicopter [ˈhelikɔptə]
　n. 直升飞机
hell [hel]
　n. 1. 地狱
　　2. 苦境
hello [ˈheləu, heˈləu]
　int. (招呼语)喂
help [help]
　v. 帮助,援助
　n. 1. 帮助,援助
　　2. 帮手,助手
　can't/couldn't ～ 禁不住,
　　不得不
helpful [ˈhelpful]
　a. (to)有帮助的,有用的
helpless [ˈhelplis]
　a. 1. 无助的
　　2. 无能的,没用的
hen [hen]
　n. 母鸡
hence [hens]
　ad. 1. 从此,以后
　　2. 因此

her [həː, hə]

pron. 1. [she 的宾格]她

2. [she 的所有格]她的

here [hiə]

ad. 1. 这里,在这里

2. 朝这里,到这里

hero ['hiərəu]

n. 1. 英雄

2. 男主角,男主人公

hers [həz]

pron. [she 的物主代词]她的

herself [həːˈself, həˈself]

pron. 1. 她自己

2. 她亲自,她本人

hesitate ['heziteit]

v. 犹豫,踌躇

hi [hai]

int. (招呼语)嗨,喂

hide [haid]

v. 1. 隐藏,躲藏

2. 隐瞒

high [hai]

a. 1. 高的

2. 高级的,高等的

ad. 高高地,高价地

highly ['haili]

ad. 1. 高度地,非常

2. 赞许地

highway ['haiwei]

n. 公路,大路

hill [hil]

n. 1. 小山,丘陵

2. 斜坡

him [him, im, əm]

pron. [he 的宾格]他

himself [him'self]

pron. 1. 他自己

2. 他亲自,他本人

hint [hint]

n. 1. 暗示

2. 指示,线索

v. 暗示

hire ['haiə]

vt. 租借,雇用

his [hiz, iz]

pron. 1. [he 的所有格]他的

2. [he 的物主代词]他的

historical [his'tɔrikəl]

a. 1. 历史(上)的

2. 有关历史的

history ['histəri]

n. 历史(学)

hit [hit]

v. 1. 打,击中

2. 碰撞

n. 一击,击中

hobby ['hɔbi]

n. 业余爱好

hold [həuld]

v. 拿着,握住

vt. 1. 保有,拥有

2. 托住,支持

3. 容纳,装得下

4. 举行

vi. 1. 有效,适用

2. 继续,持续

n. 握住,掌握

~ back 1. 阻止

2. 退缩

~ on 继续

~ onto 1. 抓住

2. 坚持

~ out 维持,支持

~ up 1. 举起

2. 阻挡

hole [həul]

n. 洞,孔

holiday ['hɔlədi, 'hɔlidei]

n. 假日,节日,假期

hollow ['hɔləu]

a. 空的,空中的

home [həum]

n. 家,家乡,本国

ad. 在家,回家,回国

a. 家庭的,家乡的,国内的

homework ['həumwəːk]

n. 1. 家庭作业

2. 准备工作

honest ['ɔnist]

a. 诚实的,正直的

honey ['hʌni]

n. (蜂)蜜

hono(u)r ['ɔnə]

n. 1. 尊敬,敬意

2. 荣誉,光荣

vt. 尊敬,给以荣誉

in ~ of 为纪念,向……表示敬意

hono(u)rable ['ɔnərəbl]

a. 1. 可敬的

2. 荣誉的,光荣的

hook [huk]

n. 钩,吊钩

v. 钩住

hope [həup]

v. & n. 希望,期望

hopeful ['həupful]

a. 1. 怀有希望的

2. 有希望的

hopeless ['həuplis]

a. 没有希望的,绝望的

horizon [hə'raizn]

a. 地平线

horror ['hɔrə]

n. 恐怖

horse [hɔːs]

n. 马

horsepower ['hɔːsˌpauə]

n. 马力

hospital ['hɔspitl]

n. 医院

host [həust]

n. 1. 主人,东道主

2. 节目主持人

hot [hɔt]

a. 1. 热的

2. 激动的,急躁的

3. (味道)刺激的,辣的

hotel [həu'tel]

n. 旅馆

hour ['auə]

n. 1. 小时

2. 时间,时刻

house [haus]

n. 1. 房子,住宅

2. 机构,所,社

vt. 给房子住

housewife ['hauswaif]

n. 家庭主妇

housework ['hauswəːk]

n. 家务劳动

how [hau]

ad. 1. 怎样,怎么

　　　2. 多么

however [hau'evə]

ad. 无论如何,不管怎样

conj. 不管用什么方法

huge [hjuːdʒ]

a. 巨大的,庞大的

human ['hjuːmən]

a. 人的,人类的

n. 人

humble ['hʌmbl]

a. 谦卑的,恭顺的

humo(u)r ['hjuːmə]

n. 幽默,诙谐

hundred ['hʌndrəd, '-drid]

num. 百,一百个

n. 1. 百

　　2. [pl.](of)数以百计,许多

hunger ['hʌŋgə]

n. 1. 饥饿

　　2. (for)欲望,渴望

hungry ['hʌŋgri]

a. 饥饿的

hunt [hʌnt]

v. & n. 1. 打猎,猎取

　　　　2. 搜索,搜寻

hurry ['hʌri]

v. (使)赶紧,(使)匆忙

n. 匆忙,仓促

in a ~ 匆忙地

hurt [həːt]

v. 1. 刺痛,伤害

　　2. (使)痛心,(使)伤感情

　　3. 危害,损害

n. 伤痛,伤害

husband ['hʌzbənd]

n. 丈夫

hut [hʌt]

n. 小屋,棚屋

hydrogen ['haidrədʒən]

n. 氢

I

I [ai]

pron. 我

ice [ais]

n. 冰,冰块

idea [ai'diə]

n. 1. 思想,概念

　　2. 想法,主意

ideal [ai'diəl]

a. 1. 理想的,完善的

　　2. 空想的,想像的

n. 理想

identify [ai'dentifai]

vt. 1. 识别,鉴别

　　2. (with)把……和……看成

　　　一样

i.e. (*id est*)

那就是,即

if [if]

conj. 1. 如果,假使

　　　2. 是否

ignore [ig'nɔː]

vt. 不理睬,忽视

ill [il]

a. 1. 有病的

　　2. 坏的,恶意的

illness ['ilnis]

n. 病,疾病

illustrate ['iləstreit]

vt. 1. (举例)说明,阐明

　　2. 图解,加插图

image ['imidʒ]

n. 1. 形象,肖像

　　2. 映像,影像

imagination [i,mædʒi'neiʃən]

n. 想像,想像力

imagine [i'mædʒin]

vt. 想像,设想

imitate ['imiteit]

vt. 1. 模仿,仿效

　　2. 仿制,仿造

immediate [i'miːdjət]

a. 1. 立即的,即时的

　　2. 直接的,最接近的

immense [i'mens]

a. 广大的,巨大的

impact ['impækt]

n. & v. 1. 影响,作用

　　　　2. 冲击,碰撞

imply [im'plai]

vt. 含有……意思,暗示

import [*v.* im'pɔːt, *n.* 'impɔːt]

vt. & n. 进口,输入

importance [im'pɔːtəns]

n. 重要(性)

important [im'pɔːtənt]

a. 1. 重要的,重大的

　　2. 有权力的,有地位的

impossible [im'pɔsəbl]

a. 不可能的,办不到的

impress [im'pres]

vt. (on) 1. 印,盖印

　　　　2. 留下印象

impression [im'preʃən]

n. 1. 印象,感想

　　2. 盖印,压痕

improve [im'pruːv]

v. 改善,改进

~ on 改进

improvement [im'pruːvmənt]

n. 改进,进步

in [in]

prep. 1. 在……里

　　　2. [表示状态]处在……中

　　　3. 在……期间,

　　　　在……以后

　　　4. 在……方面

ad. 1. 在家,在屋里

　　2. 到达,来到

　　3. 向内,在内

inch [intʃ]

n. 英寸

incident ['insidənt]

n. 事件,事变

incline [in'klain]

v. 1. (使)倾斜

　　2. (使)倾向于,赞同

include [in'kluːd]

vt. 包括,包含

income ['inkʌm]

n. 收入,收益

increase [in'kriːs]

v. & n. 增加,增长

indeed [in'diːd]

ad. 1. 真正地,实际上
　　2. 确实,实在

independent [indi'pendənt]
　a. (of)独立的

index ['indeks]
　n. 1. 索引
　　2. 指标,标志
　　3. 指数

Indian ['indjən]
　a. 1. 印度的,印度人的
　　2. 印第安人的
　n. 1. 印度人
　　2. 印第安人

indicate ['indikeit]
　vt. 1. 指出,指示
　　2. 表明,暗示

indirect [,indi'rekt]
　a. 间接的

individual [,indi'vidjuəl]
　a. 1. 个人的,单独的
　　2. 独特的
　n. 个人,个体

indoors ['in'dɔ:z]
　ad. 在室内

industrial [in'dʌstriəl]
　a. 工业的,产业的

industry [in'dʌstri]
　n. 1. 工业,产业
　　2. 勤劳,勤奋

infant ['infənt]
　n. 婴儿,幼儿
　a. 婴儿的,幼稚的,初期的

infect [in'fekt]
　vt. 1. 传染,感染
　　2. 影响

influence ['influəns]
　n. 1. (on)影响,感化
　　2. 势力,权势
　vt. 影响,感化

inform [in'fɔ:m]
　v. (of,about)通知,告诉

information [,infə'meiʃən]
　n. 1. 信息,消息,情报
　　2. 通知,告知

inhabitant [in'hæbitənt]
　n. 居民,住户

inherit [in'herit]
　vt. 继承

initial [i'niʃəl]
　a. 1. 最初的
　　2. 词首的
　n. 词首大写字母

injure ['indʒə]
　vt. 损害,伤害

ink [iŋk]
　n. 墨水

inn [in]
　n. 小旅馆,客栈

inner ['inə]
　a. 1. 内部的,里面的
　　2. 内心的

innocent ['inəsnt]
　a. 1. (of)清白的,无罪的
　　2. 天真的,无知的

inquire/enquire [in'kwaiə]
　v. (of,about) 1. 询问,打听
　　　　　2. 调查,查问

insect ['insekt]
　n. 昆虫,虫

inside ['in'said]
　a. 里面的,内部的
　ad. 在里面,在内部
　n. 里面,内部

insist [in'sist]
　v. (on)坚决要求,坚决主张,
　　坚持

inspect [in'spekt]
　vt. 检查,视察

inspire [in'spaiə]
　vt. 1. 鼓舞,激起
　　2. 给……以灵感

instal(l) [in'stɔ:l]
　vt. 安装,设置

instance ['instəns]
　n. 例子,事例
　for ～ 例如

instant ['instənt]
　a. 1. 立即的,直接的
　　2. 紧迫的
　　3. (食品)速溶的,方便的

instead [in'sted]
　ad. 代替,顶替

～ of 代替,而不是

institute ['institju:t]
　n. 学会,研究所,学院

institution [,insti'tju:ʃən]
　n. 公共机构,协会

instruction [in'strʌkʃən]
　n. 1. [pl.]指示,用法说明(书)
　　2. 教育,指导

instrument ['instrumənt]
　n. 1. 仪器,器械
　　2. 乐器

insult [*v*. in'sʌlt, *n*. 'insʌlt]
　vt. & *n*. 侮辱,凌辱

insurance [in'ʃuərəns]
　n. 保险,保险业

insure [in'ʃuə]
　vt. 给……保险

intelligence [in'telidʒəns]
　n. 智力,聪明

intelligent [in'telidʒənt]
　a. 聪明的,明智的

intend [in'tend]
　vt. 想要,打算

intense [in'tens]
　a. 1. 强烈的,剧烈的
　　2. 热切的,热情的

intention [in'tenʃən]
　n. 意图,目的

interest ['intrist]
　n. 1. (of)兴趣,关心
　　2. 重要性,影响
　　3. 利息
　　4. [常 pl.]利益,利害
　vt. (in)使发生兴趣,引起……的
　　注意

interesting ['intristiŋ]
　a. 有趣的

interfere [,intə'fiə]
　v. 1. 干涉,干预
　　2. (with)妨碍,打扰

interference [,intə'fiərəns]
　n. 1. (in)干涉,干预
　　2. (with)妨碍,打扰

intermediate [,intə'mi:djət]
　a. 中间的

internal [in'tə:nl]

a. 1. 内部的,内的

2. 内政的,国内的

international [ˌintə(:)'næʃənəl]

a. 国际的

Internet ['intənet]

n. [the ～]国际互联网,因特网

interpret [in'tə:prit]

v. 1. 解释,说明

2. 口译

interrupt [ˌintə'rʌpt]

vt. 中断,阻碍

v. 打断(话),打扰

interruption [ˌintə'rʌpʃən]

v. 中断,打断

interval ['intəvəl]

n. 1. 间隔

2. 幕间(工间)休息

at ～s 不时,时时

interview ['intəvju:]

vt. & *n*. 接见,会见

intimate ['intimit]

a. 亲密的,密切的

into ['intu, 'intə]

prep. 1. 向……内,到……里

2. 成为,转入

introduce [ˌintrə'dju:s]

vt. 1. 介绍

2. 传入,引进

introduction [ˌintrə'dʌkʃən]

n. (to) 1. 介绍

2. 传入,引进

3. 导言,导论

invade [in'veid]

v. 侵入,侵略,侵袭

invent [in'vent]

vt. 发明,创造

invention [in'venʃən]

n. 发明,创造

inventor [in'ventə(r)]

n. 发明者

invest [in'vest]

vt. 1. 投资

2. 投入(时间,精力等)

vi. (in) 投资

investigate [in'vestigeit]

v. 调查,调查研究

investment [in'vestmənt]

n. 投资

invisible [in'vizəbl]

a. 看不见的,无形的

invitation [ˌinvi'teiʃən]

n. 邀请,招待

invite [in'vait]

vt. 邀请,招待

involve [in'vɔlv]

vt. 1. 卷入,陷入

2. 包含,涉及

inward ['inwəd]

ad. 内向,在内

a. 向内的

iron ['aiən]

n. 1. 铁

2. 烙铁,熨斗

v. 熨(衣服)

island ['ailənd]

n. 岛,岛屿

isolate ['aisəleit]

vt. 隔离,孤立

issue ['isju:]

v. 1. 颁布,发布,发行

2. 流出,放出

n. 1. 发行(物),(报刊)期号

2. 问题,争论点

it [it]

pron. 1. 它

2. [作先行词引导短语或从句]

3. [作无人称动词的主语,表示时间、气候、距离等]

Italian [i'tæljən]

a. 1. 意大利(人)的

2. 意大利语的

n. 1. 意大利人

2. 意大利语

item ['aitem, 'aitəm]

n. 条,条款,条目

its [its]

pron. [it 的所有格]它的

itself [it'self]

pron. 它自己,它本身

by ～ 独自,单独

in ～ 本身

J

jacket ['dʒækit]

n. 上衣,茄克衫

jail [dʒeil]

n. 监狱,看守所

jam [dʒæm]

n. 1. 拥挤,阻塞

2. 果酱

v. (使)卡住,(使)塞满

January ['dʒænjuəri]

n. 一月

Japanese [ˌdʒæpə'ni:z]

a. 1. 日本的,日本人的

2. 日语的

n. 1. 日本人

2. 日语

jar [dʒɑ:]

n. 罐,广口瓶

jaw [dʒɔ:]

n. 颌,颚

jealous ['dʒeləs]

a. (of) 1. 嫉妒的

2. 羡慕的

jet [dʒet]

n. 1. 喷气发动机,喷气式飞机

2. 喷嘴,喷口

jewel ['dʒu:əl]

n. 宝石

job [dʒɔb]

n. 1. 职业,职位

2. 工作,活儿

join [dʒɔin]

v. 1. 参加,加入

2. 连接,接合

joint [dʒɔint]

n. 1. 接合处,接头

2. 关节,骨节

a. 联合的,共同的

joke [dʒəuk]

n. 笑话,玩笑

v. (和……)开玩笑

journal ['dʒə:nl]

n. 定期刊物,杂志

journey ['dʒə:ni]

n . 旅行, 旅程

joy [dʒɔi]

  n . 1. 欢乐, 喜悦

    2. 乐事, 乐趣

judge [dʒʌdʒ]

  n . 1. 法官, 审判员

    2. 裁判员, 评判员, 鉴定人

  v . 1. 审判, 判定

    2. 评定, 裁判

    3. 断定, 判断

judg(e)ment [ˈdʒʌdʒmənt]

  n . 1. 审判, 判决

    2. 判断力

    3. 意见, 看法

juice [dʒuːs]

  n . (水果)汁, 液

July [dʒu(ː)ˈlai]

  n . 七月

jump [dʒʌmp]

  vi . & *n* . 1. 跳跃, 跳

    2. 暴涨, 突增

June [dʒuːn]

  n . 六月

junior [ˈdʒuːnjə]

  a . 1. 年少的, 较年幼的

    2. 资历较浅的, 地位较低的

  n . 1. 年少者

    2. 地位较低者, 晚辈

    3. (美国大学或中学的)三年级学生

just [dʒʌst]

  ad . 1. 正好, 恰好

    2. 仅仅, 只是

    3. 刚才

  a . 1. 公正的, 公平的

    2. 恰当的, 应得的

justice [ˈdʒʌstis]

  n . 公正, 公平

justify [ˈdʒʌstifai]

  v . 证明……是正当的

K

keep [kiːp]

  v . 保持

  vt . 1. 保留, 保存

    2. 经营, 经售

    3. 留住, 扣留

    4. 料理, 整理

    5. 守护, 看(门)

    6. 供养, 饲养

  ~ from 防止, 预防

  ~ on 继续不断

  ~ to 坚持, 保持

  ~ up 1. 保持

    2. 继续进行

  ~ up with 向……看齐, 赶上

kettle [ˈketl]

  n . 水壶

key [kiː]

  n . 1. 钥匙

    2. (to)答案

    3. 键

    4. 关键

kick [kik]

  v . & *n* . 踢

kid [kid]

  n . 小孩, 儿童

  v . 开玩笑, 戏弄

kill [kil]

  v . 1. 杀死

    2. 毁掉

kilogram(-me) [ˈkiləgræm]

  n . 千克, 公斤

kilometre(-ter) [ˈkiləumiːtə(r)]

  n . 公里, 千米

kind [ˈkaind]

  n . 种类

  a . 仁慈的, 亲切的

kindness [ˈkaindnis]

  n . 1. 仁慈, 亲切

    2. 好意

king [ˈkiŋ]

  n . 国王

kingdom [ˈkiŋdəm]

  n . 1. 王国

    2. 领域

kiss [kis]

  v . & *n* . 吻

kitchen [ˈkitʃin]

  n . 厨房

knee [niː]

  n . 膝, 膝盖

kneel [niːl]

  vi . 跪

knife [naif]

  n . 刀, 餐刀

knit [nit]

  v . 编织, 编结

knock [nɔk]

  v . 1. 敲, 敲打

    2. (使)碰撞

  n . 敲, 击

know [nəu]

  v . 知道, 了解

  vt . 1. 精通

    2. 认识, 熟悉

  be known as 被认为是, 被称为

knowledge [ˈnɔlidʒ]

  n . 1. 知识, 学问

    2. 知道, 了解

L

laboratory (lab)

  [ləˈbɔrətəri]

  n . 实验室

labo(u)r [ˈleibə]

  n . 1. 劳动

    2. 劳力, 劳工

lack [læk]

  n . & *v* . 缺乏, 不足

ladder [ˈlædə]

  n . 梯子, 阶梯

lady [ˈleidi]

  n . 1. 女士, 夫人

    2. [pl.]女厕所, 女盥洗室

lake [leik]

  n . 湖

lamp [læmp]

  n . 灯

land [lænd]

  n . 1. 陆地, 地面

    2. 土地, 田地

    3. 国土, 国家

  v . (使)登陆, (使)着陆

landlord [ˈlændlɔːd]

  n . 房东, 地主

language [ˈlæŋgwidʒ]

  n . 语言

large [lɑːdʒ]

　a. 大的

　at ～ 一般,大体上

largely [lɑːdʒli]

　ad. 1. 主要地

　　　2. 大量地

laser [ˈleizə]

　n. 激光

last [lɑːst]

　a. 1. 最后的,惟一剩下的

　　　2. 上一个的

　ad. 1. 最后

　　　2. 最近一次,上一次

　vt. 持续,耐久

　at ～ 最后,终于

late [leit]

　a. 1. 迟的

　　　2. 晚的,晚期的

　　　3. 已故的

　ad. 迟,晚

lately [leitli]

　ad. 最近,不久前

later [ˈleitə]

　ad. 1. 后来

　　　2. 过一会儿

　a. 1. 后来的,以后的,后面的

　　　2. 新近的

　　　3. 晚年的

latter [ˈlætə]

　a. 后面的,末了的

　pron. 后者

laugh [lɑːf]

　vi. (at)笑,讥笑

　n. 笑,笑声

laughter [ˈlɑːftə]

　n. 笑,笑声

launch [lɔːntʃ, lɑːntʃ]

　vt. 1. 发射

　　　2. 使(船)下水

　　　3. 发动,开展

　n. 1. 发射

　　　2. 下水

laundry [lɔːndri]

　n. 1. 洗衣房,洗衣店

　　　2. 洗的衣服

lavatory [ˈlævəˌtəri]

　n. 厕所,盥洗室

law [lɔː]

　n. 1. 法律,法令

　　　2. 法则,规律,定律

lawyer [ˈlɔːjə]

　n. 律师

lay [lei]

　vt. 1. 放,搁

　　　2. 铺设,砌(砖)

　～ aside 1. 把……搁置一边

　　　　　2. 储蓄

　～ down 1. 放下

　　　　　2. 制定,拟定

　～ out 设计,制定

layer [ˈleiə]

　n. 层,阶层

lazy [ˈleizi]

　a. 懒惰的,懒散的

lead [liːd]

　v. 1. 领导,引导

　　　2. 领先,占首位

　vi. (to) 1. 通向

　　　　　2. 导致,引起

　n. 带领,引导

lead [liːd]

　n. 铅

leader [ˈliːdə]

　n. 领袖,领导人

leadership [ˈliːdəʃip]

　n. 领导

leading [ˈliːdiŋ]

　a. 1. 领导的

　　　2. 第一位的,最主要的

leaf [liːf]

　n. 1. 叶子

　　　2. (书刊的)一张

league [liːg]

　n. 1. 同盟,联盟

　　　2. 联合会,社团

leak [liːk]

　v. 1. 漏,渗

　　　2. 泄漏

　n. 1. 倾斜,漏隙

　　　2. 泄漏,漏出

lean [liːn]

　v. 1. 倾斜,屈身

　　　2. 依靠,依赖

　a. 瘦的

learn [ləːn]

　v. 1. 学习,学

　　　2. (of)听到,获悉

learned [ˈləːnid]

　a. 博学的,有学问的

learning [ˈləːniŋ]

　n. 1. 知识,学问

　　　2. 学习,学

least [liːst]

　a. 最小的,最少的

　ad. 最少,最小

　at ～ 至少

leather [ˈleðə]

　n. 皮革,皮革制品

leave [liːv]

　v. 离开,出发

　vt. 1. 留下,出发

　　　2. 听任,让

　　　3. 交付,委托

　n. 准假,假期

　～ behind 1. 留下

　　　　　2. 忘记带

　～ out 遗漏,略去

lecture [ˈlektʃə]

　n. 演讲,讲课

left [left]

　a. 左,左边的

　n. 左,左边

leg [leg]

　n. 腿

legal [ˈliːgəl]

　a. 法律的,法定的,合法的

leisure [ˈleʒə, ˈliːʒə]

　n. 1. 空闲,闲暇

　　　2. 悠闲,安逸

lend [lend]

　v. 借给,贷(款)

　～ itself to 适宜于,对……有用

length [leŋθ]

　n. 1. 长,长度

　　　2. 一段,一节

　at ～ 1. 终于,最后

　　　　2. 详细地

lens [lenz]

n. 透镜,镜头

less [les]

　　a. 更少的,更小的

　　ad. 更少地,更小地

　　no ～ than 1. 决不少于

　　　　　　　　 2. 不亚于,不次于

lesson [ˈlesn]

　　n. 1. 功课

　　　　 2. (一节)课

　　　　 3. [pl.]课程

　　　　 4. 教训

lest [lest]

　　conj. 惟恐,免得

let [let]

　　vt. 1. 允许,让

　　　　 2. 出租,租给

　　～ alone 更不用说

　　～ out 放掉

letter [ˈletə]

　　n. 1. 信,函件

　　　　 2. 字母,文字

level [ˈlev(ə)l]

　　n. 1. 水平

　　　　 2. 级别,等级

　　a. 水平的,平的

liberty [ˈlibəti]

　　n. 自由

librarian [laiˈbreəriən]

　　n. 图书管理员

library [ˈlaibrəri]

　　n. 图书馆,藏书室

lid [lid]

　　n. 盖子

lie [lai]

　　vi. 1. 躺

　　　　 2. 平放

　　v. 说谎,欺骗

　　n. 谎话,谎言

　　～ in 在于

life [laif]

　　n. 1. 生命

　　　　 2. 生物

　　　　 3. 一生,生涯

lift [lift]

　　v. (使)升起,举起

　　vi. 消散

n. 1. [英]电梯

　　　 2. 上升,升力

light [lait]

　　n. 1. 光,光亮

　　　　 2. 光源,灯

　　v. 1. 点(火),点燃

　　　　 2. (使)变亮,照亮

　　a. 1. 轻的

　　　　 2. 轻松的

　　　　 3. (颜色)浅的

　　　　 4. 光亮的

　　in (the) ～ of 按照,根据

　　throw/cast ～ on 阐明,使明白

lightning [ˈlaitniŋ]

　　n. 闪电

like [laik]

　　v. 1. 喜欢

　　　　 2. 希望,想要

　　prep. 好像,如,跟……一样

　　a. 相似的,同样的

likely [ˈlaikli]

　　a. 很可能的

likewise [ˈlaikˌwaiz]

　　ad. 1. 同样地,照样地

　　　　　 2. 又,也

limb [lim]

　　n. 肢,翼

limit [ˈlimit]

　　n. 界线,限度

　　vt. (to)限制,限定

limitation [ˌlimiˈteiʃən]

　　n. 限制

limited [ˈlimitid]

　　a. 有限的

line [lain]

　　n. 1. 线,绳

　　　　 2. 路线,航线

　　　　 3. 排,行

　　　　 4. 线路,电线

　　　　 5. 界线,边线

　　v. 排队

　　in ～ with 和……成直线,

　　　和……一致

link [liŋk]

　　v. 连接,联系

　　n. 链环,环节

lion [ˈlaiən]

　　n. 狮子

lip [lip]

　　n. 嘴唇

liquid [ˈlikwid]

　　n. 液体

　　a. 液体的

list [list]

　　n. 表,清单

　　vt. 把……编列成表,列入表内

listen [lisn]

　　vi. (to) 1. 听

　　　　　　 2. 听从

literary [ˈlitərəri]

　　a. 文学(上)的

literature [ˈlitəritʃə]

　　n. 文学,文学作品,文献

litre [ˈliːtə(r)]

　　n. 升(容量单位)

little [ˈlitl]

　　a. 1. 小的

　　　　 2. 很少的,几乎没有的

　　n. 没有多少,少量

　　ad. 几乎不

　　a ～ 一点,稍微

　　～ by ～ 逐渐地

live [*v*. liv, *a*. laiv]

　　vi. 1. 居住

　　　　 2. 生活,生存

　　vt. 过生活

　　a. 1. 活的

　　　　 2. 实况的

　　～ through 度过,经受住

　　～ up to 做到,不辜负

lively [ˈlaivli]

　　a. 1. 活泼的,活跃的

　　　　 2. 栩栩如生的,真实的

living [ˈliviŋ]

　　a. 1. 活(着)的,生活的

　　　　 2. 有生命力的,生动活泼的

　　n. 生计,生活

load [ləud]

　　v. 装(货),装载

　　n. 装载(量),负荷(量)

loaf [ləuf]

　　n. 一个(面包)

loan [ləun]
  n. 1. 贷款
     2. 出借,借出

local ['ləukəl]
  a. 地方的,本地的

locate [ləu'keit]
  vt. 1. 查找……的地点
     2. 使……坐落于,位于

location [ləu'keiʃən]
  n. 位置,场所

lock [lɔk]
  n. 锁
  v. 锁,锁上

lodge [lɔdʒ]
  v. 住宿,留宿

logic ['lɔdʒik]
  n. 逻辑,逻辑学

lonely ['ləunli]
  a. 孤独的,寂寞的

long [lɔŋ]
  a. 1. 长的,远的
     2. 长久的,长期的
  ad. 长久,长期地
  vi. (for)渴望
  as ～ as 只要
  before ～ 不久以后
  for ～ 长久地
  no ～er 不再
  so ～ as 只要

look [luk]
  vi. 1. (at)看,望
     2. 显得,好像
  n. 1. (at)看,望
     2. 外表,样子
  ～ after 照管,照料
  ～ back 回顾
  ～ down on 看不起,轻视
  ～ for 寻找
  ～ forward to 盼望,期望
  ～ in 顺便看望
  ～ into 调查,观察
  ～ out 留神,提防
  ～ over 检查
  ～ through 仔细察看
  ～ up 查阅,查考

loose [luːs]

  a. 松的,肥大的

lorry ['lɔri]
  n. [英]卡车

lose [luːz]
  vt. 1. 丢,丢失
     2. 迷(路)
     3. 输去,负
  vi. (钟,表)走慢

loss [lɔs]
  n. 1. 丢失,遗失
     2. 损失,亏损
  at a ～ 困惑,不知所措

lot [lɔt]
  n. 1. 许多
     2. (抽)签
  a ～ (of) 大量(的),很多(的)
  ～s of 大量的,很多的

loud [laud]
  a. 大声的,响亮的

love [lʌv]
  vt. 1. 爱,热爱
     2. 爱好,喜欢
  n. 爱,热爱

lovely ['lʌvli]
  a. 1. 可爱的,好看的
     2. 愉快的

lover ['lʌvə]
  n. 1. 爱好者
     2. 情人

low [ləu]
  a. 1. 低的
     2. 低劣的,低级的

lower ['ləuə]
  a. 较低的
  v. 降下,放低

loyal ['lɔiəl]
  a. (to)忠诚的,忠心的

luck [lʌk]
  n. 1. 运气
     2. 好运

lucky ['lʌki]
  a. 幸运的

luggage ['lʌgidʒ]
  n. 行李

lump [lʌmp]
  n. 团,块

lunch [lʌntʃ]
  n. 午餐

luxury ['lʌkʃəri]
  n. 奢侈,华贵

M

machine [mə'ʃiːn]
  n. 机器,机械
  vt. 用机器加工

machinery [mə'ʃiːnəri]
  n. [总称]机器,机械

mad [mæd]
  a. 1. 发疯的,狂怒的
     2. 狂热的,着迷的

magazine [ˌmægə'ziːn]
  n. 杂志,期刊

magic ['mædʒik]
  n. 魔法,魔术
  a. 有魔力的,魔术的

magnetic [mæg'netik]
  a. 1. 磁的,有磁性的
     2. 有吸引力的

magnificent [mæg'nifisnt]
  a. 壮丽的,宏伟的

mail [meil]
  n. 邮件
  vt. 邮寄

mailbox ['meilbɔks]
  n. 邮箱

main [mein]
  a. 主要的

mainly ['meinli]
  ad. 大体上,主要地

maintain [men'tein]
  vt. 1. 维修,保养
     2. 维持,保持
     3. 坚持,主张

major ['meidʒə]
  a. 较大的,较重要的
  n. 专业,专业学生
  vi. (in)主修,专攻

majority [mə'dʒɔriti]
  n. 多数,大多数

make [meik]
  vt. 1. 做,制造
     2. 准备,布置

3. 使，使得
4. 获得，挣得
5. 总计，等于

n. (产品)制造方法，(产品)来源

be made up of 由……构成，
　由……组成

~ for 1. 走向，驶
　　　2. 有助于，有利于

~ out 1. 辨认，区分
　　　2. 理解

~ up 1. 组成，构成
　　　2. 弥补
　　　3. 化妆

~ up for 补偿，弥补

male [meil]

a. 男的，雄的

mall [mɔːl]

n. 商业街，购物中心

man [mæn]

n. 1. 男人
　　2. 人，人类

manage ['mænidʒ]

v. 1. 经营，管理，处理
　　2. 设法，对付

vt. 操纵，运用

management ['mænidʒmənt]

n. 经营，管理，管理部门

manager ['mænidʒə]

n. 经理，管理人

mankind [mæn'kaind]

n. 人类

manner ['mænə]

n. 1. 方式，方法
　　2. [pl.]礼貌，规矩
　　3. 举止，风度

manual ['mænjuəl]

a. 手的，手工做的

n. 手册，指南

manufacture [ˌmænju'fæktʃə]

vt. 制造，加工

n. 1. 制造，制造业
　　2. 产品

manufacturer [ˌmænju'fæktʃərə]

n. 制造商，制造厂

many ['meni]

a. 许多的，多的

pron. 许多人，许多

a great/good ~ (of) 许多，大量

~ a 许多的

map [mæp]

n. 地图，图

march [mɑːtʃ]

v. (使)行军，(使)行进

n. 1. 行军，行程
　　2. [M-]三月

margin ['mɑːdʒin]

n. 1. 页边空白
　　2. 边缘

mark [mɑːk]

n. 1. 痕迹，斑点
　　2. 记号，符号
　　3. (考试等的)分数

vt. 1. 计分，打分
　　2. 标明，作记号于

market ['mɑːkit]

n. 1. 市场，集市
　　2. 销路，需要

marriage ['mæridʒ]

n. 结婚，婚姻

married ['mærid]

a. 1. 已婚的
　　2. (to)与……结婚的

marry ['mæri]

vt. 娶，嫁，和……结婚

marvel(l)ous ['mɑːviləs]

a. 奇迹般的，惊人的，妙极的

mask [mɑːsk]

n. 1. 面具，面罩，口罩
　　2. 假面具，伪装

vt. 1. 用面具遮住，遮盖
　　2. 掩饰，掩盖

mass [mæs]

n. 1. 大量，众多
　　2. 团，块
　　3. [pl.]群众，民众，大众
　　4. 质量

master ['mɑːstə]

n. 1. 男主人，雇主
　　2. 师傅，能手
　　3. [M-]硕士

vt. 精通，掌握

match [mætʃ]

n. 1. 火柴
　　2. 比赛，竞赛

v. 相配，相称

mate [meit]

n. 1. 伙伴，同事
　　2. 配偶

v. 交配，成配偶

material [mə'tiəriəl]

n. 材料，原料

a. 物质的，实体的

mathematics (maths)
[ˌmæθi'mætiks]

n. 数学

matter ['mætə]

n. 1. 物质
　　2. 麻烦事，毛病
　　3. 事情，问题

vi. 有关系，要紧

a ~ of 1. (关于……)的问题
　　　 2. 大约

as a ~ of fact 其实，事实上

no ~ + wh-word 无论

mature [mə'tjuə]

a. 1. 成熟的，熟的
　　2. 成年人的

v. (使)成熟

maximum ['mæksiməm]

n. 最大值，极限

a. 最大的，最高的

may [mei, me]

aux. v. 1. 可能，也许
　　　　 2. 可以
　　　　 3. 祝，愿

n. [M-]五月

maybe ['meibi]

ad. 大概，或许

mayor [mɛə]

n. 市长

me [miː]

pron. [I 的宾格]我

meal [miːl]

n. 膳食，一餐

mean [miːn, min]

vt. 1. 表示……意思，意思是
　　2. 意欲，打算

a. 1. 卑鄙的

2. 吝啬的,小气的

3. 平均的

n. 平均值

meaning [ˈmiːniŋ]

n. 意思,意义

means [miːnz]

n. 手段,方法

by all ～ 无论如何,必定

by ～ of 借助于,用

by no ～ 决不

meantime [ˈmiːnˈtaim]

n. 其间

meanwhile [ˈmiːnwail]

ad. 当时,同时

measure [ˈmeʒə]

v. 量,测量

n. 1. 尺寸,大小

2. [常 pl.]措施,办法

measurement [ˈmeʒəmənt]

n. 测量,度量

meat [miːt]

n. (食用)肉

mechanic [miˈkænik]

n. 1. 技工,机修工

2. [-s]力学,机械学

mechanical [miˈkænikl]

a. 1. 机械的,机械制造的

2. 机械似的,呆板的

medal [ˈmedl]

n. 奖牌,奖章,勋章

media [ˈmiːdjə]

n. 新闻媒介,传播媒介

medical [ˈmedikəl]

a. 1. 医学的,医疗的

2. 内科的

medicine [ˈmedsin]

n. 1. 内服药

2. 医学,内科学

medium [ˈmiːdjəm]

n. 1. 中间,适中

2. 媒介物,介质

a. 中等的,适中的

meet [miːt]

v. 1. (with)遇见,碰到

2. 会见,会谈

vt. 1. 迎接

2. 满足,符合

meeting [ˈmiːtiŋ]

n. 1. 会议,集会

2. 会见,会合

melt [melt]

v. (使)融化,(使)熔化

member [ˈmembə]

n. 成员,会员

memory [ˈmeməri]

n. 1. 记忆,记忆力

2. 回忆

3. 存储(器)

mend [mend]

vt. 修理,缝补

mental [ˈmentl]

a. 精神的,智力的

mention [ˈmenʃən]

vt. & *n*. 提及,说起

menu [ˈmenjuː]

n. 菜单

merchant [ˈməːtʃənt]

n. 商人

mercy [ˈməːsi]

n. 仁慈,宽恕

at the ～ of 在……支配下

mere [miə]

a. 仅仅,不过

merit [ˈmerit]

n. 优点,价值

merry [ˈmeri]

a. 欢乐的,愉快的

message [ˈmesidʒ]

n. 消息,信息

metal [ˈmetl]

n. 金属

method [ˈmeθəd]

n. 方式,方法

metre(-ter) [ˈmiːtə]

n. 米,公尺

microphone [ˈmaikrəfəun]

n. 话筒

microscope [ˈmaikrəskəup]

n. 显微镜

midday [ˈmiddei]

n. 正午

middle [ˈmidl]

n. 中间,当中

a. 中间的,中部的

midnight [ˈmidˌnait]

n. 午夜

might [mait]

aux. v. 1. [may 的过去式]

2. 可能,会

n. 力量,威力,能力

mild [maild]

a. 1. 温暖的,暖和的

2. 温和的,温柔的

3. 轻微的

mile [mail]

n. 英里

military [ˈmilitəri]

a. 军事的,军用的

milk [milk]

n. 乳,牛奶

v. (挤)奶

mill [mil]

n. 1. 磨粉机,磨坊

2. 作坊,工厂

millimetre(-ter) [ˈmiliˌmiːtə(r)]

n. 毫米

million [ˈmiljən]

num. 百万,百万个

n. [pl.](of)无数

mind [maind]

n. 1. 头脑,精神

2. 记忆

vi. 1. 注意,留心

2. 介意,反对

bear/keep in ～ 记住

have in ～ 1. 记住

2. 考虑到,想到

make up one's ～ (+ to V.) 下决
心(做)

mine [main]

pron. [I 的物主代词]我的

n. 1. 矿,矿山

2. 地雷,水雷

v. 1. 采矿

2. 布雷

mineral [ˈminərəl]

n. 矿物,矿石

minimum [ˈminiməm]

· 49 ·

n. 最小值,最低限度

a. 最小的,最低的

minister ['ministə]

n. 部长,大臣

minor ['mainə]

a. 1. 较小的,较少的

2. 较次要的

minority [mai'nɔriti]

n. 1. 少数,少数派

2. 少数民族

minus ['mainəs]

a. 负的,减的

prep. 减去

minute [*n*. 'minit, *a*. mai'nju:t]

n. 1. 分,分钟

2. 一会儿,瞬间

a. 微小的

miracle ['mirəkl]

n. 奇迹,令人惊奇的人(事)

mirror ['mirə]

n. 镜

miserable ['mizərəbl]

a. 痛苦的,悲惨的

miss [mis]

n. [M-]小姐

v. 未击中

vt. 1. 错过,未赶上

2. 惦念

3. (out)漏掉,省掉

missile ['misail, -səl]

n. 导弹,发射物

missing ['misiŋ]

a. 漏掉的,失踪的

mission ['miʃən]

n. 1. 使命,任务

2. 使团,代表团

mistake [mis'teik]

n. 错误,过失

v. 1. 弄错,误解

2. (for)把……误认为

by ~ 错误地

Mister (Mr.) ['mistə]

n. 先生

mistress ['mistris]

n. 1. 情妇

2. 女主人,主妇

misunderstand ['misʌndə'stænd]

vt. 误解,误会

mix [miks]

v. 1. 使混合

2. 混淆

mixture ['mikstʃə]

n. 1. 混合

2. 混合物,混合剂

mobile ['məubail]

a. 1. 运动的,活动的,流动的

2. 多变的,易变的

mode [məud]

n. 方式,样式

model ['mɔdl]

n. 1. 样式,型

2. 模范,典型

3. 模型,原型,模特儿

moderate ['mɔdərit]

a. 中等的,适度的

modern ['mɔdən]

a. 现代的,新式的

modest ['mɔdist]

a. 谦虚的,谦让的

modify ['mɔdifai]

vt. 更改,修改

moisture ['mɔistʃə]

n. 潮湿,湿气

molecule ['mɔlikju:l]

n. 分子

moment ['məumənt]

n. 片刻,瞬间

at the ~ 现在,此刻

for a ~ 片刻,一会儿

for the ~ 现在,暂时

in a ~ 立刻,马上

the ~ (that) 一……(就)

Monday ['mʌndei]

n. 星期一

money ['mʌni]

n. 货币,钱

monkey ['mʌŋki]

n. 猴子

month [mʌnθ]

n. 月

monthly ['mʌnθli]

a. 每月的

ad. 每月一次

n. 月刊

monument ['mɔnjumənt]

n. 纪念碑

mood [mu:d]

n. 1. 心情,情绪

2. 语气

moon [mu:n]

n. 1. 月球,月亮

2. 卫星

moral ['mɔrəl]

a. 道德(上)的

more [mɔ:(r)]

a. 更多的

n. 更多

ad. 更,更多

~ and ~ 越来越(多)

~ or less 或多或少

no ~ 不再

no ~ than 1. 不过,仅仅

2. 和……一样不

moreover [mɔ:'rəuvə]

ad. 再者,此外

morning ['mɔ:niŋ]

n. 早晨,上午

most [məust]

a. 1. 最多的

2. 多数的,大部分的

ad. 1. 最,最多

2. 很,十分

n. 大多数,大部分

at ~ 至多,不超过

mostly ['məustli]

ad. 主要地,大部分

mother ['mʌðə]

n. 母亲

motion ['məuʃən]

n. 1. (物体的)运动

2. 手势,眼色,动作

3. 提议,动议

v. 向……打手势,示意

motive ['məutiv]

n. 动机,目的

a. 发动的,运动的

motor ['məutə]

n. 发动机,电动机

mount [maunt]

  v. 登,上(山、梯等)

  vt. 安装

mountain ['mauntin]

  n. 1. 山

    2. [pl.]山脉

mouse [maus]

  n. 1. 鼠

    2. 鼠标

mouth [mauθ]

  n. 口,嘴

move [mu:v]

  vt. 1. 移动,搬动

    2. 感动,激动

  vi. 1. 迁移,搬家

    2. 活动

  n. 移动,活动

movement ['mu:vmənt]

  n. 1. 运动,活动

    2. 移动,迁移

movie ['mu:vi]

  n. 电影

much [mʌtʃ]

  a. 许多的,大量的

  ad. 1. 非常,很

    2. ……多,更加

  n. 许多,大量

mud [mʌd]

  n. 泥,泥浆

multiple ['mʌltipl]

  a. 多样的,多重的

  n. 倍数

multiply ['mʌltiplai]

  v. 1. (by)乘,使相乘

    2. 倍增

murder ['mə:də]

  vi. & *n*. 谋杀,凶杀

muscle ['mʌsl]

  n. 肌肉

museum [mju(:)'ziəm]

  n. 博物馆

music ['mju:zik]

  n. 音乐

musical ['mju:zikəl]

  a. 1. 音乐的

    2. 悦耳的

musician [mju:'ziʃən]

  n. 音乐家

must [mʌst, məst]

  aux. *v*. 1. 必须,应当

    2. 很可能,一定

my [mai, mi]

  pron. [I 的所有格]我的

myself [mai'self]

  pron. 1. 我自己

    2. 我亲自,我本人

mysterlous [mis'tiəriəs]

  a. 神秘的

mystery ['mistəri]

  n. 神秘,神秘的事物

N

nail [neil]

  n. 1. 指甲

    2. 钉

  vt. 钉,将……钉牢

naked ['neikid]

  a. 1. 裸体的

    2. 无遮蔽的,无掩饰的

name [neim]

  n. 1. 名字,名称

    2. 名义

  vt. 1. (after)给……取(命)名

    2. 叫出……的名字

narrow ['nærəu]

  a. 狭窄的

nation ['neiʃən]

  n. 民族,国家

national ['næʃənəl]

  a. 1. 民族的,国家的

    2. 全国性的,国有的

native ['neitiv]

  a. 1. 本地的,本国的

    2. 天生的

  n. 本地人,本国人

natural ['nætʃərəl]

  a. 1. 正常的,自然的

    2. 自然界的,天然的

    3. 天赋的

nature ['neitʃə]

  n. 1. 自然界,大自然

    2. 性质

in ～ 本质上

navy ['neivi]

  n. 海军

near [niə]

  prep. 靠近

  ad. 接近

  a. 接近的,近的

nearby ['niəbai]

  a. 附近的

  ad. 在附近

ncarly ['niəli]

  ad. 差不多,几乎

neat [ni:t]

  a. 整洁的,干净的

necessary ['nesisəri]

  a. 必需的,必要的

necessity [ni'sesiti]

  n. 1. 必要性,需要

    2. [pl.]必需品

neck [nek]

  n. 颈

need [ni:d]

  vt. 需要,要

  aux. *v*. 必须,不得不

  n. 需要,必要

needle ['ni:dl]

  n. 针

negative ['negətiv]

  a. 1. 否定的

    2. 负的,阴性的

  n. 1. 负数

    2. (摄影)底片

neglect [ni'glekt]

  vt. & *n*. 1. 忽视

    2. 疏忽,漏做

negotiate [ni'gəuʃieit]

  v. 协商,洽谈

Negro ['ni:grəu]

  n. 黑人

neighbo(u)r ['neibə(r)]

  n. 邻居,邻国

neighbo(u)rhood ['neibəhud]

  n. 1. 邻近

    2. 四邻,居民区

neither ['naiðə, 'ni:ðə]

  a. 两者都不

pron. 两者都不

ad. 也不

~ ...nor 既不……也不

nephew ['nevju(:),'nefju(:)]

n. 侄子,外甥

nerve [nəːv]

n. 神经

nervous ['nəːvəs]

a. 1. 神经的

2. 紧张不安的,神经过敏的

nest [nest]

n. 窝,巢

net [net]

n. 网

a. 纯净的

neutral ['njuːtrəl]

a. 1. 中立的

2. 中性的,中和的

never ['nevə]

ad. 1. 永不,从来没有

2. 不,没有

nevertheless [,nevəðə'les]

conj. 然而,不过

ad. 仍然,不过

new [njuː]

a. 新的

newly ['njuːli]

ad. 新近

news [njuːz]

n. 新闻,消息

newspaper ['njuːspeipə]

n. 报纸

next [nekst]

a. 1. 紧接(在后)的,下次的

2. 贴近的,隔壁的

ad. 1. 其次,下次

2. 贴近

nice [nais]

a. 美好的,令人愉快的

niece [niːs]

n. 侄女,外甥女

night [nait]

n. 夜,夜间

nine [nain]

num. 九,九个

nineteen ['nain'tiːn]

num. 十九,十九个

ninety ['nainti]

num. 九十,九十个

ninth [nainθ]

num. 第九

no [nəu]

a. 1. 没有

2. 决非

3. 不许

ad. 不,不是

noble [nəubl]

a. 1. 高尚的

2. 贵族的,显贵的

n. 贵族

nobody ['nəubədi]

pron. 谁也不,无人

nod [nɔd]

v. 点(头)

n. 点头

noise [nɔiz]

n. 喧闹声,噪声

noisy ['nɔizi]

a. 喧闹的

none [nʌn]

pron. 1. 没有人,没有任何东西

2. ……中任何一个都不

ad. 一点也不

nonsense ['nɔnsəns]

n. 胡说,废话

noodle ['nuːdl]

n. 面条

noon [nuːn]

n. 中午

nor [nɔː]

conj. 也不

normal ['nɔːməl]

a. 1. 正常的,普通的

2. 正规的,标准的

north [nɔːθ]

n. 北,北方,北部

a. 北方的,北部的

northeast ['nɔːθ'iːst]

n. 东北

a. 东北的

northern ['nɔːðən]

a. 北方的,北部的

northwest ['nɔːθ'west]

n. 西北方

a. 西北的

nose [nəuz]

n. 1. 鼻子

2. (飞机、船等的)前端

not [nɔt]

ad. 不,没有

~ only...but (also) 不仅……而且

note [nəut]

n. 1. 笔记,记录

2. 按语,注释

3. 便条,短笺

vt. 记下,摘下

notebook ['nəutbuk]

n. 笔记簿

nothing ['nʌθiŋ]

n. 1. 没有东西,什么也没有

2. 微不足道的事物

~ but 只有,仅仅

notice ['nəutis]

n. 1. 通知,布告

2. 注意

v. 注意到

noun [naun]

n. 名词

novel ['nɔvəl]

n. (长篇)小说

a. 新奇的,新颖的

November [nəu'vembə]

n. 十一月

now [nau]

ad. 1. 现在,目前

2. 立刻,马上

3. [用来表示语气,如命令、不满等]

conj. 既然,由于

~ and then 时而,不时

~ that 既然,由于

nowadays ['nauədeiz]

ad. 现今,现在

nowhere ['nəuhwɛə]

ad. 任何地方都不,没有地方

nuclear ['njuːkliə]

a. 1. 核心的,中心的

2. 原子核的,核能的

number ['nʌmbə]

  n. 1. 数,数字

    2. [通常略作 No.]号码,(报刊等)期

    3. 数目

  vt. 1. 给……编号

    2. 达……之数,总计

  a ～ of 若干

numerous ['nju:mərəs]

  a. 众多的,许多的

nurse [nəːs]

  n. 护士,保姆

  vt. 护理,看护

nut [nʌt]

  n. 1. 坚果

    2. 螺母,螺帽

O

obey [əuˈbei]

  v. 服从,顺从

object [əbˈdʒekt]

  n. 1. 物体

    2. 对象,客体

    3. 目的,目标

  vi. (to)反对

oblige [əˈblaidʒ]

  vt. 迫使,责成

observation [ɔbzəˈveiʃ(ə)n]

  n. 1. 观察,观测

    2. [pl.]观察资料(或报告)

observe [əbˈzəːv]

  vt. 1. 观察,观测

    2. 遵守

    3. 评述,说

observer [əbˈzəːvə(r)]

  n. 观测者,观察员

obtain [əbˈtein]

  vt. 获得,得到

obvious ['ɔbviəs]

  a. 明显的

occasion [əˈkeiʒn]

  n. 1. 场合

    2. 时机,机会

  on ～ 有时,不时

occasional [əˈkeiʒən(ə)l]

  a. 1. 偶然的,非经常的

    2. 特殊场合的,临时的

occupy ['ɔkjupai]

  vt. 1. 占,占用

    2. 占领,占据

occur [əˈkəː(r)]

  vi. 发生,出现

  ～ to 被想到,被想起

ocean ['əuʃ(ə)n]

  n. 海洋

o'clock [əˈklɔk]

  = of the clock ……点钟

October [ɔkˈtəubə(r)]

  n. 十月

odd [ɔd]

  a. 1. 奇数的,单数的

    2. 单只的,不成对的

    3. 临时的,不固定的

    4. 带零头的,余的

of [ɔv]

  prep. 1. [表示所属,性质,主客体等]……的

    2. 关于,对于

    3. 由……制成的

    4. 由于,因为

    5. 来自……的,从

    6. [引出动词不定式的逻辑主语]

    7. [表示同位关系]

    8. 在……方面

off ['ɔf]

  prep. 从……离开,脱离

  ad. 1. 距,隔开,向(左)那边

    2. [表示分离、中断]

    3. [表示离去、脱掉]

    4. [表示完成、结束]

offend [əˈfend]

  vt. 冒犯,触怒

offer ['ɔfə(r), ɔːfər]

  vt. 提供,提出

  n. 提议,提供

office ['ɔfis, ɔːfis]

  n. 1. 办公室,办事处

    2. 处,局,行

officer ['ɔfisə(r), ɔːfisər]

  n. 1. 官员,办事员

    2. 军官

official [əˈfiʃ(ə)l]

  n. 官员,行政人员

  a. 官员的,官方的,正式的

often ['ɔf(ə)n, ɔːfn]

  ad. 经常,常常

oh [əu]

  int. [表示惊讶,害怕等]哦,哎呀

oil [ɔil]

  n. 1. 油

    2. 石油

  vt. 给……加润滑油

okay(O.K., OK) [əuˈkei]

  a. & ad. 好,行

old [əuld]

  a. 1. 年老的,老的

    2. ……岁的

    3. 陈旧的,古老的

omit [əˈmit]

  vt. 1. 省略,删去

    2. 遗漏,忽略

on [ɔn]

  prep. 1. 在……上

    2. 在……旁,靠近

    3. 向,朝着

    4. 在……时候

    5. 关于,论述

    6. 根据,靠

  ad. 1. 向前,(继续)下去

    2. 在上,穿上

    3. 接通

once [wʌns]

  ad. 1. 一次,一回

    2. 曾经,一度

  conj. 一旦……(就……)

  all at ～ 1. 突然

    2. 同时

  at ～ 立刻

  ～ (and) for all 一劳永逸,限此一次

one [wʌn]

  num. 一,一个

  a. 某一

  pron. 1. 一个人,任何人

    2. 一个

  ～ another 相互

oneself [wʌnˈself]

pron. 1. 自己,自身
　　　2. 亲自
by ～ 独自,单独地

onion [ˈʌnjən]
　n. 洋葱

only [ˈəunli]
　ad. 仅仅,只不过
　a. 惟一的
　conj. 可是,不过
if ～ 只要……就好了

onto [ˈɔntu]
　prep. 到……上

open [ˈəupən]
　a. 1. 开着的,开放的
　　　2. 开阔的
　　　3. 公开的,自由出入的
　v. 打开,开
　vt. 开始,开业

opening [ˈəupəniŋ]
　n. 1. 口子,孔
　　　2. 开始,开端

opera [ˈɔpərə]
　n. 歌剧

operate [ˈɔpəreit]
　v. 1. 运转,开动
　　　2. (on)(对……)施行手术

operation [ɔpəˈreiʃ(ə)n]
　n. 1. 运转,开动
　　　2. (on)手术
　　　3. 运算
come/go into ～ 开始,运转,开工
put /bring into ～ 使投入生产,使
　运转

opinion [əˈpinjən]
　n. 意见,看法

opportunity [ɔpəˈtjuːniti]
　n. 机会

oppose [əˈpəuz]
　vt. 反对,反抗

opposite [ˈɔpəzit]
　a. (to)对面的,对立的
　n. 对立面,对立物
　prep. 在……的对面

or [ə(r),ɔː(r)]
　conj. 1. 或,或者
　　　2. 或者说,即

　　　3. [常和 else 连用]否则,要
　　　　不然

oral [ˈɔːrəl]
　a. 口头的

orange [ˈɔrindʒ]
　n. 橙,柑橘

orbit [ˈɔːbit]
　n. 轨道
　v. (使)沿轨道运行

order [ˈɔːdə(r)]
　n. 1. 命令
　　　2. 次序,顺序
　　　3. 秩序
　　　4. 正常状态,整齐
　　　5. 订购,订货
　vt. 1. 命令
　　　2. 定购
in ～ 有秩序,整齐
in ～ + to V. 为了
in ～ that 为了
out of ～ 发生故障
put in ～ 整理,检修

orderly [ˈɔːdəli]
　a. 整洁的,有条理的

ordinary
　[ˈɔːdinəri, ˈɔːdənəri]
　a. 普通的,平凡的

organ [ˈɔːgən]
　n. 1. 器官
　　　2. 口琴
　　　3. 新闻媒介,宣传工具,喉舌

organization(-isation)
　[ɔːgənaiˈzeiʃ(ə)n]
　n. 1. 组织
　　　2. 团体,机构

organize(-ise) [ˈɔːgənaiz]
　vt. 组织,创办

origin [ˈɔridʒin]
　n. 1. 起源,由来
　　　2. 出身,来历

original [əˈridʒin(ə)l]
　a. 1. 最初的,原始的
　　　2. 有独创性的
　n. 原物,原作

other [ˈʌðə(r)]
　a. 另外的,其他的

every ～ 每隔一个的
～ than 不同于

otherwise [ˈʌðəwaiz]
　ad. 1. 另外,用别的方法
　　　2. 在其他方面
　conj. 要不然,否则

ought [ɔːt]
　aux. *v*. (+ to V.)应当,应该

ounce [auns]
　n. 盎司

our [ˈauə(r)]
　pron. [we 的所有格]我们的

ours [ˈauəz]
　pron. [we 的物主代词]我们的

ourselves [auəˈselvz]
　pron. 1. 我们自己
　　　2. 我们亲自

out [aut]
　ad. 1. 在外,向外
　　　2. 显露出来,发表
　　　3. 熄灭,尽,完
～ of 1. 在……外,向……外
　　　2. 由于,出于
　　　3. 从……中
　　　4. 越出
　　　5. 丧失,失去
　　　6. 缺乏

outcome [ˈautkʌm]
　n. 结果

outdoor [ˈautdɔː(r)]
　a. 室外的,野外的

outer [ˈautə(r)]
　a. 外部的,外面的

outlet [ˈautlet]
　n. 出口,出路

outline [ˈautlain]
　n. 1. 轮廓,略图
　　　2. 大纲,梗概
　vt. 概述,略述

outlook [ˈautluk]
　n. 1. 景色,风光
　　　2. 观点,见解
　　　3. 展望,前景

output [ˈautput]
　n. 1. 产量
　　　2. 输出,输出量

outside [aut'said]

　ad. 向外面,在外面

　n. 外部,外表

　a. 外部的,外面的

outstanding [aut'stændiŋ]

　a. 突出的,显著的

outward ['autwəd]

　ad. 向外,在外

　a. 向外的

oven ['ʌv(ə)n]

　n. 炉,灶

over ['əuvə(r)]

　prep. 1. 在……上方,在……上面

　　　 2. 越过

　　　 3. 多于,……以上

　　　 4. 在……期间

　　　 5. 遍及,到处

　ad. 1. 翻转过来

　　　 2. 结束,完了

　　　 3. (越)过

　　　 4. 在那边,向那边

　　　 5. 太,过分

　　　 6. 再,重复地

　~ and ~ (again) 一再,再三

overcoat ['əuvəkəut]

　n. 大衣

overcome [əuvə'kʌm]

　vt. 战胜,克服

overlook [əuvə'luk]

　vt. 1. 忽视,忽略,未注意到

　　　 2. 俯瞰,俯视

overnight ['əuvənait, ˌəuvə'nait]

　ad. & a. 1. 在整个夜里

　　　　　　 2. 一夜之间,突然

oversea(s) ['əuvə'si:]

　ad. 海外

　a. 外国的,海外的

overtake [əuvə'teik]

　vt. 追上,赶过

owe [əu]

　vt. 1. 欠(债等)

　　　 2. (to)把……归功于

own [əun]

　a. 自己的

　vt. 有,拥有

　on one's ~ 独自地,独立地

owner ['əunə(r)]

　n. 物主,货主

ox [ɔks]

　n. 牛

oxygen ['ɔksidʒ(ə)n]

　n. 氧

P

pace [peis]

　n. 步,步伐

　keep ~ with 跟上,与……同步

pacific [pə'sifik]

　a. 1. 和平的,平静的

　　　 2. [P-]太平洋的

　n. [the P-]太平洋

pack [pæk]

　v. 1. 捆扎,打包

　　　 2. 挤(满)

　n. 包,捆

package ['pækidʒ]

　n. 包裹,包

packet ['pækit]

　n. 小包裹,小捆

pad [pæd]

　n. 1. 垫,衬垫

　　　 2. 便笺簿

page [peidʒ]

　n. 页

　vt. (通过扩音器,传呼机等)呼

　　　 叫

pain [pein]

　n. 痛,痛苦

painful ['peinful]

　a. 疼痛的,使痛苦的

paint [peint]

　n. 油漆,颜料

　v. 1. 油漆

　　　 2. (用颜料等)画,绘

painter ['peintə(r)]

　n. 1. 漆工

　　　 2. 画家

painting ['peintiŋ]

　n. 1. 上油漆,着色

　　　 2. 绘画

pair [peə(r)]

　n. 一对,一双

palace ['pælis]

　n. 宫,宫殿

pale [peil]

　a. 1. 苍白的,灰白的

　　　 2. 淡的,暗淡的

palm [pa:m]

　n. 1. 手掌

　　　 2. 掌状物

pan [pæn]

　n. 平底锅,盘子

pants [pænt]

　n. 长裤,(宽松的)便裤

paper ['peipə(r)]

　n. 1. 纸

　　　 2. 报纸

　　　 3. 试卷

　　　 4. 文章,论文

　　　 5. [pl.]官方文件

paragraph ['pærəgra:f]

　n. 段,节

parallel ['pærəlel]

　a. 1. (to, with)平行的

　　　 2. (to)相同的,类似的

　　　 3. 并联的

　n. 1. 平行线,平行面

　　　 2. 类似,相似物

parcel ['pa:s(ə)l]

　n. 小包,包裹

　vt. 打包,捆扎

pardon ['pa:d(ə)n]

　vt. & n. 原谅,饶恕

parent ['peərənt]

　n. 父亲,母亲,家长

park [pa:k]

　n. 公园

　vt. 停放

part [pa:t]

　n. 1. 部分,局部

　　　 2. 角色

　　　 3. 一方,方面

　　　 4. 零件

　v. (使)分开

　play a ~ (in) 起作用

　take ~ in 参加

partial ['pa:ʃ(ə)l]

　a. 1. 部分的,不完全的

2. 偏袒的,不公平的

participate [pɑ:'tisipeit]

vi. (in)参与,参加

particle ['pɑ:tik(ə)l]

n. 1. 粒子,微粒

2. 小品词,虚词

particular [pə'tikjulə(r)]

a. 1. 特殊的,特别的

2. 特定的,个别的

n. [pl.]细节

in ～ 特别,尤其

particularly [pə'tikjuləli]

ad. 特别,尤其

partner ['pɑ:tnə(r)]

n. 1. 合作者,合伙人

2. 舞伴

party ['pɑ:ti]

n. 1. 聚会

2. 政党,党派

pass [pɑ:s]

v. 1. 经过,穿过

2. (使)及格,批准

3. 度过,度(日)

4. 传递,传给

n. 1. 通行证

2. 关口,要隘

passage ['pæsidʒ]

n. 1. 通过,经过

2. 通道

3. (一)段,(一)节

passenger ['pæsindʒə(r)]

n. 乘客,旅客

passive ['pæsiv]

a. 被动的

passport ['pɑ:spɔ:t]

n. 护照

past [pɑ:st, pæst]

prep. 过,越过

n. 过去,昔日

a. 过去的

in the ～ 在过去

paste [peist]

n. 糊,浆糊

vt. 粘贴

pat [pæt]

v. & *n*. 轻拍,轻打

path [pɑ:θ, pæθ]

n. 1. 小路,小径

2. 路线,轨道

patience ['peiʃ(ə)ns]

n. 忍耐,耐心

patient ['peiʃ(ə)nt]

n. 病人

a. 忍耐的,耐心的

pattern ['pætən]

n. 1. 图案,图样

2. 型,式样

pause [pɔ:z]

vi. & *n*. 中止,暂停

paw [pɔ:]

n. 爪

pay [pei]

v. 支付,付出

vt. 给予(注意等),进行(访问等)

n. 工资,薪金

payment ['peimənt]

n. 1. 支付

2. 付款额

pea [pi:]

n. 豌豆

peace [pi:s]

n. 1. 和平

2. 平静,安宁

peaceful ['pi:sful]

a. 1. 和平的

2. 平静的,安宁的

peak [pi:k]

n. 山顶,最高点

a. 高峰的,最高的

pear [peə(r)]

n. 梨

peasant ['pezənt]

n. 农民

peculiar [pi'kju:liə(r)]

a. 1. 古怪的,异常的

2. 特殊的,特有的

pen [pen]

n. 钢笔

pencil ['pens(ə)l]

n. 铅笔

penetrate ['penitreit]

v. 穿过,渗透

penny ['peni]

n. 便士

people ['pi:p(ə)l]

n. 1. 人,人们

2. 人民,民众

3. 民族

pepper ['pepə(r)]

n. 胡椒,胡椒粉

per [pə(r)]

prep. 1. 每

2. 经,由

percent [pə'sent]

n. 百分之……

percentage [pə'sentədʒ]

n. 百分数,百分率

perfect [*a*. 'pə:fikt, *v*. pə'fekt]

a. 1. 完美的,无瑕的

2. 完全的,十足的

3. [语法]完成时的

vt. 使完美

perform [pə'fɔ:m]

vt. 1. 履行,执行

2. 表演,演出

performance [pə'fɔ:məns]

n. 1. 履行,执行

2. 表演,演出

3. 性能,特性

perhaps [pə'hæps]

ad. 也许,大概

period ['piəriəd]

n. 1. 时期,时代

2. 学时,课时

3. 周期

permanent ['pə:mənənt]

a. 永久的,持久的

permission [pə'miʃ(ə)n]

n. 允许,同意

permit [pə'mit]

v. 许可,允许

n. 许可证

persist [pə'sist]

vi. 1. (in)坚持

2. 持续

person ['pə:s(ə)n]

n. 1. 人

2. 本人,自身

personal [ˈpəːsən(ə)l]
  a. 1. 个人的, 私人的
       2. 亲自的

perspective [pəˈspektiv]
  n. 1. 视角, 观点, 看法
       2. 远景, 前途
       3. 透视画法, 透视图

persuade [pəˈsweid]
  v. 1. 说服, 劝导
       2. (of)(使)相信

pet [pet]
  n. 宠物, 宠儿

petrol [ˈpetr(ə)l]
  n. 汽油

petroleum [piˈtrəuliəm]
  n. 石油

phase [feiz]
  n. 1. 阶段, 时期
       2. (月)相, 相位

phenomenon [fiˈnɔminən]
  n. 现象

philosophy [fiˈlɔsəfi]
  n. 哲学

phone [fəun]
  n. 电话, 电话机
  v. (给……)打电话

photograph (photo)
  [ˈfəutəgrɑːf] ([ˈfəutəu])
  n. 照片

phrase [freiz]
  n. 短语, 词组

physical [ˈfizik(ə)l]
  a. 1. 物质的, 有形的
       2. 身体的, 肉体的
       3. 按自然法则的, 自然的
       4. 物理的

physicist [ˈfizisist]
  n. 物理学家

physics [ˈfiziks]
  n. 物理(学)

piano [piˈænəu]
  n. 钢琴

pick [pik]
  v. 1. 采摘, 摘
       2. 挑选, 选择
  n. 镐, 鹤嘴锄

~ out 1. 挑选, 拣出
       2. 辨认, 辨别出
~ up 1. 拾起
       2. 增加, 改进
       3. (偶然)得到

picnic [ˈpiknik]
  n. 野餐
  vi. (去)野餐

picture [ˈpiktʃə(r)]
  n. 1. 画, 图画
       2. 影片
       3. 美景
  vt. 画, 描述

pie [pai]
  n. 馅饼

piece [piːs]
  n. 1. 件, 块, 片
       2. 碎片, 断片
  vt. (together)拼合, 拼凑

pig [pig]
  n. 猪

pigeon [ˈpidʒ(ə)n]
  n. 鸽子

pile [pail]
  n. 堆
  v. (up)堆, 堆积

pill [pil]
  n. 药丸

pillow [ˈpiləu]
  n. 枕头

pilot [ˈpailət]
  n. 1. 飞行员
       2. 领航员, 引水员
  vt. 1. 驾驶(飞机)等
       2. 领航, 引水

pin [pin]
  n. 1. 钉, 销, 栓
       2. 大头针, 别针
  vt. (up)钉住, 别住

pink [piŋk]
  n. 桃红色, 粉红色
  a. 粉红色的

pint [paint]
  n. 品脱

pioneer [paiəˈniə(r)]
  n. 先驱, 倡导者

pipe [paip]
  n. 1. 管子
       2. 烟斗

pity [ˈpiti]
  v. (觉得)可怜
  n. 1. 憾事
       2. 怜悯

place [pleis]
  n. 1. 地方, 地点
       2. 名次
       3. 地位, 职位
  vt. 1. 放置
       2. 任命
       3. 投(资), 订(货)
  in ~ of 代替
  in the first ~ 首先, 第一
  take ~ 发生, 举行

plain [plein]
  a. 1. 明白的, 清晰的
       2. 朴素的, 平常的
  n. 平原, 旷野

plan [plæn]
  n. 1. 计划, 规划
       2. 平面图, 设计图
  v. 计划

plane [plein]
  n. 1. 飞机
       2. 平面, 水平面

planet [ˈplænit]
  n. 行星

plant [plɑːnt]
  n. 1. 植物, 作物
       2. 工厂
       3. 装置
  vt. 栽种, 播种

plastic [ˈplæstik]
  n. [常 pl.]塑料, 塑料制品
  a. 可塑的, 塑性的

plate [pleit]
  n. 1. 金属板, 片
       2. 盘子, 盆子
  vt. 电镀

platform [ˈplætfɔːm]
  n. 1. 平台, 台
       2. 站台, 月台

play [plei]

v. 1. 玩,游戏
　　2. 演奏
　　3. 扮演
n. 1. 游戏,比赛
　　2. 剧本,戏剧

player ['pleiə(r)]
n. 1. 做游戏的人,比赛者
　　2. 演员,演奏者

playground ['pleigraund]
n. 运动场,游乐场

pleasant ['plezənt]
a. 令人愉快的,舒适的

please [pliːz]
vt. 请
v. (使)喜欢,中(……的)意

pleasure ['pleʒə(r)]
n. 1. 愉快,快乐
　　2. 乐事,乐趣

plentiful ['plentiful]
a. 富裕的,丰富的

plenty ['plenti]
n. 丰富,大量

plot [plɔt]
n. 1. 秘密计划
　　2. 小块土地
　　3. 情节
vt. 标绘,绘制
v. 密谋,策划

plough [plau]
n. 犁
v. 耕,犁

plug [plʌg]
vt. 堵,塞
n. 1. 塞子
　　2. 插头

plunge [plʌndʒ]
v. (into)(使)投入,(使)插进

plural ['pluər(ə)l]
a. 复数的

plus [plʌs]
prep. 加上
a. 正的,加的

p.m. (*post meridiem*)
下午,午后

pocket ['pɔkit]
n. 袋子,小袋

a. 袖珍的,小型的
vt. 把……装入袋内

poem ['pəuim]
n. 诗

poet ['pəuit]
n. 诗人

poetry ['pəuitri]
n. 诗歌,诗集

point [point]
n. 1. 尖,尖端
　　2. 点,小数点
　　3. 条款,细目
　　4. 分(数),得分
　　5. 要点,论点
v. 1. (at, to)指向,表明
　　2. (out)指出
on the ～ of 即将……的时候
to the ～ 切题

poison ['poiz(ə)n]
n. 毒,毒物

poisonous ['poizənəs]
a. 有毒的

pole [pəul]
n. 1. 杆,柱
　　2. 极(点)
　　3. 磁极,电极

police [pə'liːs]
n. [the ～]警察当局,警方

policeman [pə'liːsmən]
n. 警察

policy ['pɔlisi]
n. 政策,方针

polish ['pɔliʃ]
vt. 1. 磨光,擦亮
　　2. 使优美,润饰

polite [pə'lait]
a. 1. 有礼貌的,客气的
　　2. 有教养的,文雅的

political [pə'litik(ə)l]
a. 政治(上)的

politician [pɔli'tiʃ(ə)n]
n. 政治家,政客

politics ['pɔlitiks]
n. 1. 政治,政治学
　　2. 政纲,政见

pollute [pə'luːt]

vt. 弄脏,污染

pollution [pə'luːʃ(ə)n]
n. 污染

pond [pɔnd]
n. 池塘

pool [puːl]
n. 1. 水池,游泳池
　　2. 合资经营,联营
vt. 合伙经营,联营

poor [puə(r)]
a. 1. 贫困的,穷的
　　2. 可怜的
　　3. 贫乏的,贫瘠的

popular ['pɔpjulə(r)]
a. 流行的,通俗的

population [pɔpju'leiʃ(ə)n]
n. 人口

pork [pɔːk]
n. 猪肉

port [pɔːt]
n. 港,港口

porter ['pɔːtə(r)]
n. 1. 守门人,门房
　　2. 行李搬运工

portion ['pɔːʃ(ə)n]
n. 一部分,一份

position [pə'ziʃ(ə)n]
n. 1. 位置,方位
　　2. 职位,职务
　　3. 形势,状况
　　4. 见解,立场

positive ['pɔzitiv]
a. 1. 确实的,明确的
　　2. 积极的,肯定的
　　3. 正的,阳性的

possess [pə'zes]
vt. 占有,拥有

possession [pə'seʃ(ə)n]
n. 1. [pl.]占有物
　　2. 所有,占有

possibility [pɔsi'biliti]
n. 可能,可能性

possible ['pɔsib(ə)l]
a. 1. 可能的
　　2. 合理的,可允许的

possibly ['pɔsibli]

ad. 1. 尽可能地
    2. 也许

post [pəust]
vt. 1. 邮寄
    2. 贴出
n. 1. 邮政,邮件
    2. 柱,标杆
    3. 职位,岗位

postage ['pəustidʒ]
n. 邮费,邮资

postcard ['pəustkɑːd]
n. 明信片

postpone [pəust'pəun]
vt. 推迟,延期

pot [pɔt]
n. 罐,壶

potato [pə'teitəu]
n. 土豆

pound [paund]
n. 1. 磅
    2. 英镑
v. (连续)猛击,(猛烈)敲打
vt. 捣碎

pour [pɔː(r)]
v. 灌注,倾泻

poverty ['pɔvəti]
n. 1. 贫穷,贫困
    2. 贫乏,缺少

powder ['paudə(r)]
n. 1. 粉末,粉
    2. 火药,炸药

power ['pauə(r)]
n. 1. 权力,政权
    2. 能力,精力
    3. 功率,动力
    4. [数字]幂,乘方

powerful ['pauəful]
a. 强大的,有力的

practical ['præktik(ə)l]
a. 1. 实际的,实践的
    2. 实用的,应用的
    3. 有实际经验的

practically ['præktikəli]
ad. 1. 实际上,事实上
    2. 几乎,简直

practice ['præktis]

n. 1. 练习,实习
    2. 实践,实际
v. = practise
bring/carry into ～ 实施,实行
in ～ 实际上

practise ['præktis]
v. 1. 练习,实习
    2. 实践,实行

praise [preiz, preis]
vt. 赞扬,歌颂
n. 赞扬,赞美的话

pray [prei]
v. 1. 请求,恳求
    2. 祈祷

precious ['preʃəs]
a. 宝贵的,珍贵的

precise [pri'sais]
a. 精确的,准确的

predict [pri'dikt]
v. 预言,预告

preface ['prefis]
n. 序言,引言

prefer [pri'fəː(r)]
vt. (to)更喜欢,宁愿

preliminary [pri'liminəri]
a. 预备的,初步的

preparation [prepə'reiʃ(ə)n]
n. 准备,预备

prepare [pri'peə(r)]
v. 准备,预备

preposition [prepə'ziʃ(ə)n]
n. 介词

prescribe [pri'skraib]
vt. 开(药),吩咐采用(某种疗法)

presence ['prezəns]
n. 出席,到场,存在

present ['preznt]
a. 1. 出席的,到场的
    2. 现在的,目前的
n. 1. 现在,目前
    2. 礼物,赠品
vt. 1. 赠送,呈现
    2. 介绍,陈述
    3. 提出,呈交
at ～ 现在
for the ～ 目前,暂时

preserve [pri'zəːv]
vt. 1. 保护,维持
    2. 保存,保藏

president ['prezidənt]
n. 1. 总统
    2. 校长,会长

press [pres]
vt. 1. 压,揿,按
    2. 压榨,压迫
n. 1. 报刊,出版社,通讯社
    2. 压榨机,压力机
    3. 压,揿,按

pressure ['preʃə(r)]
n. 1. 压(力)
    2. 强制,压迫

pretend [pri'tend]
vt. 假装,装扮

pretty ['priti]
a. 漂亮的,秀丽的
ad. 相当,颇

prevent [pri'vent]
vt. (from)预防,防止

previous ['priːviəs]
a. 先前的
～ to 在……之前

price [prais]
n. 1. 价格,价钱
    2. 代价

pride [praid]
n. 1. 自豪,自尊(心)
    2. 骄傲,傲慢
vt. (使)自豪,(使)自夸

primary ['praiməri]
a. 1. 最初的,初级的
    2. 首要的,主要的

principal ['prinsip(ə)l]
a. 最重要的,主要的
n. 1. 首长,负责人
    2. 资本,本金

principle ['prinsip(ə)l]
n. 原理,原则

print [print]
n. 印刷,印刷品
vt. 印刷,出版

prior ['praiə(r)]
a. 优先的,在前的

~ to 在……之前

prison ['priz(ə)n]

n. 监狱

prisoner ['priznə(r)]

n. 囚犯

private ['praivit]

a. 1. 私人的,个人的

　　2. 秘密的,私下的

prize [praiz]

n. 奖赏,奖金,奖品

vt. 珍视

probable ['prɔbəb(ə)l]

a. 很可能的,大概的

probably ['prɔbəb(ə)li]

ad. 大概,或许

problem ['prɔbləm]

n. 1. 问题,疑难问题

　　2. 思考题,讨论题

procedure [prə'siːdʒə(r)]

n. 过程,步骤

proceed [prə'siːd]

vi. 1. 进行,继续下去

　　2. 发生

process ['prɔuses, 'prɔses]

n. 1. 过程,进程

　　2. 工序,制作法

vt. 加工,处理

procession [prə'seʃ(ə)n]

n. 行列,队伍

produce [*v*. prə'djuːs, *n*. 'prɔdjuːs]

v. 生产,制造

n. 产品,农产品

product ['prɔdʌkt]

n. 1. 产品,产物

　　2. 乘积

production [prə'dʌkʃ(ə)n]

n. 1. 生产

　　2. 产量

　　3. 产品,作品

profession [prə'feʃ(ə)n]

n. 职业

professional [prə'feʃən(ə)l]

a. 职业的,专业的

n. 自由职业者,专业人员

professor [prə'fesə(r)]

n. 教授

profit ['prɔfit]

n. 1. 利润

　　2. 益处,得益

vi. (by, from)得益,利用

vt. 有益于,有利于

program(me) ['prəugræm]

n. 1. 节目,节目单

　　2. 计划,议程

　　3. 程序

progress [*n*. 'prəugres, *v*. prə'gres]

n. & *vi*. 前进,进步

make ~ 进步,进展

progressive [prə'gresiv]

a. 1. 进步的,先进的

　　2. 前进的

project ['prɔdʒekt]

n. 1. 方案,计划

　　2. 工程,项目

vt. 投射,放映

v. (使)凸出,(使)伸出

promise ['prɔmis]

vt. & *n*. 允诺,答应

promote [prə'məut]

vt. 1. 促进,发扬

　　2. 提升,提拔

pronoun ['prəunaun]

n. 代词

pronounce [prə'nauns]

v. 发(……的)音

vt. 宣布,宣判

pronunciation

[prənʌnsi'eiʃ(ə)n]

n. 发音,发音方法

proof [pruːf]

n. 1. 证明,证据

　　2. 校样,样张

proper ['prɔpə(r)]

a. 1. 适合的,恰当的

　　2. 合乎体统的,正当的

　　3. (to)特有的,专门的

　　4. 本身的

property ['prɔpəti]

n. 1. 财产,资产

　　2. 性质,特性

proportion [prə'pɔːʃ(ə)n]

n. 1. 比例

　　2. 部分,份儿

　　3. 均衡,相称

in ~ (to) (与……)成比例

proposal [prə'pəuz(ə)l]

n. 提议,建议

propose [prə'pəuz]

vt. 1. 提议,建议

　　2. 提名,推荐

protect [prə'tekt]

vt. (from)保护

protein ['prəutiːn]

n. 蛋白质

protest

[*v*. prə'test, *n*. 'prəutest]

vt. & *n*. 抗议,反对

proud [praud]

a. 1. (of)自豪的,得意的

　　2. 骄傲的,妄自尊大的

prove [pruːv]

vt. 1. 证明,证实

　　2. 检验,考验

vi. 原来(是),证明(是)

provide [prə'vaid]

vt. (with, for)提供,供给

vi. (for)赡养

province ['prɔvins]

n. 省

provision [prə'viʒ(ə)n]

n. 1. 供应,(一批)供应品

　　2. (for, against)预备,防备

public ['pʌblik]

a. 1. 公众的,公共的

　　2. 公开的

n. 公众,民众

in ~ 公开地,当众

publication [pʌbli'keiʃ(ə)n]

n. 1. 出版物

　　2. 出版,发行

　　3. 公布,发表

publish ['pʌbliʃ]

v. 出版,刊印

vt. 公布,发表

pull [pul]

v. 1. 拉,拖

　　2. 拔

n. 1. 拉,拖

2. 拉力,牵引力

~ down 1. 拉下,降低

      2. 推翻,拆毁

~ in (车)进站,(船)到岸

~ off 脱(帽,衣等)

~ on 穿,戴

~ up (车辆)减速并停下

pulse [pʌls]

n. 脉搏,脉冲

pump ['pʌmp]

n. 泵

vt. (用泵)抽(水)

punctual ['pʌŋktjuəl]

a. 严守时刻的,准时的

punish ['pʌniʃ]

vt. 惩罚,处罚

punishment ['pʌniʃmənt]

n. 惩罚,处罚

pupil ['pjuːpil]

n. 1. 学生,小学生

      2. 瞳孔

purchase ['pəːtʃəs]

vt. & *n*. 买,购买

pure [pjuə(r)]

a. 1. 纯的,纯洁的

      2. 纯理论的,抽象的

      3. 完全的,十足的

purple ['pəːp(ə)l]

a. 紫的

n. 紫色

purpose ['pəːpəs]

n. 1. 目的,意图

      2. 用途,效果

for (the) ~ of 为了

on ~ 故意地

with the ~ of 为了

purse [pəːs]

n. 钱包

pursue [pəˈsjuː]

vt. 1. 追赶,追踪

      2. 继续,从事

push [puʃ]

v. 1. 推

      2. 催逼,逼迫

n. 推,推力

put [put]

vt. 1. 放,摆

      2. 记下,写下,叙述

      3. 使……处于(某种状态)

~ away 1. 放好,收好

      2. 储存

~ down 1. 记下

      2. 放下

~ forward 提出

~ in 驶进

~ in for 申请

~ off 推迟,拖延

~ on 穿上

~ out 1. 熄灭

      2. 出版

      3. 生产

~ up 1. 提出

      2. 建起,架起

~ up with 忍受

puzzle ['pʌz(ə)l]

n. 难题,谜

v. (使)迷惑,(使)为难

Q

qualification [kwɔlifiˈkeiʃ(ə)n]

n. 资格,资格证明,合格证书

qualify ['kwɔlifai]

v. (使)具有资格,证明合格

vt. 限制,限定

quality ['kwɔliti]

n. 1. 质量

      2. 品质,特性

quantity ['kwɔntəti]

n. 量,数量

quarrel ['kwɔːrəl]

vi. (about, over)争吵,争论

n. 争吵,口角

quarter ['kwɔːtə(r)]

n. 1. 四分之一

      2. [常 pl.]方向,地区

      3. 季,季度

      4. 一刻钟

queen [kwiːn]

n. 王后

question ['kwestʃ(ə)n]

n. 1. 问题,议题

      2. 发问,询问

vt. 1. 询问,审问

      2. 怀疑,对……表示疑问

in ~ 正在考虑

out of ~ 毫无疑问

out of the ~ 毫无可能的,绝对

      做不到的

queue [kjuː]

n. (人或车辆的)行列,长队

vt. (up)排(成)队(等候)

quick [kwik]

a. 1. 快的,迅速的

      2. 灵敏的,敏捷的

quickly ['kwikli]

ad. 快,迅速

quit [kwit]

v. 1. 停止,放弃

      2. 离开,辞(职)

quiet ['kwaiət]

a. 安静的,平静的

n. 寂静,平静

quite [kwait]

ad. 1. 十分,完全

      2. 相当,颇

      3. 的确,真正

quiz [kwiz]

n. 1. 智力竞赛,答问比赛

      2. 小测验

quote [kwəut]

v. 引用,援引

R

rabbit ['ræbit]

n. 兔子

race [reis]

n. 1. (速度上的)比赛

      2. 人种,种族

vi. 全速行进

v. (使)比速度,竞赛

radar ['reidə]

n. 雷达

radio ['reidiəu]

n. 1. 收音机

      2. 无线电报,无线电话

vi. 用无线电通讯

rag [ræg]

n. 碎布,破布

rail [reil]

　n. 1. 铁路

　　　2. 铁轨,轨道

　　　3. 横杆,栏杆

railroad ['reilrəud]

　n. = railway

railway ['reilwei]

　n. 铁道

rain [rein]

　n. 雨

　vi. 下雨

raincoat ['reinkəut]

　n. 雨衣

rainy ['reini]

　a. 下雨的

raise [reiz]

　vt. 1. 举起,抬高

　　　2. 提高,增加

　　　3. 饲养,养育

　　　4. 引起,惹起

　　　5. 竖起,建立起

range [reindʒ]

　vi. 1. 延伸,绵亘

　　　2. (在某范围内)变动,变化

　vt. 排列成行

　n. 1. 幅度,范围

　　　2. 排列,绵亘

rank [ræŋk]

　n. 1. 军衔,社会阶层

　　　2. 排,横列

　vt. 1. 分等级,把……分类

　　　2. 排列

rapid ['ræpid]

　a. 快的,迅速的

　n. [pl.]急流,湍滩

rare [rɛə]

　a. 1. 稀有的,难得的

　　　2. 稀薄的,稀疏的

rarely ['rɛəli]

　ad. 1. 很少,难得

　　　2. 非凡地,非常地

rat [ræt]

　n. 老鼠

rate [reit]

　n. 1. 率,比率

　　　2. 等级

　v. 估价

　at any ～ 无论如何

rather ['rɑːðə]

　ad. 1. 相当,有一点儿

　　　2. 宁愿,宁可

　had /would ～ (...than)

　　　宁愿……(而不愿)

　～ than 而不是

ratio ['reiʃiəu]

　n. 比,比率

raw [rɔː]

　a. 1. 未煮过的,生的

　　　2. 未加过工的,未经训练的

ray [rei]

　n. 光线,射线

reach [riːtʃ]

　v. 1. 抵达,达到

　　　2. (out)伸出(手)

　n. 达到的区域,影响范围

react [ri'ækt]

　vt. 1. 起反应,起作用

　　　2. (against)反抗,起反抗

　　　作用

reaction [ri(ː)'ækʃən]

　n. 1. 反应,反作用

　　　2. 反动

read [riːd]

　v. 读,阅读

　vt. 1. 看懂,理解

　　　2. 指明,表明

reader [riːdə]

　n. 1. 读者

　　　2. 读物,读本

readily ['redili]

　ad. 1. 乐意地,欣然地

　　　2. 容易地

reading ['riːdiŋ]

　n. 1. 阅读,读书

　　　2. 读物,阅读材料

　　　3. 读数,仪器指示数

ready ['redi]

　a. 1. (for)准备好的

　　　2. (to V.)乐意的,甘心的

real ['riəl]

　a. 1. 现实的,实际的

　　　2. 真正的,真实的

reality [ri(ː)'æliti]

　n. 现实,真实

realize(-ise) ['riəlaiz]

　vt. 1. 认识到,了解

　　　2. 实现,实行

really ['riəli]

　ad. 1. 真正地

　　　2. 实在地

　　　3. [表示关心,惊讶,怀疑等]

　　　真的吗?

rear [riə]

　a. 后部的,后面的

　n. 后部,后面

　v. 抚养,饲养,种植

reason ['riːzn]

　n. 1. 理由,原因

　　　2. 理智,理性

　v. 1. 推论,推理

　　　2. 说理,评理

　by ～ of 由于

reasonable ['riːznəbl]

　a. 1. 合理的,有道理的

　　　2. 通情达理的,讲道理的

recall [ri'kɔːl]

　vt. 回忆,回想

receipt [ri'siːpt]

　n. 1. 收条,收据

　　　2. 收到

receive [ri'siːv]

　vt. 1. 收到,接到

　　　2. 遭受,受到

　　　3. 接待,接见

receiver [ri'siːvə]

　n. 1. 收受者

　　　2. 接收器

recent ['riːsnt]

　a. 新近的,近来的

recently ['riːsəntli]

　ad. 新近,最近

reception [ri'sepʃən]

　n. 1. 接待,招待会,接待处

　　　2. 接收

recognize(-ise) ['rekəgnaiz]

　vt. 1. 认出,辨认

　　　2. 承认,认可

recommend [rekə'mend]

vt. 1. 推荐,介绍
    2. 劝告,建议

record [*n*.'rekɔːd, *v*.ri'kɔːd]

n. 1. 记录,记载
    2. 最高记录,最佳成绩
    3. 履历,经历

v. 1. 记录,登记
    2. 录音

recorder [ri'kɔːdə]

n. 1. 记录员
    2. 录音机

recover [ri'kʌvə]

v. (from)(使)痊愈,(使)复元

vt. 1. 重新获得,重新找到
    2. 恢复

recovery [ri'kʌvəri]

n. 1. 痊愈,复元
    2. 重获,恢复

red [red]

a. 红色的

n. 红色

reduce [ri'djuːs]

vt. 1. 减少,缩减
    2. 简化,还原

reduction [ri'dʌkʃən]

n. 减少,缩小

refer [ri'fəː]

v. (to) 1. 参考,参阅
    2. 涉及,提到
    3. 把……提交,
      让……查询

~ to...as 把……称作,
把……当作

reference ['refrəns]

n. 1. 提及,涉及
    2. 参考,参考书目
    3. 证明书(人),介绍信(人)

refine [ri'fain]

vt. 精炼,精制

reflect [ri'flekt]

v. 1. 反射
    2. 反映,表现
    3. 反省,细想

reflection [ri'flekʃən]

n. 1. 反射
    2. 反映,倒影

    3. 反省,沉思

reform [ri'fɔːm]

v. 改革,改进,改造

refrigerator [ri'fridʒəreitə]

n. 冰箱,冷藏库

refuse [ri'fjuːz]

vt. 拒绝,谢绝

regard [ri'gɑːd]

n. 1. 尊敬,尊重
    2. 考虑,关心
    3. [pl.]致意,问候

vt. (as)把……看作为,把……认
    为

as ~s 关于,至于

with/in ~ to 1. 对于
        2. 就……而论

regarding [ri'gɑːdiŋ]

prep. 关于

regardless [ri'gɑːdlis]

a. 不留心的,不注意的

~ of 不顾,不管

region ['riːdʒən]

n. 地区,区域

register ['redʒistə]

vt. 1. 登记,注册
    2. (仪表等)指示,自动记下
    3. 把(邮件)挂号

n. 登记,注册

regret [ri'gret]

vt. 1. 抱歉,遗憾
    2. 懊悔,悔恨

n. 抱歉,遗憾

regular ['regjulə]

a. 1. 有规律的,有规则的
    2. 整齐的,匀称的

reject [ri'dʒekt]

vt. 1. 拒绝,抵制
    2. 丢弃

relate [ri'leit]

vt. 1. 叙述,讲
    2. (to)使联系

relation [ri'leiʃən]

n. 1. 关系,联系
    2. 亲属,亲戚

in/with ~ to 关系到

relationship [ri'leiʃənʃip]

n. 关系,关联

relative ['relətiv]

n. 亲属,亲戚

a. 1. (to)有关系的,相关的
    2. 相对的,比较的

relax [ri'læks]

v. (使)松弛,放松

release [ri'liːs]

vt. 1. 释放,解放
    2. 发表,发行

reliable [ri'laiəbl]

a. 可靠的

relief [ri'liːf]

n. 1. (痛苦等)减轻,解除
    2. 援救,救济

religion [ri'lidʒən]

n. 宗教,信仰

rely [ri'lai]

vi. (on) 1. 依赖,依靠
    2. 信赖,信任

remain [ri'mein]

vi. 1. 逗留
    2. 继续存在,仍是
    3. 剩余,遗留

remark [ri'mɑːk]

n. (about,on)评论,议论

vi. (on)评论,谈论

vt. 注意到,察觉

remarkable [ri'mɑːkəbl]

a. 1. 异常的,非凡的
    2. 值得注意的

remedy ['remidi]

n. 1. 治疗,药物
    2. 补救(措施)

vt. 1. 治疗,医治
    2. 纠正,补救

remember [ri'membə]

v. 记起,记得

vt. (to)代……致意,代……问好

remind [ri'maind]

vt. (of)提醒,使想起

remote [ri'məut]

a. 遥远的,长久的

remove [ri'muːv]

vt. 去掉,消除

v. 移动,迁居

render [ˈrendə]
　vt. 1. 使得，致使
　　　2. 提出
renew [riˈnju:]
　v. (使)更新，恢复
rent [rent]
　v. 租
　n. 租金
repair [riˈpɛə]
　n. 修理，修补
　vt. 1. 修理，修补
　　　2. 补救，纠正
repeat [riˈpi:t]
　v. 反复，重复，重说
　n. 重复
repetition [ˌrepiˈtiʃən]
　n. 1. 重复，重说，重做
　　　2. 重复的事情，复制品
replace [ri(:)ˈpleis]
　vt. 1. 取代，替换
　　　2. 把……放回原处
reply [riˈplai]
　v. & n. (to)回答，答复
report [riˈpɔ:t]
　n. 1. 报告，汇报
　　　2. 传说，传闻
　v. 报告，汇报
　vi. 报到
reporter [riˈpɔ:tə]
　n. 记者
represent [ˌri:priˈzent]
　vt. 1. 描述，表示
　　　2. 代表，代理
representative [ˌrepriˈzentətiv]
　n. 代表
　a. (of)典型的，有代表性的
republic [riˈpʌblik]
　n. 共和国，共和政体
request [riˈkwest]
　vt. & n. 请求，要求
require [riˈkwaiə]
　vt. 1. 需要
　　　2. 要求，命令
rescue [ˈreskju:]
　vt. & n. 援救，营救
research [riˈsə:tʃ]

　n. 研究，调查
　vi. (into, on)研究，调查
resemble [riˈzembl]
　vt. 好像，类似
reserve [riˈzə:v]
　n. 储备(物)，储藏量
　vt. 1. 储备，保存
　　　2. 预定，预约
reservoir [ˈrezəvwɑ:]
　n. 水库，蓄水池
residence [ˈrezidəns]
　n. 1. 居住
　　　2. 住处
resist [riˈzist]
　vt. 1. 抵抗，反抗
　　　2. 抗，忍得住
resistance [riˈzistəns]
　n. (to) 1. 反抗，抵抗
　　　　　2. 抵抗力，阻力，电阻
resolution [ˌrezəˈlu:ʃən]
　n. 1. 坚定，决心
　　　2. 决定，决议
resolve [riˈzɔlv]
　v. 1. 决心，决定
　　　2. (使)分解，溶解
　vt. 解决
resource [riˈsɔ:s]
　n. 1. [pl.]资源，财力
　　　2. 办法，智谋
respect [risˈpekt]
　vt. 尊敬，尊重
　n. 1. 尊敬，尊重
　　　2. [pl.]敬意，问候
　　　3. 方面
　with ~ to 关于
respective [risˈpektiv]
　a. 各自的，各个的
respond [risˈpɔnd]
　v. 回答，响应
　vi. (to)有反应
response [risˈpɔns]
　n. 1. 回应，答复
　　　2. 反应，响应
responsibility [risˌpɔnsəˈbiliti]
　n. 1. 责任，责任心
　　　2. 职责，任务

responsible [risˈpɔnsəbl]
　a. 1. (for, to)有责任的
　　　2. 可靠的，可信赖的
rest [rest]
　n. 1. 休息，睡眠
　　　2. 停止，静止
　　　3. 剩余部分，其余
　vi. 休息，睡
　v. (使)搁在
restaurant [ˈrestərɔnt]
　n. 餐馆，饭店
restore [risˈtɔ:]
　vt. 1. 恢复，使回复
　　　2. 归还，交还
　　　3. 修复，重建
restrict [risˈtrikt]
　vt. 限制，约束
result [riˈzʌlt]
　n. 结果，成果
　vi. 1. (in)导致，结果是
　　　2. (from)起因于，因……而
　　　　造成
　as a ~ 因此，结果
　as a ~ of 由于……的结果
resume [riˈzju:m]
　v. (中断后)重新开始，继续，恢复
　n. 1. 概要，摘要
　　　2. 简历
retain [riˈtein]
　vt. 保持，保留
retire [riˈtaiə]
　vi. 1. 退休，引退
　　　2. 退却，撤退
retreat [riˈtri:t]
　vi. & n. 撤退，退却
return [riˈtə:n]
　vi. 返回，回来
　v. 归还，送还
　n. 1. 返回，归来
　　　2. 偿还，归还
reveal [riˈvi:l]
　vt. 1. 展现，显示
　　　2. 揭示，揭露
reverse [riˈvə:s]
　n. 1. 相反
　　　2. 背面，反面

a. 相反的,倒转的

vt. 颠倒,倒转

review [ri'vju:]

vt. 回顾,复习

n. 1. 回顾,复习

　　 2. 评论

revise [ri'vaiz]

vt. 1. 修订,校订

　　 2. 修正,修改

revolution [ˌrevə'lu:ʃən]

n. 1. 革命

　　 2. 旋转

revolutionary [ˈrevə'lu:ʃənəri]

a. 革命(性)的

reward [ri'wɔːd]

n. (for)报酬,赏金,奖赏

vt. (for)酬劳,奖赏

ribbon [ˈribən]

n. 1. 缎带,丝带

　　 2. 带,带状物

rice [rais]

n. 稻,米

rich [ritʃ]

a. 1. 富的,有钱的

　　 2. 富饶的,肥沃的

　　 3. (in)充足的,丰富的

rid [rid]

vt. (of)使摆脱,使去掉

get ～ of 除去,摆脱

ride [raid]

v. & *n*. 骑,乘

rifle [ˈraifl]

n. 步枪

right [rait]

a. 1. 正确的,对的

　　 2. 合适的,恰当的

　　 3. 右边的,右方的

　　 4. 正常的,健康的

　　 5. 直角的,直的

ad. 1. 对,不错

　　 2. 直接,径直地

　　 3. 正好,完全

n. 权力,法权

all ～ 好,行

ring [riŋ]

n. 1. 卷,环

2. 戒指

3. 铃声,按铃

v. 按(铃),敲(钟)

vt. (up)打电话

ripe [raip]

a. 1. 熟的,成熟的

　　 2. (for)时机成熟的

rise [raiz]

vi. 1. 升起,上升

　　 2. 起立,起床

　　 3. 上涨,增长

　　 4. 起义,奋起

n. 上涨,增高

give ～ to 引起,使发生

risk [risk]

vt. 冒……的危险

n. 冒险

river [ˈrivə]

n. 河流

road [rəud]

n. 道路,路

roar [rɔː]

vi. & *n*. 吼叫,怒号

roast [rəust]

v. 烤,炙,烘

n. 烤肉

a. 烤过的,烘过的

rob [rɔb]

vt. (of)1. 抢劫,盗取

　　　　 2. 非法剥夺

rock [rɔk]

n. 岩石,石块

v. 摇,摇动

rocket [ˈrɔkit]

n. 火箭

rod [rɔd]

n. 杆,棒

role [rəul]

n. 1. 角色

　　 2. 作用,任务

roll [rəul]

v. 1. 滚动,滚转

　　 2. (使)摇摆,(使)摇晃

　　 3. (up)卷起,卷缩

vt. 辗,轧

n. (一)卷,卷形物

roof [ru:f]

n. 屋顶,顶

room [ru:m]

n. 1. 房间,室

　　 2. 空间,地方

　　 3. 余地,机会

root [ru:t]

n. 1. 根,根部

　　 2. 根本,根源

v. (使)生根,(使)扎根

rope [rəup]

n. 绳,索

rose [rəuz]

n. 蔷薇,玫瑰

rough [rʌf]

a. 1. 粗糙的

　　 2. 粗略的,大致的

　　 3. 粗野的,粗暴的

round [raund]

a. 圆的,球形的

prep. 围绕

ad. 周围

vt. 1. 绕行

　　 2. 使成圆形,弄圆

n. (一)回合,(一)场,(一)圈

route [ru:t]

n. 路线,路程

routine [ruː'tiːn]

n. 例行公事,惯例,惯常的程序

a. 例行的,日常的,常规的

row [rau]

n. 排,行

v. 划(船)

royal [ˈrɔiəl]

a. 1. 王室的,皇家的

　　 2. 第一流的,高贵的

rub [rʌb]

v. 擦,摩擦

rubber [ˈrʌbə]

n. 橡皮,橡胶

rubbish [ˈrʌbiʃ]

n. 1. 垃圾,废物

　　 2. 废话

rude [ru:d]

a. 粗鲁的,不礼貌的

rug [rʌg]

n. (小)地毯

ruin [ruin]

vt. 毁灭,毁坏

v. (使)破产,(使)堕落

n. 1. 毁灭,崩溃

2. [pl.]废墟,遗迹

rule [ru:l]

v. 统治,控制

n. 1. 规章,条例

2. 习惯,通例

3. 统治,管辖

as a ～ 通常,照例

ruler ['ru:lə]

n. 1. 统治者

2. 直尺

run [rʌn]

v. 1. (使)跑,(使)奔跑

2. 行驶,驾驶

3. 运转,开动

4. 蔓延,伸展

vt. 1. 经营,管理

2. 运载,运送

n. 运行,运转

～ down 撞倒,停掉

～ into 撞上,偶然碰见

～ out of 用完,用尽

～ over 1. 溢出,满出

2. 略读,略述

3. 辗过

rural ['ruər(ə)l]

a. 农村的

rush [rʌʃ]

v. (使)冲,(使)突进

n. 1. 冲,急速行进

2. 匆忙,急迫

3. (交通,事物等的)繁忙

Russian ['rʌʃən]

a. 1. 俄罗斯的,俄国的,

俄国人的

2. 俄语的

n. 1. 俄罗斯人,俄国人

2. 俄语

rust [rʌst]

n. 铁锈

v. (使)生锈

S

sack [sæk]

n. 袋,包

vt. 解雇

sad [sæd]

a. 悲哀的,悲痛的

saddle ['sædl]

n. 鞍,鞍状物

safe [seif]

a. 1. 安全的,平安的

2. 谨慎的,可靠的

safety ['seifti]

n. 1. 安全,保险

2. 安全保险,保险装置

sail [seil]

v. 航行(于)

vi. 启航,开船

n. 1. 帆,篷

2. 航行

sailor ['seilə]

n. 水手,海员

sake [seik]

n. 缘故,理由

for the ～ of 为了……起见

salad ['sæləd]

n. 凉拌菜,色拉

salary ['sæləri]

n. 薪水,工资

sale [seil]

n. 1. 出售,卖出

2. 贱卖,廉价出售

3. 销路,销售额

on ～ 减价出售

salesman ['seilzmən]

n. 售货员,推销员

salt [sɔ:lt]

n. 盐

vt. 腌,盐渍

same [seim]

a. 相同的,同样的

pron. 同样的人,同样的事物

the ～ as 与……一致的,

与……相同的

sample ['sæmpl]

n. 样品,试样

vt. 抽样试验,抽样调查

sand [sænd]

n. 1. 沙

2. [pl.]沙滩,沙地

sandwich ['sænwitʃ]

n. 夹心面包,三明治

vt. 夹入中间

satellite ['sætəlait]

n. 卫星

satisfaction [ˌsætis'fækʃən]

n. 1. 满意,满足

2. 令人满意的事物

satisfactory [ˌsætis'fæktəri]

a. 令人满意的

satisfy ['sætisfai]

vt. 1. 满足,使满意

2. 说服,使相信

Saturday ['sætədi]

n. 星期六

saucer ['sɔ:sə]

n. 茶托,碟子

sausage ['sɔsidʒ]

n. 香肠

save [seiv]

v. 1. 救,拯救

2. 储蓄,储存

3. 节省

saving ['seiviŋ]

n. 1. [pl.]储蓄,存款

2. 节省

saw [sɔ:]

n. 锯子,锯床

v. 锯,锯开

say [sei]

v. 说,讲

vt. 说明,表明

n. 发言权,意见

scale [skeil]

n. 1. 刻度,标度

2. [pl.]天平,磅秤

3. 比例,比例尺

4. 大小,规模

on a large ～ 大规模地

scarce [skɛəs]

a. 1. 缺乏的,不足的

2. 稀有的

· 66 ·

scarcely ['skɛəsli]

  ad. 几乎不,简直没有

scare [skɛə]

  v. 惊吓,受惊

  n. 惊恐,恐慌

scatter ['skætə]

  v. 分散,散开,撒开

scene [si:n]

  n. 1. 景色,景象

     2. 舞台,发生地点

     3. (戏剧等中)一场

scenery ['si:nəri]

  n. 1. 风景,景色

     2. 舞台布景

schedule ['skedʒjul]

  n. 时间表,日程安排表

  v. 安排,排定

  on ~ 按时间表,及时,准时

scheme [ski:m]

  n. 1. 计划,规划

     2. 诡计,阴谋

     3. 配置,安排

scholar ['skɔlə]

  n. 学者

school [sku:l]

  n. 1. 学校

     2. (大学里的)学院

     3. 学派,流派

science ['saiəns]

  n. 1. 科学

     2. 学科

scientific [saiən'tifik]

  a. 科学的

scientist ['saiəntist]

  n. 科学家

scissors ['sizəz]

  n. 剪刀

scold [skəuld]

  v. 责骂,申斥

scope [skəup]

  n. 1. (活动,影响等的)范围

     2. (发挥能力等的)余地,

      机会

score [skɔ:]

  n. 1. 得分,分数

     2. 二十

  v. 得(分),记(……的)分数

scratch [skrætʃ]

  v. 抓,搔,抓伤

  n. 抓,搔,抓痕

scream [skri:m]

  v. 尖声叫

  n. 尖叫声

screen [skri:n]

  n. 1. 屏幕

     2. 帘

  vt. 掩蔽,遮

screw [skru:]

  n. 螺旋,螺钉

  v. 拧,拧紧

sea [si:]

  n. 海,海洋

seal [si:l]

  n. 1. 封铅,封条

     2. 印,图章

  vt. 封,密封

search [sə:tʃ]

  v. & *n*. (for)搜查,搜寻

season ['si:zn]

  n. 季,季节

seat [si:t]

  n. 1. 座,座位

     2. 所在地,场所

  vt. 使坐下

second ['sekənd]

  num. 第二

  a. 二等的,次等的

  n. 秒

secondary ['sekəndəri]

  a. 1. 次要的,二级的

     2. 中级的,第二的

secret ['si:krit]

  a. 秘密的,机密的

  n. 秘密,奥秘

secretary ['sekrətri]

  n. 1. 秘书

     2. 书记

section ['sekʃən]

  n. 1. 部分

     2. 断面,剖面

     3. 部门,科

secure [si'kjuə]

  a. 1. (from, against)安全的,

      可靠的

     2. 放心的,无虑的

security [si'kjuəriti]

  n. 安全

see [si:]

  v. 1. 看,看见

     2. 领会,理解

     3. 获悉,知道

  vt. 1. 会见,访问

     2. 目睹,经历

  ~ off 送行

  ~ to 注意,务必

seed [si:d]

  n. 种子

  vi. 结实,结籽

  v. 播(种)

seek [si:k]

  v. (after, for)寻找,探索

seem [si:m]

  vi. 好像,似乎

seize [si:z]

  v. 抓住,逮住

  vt. 没收,查封

seldom ['seldəm]

  ad. 很少,不常

select [si'lekt]

  vt. 选择,挑选

  a. 精选的

selection [si'lekʃən]

  n. 1. 选择,挑选

     2. 选集,精选品

self [self]

  n. 自我,自己

selfish ['selfiʃ]

  a. 自私的

sell [sel]

  v. 出售,卖

senate ['senit]

  n. 参议院,上院

send [send]

  vt. 1. 送,寄

     2. 派遣,打发

  ~ for 派人去请

senior ['si:njə]

  a. 1. 年长的

2. 资格较老的,地位较高的

sense [sens]

n. 1. 感官,官能

2. 感觉

3. 判断力,见识

4. 意义,意思

vt. 觉得,意识到

make ~ 讲得通,有意义

sensitive ['sensitiv]

a. (to)1. 敏感的

2. 易受伤害的

3. 灵敏的

sentence ['sentəns]

n. 1. 句子

2. 判决,宣判

vt. 宣判,判决

separate ['sepəreit]

a. (from)分离的,分开的

v. (from)分离,分开

September [səp'tembə]

n. 九月

series ['siəri:z]

n. 1. 系列,连续

2. 丛书

a ~ of 一系列,一连串

serious ['siəriəs]

a. 1. 严肃的,庄重的

2. 严重的,危急的

3. 认真的

servant ['sə:vənt]

n. 仆人

serve [sə:v]

v. 1. 服务,尽责

2. 招待,伺候

3. 符合,适用

4. 供应(饭菜)

~ as 作为,用作

service ['sə:vis]

n. 1. [常 pl.]服务,帮助

2. 公共设施,公用事业

3. 维修,保养

4. 行政部门,服务机构

vt. 维修,保养

set [set]

n. 1. (一)套,(一)副,(一)批

2. 机组,设备

vt. 1. 安置,放

2. 树立,创造

3. 调整,校正

vi. (日、月)沉落,下沉

a. 不变的

~ aside 1. 拨出,留出

2. 拒绝,驳回

~ down 1. 卸下,放下

2. 记下,记入

~ forth 阐明,陈述

~ off 1. 出发,动身

2. 引起,使发生

~ out 1. 陈列,显示

2. 动身,起程

~ out + to V. 打算,着手

~ up 创立,建立

settle ['setl]

v. 1. 解决,决定

2. 稳定,(使)镇静

3. 支付,结算

4. (down)(使)定居,(使)安家

vi. 停留,停息

seven ['sevən]

num. 七,七个

seventeen ['sevən'ti:n]

num. 十七,十七个

seventh ['sevənθ]

num. 第七

seventy ['sevənti]

num. 七十,七十个

several ['sevərəl]

a. 几个,数个

severe [si'viə]

a. 1. 严厉的,严格的

2. 剧烈的,严重的,严峻的

sew [sju:]

v. 缝制,缝纫

sex [seks]

n. 性别,性

sexual ['seksjuəl]

a. 1. 性的,两性的

2. 性别的

shade [ʃeid]

n. 1. 荫,阴暗

2. 遮光物

vt. 遮蔽,遮光

shadow ['ʃædəu]

n. 阴影,荫,影子

shake [ʃeik]

v. & *n*. 1. 摇动,摇

2. 擅抖,震动

shall [ʃæl,ʃəl,ʃl]

aux. *v*. 1. 将,将要

2. 应,必须

shallow ['ʃæləu]

a. 1. 浅的

2. 浅薄的

shame [ʃeim]

n. 1. 羞耻,羞愧

2. 可耻的人(事物)

shape [ʃeip]

n. 1. 形状,外形

2. 情况,状态

3. 种类

v. 成型,塑造

share [ʃɛə]

v. (with)分摊,分享,共用

n. 1. 一份,份额

2. 股份

sharp [ʃɑ:p]

a. 1. 锋利的,锐利的

2. 轮廓分明的

3. 陡的,急转的

4. 刺耳的

5. 敏锐的,机警的

ad. (指时刻)正,准

shave [ʃeiv]

v. 剃,刮

vt. 刨,剥

n. 刮脸

she [ʃi:,ʃi]

pron. 她

shed [ʃed]

vt. 1. 流出

2. 发散,散发

sheep [ʃi:p]

n. 羊,绵羊

sheet [ʃi:t]

n. 1. (一)片,(一)张,薄片

2. 被单

shelf [ʃelf]

n. 架子

shell [ʃel]

  n. 1. 壳

    2. 炮弹

shelter [ˈʃeltə]

  n. 1. 掩蔽处,躲避处

    2. 掩蔽,保护

  v. 掩蔽,躲避

shield [ʃiːld]

  n. 1. 防护物,护罩

    2. 盾,盾状物

  vt. (from)保护,防护

shift [ʃift]

  v. 替换,转换

  n. 1. 转换,转变

    2. 轮班,换班

shine [ʃain]

  v. 照耀,发光

  vt. 擦亮

  n. 光泽

ship [ʃip]

  n. 船,船舶

  vt. 用船运,装运

shirt [ʃət]

  n. 衬衫

shiver [ˈʃivə]

  vi. & n. 战栗,发抖

shock [ʃɔk]

  n. 1. 震动,冲击,休克

    2. 电击,触电

    3. 震惊,激动

  v. (使)震惊,(使)激动

shoe [ʃuː]

  n. 鞋

shoot [ʃuːt]

  v. (at)发射,射击

  vt. 掠过,迅速穿过

  n. 1. 嫩枝,苗

    2. 射击,发射

shop [ʃɔp]

  n. 商店,店铺

  vi. 买东西,购货

shore [ʃɔː, ʃəə]

  n. 滨,岸

short [ʃɔːt]

  a. 1. 短的,矮的

    2. (of)短缺的,不足的

cut ~ 1. 中断

    2. 简化

in ~ 简言之,简单地说

shortage [ˈʃɔːtidʒ]

  n. 不足,缺少

shortcoming [ˈʃɔːtkʌmiŋ]

  n. 缺点,短处

shortly [ˈʃɔːtli]

  ad. 1. 立刻,不久

    2. 简略地,简言之

shot [ʃɔt]

  n. 1. 开枪,射击

    2. 子弹,炮弹

should [ʃud]

  aux. v. 1. shall 的过去式

    2. 应该

shoulder [ˈʃəuldə]

  n. 肩,肩部

  vt. 肩负,承当

shout [ʃaut]

  v. & n. 呼喊,呼叫

show [ʃəu]

  v. 呈现,显示

  vt. 表明,说明

  n. 1. 展览,展览会

    2. 演出

shower [ˈʃauə]

  n. 1. 阵雨

    2. 淋浴

    3. (一)阵,(一)大批

shrink [ʃriŋk]

  v. 收缩,(使)皱缩

shut [ʃʌt]

  v. 关上,闭上

shy [ʃai]

  a. (of)怕羞的,畏缩的

sick [sik]

  a. 1. 有病的

    2. 恶心的,想呕吐的

side [said]

  n. 1. 侧面,旁边

    2. 坡,岸

    3. 一边,一方

  v. (with)同意,站在……的一边

~ by ~ 并列,并肩

sight [sait]

n. 1. 视力,视觉

    2. 见,瞥见

    3. 视域,眼界

at first ~ 乍一看,初看起来

sightseeing [ˈsaitsiːiŋ]

  n. 观光,游览

sign [sain]

  n. 1. 标记,标志

    2. 符号,记号

    3. 征兆,迹象

  v. 签名(于),署名(于)

signal [ˈsignl]

  n. 信号

  v. 发信号,用信号通知

signature [ˈsignitʃə]

  n. 签名,署名

significance [sigˈnifikəns]

  n. 1. 意义

    2. 重要性

silence [ˈsailəns]

  n. 1. 静,寂静

    2. 沉默

  vt. 使沉默,使安静

silent [ˈsailənt]

  a. 1. 寂静的

    2. 沉默的

silk [silk]

  n. 丝,绸

silly [ˈsili]

  a. 傻的,糊涂的

silver [ˈsilvə]

  n. 银

  vt. 镀银

similar [ˈsimilə]

  a. (to)相似的,类似的

simple [ˈsimpl]

  a. 1. 简单的,简易的

    2. 朴素的,俭朴的

    3. 单纯的,直率的

simply [ˈsimpli]

  ad. 1. 简单地

    2. 完全,简直

    3. 仅仅,不过

    4. 朴素地

since [sins]

  prep. 从……以来,自从

conj. 1. 从……以来,自从
　　　 2. 因为,既然
ad. 从那以后,后来
ever ～ 从那时起,自那时以来

sincere [sin'siə]
　a. 诚挚的,真实的

sing [siŋ]
　v. 唱,演唱

single ['siŋgl]
　a. 1. 单人的
　　　 2. 单一的,单个的
　　　 3. 未婚的,独身的

sink [siŋk]
　v. 沉没,(使)下沉
　n. 水槽,水池

sir [sə:, sə]
　n. 先生

sister ['sistə]
　n. 姐妹

sit [sit]
　v. 就座,坐

site [sait]
　n. 位置,地点

situation [ˌsitju'eiʃən]
　n. 1. 状况,处境
　　　 2. 位置,地点

six [siks]
　num. 六,六个

sixteen ['siks'ti:n]
　num. 十六,十六个

sixth [siksθ]
　num. 第六

sixty ['siksti]
　num. 六十,六十个

size [saiz]
　n. 大小,尺寸

skate [skeit, skit]
　vi. 溜冰,滑冰
　n. 冰鞋

sketch [sketʃ]
　n. 1. 略图,草图
　　　 2. 概略,梗概
　vi. 绘略图,素描

ski [ski:]
　vi. 滑雪
　n. 滑雪板

skill [skil]
　n. 1. 技能,技巧
　　　 2. 熟练

skilled [skild]
　a. 1. 熟练的,有技能的
　　　 2. 需要技能的

skil(l)ful ['skilful]
　a. (in, at)灵巧的,熟练的

skin [skin]
　n. 1. 皮,皮肤
　　　 2. 兽皮,皮毛
　　　 3. 外皮,外壳

skirt [skə:t]
　n. 裙子

sky [skai]
　n. 天,天空

slave [sleiv]
　n. 奴隶

sleep [sli:p]
　vi. 睡
　n. 睡眠

sleeve [sli:v]
　n. 袖子

slide [slaid]
　v. (使)滑动,(使)滑行
　n. 1. 滑坡,滑道
　　　 2. 滑,滑动
　　　 3. 幻灯片

slight [slait]
　a. 轻微的,微小的

slim [slim]
　a. 1. 苗条的
　　　 2. 薄的
　　　 3. (机会等)小的, 少的

slip [slip]
　vi. 1. 滑倒
　　　 2. 滑落,滑掉
　　　 3. 溜,溜走
　n. 疏忽,小错

slope [sləup]
　n. 1. 斜坡,斜面
　　　 2. 倾斜
　v. (使)倾斜

slow [sləu]
　a. 1. 慢的
　　　 2. 迟钝的,不活跃的

v. (down) (使)慢下来,(使)减速

small [smɔ:l]
　a. 小的,少的

smart [sma:t]
　a. 1. 漂亮的,潇洒的
　　　 2. 聪明的,巧妙的

smell [smel]
　n. 1. 气味,臭味
　　　 2. 嗅觉
　v. 1. 嗅,闻到
　　　 2. 散发(……的)气味,
　　　　 有(……的)气味

smile [smail]
　vi. (at)微笑
　n. 微笑

smoke [sməuk]
　n. 烟,烟尘
　v. 抽(烟),吸(烟)
　vi. 冒烟

smooth [smu:ð]
　a. 1. 光滑的,平滑的
　　　 2. 平稳的,平静的
　　　 3. 流畅的,柔和的

snake [sneik]
　n. 蛇

snow [snəu]
　n. 雪
　vi. 下雪

so [səu]
　conj. 1. 因而,所以
　　　　 2. 那样,这样看来
　ad. 1. [表示程度]如此,那么
　　　　 2. 非常,很
　　　　 3. [表示方式]这样,那样
and ～ on/forth 等等
ever ～ 非常,极其
or ～ 左右,大约
～ as + to V. 结果是,以致

soap [səup]
　n. 肥皂

so-called [səu'kɔ:ld]
　a. 所谓的

social ['səuʃəl]
　a. 社会的

socialism ['səuʃəlizəm]
　n. 社会主义

socialist ['səuʃəlist]

　　n. 社会主义者

　　a. 社会主义的

society [sə'saiəti]

　　n. 1. 社会

　　　　2. 团体,会,社

sock [sɔk]

　　n. 短袜

soda ['səudə]

　　n. 苏打,汽水

sofa ['səufə]

　　n. (长)沙发

soft [sɔft]

　　a. 1. 软的,柔软的

　　　　2. 温和的,温柔的

　　　　3. 不含酒精的

soil [sɔil]

　　n. 泥土,土壤

　　v. 弄脏,(使)变脏

solar ['səulə]

　　a. 太阳的,日光的

sole [səul]

　　a. 1. 单独的, 惟一的

　　　　2. 独有的

　　n. 脚底,鞋底,袜底

soldier ['səuldʒə]

　　n. 士兵,军人

solid ['sɔlid]

　　a. 1. 固体的

　　　　2. 实心的

　　　　3. 结实的,坚固的

　　n. 固体

solution [sə'lu:ʃn]

　　n. 1. 解答,解决办法

　　　　2. 溶解,溶液

solve [sɔlv]

　　vt. 解决,解答

some [sʌm,səm,sm]

　　a. 1. 一些,若干

　　　　2. 某一

　　pron. 一些,若干

　　ad. 1. 大约

　　　　2. 稍微

somebody ['sʌmbədi]

　　pron. 某人,有人

somehow ['sʌmhau]

　　ad. 1. 设法,以某种方式

　　　　2. 不知怎么地

someone ['sʌmwʌn]

　　pron. 某人,有人

something ['sʌmθiŋ]

　　pron. 某事,某物

sometime ['sʌmtaim]

　　ad. 在某一时候,曾经,有一天

sometimes ['sʌmtaimz]

　　ad. 不时,有时

somewhat ['sʌmwɔt]

　　ad. 稍微,有点

somewhere ['sʌmwɛə]

　　ad. 在某处,到某处

son [sʌn]

　　n. 儿子

song [sɔŋ]

　　n. 歌,歌曲

soon [su:n]

　　ad. 1. 不久,即刻

　　　　2. 早,快

　　as ～ as 一……就,刚……便

　　no ～er...than 一……就,

　　　　刚……便

　　～er or later 迟早

sore [sɔ,sɔə]

　　a. 1. 疼痛的

　　　　2. 痛心的

　　n. 痛的地方,痛处

sorrow ['sɔrəu]

　　n. 悲哀,悲痛

sorry ['sɔri]

　　a. (for, about)

　　　　1. 遗憾的,对不起的

　　　　2. 可怜的

sort [sɔ:t]

　　n. 种类,类别

　　vt. 分类,整理

soul [səul]

　　n. 1. 灵魂, 心灵

　　　　2. 精神, 精力

　　　　3. 人

sound [saund]

　　n. 声音

　　v. (使)发声,(弄)响

　　vi. 听起来

sound

　　a. 1. 健全的,完好的

　　　　2. 正确的,稳妥的

soup [su:p]

　　n. 汤

sour ['sauə]

　　a. 1. 酸的

　　　　2. 发酵的,酸腐的

source [sɔ:s]

　　n. 1. 源,源泉

　　　　2. 来源,出处

south [sauθ]

　　n. 南,南方,南部

　　a. 南方的,南部的

southeast ['sauθ'i:st]

　　n. 东南

　　a. 东南的

southern ['sʌðən]

　　a. 南方的,南部的

southwest ['sauθ'west]

　　n. 西南

　　a. 西南的

sow [sau]

　　v. 播(种)

space [speis]

　　n. 1. 间隔,距离

　　　　2. 空地,余地

　　　　3. 空间,太空

spade [speid]

　　n. 铲,锹

Spanish ['spæniʃ]

　　a. 1. 西班牙(人)的

　　　　2. 西班牙语的

　　n. 西班牙语

spare [spɛə]

　　a. 多余的,剩下的

　　v. 节约,节省

spark [spɑ:k]

　　n. 火星,火花

speak [spi:k]

　　v. 说,说话

　　vi. 1. 表示意见

　　　　2. 演说,发言

special ['speʃəl]

　　a. 1. 特殊的,专门的

　　　　2. 额外的,附加的

specialist ['speʃəlist]

n. 专家

specific [spəˈsifik]

　a. 1. 明确的,具体的

　　　2. 特有的,特定的

speech [spiːtʃ]

　n. 演说,讲话

speed [spiːd]

　n. 1. 速度

　　　2. 迅速,快

　vi. 迅速前进,快行

　vt. 加速,催

spell [spel]

　vt. 拼写

spelling [ˈspeliŋ]

　n. 拼法,拼写法

spend [spend]

　v. 1. 花费

　　　2. 消耗,用尽

　vt. 度过,消磨

sphere [sfiə]

　n. 1. 球,球体

　　　2. 范围,领域

spider [ˈspaidə]

　n. 蜘蛛

spill [spil]

　v. 溢出,溅出

spin [spin]

　v. 1. 旋转

　　　2. 纺,纺纱

　n. 旋转

spirit [ˈspirit]

　n. 1. 精神

　　　2. 气概,志气

spit [spit]

　v. 吐(唾沫)

　n. 唾液

spite [spait]

　in ～ of 不顾,不管(介词短语)

splendid [ˈsplendid]

　a. 1. 壮丽的,辉煌的

　　　2. 极好的

split [split]

　v. 1. 劈开,(使)裂开

　　　2. 分裂,分离

　n. 裂开,裂口

spoil [spoil]

　vt. 1. 损坏,搞糟

　　　2. 宠坏,溺爱

spoon [spuːn]

　n. 匙,调羹

sport [spɔːt]

　n. 1. 运动

　　　2. [pl.] 运动会

sportsman [ˈspɔːtsmən]

　n. 运动员

spot [spɔt]

　n. 1. 斑点,污点

　　　2. 地点,场所

　v. 玷污,弄脏

　vt. 认出,发现

spray [sprei]

　v. 喷,(使)溅散

　n. 1. 浪花,水花,飞沫

　　　2. 喷雾

spread [spred]

　v. & *n*. 1. 伸开,伸展,铺开

　　　　　 2. 散布,传播

spring [spriŋ]

　n. 1. 春,春季

　　　2. 跳,跃

　　　3. 泉,源泉

　　　4. 弹簧

　vi. 跳,跳跃

square [skwɛə]

　n. 1. 正方形

　　　2. 广场

　a. 1. 正方形的

　　　2. 平方的

squeeze [skwiːz]

　v. & *n*. 压榨,挤

stable [ˈsteibl]

　n. 稳定的

staff [stɑːf]

　n. 全体职工,全体人员

stage [steidʒ]

　n. 1. 舞台

　　　2. 阶段,时期

stain [stein]

　n. 污点,瑕疵

　v. 污染

stair [stɛə]

　n. [pl.]楼梯

stale [steil]

　a. 1. 变质的,不新鲜的

　　　2. 陈腐的,陈旧的

stamp [stæmp]

　n. 1. 邮票,印花

　　　2. 印,图章

　　　3. 标志,印记

　　　4. 踩脚,顿足

　v. 踩(脚),顿(足)

stand [stænd]

　vi. 1. 站,站立

　　　2. 坐落,位于

　　　3. 坚持,维持原状

　vt. 忍受,经受

　n. 台,架

　～ by 支持,帮助

　～ for 1. 代表,表示

　　　　2. 主张,主持

　～ out 突出,出色

　～ up 1. 站起来

　　　　2. 耐用

　～ up to 经得住

standard [ˈstændəd]

　n. 标准,规格

　a. 标准的

star [stɑː]

　n. 1. 星,恒星

　　　2. 明星,名角

stare [stɛə(r)]

　v. (at)凝视,盯着看

start [stɑːt]

　v. 1. 开始,着手

　　　2. 惊起,吃惊

　vi. 出发,动身

　n. 1. 开端,起点

　　　2. 惊起,吃惊

starve [stɑːv]

　v. (使)饿死,(使)饿

state [steit]

　n. 1. 状态,情况

　　　2. 国家,(美国的)州

　vt. 陈述,说明

statement [ˈsteitmənt]

　n. 声明,陈述

station [ˈsteiʃən]

　n. 1. 车站

2. 所,站

statistic [stə'tistik]

  n. 1. 统计数字,统计资料

     2. [-s]统计学

stay [stei]

  vi. 1. 停留,暂住

     2. 保持下去,能持续

     3. 停止,站住

  n. 逗留,停留

steady ['stedi]

  a. 1. 稳固的,稳定的

     2. 坚定的,扎实的

  v. (使)稳定,(使)稳固

steak [steik]

  n. 牛排,肉排,鱼排

steal [sti:l]

  v. 偷,窃取

steam [sti:m]

  n. 蒸汽,水汽

  vi. 蒸发

  vt. 蒸

steamer ['sti:mə]

  n. 汽船

steel [sti:l]

  n. 钢

steep [sti:p]

  a. 陡峭的,险峻的

stem [stem]

  n. 茎,干

step [step]

  n. 1. 步,脚步

     2. 梯级,台阶

     3. 步骤,措施

  v. 踏,走

  ~ by ~ 逐步地

stick [stik]

  n. 棍,棒,手杖

  v. 粘住,粘贴

  vt. 刺,戳

stiff [stif]

  a. 1. 硬的,僵直的

     2. 拘谨的,呆板的

     3. 艰难的,费劲的

still [stil]

  ad. 1. 还,仍旧

     2. 更,还要

a. 静止的,寂静的

  n. 寂静

stir [stə:]

  vt. 1. 搅拌,搅动

     2. 动,摇动

     3. 煽动,鼓动

stock [stɔk]

  n. 1. 库存,储品

     2. 公债,股票

  vt. 储存

stocking ['stɔkiŋ]

  n. 长袜

stomach ['stʌmək]

  n. 胃,胃口

stone [stəun]

  n. 1. 石,石头

     2. 宝石

stoop [stu:p]

  v. 俯(身),弯(腰)

  n. 弯腰,曲背

stop [stɔp]

  v. 1. 停止,中止

     2. 塞住,堵塞

  vt. 阻止,阻挡

  n. 1. (公共汽车的)站

     2. 停止,中止

store [stɔ:]

  vt. 储藏,储备

  n. 1. 商店,店铺

     2. 储藏,储备

stor(e)y ['stɔ:ri]

  n. 楼,层

storm [stɔ:m]

  n. 暴风雨,暴风雪

story ['stɔ:ri]

  n. 1. 故事,传说

     2. = storey

stove [stəuv]

  n. 炉

straight [streit]

  a. 1. 直的,笔直的

     2. 整齐的,端正的

     3. 正直的

  ad. 直接

strain [strein]

  n. 1. 过度的疲劳,紧张

2. 张力,应变

  vt. 扭伤,损伤

  v. 1. 拉紧,扯紧

     2. (使)紧张,尽力

strange [streindʒ]

  a. 1. 奇异的,奇怪的

     2. 陌生的,不习惯的

stranger ['streindʒə]

  n. 陌生人

strategy ['strætidʒi]

  n. 战略,策略

straw [strɔ:]

  n. 稻草,麦秆

stream [stri:m]

  n. 1. 溪,川

     2. 流,一股,一串

  v. 流,涌

street [stri:t]

  n. 街,街道

strength [streŋθ]

  n. 力量,实力,强度

strengthen ['streŋθən]

  v. 加强,巩固

stress [stres]

  n. 1. 压力,应力

     2. 重音

stretch [stretʃ]

  v. 伸展,伸长

  n. 一段时间,一段路程

strict [strikt]

  a. 1. (with)严格的,严厉的

     2. 严谨的,精确的

strike [straik]

  v. 1. 击,撞

     2. 罢工

     3. (使)产生印象,打动

     4. 敲(响)

  vt. 发现,找到

  n. 罢工

string [striŋ]

  n. 1. 线,细绳

     2. 一串,一行

stripe [straip]

  n. 条纹

stroke [strəuk]

  n. 1. 击,敲

2. 报时的钟声

3. 一击,一划,一笔,一次努力

4. 中风

vt. 抚摸

strong [strɔŋ]

a. 1. 强壮的,强大的

2. 强烈的,浓的

structure [ˈstrʌktʃə]

n. 1. 结构,构造

2. 结构物,建筑物

vt. 构造,建造

struggle [ˈstrʌgl]

n. & *vi*. 斗争,奋斗

student [ˈstjuːdənt]

n. 学生,大学生

study [ˈstʌdi]

v. 学习,研究

vt. 细察,仔细端详

n. 1. 学习

2. 书房

stuff [stʌf]

n. 原料,材料,东西

vt. 塞满,填满

stupid [ˈstjuːpid]

a. 愚蠢的,笨的

style [stail]

n. 1. 风格,文体

2. 式样,类型

subject [ˈsʌbdʒikt]

n. 1. 主题,题目

2. 学科,科目

vi. (to)使遭到,使受到

a. (to)受制于……的,受……影响的,易受……的

submarine

[*n*. ˈsʌbməriːn, *a*. sʌbməˈriːn]

n. 潜水艇

a. 水下的,海底的

submit [səbˈmit]

v. (to)(使)服从,(使)顺从

vt. (to)提交,递交

substance [ˈsʌbstəns]

n. 1. 物质

2. 实质,主旨

substitute [ˈsʌbstitjuːt]

n. 代用品,代替者

v. (for)代替,替换

subtract [səbˈtrækt]

v. (from)减去,减

suburb [ˈsʌbəːb]

n. 市郊,郊区

subway [ˈsʌbwei]

n. 地道,地铁

succeed [səkˈsiːd]

vi. (in)成功

v. 继……之后,继任,继承

success [səkˈses]

a. 成功,成就

successful [səkˈsesful]

a. 成功的

successive [səkˈsesiv]

a. 连续的,接连的

such [sʌtʃ]

ad. 那么

a. 1. 这样的,这种的

2. 上述的,该

pron. 这样的人(物),上述事物

~ ... as 像……这样的

~ as 例如

sudden [ˈsʌdn]

a. 突然的,意外的

suffer [ˈsʌfə]

vi. (from) 1. 受痛苦,患病

2. 受损失

vt. 1. 遭受,蒙受

2. 忍受,忍耐

sufficient [səˈfiʃənt]

a. (for)足够的,充分的

sugar [ˈʃugə]

n. 糖

suggest [səˈdʒest]

vt. 1. 建议,提出

2. 使想起,暗示

suggestion [səˈdʒestʃən]

n. 建议,意见

suit [sjuːt]

v. 1. 合适,适合

2. 相配,配合

n. 一套衣服

suitable [ˈsjuːtəbl]

a. (for)合适的,适宜的

sum [sʌm]

n. 1. 总数,和

2. 金额

v. 总计,合计

in ~ 总而言之

~ up 总结,概括

summarize(-ise) [ˈsʌməraiz]

vt. 概括,总结

summary [ˈsʌməri]

n. 摘要,概要

summer [ˈsʌmə]

n. 夏,夏季

sun [sʌn]

n. 太阳,日

Sunday [ˈsʌndi]

n. 星期日

sunlight [ˈsʌnlait]

n. 日光,阳光

sunrise [ˈsʌnraiz]

n. 日出

sunset [ˈsʌnset]

n. 日落

sunshine [ˈsʌnʃain]

n. 阳光

superior [sjuːˈpiəriə]

a. 1. 优良的,卓越的

2. (to)较……多的,优……于的

3. (to)在上的,上级的

n. 上级,长官

supermarket [ˈsjuːpəmɑːkit]

n. 超级市场

supper [ˈsʌpə]

n. 晚餐

supply [səˈplai]

vt. 1. (with, to)供给,供应

2. 满足(需要)

n. 供给,供应量

support [səˈpɔːt]

vt. 1. 支撑,支承

2. 支持,拥护

3. 供养,维持

n. 1. 支持者,支撑物

2. 支撑,支持

suppose [səˈpəuz]

v. 料想,猜想

vt. 1. 假定

2. [用于祈使语句]让,设

supreme [sjuːˈpriːm]

  a. 1. 极度的,极大的

    2. 至高的,最高的

sure [ʃuə]

  a. 1. (of)肯定的,确信的

    2. 可靠的,稳当的

make ~ of/that 确信,确定,务必

surface [ˈsəːfis]

  n. 1. 表面,面

    2. 外表,外观

surprise [səˈpraiz]

  vt. 使惊奇,使惊讶

  n. 惊奇,诧异

surround [səˈraund]

  vt. 包围,环绕

survey [*v.* səˈvei, *n.* ˈsəːvei]

  vt. 1. (向公众)调查

    2. 测量,勘定

  n. 1. 公众调查

    2. 测量,测量图

survive [səˈvaiv]

  v. 幸免于,幸存

suspect [səsˈpekt]

  vt. 猜疑,怀疑

  n. 嫌疑犯,可疑分子

swallow [ˈswɔləu]

  v. 吞,咽

  n. 1. 吞,咽

    2. 燕子

sway [swei]

  v. 摇摆,摇动

swear [swɛə]

  vi. (at)诅咒

  v. 宣誓,发誓

sweat [swet]

  n. 汗

  v. (使)出汗

sweep [swiːp]

  v. 1. 扫,打扫

    2. 席卷,冲光

    3. 扫过,掠过

sweet [swiːt]

  a. 1. 甜的

    2. 可爱的,美好的

    3. 芳香的

  n. 1. [常 pl.]糖果

    2. 甜食

swift [swift]

  a. 快速的,敏捷的

swim [swim]

  vi. & *n.* 游泳

swing [swiŋ]

  v. 1. 摇摆,摆动

    2. 回转,旋转

  n. 1. 秋千

    2. 摇摆,摆动

switch [switʃ]

  n. 1. 开关,电闸

    2. 转换

  vt. 转换

  ~ off 断开

  ~ on 接通

symbol [ˈsimbəl]

  n. 1. 符号,记号

    2. 象征

sympathy [ˈsimpəθi]

  n. 同情,同情心

symptom [ˈsimptəm]

  n. 1. 症状

    2. 征候,征兆

synthetic [sinˈθetic]

  a. 1. 合成的,人造的

    2. 综合的

system [ˈsistəm]

  n. 1. 系统,体系

    2. 制度,体制

T

table [ˈteibl]

  n. 1. 桌子,台子

    2. 表格

tail [teil]

  n. 1. 尾巴

    2. 后部,尾部

tailor [ˈteilə(r)]

  n. 裁缝

  vt. 剪裁,缝制

take [teik]

  vt. 1. 拿,取

    2. 带去,携带

    3. 吃,服用

    4. 记录,拍摄

    5. 取得,接受

    6. 需要,花费

    7. 捕获,抓住

  ~ ...as 把 ……作为

  ~ away 1. 清除

     2. 拿走

  ~ ...down 记下,写下

  ~ ...for 把……认为是,

     把……看成为

  ~ in 1. 吸收

     2. 了解,听懂

  ~ off 1. 脱下

     2. 起飞

  ~ on 1. 呈现

     2. 承担

  ~ over 接办,代理

  ~ up 1. 拿起

     2. 占有,占据

tale [teil]

  n. 故事,传说

talk [tɔːk]

  v. 1. 谈话,讲

    2. (over)谈论,议论

  n. 1. 谈话,会谈

    2. 演讲,讲话

tall [tɔːl]

  a. 高的,身材高的

tame [teim]

  a. 驯服的,温顺的

  vt. 驯服,制服

tank [tæŋk]

  n. 1. 罐,槽

    2. 坦克

tap [tæp]

  n. 1. 塞子,龙头

    2. 轻叩,轻拍

  v. 1. 轻叩,轻敲

    2. 利用,开发

tape [teip,tep]

  n. 1. 带,带子

    2. 录音带

  vt. 录音

target [ˈtɑːgit]

  n. 目标,对象

task [tɑːsk]

n. 任务,作业

taste [teist]

  v. 1. 品尝,辨味

      2. (of)有……味道

  vt. 体验,感到

  n. 味道,味觉

tax [tæks]

  n. 税,税款

  vt. 1. 对……征税

      2. 使负重担

taxi ['tæksi]

  n. 出租汽车

tea [ti:]

  n. 1. 茶,茶叶

      2. 茶点

teach [ti:tʃ]

  v. 教,讲授

teacher ['ti:tʃə]

  n. 教师

team [ti:m]

  n. 队,组

tear [tiə]

  n. 眼泪

  v. 撕开,撕碎

technical ['teknikəl]

  a. 技术的

technique [tek'ni:k]

  n. 技术,技能

technology [tek'nɔlədʒi]

  n. 工艺,技术

telegram ['teligræm]

  n. 电报

telephone ['telifəun]

  n. 电话,电话机

  v. 打电话

telescope ['teliskəup]

  n. 望远镜

television (TV) ['teliviʒən]

  n. 电视,电视机

tell [tel]

  v. 说,讲述

  vt. 1. 告诉

      2. 吩咐,命令

      3. (from)辨别,区别

temper ['tempə]

  n. 脾气,情绪

temperature ['tempritʃə(r)]

  n. 温度

temple ['templ]

  n. 庙宇,神殿,寺院

temporary ['tempərəri]

  a. 暂时的,临时的

temptation [temp'teiʃən]

  n. 诱惑,引诱

ten [ten]

  num. 十,十个

tend [tend]

  vi. 趋向,往往是

  vt. 照管,护理

tendency ['tendənsi]

  n. 趋向,趋势

tender ['tendə]

  a. 1. 嫩的

      2. 温柔的

tennis ['tenis]

  n. 网球

tense [tens]

  a. 拉紧的,紧张的

  n. [动词的]时态

tent [tent]

  n. 帐篷

tenth [tenθ]

  num. 第十

term [tə:m]

  n. 1. 学期

      2. 期限,期间

      3. [pl.]条款,条件

      4. 术语

in ~s of 1. 依据,按照

         2. 用……措词

terrible ['terəbl]

  a. 1. 很糟的,极坏的

      2. 可怕的,骇人的

territory ['teritəri]

  n. 领土,版图

terror ['terə]

  n. 恐怖

test [test]

  n. & *v*. 测试,试验,检验

text [tekst]

  n. 1. 正文,原文

      2. 课文,课本

than [ðæn, ðən, ðn]

  conj. 比

thank [θæŋk]

  vt. (for)感谢

  n. [pl.]感谢,谢谢

  ~s to 由于,多亏

that [ðæt]

  a. & *pron*. 那,那个

  conj. [引导从句]

  so ~ 1. 为的是,使得

        2. 结果是,以致

the [ði:, ði, ðə, ð]

  art. 这,那

theatre(-ter) ['θiətə(r)]

  n. 1. 戏院

      2. 阶梯教室

      3. 戏剧

their [ðɛə, ðər]

  pron. [they 的所有格]他(她,它)们的

theirs [ðɛəz]

  pron. [they 的物主代词]他(她,它)们的

them [ðəm]

  pron. [they 的宾格]他(她,它)们

themselves [ðəm'selvz]

  pron. 1. 他(她,它)们自己

      2. 他(她,它)们亲自

then [ðen]

  ad. 1. 当时,在那时

      2. 那么,因而

      3. 然后,于是

  and ~ 其次,然后,于是

theory ['θiəri]

  n. 1. 理论,原理

      2. 学说

there [ðɛə, ðə]

  ad. 1. 在那里,往那里

      2. 在这方面,在这点上

      3. [用于引起注意]

      4. [与 be 连用,表示"有"]

therefore ['ðɛəfɔ:]

  ad. 因此,所以

thermometer [θə'mɔmitə(r)]

  n. 温度计

these [ði:z]

a. & *pron.* 这些

they [ðei, ðe]

  pron. 他(她,它)们

thick [θi:k]

  a. 1. 厚的,粗的

    2. 稠的,浓的

thief [θi:f]

  n. 小偷,贼

thin [θin]

  a. 1. 薄的,细的

    2. 稀薄的,淡的

    3. 瘦的

thing [θiŋ]

  n. 1. 东西,物

    2. [pl.]所有物,用品

    3. 事,事情,事件

    4. [pl.]事态,情况

think [θiŋk]

  v. 想,思索

  vt. 认为,以为

  ~ of 1. 想起,考虑到

    2. 想一想

  ~ of...as 把……看做是,

    以为……是

third [θə:d]

  num. 第三

thirsty [ˈθə:sti]

  a. 1. 口渴的

    2. (for)渴望的,热望的

thirteen [ˈθə:ˈti:n]

  num. 十三,十三个

thirty [ˈθə:ti]

  num. 三十,三十个

this [ðis]

  a. 1. 这,这个

    2. 今,本

  pron. 这,这个

thorough [ˈθʌrə]

  a. 彻底的,完全的

those [ðəuz]

  a. & *pron.* 那些

though [ðəu, ðə]

  conj. 虽然,尽管

  ad. 可是,然而

  as ~ 好像

thought [θɔ:t]

n. 1. 思想

  2. 思维,思维活动

  3. 想法,打算

thoughtful [ˈθɔ:tful]

  a. 1. 认真思考的,沉思的

    2. 体贴的

thousand [ˈθauzənd]

  num. 一千,一千个

  n. 1. 千

    2. [pl.](of)许多,无数

thread [θred]

  n. 1. 线,细丝

    2. 线索,思路

threat [θret]

  n. 1. 恐吓,威胁

    2. 恶兆,坏兆头

threaten [ˈθretn]

  vt. 1. 恐吓,威胁

    2. 预示(危险)

three [θri:]

  num. 三,三个

throat [θrəut]

  n. 咽喉

through [θru:]

  prep. 1. 穿过,通过

    2. 从开始到结束

    3. 经由,以

  ad. 1. 从头到尾,自始至终

    2. 直达地

    3. 彻底,完全

  a. 直达的,直通的

throughout [θru(:)ˈaut]

  prep. 遍及,贯穿

  ad. 到处,始终,全部

throw [θrəu]

  v. 扔,抛

thrust [θrʌst]

  v. 戳,刺,插入

  n. 推力

thumb [θʌm]

  n. 拇指

thunder [ˈθʌndə]

  n. 1. 雷,雷声

    2. 轰隆声

  vi. 打雷,雷鸣

Thursday [ˈθə:zdi]

n. 星期四

thus [ðʌs]

  ad. 1. 因而,从而

    2. 这样,如此

ticket [ˈtikit]

  n. 票,入场券

tide [taid]

  n. 1. 潮,潮汐

    2. 潮流,趋势

tidy [ˈtaidi]

  a. 整洁的,整齐的

  vt. 整理,弄整洁

tie [tai]

  n. 1. 领带,领结

    2. 联系,关系

    3. 束缚,约束

  vt. 扎,束紧

tiger [ˈtaigə]

  n. 虎

tight [tait]

  a. 1. 紧的

    2. 紧身的,装紧的

    3. 密封的,不透……的

till [til]

  prep. & *conj.* 直到……为止

time [taim]

  n. 1. 时候,时刻

    2. 时间,光阴

    3. 次,回

    4. 时机,机会

    5. 倍,乘

    6. [常 pl.]时代

  all the ~ 一直,始终

  at a ~ 每次,一次

  at no ~ 从不,决不

  at one ~ 1. 同时

    2. 曾经,从前

  at the same ~ 同时,然而

  at ~s 有时,不时

  from ~ to 有时,不时

  in no ~ 立即

  in ~ 及时

  on ~ 准时

tin [tin]

  n. 1. 罐头

    2. 锡

tiny [ˈtaini]

  a. 极小的，微小的

tip [tip]

  n. 1. 末端，尖端

    2. 小费

    3. 指点，小窍门

  vt. 轻叩，轻击

tired [ˈtaiəd]

  a. 疲劳的，累的

tissue [ˈtisjuː]

  n. 1. 组织

    2. 薄纱，薄纸，手巾纸

title [ˈtaitl]

  n. 1. 标题，书名

    2. 衔头，称号

to [tuː, tu, tə]

  prep. 1. 向往

    2. 给……，于……

    3. 直到……为止，

      在……之前

    4. 比，对

    5. [表示程度，范围] 到，达

    6. [不定式的符号]

tobacco [təˈbækəu]

  n. 烟草，烟叶

today [təˈdei]

  ad. & n. 1. 今天

        2. 现今

toe [təu]

  n. 脚趾，足尖

together [təˈgeðə]

  ad. 1. 共同，一起

    2. 合起来，集体地

toilet [ˈtɔilit]

  n. 盥洗室

tolerate [ˈtɔləreit]

  vt. 忍受，容忍

tomato [təˈmɑːtəu, təˈmeitəu]

  n. 西红柿

tomorrow [təˈmɔrəu, tuˈmɔrəu]

  ad. 明天

  n. 1. 明天

    2. 未来

ton [tʌn]

  n. 1. 吨

    2. [pl.] 大量，许多

tone [təun]

  n. 1. 音调，音色

    2. 风气，气氛

tongue [tʌŋ]

  n. 1. 舌

    2. 语言

tonight [təˈnait]

  ad. & n. 今晚

too [tuː]

  ad. 1. 也

    2. 太，过分

tool [tuːl]

  n. 工具，用具

tooth [tuːθ]

  n. 牙齿，齿

top [tɔp]

  n. 1. 顶，顶端，顶点

    2. 上边，上面

    3. 首位，最高位

  vt. 1. 高过，超过

    2. 到达……的顶部

topic [ˈtɔpik]

  n. 话题，主题

torch [tɔːtʃ]

  n. 1. 手电筒

    2. 火炬，火把

total [ˈtəutl]

  n. 总数，合计

  a. 总的，全部的

  v. 合计，总数达

touch [tʌtʃ]

  v. 触，碰及

  vt. 1. 触动，感动

    2. 涉及，论及

  n. 1. 触动，碰到

    2. 少许，一点

  in ～ (with) 联系，接触

  ～ on 谈到，论及

tough [tʌf]

  a. 1. 坚韧的

    2. 棘手的，难办的

    3. 强健的，吃苦耐劳的

    4. 粗暴的，凶恶的

tour [tuə]

  n. & v. 旅行，游历

tourist [ˈtuərist]

  n. 旅行者

toward(s) [təˈwɔːd, təˈwɔːdz]

  prep. 1. 向，朝

    2. 对于

    3. 接近，将近

towel [ˈtauəl, taul]

  n. 毛巾

tower [ˈtauə]

  n. 塔

town [taun]

  n. 市镇，城镇

toy [tɔi]

  n. 玩具

trace [treis]

  n. 1. 痕迹，踪迹

    2. 极少量，微量

  vt. 1. 描绘

    2. 跟踪，追踪

track [træk]

  n. 1. 跑道，小路

    2. 轨迹，轮距

  v. 跟踪

tractor [ˈtræktə]

  n. 拖拉机

trade [treid]

  n. 1. 贸易，商业

    2. 职业，行业

  vi. 经商，交易

tradition [trəˈdiʃən]

  n. 传统，惯例

traditional [trəˈdiʃən(ə)l]

  a. 传统的，惯例的

traffic [ˈtræfik]

  n. 交通，车辆行人

trail [treil]

  n. 踪迹，痕迹

  vt. 跟踪，追踪

train [trein]

  n. 1. 列车，火车

    2. 行列，系列

  v. 训练，培养

training [ˈtreiniŋ]

  n. 训练，培养

transfer [trænsˈfəː(r)]

  v. 转移，调动

  vi. 转车，转业，转学

transform [træns'fɔːm]

vt. 1. 改变,变换,转化

2. 改造,改革

transistor [træn'sistə(r)]

n. 晶体管,晶体管收音机

translate [trænz'leit]

v. 翻译

translation [trænz'leiʃ(ə)n]

n. 1. 翻译

2. 译本,译文

transmit [trænz'mit]

vt. 1. 播出,发送

2. 传送,传递,传染

transport

[*v*. træn'spɔːt, *n*.'trænspɔːt]

vt. 运输,运送

n. 1. 运输系统,运输工具

2. 运输,运送

trap [træp]

n. 陷阱,圈套

vt. 诱捕

travel [trævl]

v. 旅行

vi. 行进,传播

tray [trei]

n. 盘,碟

treasure ['treʒə(r)]

n. 1. 财宝,财富

2. 珍品

vt. 珍爱,珍惜

treat [triːt]

vt. 1. 对待

2. 处理,治疗

3. 论述,探讨

treatment ['triːtmənt]

n. 1. 待遇,对待

2. 处理,治疗

tree [triː]

n. 树

tremble ['tremb(ə)l]

vi. 1. 发抖,颤抖

2. 摇动,晃动

tremendous [tri'mendəs]

a. 极大的,巨大的

trend [trend]

n. 倾向,趋势

vi. 伸向,倾向

trial ['traiəl]

n. 1. 试验,考验

2. 审判

triangle ['traiæŋg(ə)l]

n. 三角形

trick [trik]

n. 1. 诡计,骗局

2. 恶作剧

3. 窍门,诀窍

vt. 欺骗,哄骗

trim [trim]

a. 整齐的,整洁的

vt. 整理,修整

trip [trip]

n. 旅行,远足

triumph ['traiəmf]

n. 胜利,成功

troop [truːp]

n. 1. 军队,部队

2. (一)队,(一)群

trouble ['trʌb(ə)l]

n. 1. 烦恼,麻烦

2. 动乱,纠纷

3. 疾病,故障

vt. 使烦恼,麻烦

trousers ['trauzəz]

n. 裤子

truck [trʌk]

n. 卡车,载重汽车

true [truː]

a. 1. 真实的,真正的

2. 忠实的,忠诚的

3. 正确的

trumpet ['trʌmpit]

n. 喇叭

trust [trʌst]

vt. 1. 信任,信赖

2. 盼望,希望

n. (in)信任,信赖

truth [truːθ]

n. 1. 真实,真相

2. 真实性,忠实性

3. 真理

in ~ 实际上,的确

try [trai]

v. 1. 试图,努力

2. 试用,试验

3. 审判

~ on 试穿

~ out 试验

tube [tjuːb, tuːb]

n. 1. 管(子)

2. 地铁

Tuesday ['tjuːzdei]

n. 星期二

tune [tjuːn, tuːn]

n. 1. 曲调,调子

2. 和谐,协调

vt. 调音,调整

tunnel ['tʌn(ə)l]

n. 隧道,地道

turn [təːn]

v. 1. 转动,(使)旋转

2. 翻,翻转

3. (使)变化,(使)变成

n. 1. 转向,转变

2. 转动,旋转

3. 轮到,(顺)次

in ~ 依次,轮流

~ down 拒绝,驳回

~ off 关掉,断开

~ on 接通,打开

~ out 1. 制造,生产

2. 结果是

~ to 1. 变成

2. 求助于,借助于

~ up 1. 开大,调大

2. 出现,来到

twelfth [twelfθ]

num. 第十二

twelve [twelv]

num. 十二,十二个

twentieth ['twentiəθ]

num. 第二十

twenty ['twenti]

num. 二十,二十个

twice [twais]

ad. 两次,两倍

twin [twin]

a. 1. 双的,成对的

2. 孪生的

twist [twist]

　　vt. 1. 捻,搓

　　　　2. 绞,拧

two [tu:]

　　num. 二,两个

　　n. 俩,两个东西

type ['taip]

　　n. 1. 型,类型

　　　　2. 铅字

　　v. 打字

typewriter ['taipraitə(r)]

　　n. 打字机

typical ['tipik(ə)l]

　　a. (of)典型的,有代表性的

tyre ['taiə(r)]

　　n. 轮胎

U

ugly ['ʌgli]

　　a. 丑陋的,难看的

umbrella [ʌm'brelə]

　　n. 伞,雨伞

unable ['ʌn'eibl]

　　a. (+ to V.)不能的,不会的

uncle ['ʌŋkl]

　　n. 伯父,叔父,舅父,姑父,姨父

uncomfortable ['ʌn'kʌmfətəbl]

　　a. 不舒服的,不自在的

under ['ʌndə]

　　prep. 1. 在……下面

　　　　　2. 少于,低于

　　　　　3. 在……情况下,

　　　　　　 在……中

undergo [ʌndə'gəu]

　　vt. 经历,承受

underground ['ʌndəgraund]

　　a. 1. 地下的,地面下的

　　　　2. 秘密的

　　n. 地铁

　　ad. 1. 在地下

　　　　 2. 秘密地

underline [ʌndə'lain]

　　vt. 1. 在……下面划线

　　　　2. 强调

underneath [ʌndə'ni:θ]

　　prep. 在……下面

　　ad. 在下面,在底下

understand [ʌndə'stænd]

　　v. 懂得,理解

　　vt. 获悉,听说

understanding [ʌndə'stændiŋ]

　　a. 了解的,通情达理的

　　n. 1. 理解,领会

　　　　2. 协议,谅解

undertake [ʌndə'teik]

　　vt. 1. 承担,担任

　　　　2. 许诺,保证

uneasy [ʌn'i:zi]

　　a. 心神不安的, 担心的, 忧虑的

unexpected ['ʌniks'pektid]

　　a. 想不到的,意外的

unfair [ʌn'fɛə]

　　a. 不公平的

unhappy [ʌn'hæpi]

　　a. 不幸的,悲惨的

uniform ['ju:nifɔ:m]

　　n. 制服,军服

　　a. 相同的,一律的

union ['ju:njən]

　　n. 1. 协会,同盟

　　　　2. 联合,合并

　　　　3. 一致,融洽

unique [ju:'ni:k]

　　a. 惟一的,独特的

unit ['ju:nit]

　　n. 1. 单位

　　　　2. 机组,装置

unite [ju(:)'nait]

　　v. 联合,团结

unity ['ju:niti]

　　n. 团结,联合

universe ['ju:nivə:s]

　　n. 宇宙,世界

university [ju:ni'və:siti]

　　n. 大学

unknown ['ʌn'nəun]

　　a. 不知道的,未知的

unless [ən'les, ʌn'les]

　　conj. 除非,如果不

unlike [ʌn'laik]

　　a. 不同的,不相似的

　　prep. 不像……,和……不同

unnecessary [ʌn'nesisəri]

　　a. 不必要的,多余的

unpleasant [ʌn'pleznt]

　　a. 使人不愉快的,讨厌的

until [ən'til, ʌn'til]

　　prep. & *conj*. 直到……为此

unusual [ʌn'ju:ʒl]

　　a. 不平常的,与众不同的

up [ʌp]

　　prep. 向……上

　　ad. 1. 向上,在上面

　　　　2. 往上游,往北,往城里

　　　　3 [表示发生,增强,激化等]

　　　　4. ……光,……完

　　~ to 1. 直到

　　　　 2. 适于,胜任

upon [ə'pɒn]

　　prep. = on

upper ['ʌpə]

　　a. 上面的,上部的

upset [ʌp'set]

　　vt. 扰乱,使……心烦意乱

　　v. 打翻,推翻

upstairs [ʌp'stɛəz]

　　ad. 向楼上,在楼上

　　a. 楼上的

up-to-date ['ʌptə'deit]

　　a. 时新的,最新式的

upward ['ʌpwəd]

　　ad. 向上,往上

　　a. 向上的

urban ['ə:bən]

　　a. 城市的

urge [ə:dʒ]

　　vt. 催促,力劝

　　n. 强烈欲望,迫切要求

urgent [ə:dʒənt]

　　a. 急迫的,紧急的

us [ʌs, əs]

　　pron. [we 的宾格]我们

use [ju:s]

　　vt. 1. 使用,应用

　　　　2. 耗费,消费

　　n. 1. 使用,应用

　　　　2. 用途,效用

　　make ~ of 利用

used [ju:st]

  v. (～ to V.)过去常常,过去惯常

  a. 1. 用旧了的,用过的

     2. (to)习惯于

useful [ˈju:sful]

  a. 有用的,有益的

useless [ˈju:slis]

  a. 无用的,无效的

usual [ˈju:ʒuəl]

  a. 通常的,平常的

  as ～ 照常,照例

usually [ˈju:ʒuəli]

  ad. 通常,平常

utmost [ˈʌtməust]

  a. 1. 最远的

     2. 极度的,极端的

V

vacation [vəˈkeiʃ(ə)n]

  n. 假期

vacuum [ˈvækjuəm]

  n. 1. 真空

     2. 真空吸尘器

  v. 用真空吸尘器清扫

vain [vein]

  a. 1. 徒劳的,徒然的

     2. 自负的

  in ～ 徒劳

valley [ˈvæli]

  n. 1. (山)谷

     2. 流域

valuable [ˈvæljuəb(ə)l]

  a. 贵重的,有价值的

value [ˈvælju:]

  n. 1. 价格

     2. 价值

vanish [ˈvæniʃ]

  vi. 消失

vapo(u)r [ˈveipə(r)]

  n. 蒸汽

variety [vəˈraiəti]

  n. 1. 种种,多种多样

     2. 种类,品种

  a ～ of 种种,各种

various [ˈveəriəs]

  a. 各种各样的,不同的

vary [ˈveəri]

  v. 改变,(使)变化

vast [vɑ:st]

  a. 1. 巨大的,辽阔的

     2. 大量的,巨额的

vegetable [ˈvedʒitəb(ə)l]

  n. 蔬菜

  a. 蔬菜的

vehicle [ˈvi:ik(ə)l]

  n. 1. 运载工具,车辆

     2. 媒介,载体

verb [və:b]

  n. 动词

version [ˈvə:ʃ(ə)n]

  n. 1. 版本,译本

     2. 说法

vertical [ˈvə:tik(ə)l]

  a. 垂直的

  n. 垂线

very [ˈveri]

  ad. 非常,很

  a. 真的,恰好的

vessel [ˈves(ə)l]

  n. 1. 容器,器皿

     2. 船,舰

vice [vais]

  n. 1. 邪恶,坏事

     2. 恶习

     3. 台钳,老虎钳

victim [ˈviktim]

  n. 牺牲品,受害者

victory [ˈviktəri]

  n. 胜利

video [ˈvidiəu]

  n. 电视,录像

view [vju:]

  n. 1. 景色,风景

     2. 观点,见解

     3. 观察,观看

  vt. 观察,观看

village [ˈvilidʒ]

  n. 农村,村庄

vinegar [ˈvinigə(r)]

  n. 醋

violence [ˈvaiələns]

  n. 1. 暴力,强暴

     2. 猛烈,剧烈,强烈

violent [ˈvaiələnt]

  a. 1. 暴力引起的,强暴的

     2. 猛烈的,剧烈的,强烈的

violet [ˈvaiələt]

  a. 紫色的

violin [vaiəˈlin]

  n. 小提琴

virtue [ˈvə:tju:]

  n. 1. 美德,德行

     2. 优点,长处

  by ～ of 由于

visible [ˈvizəb(ə)l]

  a. 看得见的,可见的

visit [ˈvizit]

  n. 访问,参观

  v. 1. 访问,参观

     2. 观察,巡视

visitor [ˈvizitə(r)]

  n. 访问者,参观者

vital [ˈvait(ə)l]

  a. 1. 生死攸关的,重大的

     2. 生命的,生机的

vitamin [ˈvaitəmin]

  n. 维生素

voice [vois]

  n. 声音

  vt. 说出,表达

volume [ˈvolju:m]

  n. 1. 容积,体积

     2. 卷,册

     3. 音量,响度

volunteer [volənˈtiə(r)]

  n. 1. 志愿者,志愿兵

  vt. 1. 自愿(做)

     2. 自愿提供

  vi. 自愿,当志愿兵

vote [vəut]

  n. 1. 投票,表决

     2. 选票,选票数

  v. 投票,表决

voyage [ˈvoiidʒ]

  n. & *vi*. 航海,航行,旅行

W

wage [weidʒ]

n.[常 pl.]工资

wag(g)on ['wægən]

　　n.敞篷货运车,大篷车

wait [weit]

　　v.(for)等候,等待

　　n.等待,等待时间

waiter ['weitə]

　　n.侍者,服务员

wake [weik]

　　vi.醒来

　　vt.唤醒

waken ['weik(ə)n]

　　vi.醒来

　　vt.唤醒

walk [wɔ:k]

　　vi.步行,走

　　n.1.步行,散步

　　　　2.步行道

wall [wɔ:l]

　　n.墙,壁

wander ['wɒndə(r)]

　　vi.1.漫步,徘徊

　　　　2.迷路,迷失方向

　　　　3.离题

want [wɒnt]

　　vt.1.想要,希望

　　　　2.需要

　　　　3.短缺,缺少

　　n.需要,短缺

war [wɔ:(r)]

　　n.战争

warm [wɔ:m]

　　a.1.温暖的,暖和的

　　　　2.热心的,热情的

　　v.(使)变暖

warmth [wɔ:mθ]

　　n.1.暖和,温暖

　　　　2.热心,热情

warn [wɔ:n]

　　vt.警告,告诫

wash [wɒʃ]

　　v.&*n*.洗,洗涤

waste [weist]

　　v.浪费

　　a.1.无用的,废弃的

　　　　2.荒芜的

n.1.浪费

　　2.废物

watch [wɒtʃ]

　　n.1.表

　　　　2.看管,监视

　　v.1.看,注视

　　　　2.看守,监视

water ['wɔ:tə(r)]

　　n.水

　　vt.洒水,浇水

waterproof ['wɔ:təpru:f]

　　a.防水的,不透水的

wave [weiv]

　　n.1.波,波浪

　　　　2.(挥手)示意,致意

　　vi.1.(挥手)示意,致意

　　　　2.波动,飘动

wax [wæks]

　　n.蜡

way [wei]

　　n.1.道路,路线

　　　　2.方向,方面

　　　　3.方法,方式

　　　　4.状况,情形

　　by the ~ 顺便说,附带说一下

　　by ~ of 经由,通过

　　give ~ 让路,让步

　　in no ~ 决不

　　in the ~ of 妨碍

we [wi:, wi]

　　pron.我们

weak [wi:k]

　　a.1.虚弱的,弱的

　　　　2.差的,不够标准的

　　　　3.淡薄的,稀的

weakness ['wi:knis]

　　n.1.虚弱,软弱

　　　　2.弱点,缺点

wealth [welθ]

　　n.1.财富,财产

　　　　2.大量

wealthy ['welθi]

　　a.富裕的,丰富的

weapon ['wepən]

　　n.武器

wear [weə(r)]

vt.穿,戴

　　v.(out)磨损,用旧

weather ['weðə(r)]

　　n.天气,气象

weave [wi:v]

　　v.织(布),编织

web [web]

　　n.1.(蜘蛛等的)网

　　　　2.网络

　　　　3.错综复杂的事物

wedding ['wediŋ]

　　n.婚礼

Wednesday ['wenzdei]

　　n.星期三

weed [wi:d]

　　n.野草,杂草

　　v.除草

week [wi:k]

　　n.星期,周

weekday ['wi:kdei]

　　n.工作日

weekend ['wi:kend]

　　n.周末

weekly ['wi:kli]

　　a.每星期的,一周的

　　ad.每周一次

　　n.周刊,周报

weigh [wei]

　　vt.称……重量

　　vi.重(若干)

weight [weit]

　　n.1.重量,重力

　　　　2.负荷,重担

　　　　3.重要性,分量

　　　　4.砝码,秤砣

welcome ['welkəm]

　　n.,*vt*.&*int*.欢迎

　　a.受欢迎的

welfare ['welfeə]

　　n.1.福利

　　　　2.福利救济

well [wel]

　　ad.1.好,好好地

　　　　2.充分地,彻底地

　　a.健康的

　　int.[表示宽慰、惊讶等]好啦,

那么,嗯

n. 井

west [west]

n. 西,西方,西部

a. 西方的,西部的

western ['westən]

a. 西方的,西部的

wet [wet]

a. 1. 湿的,潮湿的

2. 有雨的,多雨的

vt. 弄湿

what [wɔt]

pron. 1. 什么

2. 所……的事物

a. 1. 多么,何等

2. 什么,怎样的

3. 所……的

whatever [wɔt'evə]

pron. 无论什么,不管什么

a. 无论什么样的

wheat [wiːt]

n. 小麦

wheel [wiːl]

n. 轮,车轮

when [wen]

ad. 1. 什么时候,何时

2. 当……的(时候)

conj. 1. 当……时

2. 那时,然后

3. 可是,然而

whenever [wen'evə]

conj. 无论何时,随时

where [weə(r)]

ad. 1. 在哪里,往哪里

2. 在……的(地方)

conj. 在……地方,到……地方

wherever [wɛər'evə]

conj. 无论在哪里,无论到哪里

whether ['weðə]

conj. 是否

which [witʃ]

conj. 1. 哪一个,哪一些

2. 那一个,那一些

a. 哪一个,哪一些

whichever [witʃ'evə]

pron. 无论哪个,无论哪些

a. 无论哪个的,无论哪些的

while(whilst) [wail],[wailst]

conj. 1. 当……时,和……同时

2. 而,然而

3. 尽管,虽然

n. 一段时间,一会儿

for a ~ 暂时,一时

once in a ~ 偶尔

whip [wip]

n. 鞭子

v. 鞭打,抽打

whisper ['wispə(r)]

v. & n. 耳语,轻声说

whistle [wisl]

n. 1. 口哨,汽笛

2. 口哨声,汽笛声

v. 吹口哨,鸣汽笛

white [wait]

a. 白色的,白的

n. 白色

who [huː]

pron. 1. 谁

2. ……的人,该人

whoever [huː(:)'evə]

pron. 不论谁,任何人

whole [həul]

a. 1. 完整的,无缺的

2. 全部的,全体的

on the ~ 总的来说,大体上

wholly ['həulli]

ad. 完全地,全部

whom [hum]

pron. [who 的宾格]谁

whose [huz]

pron. 1. [who 的所有格]谁的

2. 那个人的,那些人的

why [wai]

ad. 1. 为什么

2. ……的理由

wicked ['wikid]

a. 1. 邪恶的,恶劣的

2. 恶意的

wide [waid]

a. 1. 宽阔的

2. 广泛的

widely ['waidli]

ad. 广泛地

widespread ['waidspred]

a. 分布广泛的,普遍的

width [widθ, wiθ, witθ]

n. 1. 宽阔,广阔

2. 宽度

wife [waif]

n. 妻子

wild [waild]

a. 1. 野性的,野生的

2. 野蛮的

3. 狂热的,疯狂的

will [wil]

aux. v. 1. 将,会

2. 要,愿意

3. 总是,经常是

4. 决心要,下决心

n. 1. 意志,决心

2. 遗嘱

willing ['wiliŋ]

a. 情愿的,乐意的

win [win]

v. (获)胜,赢得

n. 赢,胜利

wind [wind]

n. 风

v. 1. 绕,缠

2. 上发条

window ['windəu]

n. 窗户,窗口

wine [wain]

n. 葡萄酒,酒

wing [wiŋ]

n. 翼,翅膀

winter ['wintə]

n. 冬,冬季

wipe [waip]

v. 擦

~ out 1. 擦去,除去

2. 消灭

wire ['waiə]

n. 1. 金属丝,电线

2. 电报

v. 发电报(给)

wisdom ['wizdəm]

n. 智慧,明智

wise [waiz]

　a. 有智慧的,聪明的

wish [wiʃ]

　vt. 1. 但愿

　　　2. 祝愿,祝贺

　　　3. 希望,愿望

　n. 愿望,希望

wit [wit]

　n. 智力,才智

with [wið]

　prep. 1. 带有,具有

　　　　2. 用,以

　　　　3. 和……一起,同

　　　　4. 对……,关于

　　　　5. 虽然,尽管

withdraw [wið'drɔː]

　vt. 收回,撤销

　vi. 缩回,退回

within [wið'in]

　prep. 在……里面,在……内

without [wið'aut]

　prep. 无,没有

witness ['witnis]

　n. 1. 目击者,证人

　　　2. 证据,证明

　vt. 1. 目击,目睹

　　　2. 作证

wolf [wulf]

　n. 狼

woman ['wumən]

　n. 女人,妇女

wonder ['wʌndə]

　vt. (at)(对……)感到惊奇,惊叹

　vt. 想知道

　n. 1. 惊异,惊奇

　　　2. 奇迹,奇事

wonderful ['wʌndəful]

　a. 1. 惊人的,奇妙的

　　　2. 极好的

wood [wud]

　n. 1. 木头,木材

　　　2. [常 pl.]林地,树林

wooden ['wudn]

　a. 木(制)的

wool [wul]

　n. 羊毛

word [wəːd]

　n. 1. 词,单词

　　　2. [常 pl.]话

　　　3. 消息,传说

　　　4. 诺言

　in a ～ 简言之,一句话,总之

　in other ～s 换句话说

　～ for ～ 逐字地

work [wəːk]

　n. 1. 工作,劳动

　　　2. 职业

　　　3. 产品,工艺品

　　　4. [常 pl.]著作,作品

　　　5. [pl.]工厂

　　　6. 功

　v. 1. (使)工作

　　　2. (使)运转

　～ at 1. 从事于

　　　　2. 学习研究

　～ out 1. 算出

　　　　2. 制定,拟定

worker ['wəːkə]

　n. 工人

workman ['wəːkmən]

　n. 工人,工作者

workshop ['wəːkʃɔp]

　n. 车间,工场

world [wəːld]

　n. 1. 世界,地球

　　　2. 世间,人间

　　　3. ……界,领域

worm [wəːm]

　n. 虫,蠕虫

worry ['wʌri]

　vt. 使烦恼,使发愁

　vi. (about)对……感到烦恼,

　　　对……发愁

　n. 烦恼,焦虑

worse [wəːs]

　a. 更坏的,较差的

　ad. 较坏,较差

worship ['wəːʃip]

　n. & *vt*. 崇拜,敬仰

worst [wəːst]

　a. 最坏的,最差的

　ad. 最坏,最差

worth [wəːθ]

　a. 1. 值……的,价值……的

　　　2. 值得……的

　n. 价值

worthwhile ['wəːθ'(h)wail]

　a. 值得做的

worthy ['wəːði]

　a. 1. (of)值得……的,

　　　　配得上……的

　　　2. 可尊敬的,有价值的

would [wud, wəd]

　aux. v. 1. will 的过去时

　　　　　2. [表示语气婉转的请

　　　　　　求]愿

　　　　　3. [表示过去的习惯]

　　　　　　常常

　　　　　4. 大概

wound [wuːnd]

　n. 创伤,伤口

　vt. 伤,伤害

wrap [ræp]

　vt. 裹,缠,包装

wrist [rist]

　n. 腕

write [rait]

　v. 1. 写字,书写

　　　2. 写信(给),函告

　　　3. 写(文章)等

writer ['raitə]

　n. 作者,作家

wrong [rɔŋ]

　a. 1. 错误的,不正确的

　　　2. 不道德的,不正当的

　go ～ 发生故障,出毛病

X

X-ray ['eksrei]

　n. X 射线,X 光

Y

yard [jɑːd]

　n. 1. 院子

　　　2. 码

year [jəː, jiə]

　n. 年

yearly ['jəːli]

a . 每年的,一年一次的

ad . 每年,年年

yellow [ˈjeləu]

a . 黄的

n . 黄色

yes [jes]

ad . 是的

yesterday [ˈjestədi]

ad . & *n* . 昨天

yet [jet]

ad . 1. 尚,仍然,还

　　2. 已经

conj . 然而,但是

and ~ 可是,然而

as ~ 到目前为止,到那时为止

yield [jiːld]

v . 出产,生长

vi . (to)屈服,屈从

n . 产量,收益

you [juː, ju]

pron . 你(们)

young [jʌŋ]

a . 年轻的,青年的

n . 青年人

your [jɔː, juə]

pron . [you 的所有格]你(们)的

yours [jɔːz, juəz]

pron . [you 的物主代词]你(们)的

yourself [jɔːˈself]

pron . 1. 你(们)自己

　　2. 你(们)亲自

youth [juːθ]

n . 1. 青春,少年时代

　　2. 小伙子,年轻人

　　3. 青年(男女)

Z

zero [ˈziərəu]

n . 零点,零度

num . 零

zone [zəun]

n . 地区,区域

zoo [zuː]

n . 动物园

词 组 表

a **few**	all **right**	as **though**
a good **deal**	all the **time**	**as** to
a good **deal** of	**along** with	as **usual**
a good **many**	and **so** forth	as **well**
a great **deal**	and **so** on	**as** well as
a great **deal** of	and **then**	as **yet**
a great **many**	and **yet**	**aside** from
a **little**	**anything** but	at a **loss**
a **lot**	**arrive** at	at a **time**
a **lot** of	**as...as**	at all **costs**
a **matter** of	as a **matter** of fact	at all **events**
a **number** of	as a **result**	at any **rate**
a **series** of	as a **result** of	at **best**
a **variety** of	as a **rule**	at **first**
above all	as **far** as	at first **sight**
according to	as far as...be **concerned**	at **hand**
account for	as **follows**	at **intervals**
add up to	**as** for	at **large**
after **all**	as **good** as	at **last**
ahead of	as **if**	at **least**
all at **once**	as **long** as	at **length**
all but	as **regards**	at **most**
all over	as **soon** as	at no **time**

at once
at one time
at present
at the cost of
at the mercy of
at the moment
at the same time
at times
back and forth
be able + to V.
be about + to V.
be absorbed in
be attached to
be concerned with
be known as
be made up of
bear in mind
because of
before long
both...and
break down
break off
break out
break up
bring about
bring down
bring forth
bring forward
bring into effect
bring into operation
bring into practice
bring up
build up
burn up
but for
by accident
by all means
by comparison
by far
by itself
by means of
by mistake
by on means
by oneself

by reason of
by the way
by virtue of
by way of
call for
call forth
call off
can't/couldn't help
carry into effect
carry into practice
carry off
carry on
carry out
cast light on
catch up with
check in
check out
clear away
clear up
come into effect
come into force
come into operation
come off
come on
come out
come to
come up
come up to
come up with
consist in
consist of
count on
cut down
cut off
cut out
cut short
deal with
depend on
do away with
do one's best (+ to V.)
do without
drop in
drop off
drop out

due to
each other
either...or...
even if
even then
even though
ever since
ever so
every other
except for
fall in with
far from
feel like
figure out
fill in
fill out
find out
first of all
for a moment
for a while
for ever
for example
for good
for instance
for long
for purpose of
for the better
for the moment
for the present
for (the) purpose of
for the sake of
from time to time
gain access to
gain an advantage over
get along
get along with
get at
get by
get by heart
get down
get in
get into
get off
get on

get on with	hardly any	in itself
get over	have access to	in line with
get rid of	have an advantage over	in nature
get the best of	have got	in no case
get the better of	have got + to V.	in no time
get through	have in mind	in no way
get up	have nothing to do with	in order
give away	have something to do with	in order + to V.
give in	head for	in order that
give off	hold back	in other words
give out	hold on	in particular
give rise to	hold on to	in place of
give up	hold out	in practice
give way	hold up	in proportion (to)
go after	if only	in public
go back on	improve on	in question
go by	in a hurry	in regard to
go down	in a moment	in relation to
go in for	in a word	in short
go into	in addition	in spite of
go into effect	in addition to	in sum
go into force	in all	in terms of
go into operation	in any case	in the course of
go off	in any event	in the distance
go in	in brief	in the event of
go out	in case	in the face of
go over	in case of	in the first place
go through	in charge of	in (the) future
go up	in common	in the light of
go with	in conclusion	in the past
go without	in consequence	in the way of
go wrong	in consequence of	in time
had better	in contrast to	in touch with
had rather	in contrast with	in turn
had rather...than	in detail	in vain
hand down	in effect	instead of
hand in	in fact	keep from
hand in hand	in favour of	keep in mind
hand on	in force	keep one's head
hand out	in front of	keep pace with
hand over	in future	keep on
hang on	in general	keep to
hardly...before	in hand	keep up
hardly...when	in honour of	keep up with

lay aside
lay down
lay out
lead to
learn by **heart**
leave behind
leave out
lend itself to
let alone
let out
lie in
little by **little**
live through
live up to
look after
look back
look down on
look for
look forward to
look in
look into
look out
look over
look through
look up
lose one's **head**
lots of
major in
make for
make out
make **propress**
make **sense**
make **sure** of
make **sure** that
make the **best** of
make up
make up for
make up one's **mind**(+ to V.)
make **use** of
many a
more and **more**
more or less
neither... nor
no **doubt**

no **less** than
no **longer**
no **matter** + wh-word
no **more**
mo **more** than
no **sooner**... than
not at **all**
not only... but
not only... but also
nothing but
now and then
now that
occur to
of **course**
off **duty**
on a large **scale**
on **account** of
on an **average**
on **board**
on **business**
on **condition** that
on **duty**
on **hand**
on **occasion**
on one's **own**
on **purpose**
on **sale**
on the **average**
on the **basis** of
on the **contrary**
on the **ground(s)** of
on (the) one **hand**, on the
    other **hand**
on the **point** of
on the **whole**
on **time**
once (and) for all
once in a **while**
one another
or **else**
or **so**
other than
out of
out of **date**

out of **order**
out of **question**
out of the **question**
over and **over**
over and **over** again
per **cent**
pick out
pick up
play a **part** (in)
previous to
prior to
pull down
pull in
pull off
pull on
pull up
put away
put down
put forward
put in
put in for
put in **order**
put into **operation**
put off
put on
put out
put up
put up with
rather than
refer to
refer to... as
regardless of
rely on
right **away**
run down
run into
run out of
run over
see off
see to
send for
serve as
set aside
set down

set forth	take. . . for	touch on
set off	take advantage of	try on
set out	take away	try one's best(+ to V.)
set out + to V.	take care	try out
set up	take care of	turn down
side by side	take charge of	turn off
so as + to V.	take down	turn on
so far	take effect	turn out
so far as. . . be concerned	take for granted	turn to
so long as	take in	turn up
so that	take into account	up to
sooner or later	take off	up to date
stand by	take on	wipe out
stand for	take over	with regard to
stand out	take part in	with relation to
stand up	take place	with respect to
stand up to	take up	with the exception of
step by step	the moment (that)	with the purpose of
such. . . as	the same as	word for word
such as	thanks to	work at
sum up	think of	work out
switch off	think of. . . as	would rather
switch on	throw light on	would rather. . . than
take. . . as	to the point	

2002 年 1 月浙江省大学英语三级考试试卷

Part Ⅰ Listening Comprehension

Section A

Directions: *In this section, you will hear 10 short conversations. At the end of each conversation, a question will be asked about what was said. You will hear the conversation and the question only once. After each question there will be a pause. During the pause, you must read the four choices marked A), B), C) and D), and decide which is the best answer. Then mark the corresponding letter on the Answer Sheet with a single line through the center.*

1. A) By bus.
   C) On foot.
   B) By taxi.
   D) By train.

2. A) To the drugstore.
   C) To her office.
   B) To the lab.
   D) To her mother's.

3. A) 3 pence.
   C) 4 pence.
   B) 7 pence.
   D) 10 pence.

4. A) She will join the man for dinner.
   C) She's going to have a walk.
   B) She will have to study.
   D) She will go to the concert.

5. A) Milk.
   C) Bread.
   B) Eggs.
   D) Fruit.

6. A) Jack.
   C) Alice.
   B) Tom.
   D) Jane.

7. A) Inside the Central Building.
   B) Opposite the Central Building.
   C) Close to the Central Building.
   D) Two blocks away from the Central Building.

8. A) Light.
   C) Interesting.
   B) Well-paid.
   D) Boring.

9. A) A secretary.
   C) A customer.
   B) A waitress.
   D) A housewife.

10. A) It is more thoughtful.
    B) It is less popular.
    C) It is the same as the popular music.
    D) She has no idea.

Section B

Directions: *In this section, you will hear 3 short passages. The passages will be read twice. At the end of each passage, you will hear some questions, which will be read only once. After you hear a question, you must choose the best answer from the four choices marked A), B), C) and D). Then mark the corresponding letter on the Answer Sheet with a single line through the center.*

Passage One

Questions 11 to 13 are based on the passage you have just heard.

11. A) Sleeping.   B) Dreams.
    C) Interests.   D) Experiences.

12. A) Dreams reflect one's future life.
    B) Your dreams may come from your past experiences.
    C) Prisoners never dare to dream of freedom.
    D) We always dream about what we wish for.

13. A) Families.   B) Food.
    C) Exams.   D) Freedom.

Passage Two

Questions 14 to 16 are based on the passage you have just heard.

14. A) 1 kilogram.   B) 5 kilograms.
    C) 15 kilograms.   D) 50 kilograms.

15. A) Wood of trees.   B) Hair-like parts of certain plants.
    C) Roots of trees.   D) Hair of certain animals.

16. A) Because they are forest countries.
    B) Because there are many people in those countries.
    C) Because most people in those countries are well-educated.
    D) Because they are short of paper.

Passage Three

Questions 17 to 20 are based on the passage you have just heard.

17. A) The relationship between the speaker and Susan.
    B) The arrangement of the speaker's wedding.
    C) The speaker's parents' opinion of Susan.
    D) The speaker's plan for the future.

18. A) At Susan's home.   B) In a swimming pool.
    C) On a tennis court.   D) At a dance.

19. A) Her boyfriend talks about marriage.
    B) Her boyfriend's parents don't like her.

C) Her boyfriend is not very smart.

D) Her boyfriend works as a salesman.

20. A) The speaker wants to forget Susan.

B) Susan may lose her job.

C) The speaker and Susan are of the same age.

D) Susan has saved enough money for her future.

Part II Vocabulary

Directions: *There are 20 incomplete sentences in this part. For each sentence there are four choices marked A), B), C) and D). Choose the ONE answer that best completes the sentence. Then mark the corresponding letter on the Answer Sheet with a single line through the center.*

21. After a successful career in business, he was _____ the chairman of the committee.

A) appointed   B) adopted

C) adjusted   D) achieved

22. These programs are designed for those young people who want to _____ higher education but do not have enough time to go to university.

A) insure   B) persist

C) inquire   D) pursue

23. The workers are _____ young people between the ages of sixteen and twenty.

A) most   B) much

C) mostly   D) more

24. It was difficult to guess what her _____ to the news would be.

A) impression   B) reaction

C) comment   D) opinion

25. We are interested in the weather because it _____ us so directly—what we wear, what we do, and even how we feel.

A) benefits   B) affects

C) guides   D) effects

26. There was no news from her son for quite a few years; _____, Susan went on hoping.

A) nevertheless   B) furthermore

C) consequently   D) therefore

27. He was _____ of robbery and was sentenced to ten year's imprisonment.

A) assured   B) charged

C) confirmed   D) accused

28. Thoughts are expressed _____ means of words.

A) by   B) with

C) in   D) on

29. There is no _____ in going to the cinema now as the film has already started.

A) reason   B) cause

C) motive   D) point

30. American students seldom live on campus. _____, they live at home and travel to classes.

A) Instead   B) For example

C) What's more   B) However

31. Will you please _____ my paper to find out whether I've made any mistakes?

A) look out   B) look into

C) look through   D) look up at

32. We must _____ what's the matter with the computer.

A) give out   B) figure out

C) run out   D) fill out

33. He couldn't _____ his failure in the English test.

A) account for   B) account to

C) aware of   D) according to

34. The nurses should _____ it that the children are fed and dressed properly.

A) see in   B) see to

C) see out   D) see off

35. I _____ an old friend when I was visiting London last week.

A) ran into   B) ran over

C) ran through   D) ran along

36. Many people complain of the rapid _____ of modern life.

A) rate   B) speed

C) pace   D) growth

37. I like this house better because it has a fine _____ of the green hills.

A) look   B) view

C) sight   D) point

38. She entered a poetry competition and won the first _____.

A) name   B) price

C) order   D) prize

39. If we _____ to deal with these problems now, things will get out of control.

A) fail   B) miss

C) delay   D) deny

40. If you _____ to see Jane, please ask her to give me a call this evening.

A) happen   B) mind

C) occur   D) appear

Part Ⅲ Structure

Directions: *There are 20 incomplete sentences in this part. For each sentence there are four choices marked A), B), C) and D). Choose the ONE answer that best completes the sentence. Then mark the corresponding letter on the Answer Sheet with a single line through the center.*

41. Never before that night _____ the extent of my own power.
    A) I had felt   B) I felt
    C) did I feel   D) had I felt

42. She spent a lot of time in that small town _____ she was born.
    A) which   B) when
    C) where   D) that

43. It was because she was ill _____ she didn't attend the conference yesterday.
    A) that   B) so
    C) then   D) when

44. I have learned that he is going to the United States, but _____ is his own decision.
    A) when leaving   B) when does he leave
    C) when he leaves   D) when he leaving

45. They didn't pass the exam last time; I regretted _____ them.
    A) to be not able to help   B) being unable to help
    C) being not able to helping   D) not to be able to help

46. Your hair needs _____. You'd better have it _____ tomorrow.
    A) cutting; do   B) cutting; done
    C) being cut; done   D) to be cut; to be done

47. Not only the sailors but also the captain of the ship _____ frightened during that voyage.
    A) has   B) have
    C) was   D) were

48. I'd rather you _____ by train, because I can't bear the idea of your flying in an airplane in such bad weather.
    A) would go   B) will go
    C) went   D) go

49. Be sure to come to see us this Sunday, _____?
    A) will you   B) aren't you
    C) are you   D) don't you

50. The flowers _____ because no one watered them.
    A) may die   B) must have died
    C) must die   D) can have died

51. Rose told the teacher all _____ to Oliver.
    A) which happened   B) that had happened
    C) which had happened   D) what had happened

52. Millions of $ dollars in the bank is said _____ yesterday.
    A) having stolen   B) stolen
    C) to have been stolen   D) to be stolen

53. London is the city _____ she is longing to visit.
    A) where   B) in which
    C) what   D) that

54. I appreciate _____ to your school to give a lecture.
    A) to be invited   B) to have invited
    C) having invited   D) being invited

55. Not until 1868 _____ made the capital of the state of Georgia.
    A) was Atlanta   B) when Atlanta was
    C) Atlanta was   D) was when Atlanta

56. The government didn't expect that the fall in the price of oil _____ such serious conse-
    quences for the economy.
    A) will cause   B) would cause
    C) causes   D) has caused

57. People don't want there _____ another war in their country.
    A) being   B) is
    C) to be   D) will be

58. Because he did not like the first kind of flower, he asked the salesgirl to show him _____.
    A) another kinds   B) the others ones
    C) other kind   D) another kind

59. A good dictionary can be _____ great help to learners of language.
    A) with   B) about
    C) on   D) of

60. "You know, I have our tickets."
    "That's good. I was afraid that you _____ them."
    A) had forgotten   B) forgot
    C) have forgotten   D) would have forgotten

Part Ⅳ   Reading Comprehension

Directions: *There are 3 passages in this part. Each passage is followed by some questions or*
unfinished statements. For each of them there are four choices marked A), B), C)
and D). You should decide on the best choice and mark the corresponding letter on
the Answer Sheet with a single line through the center.

Passage One
Questions 61 to 65 are based on the following passage:

Industrial pollution is not only a problem for the countries of Europe and North America. It
is also an extremely serious problem in some developing countries. For these countries, economic

growth is a very important goal. They want to attract new industries, and so they put few controls on industries which cause pollution.

Cubatao, an industrial town of 85,000 people in Brazil, is an example of the connection between industrial development and pollution. In 1954, Cubatao had no industry. Today it has more than twenty large factories, which produce many pollutants (污染物质). The people of the town are exposed to a large number of poisonous substances in their environment and the consequences of this exposure can be clearly seen. Birth defects are extremely common. Among children and adults, lung problems are sometimes twelve times more common in Cubatao than in other places.

It is true that Brazil, like many other countries, has laws against pollution, but these laws are not *enforced* strictly enough. It is cheaper for companies to ignore the laws and pay the fines than to buy the expensive equipment that will reduce the pollution. It is clear, therefore, that economic growth is more important to the government than the health of the workers. However, the responsibility does not completely lie with the Brazilian government. The example of Cubatao shows that international companies are not acting in a responsible way, either. A number of the factories in the town are owned by large companies from France, Italy, and the U.S. They are doing things in Brazil that they would not be able to do at home. If they caused the same amount of pollution at home, they would be severely punished or even put out of business.

61. Why don't developing countries have strict pollution controls?
   A) Because the new industries they want to attract do not cause much pollution.
   B) Because pollution is not a serious problem for developing countries.
   C) Because they fail to realize that the balance of nature will be disturbed by some pollutants.
   D) Because if developing countries put stricter controls on industry, fewer companies would build new plants there.

62. What is the author's purpose in mentioning Cubatao?
   A) To show that industrial development can progress very quickly in developing countries.
   B) To show that the pollution problem in Brazil is extremely serious.
   C) To show that industrial growth causes pollution problems for developing countries.
   D) To show that pollution is threatening the lives of many people and the whole economy of Brazil.

63. Why do some foreign companies like to set up their plants in Brazil?
   A) Because the investment environment in Brazil is suitable for them.
   B) Because they will not be severely punished if they cause pollution in Brazil.
   C) Because they can make a big profit as the labour cost in Brazil is relatively low.
   D) Because they can act in an irresponsible way in Brazil because there are no pollution laws there.

64. The word *"enforced"* (L.2, Para.3) could best be replaced by which of the following?
   A) carried out   B) drawn up
   C) looked over   D) put out

65. What can we conclude from the passage?

   A) In Brazil, companies which ignore pollution laws have to pay fines.

   B) The Brazilian government pays great attention to the health of workers.

   C) Many foreign companies are out of business in Brazil for their pollution.

   D) Most international companies act responsibly in Brazil.

Passage Two

Questions 66 to 70 are based on the following passage:

In 1947 Angela Mortimer was captain of the team which won the Plymouth Interschools' Championship. From the moment she stepped forward to receive the silver cup, she was determined to become a Wimbledon Champion.

Encouraged by her school championship success, Angela decided that she should have proper coaching. She heard that there was a good tennis coach at Torquay, a Mr. Roberts, who was prepared to give free tennis lessons to promising youngsters under twelve years of age and living in the Torquay area. The fact that Angela was over fifteen did not stop her. One Saturday, she made the forty-mile journey from Plymouth to Torquay and introduced herself to Mr. Roberts. Arthur Roberts was not impressed. He played a few shots to Angela and then told her directly that she knew nothing about the game and was too old to learn. He also reminded her that she lived in Plymouth, which could hardly be considered in the Torquay area.

If Arthur Roberts thought he had got rid of Angela, he was very much mistaken. For her part Angela had been greatly impressed by Mr. Roberts. She made up her mind that she was not too old to learn tennis and that Arthur Roberts was the man to teach her. However, her school certificate examination was appearing ahead and she was determined to work hard. Although the headmaster wanted her to stay on at school for another year before taking her examination, Angela begged to be allowed to sit. She surprised everyone by passing with credit in five subjects.

Angela then had a stroke of luck. She managed to persuade her family to move nearer to Torquay. Despite what had taken place at their last meeting, Angela properly presented herself to Arthur Roberts and asked him for free coaching. Arthur's welcome was not a warm one. His time was fully occupied in coaching some promising young players. However, he had to admire Angela. Whatever else she lacked, she was obviously a girl of courage and determination. Arthur liked these qualities in a pupil. "You can play against the wall," he said, "and if you improve I might help you."

Angela's heart leapt with joy. "I'll show him," she said to herself. "I will certainly show him."

66. According to the passage, Arthur Roberts _____.

   A) was a good tennis coach from Plymouth

   B) taught tennis to anybody who could pay

   C) promised to give free tennis lessons to all school children in Torquay

   D) gave free lessons to young children who he thought would one day be good players

67. What is TRUE about Angela's first meeting with Mr. Roberts?

A) Roberts told Angela that he couldn't help her unless she moved to Torquay.

B) Mr. Roberts refused to coach Angela for three reasons.

C) Angela was told to come and see Mr. Roberts when she graduated from school.

D) Angela was unimpressed by Mr. Roberts when she first met him.

68. According to the passage, Angela's headmaster _____.

A) wanted Angela to take her examination early

B) allowed Angela to take her examination a year earlier

C) forced Angela to take her examination a year later

D) wanted Angela to stay on at school after her examination

69. Why did Angela's parents move away from Plymouth?

A) Because Plymouth was too far from Wimbledon.

B) Because Angela wanted to move closer to Mr. Roberts.

C) Because Angela was asked by Mr. Roberts to do so.

D) Because they would send Angela to a better school there.

70. What can we infer from this passage about Mr. Roberts?

A) He believed Angela could improve by playing against the wall.

B) He thought Angela lacked courage and determination.

C) He would possibly help Angela later.

D) He was too busy to coach Angela.

Passage Three

Questions 71 to 75 are based on the following passage:

All over the world, telecommunications companies are thinking wireless. They are spending billions of dollars building transmission towers (发射塔), launching satellites and developing low-cost hand-held phones, all with the goal of ending the century and a half old dominance (主宰) of the wire.

Since telegraph service began in 1844, most two-way communications have been not person-to-person but place-to-place. If two people aren't in the *spots* that the wire links, they don't connect.

Now, with advances in microelectronics and satellite technology, companies are producing systems that seek out people wherever they are, keeping them in touch. The services are coming into use rapidly in the United States, Europe and the growing economies of East Asia.

Mobile phones are the most dramatic example to date. The number in use in the United States passed the 25 million mark last month, with no end to the growth in sight. In little more than a decade, the mobile phone has developed from expensive business tool and status symbol to something used by roughly one in 10 Americans.

Not everyone welcomes the change. Wireless phones are showing up in churches, courtrooms and airplanes, places where the noise of the outside world was once shut out. Nevertheless, there is no stopping the technology's advance.

"It's coming down to the lower-income levels," said Tom Ross of MTA-EMCI, a Washington-based telecommunications company. "It's slowly becoming a necessity of life."

Now authorities in many countries are clearing up new space on the radio spectrum (无线电频谱) for a new collection of wireless services. *They* are known as personal communications services, or PCS. In its simplest form, PCS is just another name for pocket phones. But companies are preparing a wide variety of "smart networks" and data services that will do things that ordinary mobile phones can't.

71. The word "*spots*" (L.2, Para.2) is closest in meaning to _____.

    A) stations   B) grounds

    C) locations   D) lines

72. Mobile phones are mentioned as an example of _____.

    A) something that not everyone likes

    B) something that not everyone can afford

    C) the use of the fast-developing wireless systems

    D) the rise in people's living standards in America and Europe

73. Which of the following is true according to Tom Ross?

    A) Mobile phones should not be used in churches.

    B) Ordinary American consumers can afford mobiles phones.

    C) The mobile phone is regarded as a symbol of wealth.

    D) Few Americans find it necessary to have a mobile phone.

74. The word "*They*" (L.2, Para.7) refers to _____.

    A) authorities   B) pocket phones

    C) companies   D) wireless services

75. The main point discussed in the passage is _____.

    A) the fast development of wireless communications

    B) new developments in the world's smart networks

    C) disagreements over the development of the telecommunications industry

    D) new advances in American microelectronics

Part Ⅴ Translation from English into Chinese

Directions: *In this part there is a passage with 5 underlined sections, numbered 76 to 80. After reading the passage carefully, translate the underlined sections into Chinese. Remember to write your translation on the Translation Sheet.*

Many changes are taking place in "food styles" in the United States. The United States is traditionally famous for its unchanging diet of meat and potatoes, but now we have a great variety of food to choose from: various ethnic (民族的) food, health food, and fast food, in addition to the traditional home-cooked meal. Ethnic restaurants and supermarkets are commonplace in the United States. (76) Because the United States is a country of immigrants(移民), there is an immense variety of food styles and any large American city is filled with restaurants serving international cooking. Many cities even have ethnic sections: Chinatown, Little Italy, or Germantown. With this vast ethnic choice, we can enjoy food from all over the world. (77) This is a pleasant thought for those who come here to travel or to work; they can usually find their native specialties. Besides sections of the cities, there are regions, which are well known for certain food because of the people who settled there. For example, southern California has many Mexican restaurants.

(78) Health food gained popularity when people began to think more seriously about the possible effect of food on their health. The very term "health food" is ironic because it implies that there is also "unhealthy" food. (79) Health food includes natural food with little processing, that is, there are no chemicals to help it last longer or to make it taste or look better. Most health food enthusiasts are vegetarians: they eat no meat; they prefer to get their proteins from other sources, such as beans, cheese and eggs.

(80) Fast-food restaurants are now expanding rapidly all over the United States, where speed is a very important factor. People usually have a short lunch break or they just do not want to waste their time eating. Fast-food restaurants are places which take care of hundreds of people in a short time. There is usually very little waiting, and the food is always cheap. Some examples are burger and pizza places.

Part VI Translation from Chinese into English

Directions: *In this part there are 5 sentences, numbered 81 to 85, in Chinese. Translate these sentences into English on the Translation Sheet.*

81. 如果你在阅读中碰到生词,有时候你可以不查词典。
82. 她正在找工作,我想她可能已从大学毕业了。
83. 学习英语需要耐心和努力;若想在几个月内掌握一门外语是不可能的。
84. 我昨晚兴奋得睡不着觉,因为我的设计被采纳了。
85. ——你们什么时候熄灯就寝?
    ——10点半,但周末例外。

【听力录音文稿】

Section A

1. M: Do you still go to work on foot?
   W: I used to. But now I usually go by bus, and sometimes by taxi.
   Q: How does the woman usually go to work?
2. M: Can't you stay a bit longer?
   W: No, I have to go to the chemist's to get some medicine for my mother.

Q: Where does the woman have to go?

3. M: Why are you angry, Mary?

   W: Bus tickets cost 3 pence last week, but now they cost 7 pence.

   Q: By how much does the cost of bus tickets rise?

4. M: I wonder if you'd like to come around for dinner tonight?

   W: I'd love to. But I'm sorry I have to go to class tonight.

   Q: What will the woman most probably do tonight?

5. M: Do you have much shopping to do?

   W: Yes. Quite a lot today. I need some oranges, milk, and a dozen eggs.

   Q: Which of the following is the woman NOT going to buy?

6. M: Jack does better at Chinese than Tom and Jane.

   W: Yes. But he is not as good as Alice.

   Q: Who does the best at Chinese?

7. W: Can you tell me where the nearest TV repair shop is?

   M: Yes. Take the second turning on the right, and you'll find it next to the Central Build-
      ing.

   Q: Where is the TV repair shop?

8. M: How do you like your new job?

   W: My pay is pretty good, though I have to work long hours.

   Q: How does the woman think of her job?

9. M: What kind of soup would you recommend?

   W: We have very nice tomato soup and clear soup, sir.

   Q: Who is the woman?

10. M: Classical music is more thoughtful than popular music.

    W: I can't help thinking the same.

    Q: How does the woman think about classical music?

Section B

Passage One

All our dreams have something to do with our emotions, fears, longings, wishes, needs and memories. But something on the outside may influence what we dream. If a person is hungry, or tired, or cold, his dreams may include this feeling. If the covers have slipped off your bed, you may dream you are on ice. The material from the dream you have tonight is likely to come form the experiences you'll have today. So your dreams come from something that affects you while you are sleeping and it may also use your past experiences and interests you now have. This is why very young children are likely to dream of sweets, other children of school exams, hungry people of food, homesick soldiers of their families, and prisoners of freedom.

During sleep, we can express or feel what we really want to.

Questions 11 to 13 are based on the passage you have just heard.

11. What is the passage mainly about?

12. Which of the following is true?

13. What are soldiers likely to dream of?

Passage Two

How much paper do you use every year? In 1900, the world's use of paper was about one kilogram for each person in a year. Now some countries use as much as fifty kilograms of paper for each person in a year. The amount of paper a country uses shows how advanced the country is. It is difficult to say whether this is true. Different people mean different things by the word "advanced", but countries like the United States, England and Sweden use more paper than other countries.

Paper, like many other things that we use today, was first made in China. In Egypt and the West, paper was not very commonly used before the year 1400. The Chinese still have pieces of paper which were made as long ago as that. But Chinese paper was not made from the wood of trees. It was made from the hair—like parts of certain plants. It was a German who found out that one could make the best paper from trees. After that the forest countries like Canada, Sweden, Norway, Finland and the United States became the most important in paper making.

Questions 14 to 16 are based on the passage you have just heard.

14. How much paper does a person use every year in some countries according to the passage?

15. What was paper made from in ancient China?

16. Why are countries like Canada, Sweden and the United States the most important in making paper?

Passage Three

I met Susan at a dance about six months ago. We get along well together since we like music, dancing, swimming, and tennis. But whenever I start to get serious about our relationship and try to discuss with her how she feels about me, and whether we might consider marriage, she gets angry and refuses to talk about it. Usually she says something like: "I'm not the marrying kind," or "we're having too much fun to be serious." Besides all this, I don't think that my parents like her very much. They think that she is not very smart. Do you think that I should continue to keep the relationship or should I forget her? We are both 22, but I'm ready to settle down and establish a home. I have a good job as a salesman, and by the time I'm 24, I hope to have saved enough money to start my own business.

Questions 17 to 20 are based on the passage you have just heard.

17. What is the main topic of the letter?

18. Where did the speaker meet Susan?

19. Why does Susan get angry sometimes?

20. Which of the following is true according to the talk?

【试题解析】

第一部分　听力理解

1. 正确答案:C。男士说:"你现在仍然走路上班吗?"女士说:"我以前是。"

2. 正确答案:A。chemist's 是"药店"的意思。

3. 正确答案:C。女士说:"上周公共汽车票还是 3 便士,现在 7 便士了。"可知上涨了 4 便士。

4. 正确答案:B。女士说:"今晚要去上课。"

5. 正确答案:C。女士说:"我要买很多东西。有橘子、牛奶、鸡蛋。"她没有提到面包。

6. 正确答案:C。男士说:"在中国,Jack 比 Tom 和 Jane 的情况都好"女士说:"他没 Alice 好。"

7. 正确答案:C。next to the Central Building 是"中央大厦隔壁"的意思。

8. 正确答案:B。她认为"薪水很高,但工作时间长"。

9. 正确答案:B。男士说:"有什么可推荐的?"女士说:"有马铃薯汤和清汤。"

10. 正确答案:A。I cannot help thinking the same 意思是"我也不禁这样认为"。

11. 正确答案:B。整段都在谈论"梦境"。

12. 正确答案:B。录音中谈到:"外界的东西也会影响我们梦的内容。"

13. 正确答案:A。录音中谈到:"想家的士兵会梦到家人。"

14. 正确答案:D。现在一些国家的一年人均用纸量是 50 公斤。

15. 正确答案:B。录音中谈到:"古代中国用某些植物毛状物做纸。"

16. 正确答案:A。自从德国人发现用木材可以做纸后,那些森林国家就变成用纸国了。

17. 正确答案:A。整篇都在谈论"我"与苏珊的恋爱关系。

18. 正确答案:D。他六个月前在一个舞会上认识了苏珊。

19. 正确答案:A。录音中谈到,只要一提到婚姻,苏珊便开始不高兴。

20. 正确答案:C。录音中提到,他和苏珊都 22 岁。

第二部分　词　　汇

21. 正确答案:A。句意为:有了商界成功的生涯,他被任命为委员会主席。
    appoint 任命,指派 / adopt 采纳,采取 / adjust 调整 / achieve 取得。例:He was appointed as the monitor of the class recently. 他最近被任命为班长。They adopted new methods to solve the problem. 他们采用了新的方法来解决这个问题。This kind of desk can be adjusted to the height you need. 这种书桌的高低可以按你的需要调整。They have achieved decisive progress in the experiment. 他们已在实验上取得了决定性的进展。

22. 正确答案:D。句意为:这些大纲是为那些追求高等教育,却没有时间去大学读书的年轻人设计的。
    insure 给……保险,保障 / persist 坚持 / inquire 询问,咨询 / pursue 追求,寻求。例:I've insured my house against fire. 我已给自己的房屋保了火险。She persists in wearing that old-fashioned hat. 她坚持戴那顶老式帽子。I inquired of him about their work. 我向他了解他们的工作情况。

23. 正确答案:C。句意为:工人们大部分是年轻人,年龄在 16 岁到 20 岁之间。

most 大部分(名词,作主语或宾语,一般不作修饰名词的定语)/mostly 大部分(副词)/ much 很多(修饰不可数名词)/ more 更多的。

24. 正确答案:B。句意为:很难猜测她对这个消息的反应是什么。

impression 印象(后跟介词 on 或 of)/ reaction 反应(后跟介词 to)/ comment 评价(后跟介词 on)/ opinion 意见(后跟介词 on 或 about)。

25. 正确答案:B。句意为:我们对天气都感兴趣,因为它直接影响我们——像我们穿什么衣服,我们做什么,甚至于我们的感觉。

benefit 得益,受益 / affect 影响 /guide 指导,引导 / effect 产生。例:We all benefited from her success. 我们大家都得益于她的成功。Will the change affect your plan? 这种变动会影响你的计划吗? Will you guide him to the General Manager's office? 你领他去总经理办公室好吗? Economic reform has effected great changes in China; 经济改革使中国发生巨大的变化。

26. 正确答案:A。句意为:她的儿子杳无音讯多年了,尽管如此,Susan 仍满怀着希望。

nevertheless 尽管如此(转折) /furthermore 再则,而且(递进) /consequently 结果(因果) / therefore 因此(因果)。例:None of them had much experience in that kind of work. They decided to try, nevertheless. 他们当中谁对那项工作也没有多少经验,但他们还是决定试一下。They cannot do it, and furthermore, no one else appears to want to do it either.他们做不了此事,而且看来也没有其他人愿意做。He was often late for work and was fired consequently. 他上班常迟到,结果被解雇了。We have a growing population and therefore we need more food.我们的人口在增长,因此,我们需要更多的食物。

27. 正确答案:D。句意为:他被指控盗窃,判了 10 年监禁。

assure 保证/ charge 指控,告发(后跟 with) /confirm 确认 /accuse 指控(后跟 of)。这种搭配和结构要特别注意学习、掌握。

28. 正确答案:A。句意为:思想是通过文字表达的。

by means of 是固定短语,意为"通过,靠"。例:You can do it by means of their help. 你可以通过他们的帮助做这件事。

29. 正确答案:D。句意为:现在去电影院已没意义了,因为电影已经开始了。

there is no point in doing sth. 为固定表达法,意为"没必要做某事"或"做某件事没意义"。例:What's your point in doing that? 你做那事的目的是什么?

30. 正确答案:A。句意为:美国学生很少住在校园里,而是住在家里,再去学校上课。

instead 替代,而是/ for example 举例 /what's more 再则 / however 然而。例:He is tired , let me go there instead. 他累了,让我替他去吧。He is only a child. What's more, he is strange to that place. How can you let him go there alone? 他只个孩子。再则,人生地不熟。你怎么能让他一个人去那儿? He didn't feel well that day. However, he still attended the party.他那天感觉不舒服,但仍参加了聚会。

31. 正确答案:C。句意为:请你浏览一下我的论文,看看有没有错误,好吗?

look out 注意,留神/ look into 调查 / look through 浏览,检查/ look up 抬头看着。例:If you don't look out, you'll hurt yourself. 如果你不当心,就会伤了自己。An official was sent here to look into this matter. 一位官员被派来调查此事。I haven't looked through the book yet. 我还没看完这本书。The son looked up at his mother in surprise. 儿子惊讶地抬头看看母亲。

32. 正确答案:B。句意为:我们必须搞清楚计算机出了什么毛病。

give out 散发,分发/ figure out 想出,解答/ run out 用完/ fill out 填写。Can you help me give out the exam papers to the students? 你能帮我把试卷发给学生吗? We tried to figure out a way to solve the problem. 我们试图想出个办法解决这个问题。It would be difficult to figure out the losses at that time. 在那时很难算出损失多少。Our time is running out. 我们的时间不多了。He filled out an application form for club membership. 他填写了一张俱乐部会员的申请表格。

33. 正确答案:A。句意为:他说不清为什么英语考试不及格。

account for 解释,说明原因/ account to(无此搭配用法)/ aware of 意识到/ according to 根据。例:The police tried to account for the blood stain. 警察试图解释这血迹是怎么来的。I was quite aware of this before we married. 在我们结婚前,我就知道这一点。According to the investigation by the police, he was declared to be innocent. 根据警察的调查,他被宣布无罪。

34. 正确答案:B。句意为:护士应该保证使孩子吃得适量,穿得适度。

see to it that... 是固定句型,意为"务必做到,保证使"。例:See to it that you are here punctually tomorrow morning. 你明天上午务必准时到达这里。

35. 正确答案:A。句意为:上个星期我在伦敦游览时,碰巧遇到了我的一位老朋友。

run into 偶遇/ run over 碾过/ run through 贯穿,浏览/ run along 沿着……跑。例:I ran into a waif in the street the other day. 那天我在街上偶然遇到了一位流浪儿。The truck nearly ran over a cyclist. 那辆卡车差点儿把一个骑自行车的人压着了。A keen humor runs through his writings. 他的文章始终有一种辛辣的幽默。He runs along the seaside everyday. 他每天沿着海边跑步。

36. 正确答案:C。句意为:许多人在抱怨现代生活的快节奏。

rate 比率,速率(用与其他事物的关系来衡量速度、价值、成本等的比值)/ speed 速度(常指任何事物持续运动时的速度,尤指车辆、机器等无生命事物的运动速度)/ pace 步速(多指走路、跑步的行速。用于比喻时,则指社会、生产效率等发展的速度)/ growth 增长,发展(常指社会经济的增长)。例:What is the interest rate of loans in China now ? 中国目前的贷款利率是多少? This kind of car can run at an extremely fast speed. 这种小车可以跑得飞快。We should quicken the pace of technical innovation. 我们应加速技术革新的步伐。Childhood is a period of rapid growth. 幼年是生长迅速的时期。

37. 正确答案:B。句意为:我更喜欢这幢房子,因为它能很好地观赏青山美景。

look 看,外表/ view 风景(尤指美丽的乡村风景),景色(常指从远处或高处看到的景色)/ sight 景象,情景(指值得一看的东西)/ point 点。例:There is no view from my bedroom window except for some factory chimneys. 从我卧室的窗子望去,除了一些工厂的烟囱外,看不到什么东西。The Great Wall is one of the best-known sights of the world. 长城是世界名胜之一。

38. 正确答案:C。句意为:她参加了一个诗歌比赛,并赢得了头奖。

name 名字/ price 价格/ order 订单/ prize 奖,奖赏。

39. 正确答案:A。句意为:如果我们现在不解决这些问题,局面会失控的。

fail 不能,不(用法常是:fail to do sth.)/ miss 丢失 / delay 耽搁(用法常是:delay doing sth.)/ deny 否认。例:They all failed to pass the preliminary test. 他们初试都未通过。Don't delay answering his letter. 不要耽搁给他复信。

40. 正确答案:A。句意为:如果你碰巧看到 Jane,告诉她晚上给我打个电话。

happen 碰巧 / mind 介意 / occur 发生 / appear 看起来。例:What occurred to her recently? She looks so upset. 她最近发生了什么吗?看起来总那么心神不定。

第三部分　语法结构

41. 正确答案:D。句意为:那天晚上之前,我从未感觉到我有如此大的权力。

以否定副词 never, scarcely, hardly 等开头的句子,主谓应倒装。例:Not once did he talk to me. 他一次也没有和我谈过。Never did he speak about his own merits. 他从不讲他自己的功绩。

42. 正确答案:C。句意为:她在自己出生的那个小镇呆了很长时间。

where 在此相当于 in which,它引导定语从句,在从句中用作地点状语,其先行词(即被定语从句修饰的名词)须是表示地点的名词。例:The place where Macbeth met the witches was a desolate heath. Macbeth 遇见女巫的地方是一片荒原。

43. 正确答案:A。句意为:就是因为她病了,所以才没来参加昨天的会议。

it is(was)...that...是一种强势句,强调的是 be 动词与 that 之间的成分。例:It is Mrs. White that makes the decisions in the family, not her meek little husband. 在那个家庭里,作决定的是怀特太太,而不是她那个温顺的小个子丈夫。需特别注意的是,不要将这类句子与定语从句相混淆。这类句子不管强调的是人、时间、地点、原因,还是其他什么成分,后面的句子都只能以 that 引导,但在强调人时,也可用 who,但 that 更多见。

44. 正确答案:C。句意为:我听说他要去美国,但什么时候走由他自己定。

when he leaves 为从句作主语。例:Why she left China is still a mystery. 她为什么离开中国仍是个谜。

45. 正确答案:B。句意为:他们上次没通过考试;我后悔没能帮上他们。

regret doing sth. 表示后悔做某事,而 regret to tell(inform)...表示遗憾。

46. 正确答案:B。句意为:你的头发该理了。你最好明天请人剪剪。

sth. needs doing = sth. needs to be done。例:My coat needs mending. = My coat needs to be mended. 我的上衣需要补一补。have sth. done = ask sb. else to do the thing. 请他人做这件事. have the hair cut 理发,该句型是:have + 名词 + 过去分词。

47. 正确答案:C。句意为:在那次航行中,不仅水手们,连船长也受到了惊吓。

not only...but also...分别修饰单数名词与复数名词时,谓语动词的时态、数应与靠动词最近的被修饰名词的时态、数相一致。例:Not only the teacher but also his students like to play tricks. 此句中,students 离动词近,所以用 like,而不是 likes.

48. 正确答案:A。句意为:我宁愿你坐火车去,因为一想起你在这样糟糕的天气乘飞机,我就坐立不安。

would rather 宁愿(后跟从句,用虚拟语气,表示愿望。从句的时态应视情况用过去时、过去完成时或过去将来时等)。例:I would rather you lived closer to us. 我倒希望你住得离我们近些。与现在情况相反,所以从句用过去式。

49. 正确答案:A。句意为:你这个星期天一定来看我们,好吗?

此句为反意疑问句。它附在陈述句之后,对陈述句所说的事实或观点提出疑问。这种疑问句由助动词或情态动词加主语(常与陈述句的主语相同)构成,前有逗号,后有问号。此考题中,陈述句其实是一个祈使句,它的主语为第二人称 you,但被省略。所以在反意问句中用 will you? 好吗?(征求对方的意见)

50. 正确答案:B。句意为:花肯定都死了,因为没人给它们浇水。

must 在此表示猜测。must + 现在完成时,表示"某件事肯定已发生了"。例:It is already six o'clock. She must have come home. 现在已是六点了。她一定到家了。

51. 正确答案:B。句意为:Rose 把 Oliver 遭遇到的一切都告诉了老师。

在定语从句中,如果先行词(被定语从句修饰的那个词)是不定代词(nothing, everything, anything, all 等),则必须用 that,而不能用 which 来引导定语从句。例:All that she has experienced will make a good story. 她所经历的一切将成为一个动人的传奇故事。

52. 正确答案:C。句意为:据说,昨天银行被盗几百万美元。

动词不定式可表示将来会发生的事。例:He was told to see his grandfather. 他们叫他去看看他的祖父。如果要用动词不定式表示一件已发生的事,就要用 to + 现在完成时。例:Ten passengers are reported to have been killed in the road accident. 据报道 10 名乘客在车祸中丧生。

53. 正确答案:D。句意为:伦敦是她一直都渴望去的城市。

此句 city 后跟一个定语从句,尽管 city 是一个地点名词,究竟用 where 还是用 that 来引导定语从句,还需看先行词在从句中究竟作宾语还是作状语。此句中 city 在从句中作宾语,所以用 that 引导。例:This is the place that we both like very much.(that 在从句中作宾语)这是我们俩都很喜欢的地方。This is the place where we met for the first time. 这是我们第一次相遇的地方。(where = in which)

54. 正确答案:D。句意为:谢谢邀请我到你们学校讲课。

appreciate doing sth. 是固定用法。being invited 是动名词的被动形态。例:We appreciate your helping us. 我们感谢他们对我们的帮助。

55. 正确答案:A。句意为:直到 1868 年,Atlanta 才被定为 Georgia 州的州府。

以否定词(not, scarcely, hardly, never 等)开头的句子应倒装。

56. 正确答案:B。句意为:政府没有料到油价的下跌会给经济带来如此严重的后果。

此句带宾语从句,应特别注意主句与从句时态的一致。主句为过去时,从句也应作相应选择。would cause 为过去将来时。

57. 正确答案:C。句意为:人们不想在他们的国家中又发生一场战争。

这是 want to do sth. 的变态句型,中间插入 there,与 there is(are) 句型组合而成。

58. 正确答案:D。句意为:因为他不喜欢第一种花,他要销售小姐给他看看另一种。

another 另一个(不特指,后一般跟单数),the other 另一个(特指两个中的另一个),other 其他的(后跟复数)。

59. 正确答案:D。句意为:一本好词典对于语言学习者来说有很大帮助。

be + of + 名词,是书面正式用法,相当于 be + 形容词的用法。例:This point is of vital importance(= This point is very important)to us.

60. 正确答案：A。句意为："你看，我们的票在这里。""很好。我还担心你忘记拿了呢！"
此句同样为主从句时态一致的考题。因为主句 I was afraid 用了过去时，从句 forget 的动作应在此之前发生，所以应用过去完成时。

第四部分 阅读理解

第一篇短文参考译文及语言注释

工业污染不仅对欧洲和北美国家来说是个问题，对某些发展中国家来说也是极其严重的问题。对这些国家来讲，经济发展是非常重要的目标。它们想吸引新产业，因此较少控制工业污染问题。

Cubatao，巴西的一个拥有 85000 人的工业小镇，便是工业发展与污染相关的例子。1954年，Cubatao 还没有工业。今天，它有了 20 多家排出污染物的大工厂。镇上的人在这样的环境中受到大量有害物质的侵袭，其结果是显而易见的。婴儿残疾比比皆是。在儿童与成年人中，肺病发生率有时是其他地方的 12 倍。

像其他国家一样，巴西确实也有反污染法，但执法不严。对公司来说，违法挨罚比买那些昂贵的环境保护设备要划算得多。因此，很明显，对政府来说，经济发展比工人的健康更重要。然而，责任并不完全在巴西政府。Cubatao 的例子也表明跨国公司没有以负责任的态度在运作。这个镇上的一些公司由法国、意大利和美国大公司所拥有。它们在巴西做本国不能做的事。如果它们在本国引起了同样程度的污染，会被严惩，甚至勒令停业。

be exposed to 暴露于。birth defects 生育缺陷。twelve times 12 倍。pay the fines 付罚款。The responsibility does not completely lie with the Brazilian government. 句中的 lie with 表示"是……的责任"。be put out of business 此处指"停业"。

试题解答

61. 正确答案：D。短文第一段最后两句解答了这个问题。

62. 正确答案：C。Cubatao 只是一个发展中国家的城市，提到它是为了说明发展中国家的城市在经济发展中所面临的环境污染问题。

63. 正确答案：B。短文第三段第一句提到"巴西有反污染法，但执法不严"。第三段最后两句谈到"这些跨国公司在巴西做本国不能做的事"，"如果它们在本国引起同样程度的污染，会被严惩，甚至勒令停业"。

64. 正确答案：A。enforce 强加，执行。

65. 正确答案：A。短文第三段第二句谈到"对公司来说，违法挨罚比买那些昂贵的环境保护设备要划算得多"。其他三个答案明显是错误的。

第二篇短文参考译文及语言注释

1947 年，Angela Mortimer 率领她的球队赢得了 Plymouth 校际冠军杯。在走向前领取银杯的那一刻，她就下定决心要成为温布尔顿网球赛冠军。

受到冠军杯胜利的鼓舞，Angela 决定请一个好教练。她听说在 Torquay 有位优秀的网球教练 Roberts 先生。他免费给住在 Torquay 地区的 12 岁以下有潜质的孩子教授网球。尽管 Angela 已过 15 岁，但这并未阻碍她的决心。一个星期六，她从 Plymouth 步行了 40 英里路程来到 Torquay，向 Roberts 先生毛遂自荐。Arthur Roberts 对她并未留下什么印象。他发了些球给 Angela，直截了当地告诉她，她不懂这项运动，而且现在学年纪也太大了。他还提醒她，因为她住在 Plymouth，Torquay 地区也不会考虑接受她。

如果 Arthur Roberts 以为就这样能把 Angela 给打发了，那他就大错特错了。对于 Angela 来说，她已对 Roberts 先生留下了深刻的印象。她认定自己学网球年纪并不太大，而且一定要 Arthur Roberts 教她。但是，学校的证书考试就在眼前，她决心下苦功夫。尽管校长要她在学校学一年后再参加考试，但 Angela 请求允许参加这次考试。令人惊讶的是，她通过了五门课的考试，拿到了学分。

而后，幸运之神降临在 Angela 身上。她成功地说服家人搬到 Torquay 附近居住。不管上次会面发生了什么，Angela 这回又得体地出现在 Arthur Roberts 面前，再次请求接受她。Arthur 给了她不热烈的迎接。他的时间已被训练那些有前途的孩子占满。不过，他不得不欣赏 Angela。不管缺什么，显然她不缺勇气与决心。Arthur 喜欢学生身上的这些特质。"你可以对着墙打，"他说，"如果你进步了，我也许会帮助你。"

Angela 心情雀跃。"我会让你看到的，"她对自己说，"我一定会让你看到的。"

championship 冠军。promising 有培养前途的，是形容词。The fact <u>that</u> Angela was over fifteen did not stop her. 句中 that 引导的是同位语从句，说明 fact 的内容。play a few shots 击了几个球。He also reminded her that she lived in Plymouth, <u>which</u> could hardly be considered in the Torquay area. 句中 which 引导的是非限制性定语从句，补充说明情况。be mistaken 搞错了。for one's part 在某人一方，就某人而言。sit 此处表示"参加考试"，例：He sat for a scholarship. 他为获奖学金而参加考试。a stroke of luck 走运。be fully occupied in doing sth. 忙于某事。

试题解答

66. 正确答案：D。短文第二段第二句谈到"Roberts 先生免费为居住在 Torquay 地区的 12 岁以下有培养前途的儿童教授网球"。

67. 正确答案：B。短文第二段解答了这个问题。三个理由是：一，她不懂网球；二，她年纪太大了；三，她不住在 Torquay。

68. 正确答案：B。短文第三段最后两句谈到，尽管校长要她等一年再考，但她请求校长同意让她现在考。结果她五课成绩都通过，并拿到了学分。

69. 正确答案：B。Roberts 先生不教她的理由之一，就是她不住在 Torquay 地区。搬离原居住地后，就消除了一个不接受的理由。

70. 正确答案：C。短文第四段最后一句谈到 Roberts 先生说"如果你进步了，我也许会帮你"。

第三篇短文参考译文及语言注释

全世界的通讯公司都在想着开展无线业务。它们花费了几十亿美元建设发射塔，发射卫星，开发低成本的手提电话，目的只有一个，结束一个半世纪来被有线主宰的局面。

自 1844 年电报业务诞生以来，大部分双向交流并非人对人，而是地对地。如果两个人所在的地方没有有线连接，他们便无法通话。

现在，随着微电子和卫星技术的发展，一些公司正在生产可定位系统，能找到人的所在，可保持联系。这些服务很快在美国、欧洲和东亚发展中国家得以使用。

移动电话是当今最具戏剧性的一个例子。在美国，移动电话用户上月已超过 2500 万，而且未来的增长仍难以估量。在十多年的时间里，移动电话已从奢侈的商务用具和身份象征，发展到差不多每十个美国人中就有一个移动电话用户。

不是每个人都欢迎这样的变化的。在教堂、法庭和飞机上,在那些本来拒绝外界喧哗的地方,无线电话叫个不停。然而,人们无法阻止这项技术的发展。

"它渐渐进入低收入阶层,"华盛顿 MTA-EMCI 通讯公司的 Tom Ross 说,"它慢慢地变成了生活的必需品。"

现在,许多国家的官方机构正在清扫无线电频谱,以腾出新空间发展一系列新的无线电业务。它们被称为个人通讯服务,或 PCS。简单看来,PCS 就是袖珍电话的别名。但是通讯公司正准备开发广泛的"智能网络"和普通移动电话无法提供的数据服务。

hand-held phones 手提电话。all with the goal of ... 所有的目的都在于。keep sb. in touch 与某人保持联系。come into use 正式启用。economies 经济实体,为可数名词。to date 至今,到现在。status symbol 身份象征。show up 出现,露面。例:He didn't show up at the last faculty meeting. 上次教师大会上,他没有到会。

试题解答

71. 正确答案:C。spots 点,地点。

72. 正确答案:C。整篇文章的主题就是谈无线业务的发展。虽然其他三个选择的内容在文章中都有提及,但不是主要的。

73. 正确答案:B。Tom 说:"移动电话渐渐进入低收入阶层,它慢慢地变成了生活的必需品。"

74. 正确答案:D。回答问题时,必须注意寻找前面出现过的复数名词,因为 they 是复数代词。

75. 正确答案:A。答案明显是第一个。其他三个都不对。

第五部分　英译汉

76. 因为美国是个移民国家,因此菜肴的风格五花八门,而且任何美国大城市里都有很多国际风味的餐馆。

77. 对那些来这儿旅游或工作的人,一想起他们还可以在这儿找到家乡特色菜便备感欣慰。

78. 当人们开始更严肃地考虑食物对健康可能造成的影响时,健康食品便受人欢迎了。

79. 健康食品包括未经精加工的天然食品,也就是,不用化学制品使其保鲜、美味或美观。

80. 快餐店在美国正遍地开花。在那儿,快速是很重要的因素。

第六部分　汉译英

81. When you come across new words in reading, sometimes you may not consult dictionaries for them.

82. She is looking for a job. I think she may have graduated from college.

83. Learning English needs patience and efforts; it is impossible to have a good command of a foreign language within a few months.

84. I was too excited to fall asleep last night because my design had been accepted.

85. —When do you turn off the light and go to bed?
    —At half past ten except on weekend.

2002年6月浙江省大学英语三级考试试卷

Part Ⅰ　Listening Comprehension

Section A

Directions: *In this section, you will hear* 10 *short conversations. At the end of each conversation, a question will be asked about what was said. You will hear the conversation and the question only once. After each question there will be a pause. During the pause, you must read the four choices marked A), B), C) and D), and decide which is the best answer. Then mark the corresponding letter on the Answer Sheet with a single line through the center.*

1. A) Warm.
   C) Mild.
   B) Hot.
   D) Cold.

2. A) In an office.
   C) In a classroom.
   B) In a library.
   D) In a bookstore.

3. A) By sea.
   C) By bus.
   B) By train.
   D) By air.

4. A) He is doubtful about the one-bedroom apartment.
   B) He's prepared to pay more for the bigger apartment.
   C) There is a big difference between the two apartments.
   D) The one-bedroom apartment is better as it is cheaper.

5. A) The train may arrive but the woman is not sure.
   B) The train will probably arrive at 10:45.
   C) The train broke down and will not arrive.
   D) The train will probably arrive at 9:45.

6. A) She will help him next week.
   B) She has finished her work quickly.
   C) She had her work done a week ago.
   D) She did her work carelessly.

7. A) She likes it as well as the man.
   C) She prefers summer.
   B) She takes her vacations in autumn.
   D) She doesn't like it.

8. A) He'll play the game.
   C) He'll watch the game on TV.
   B) He won't watch the game standing.
   D) He has little knowledge of the game.

9. A) To learn another language.
   C) To give up French.
   B) To practice the dialogues.
   D) To give up practicing.

10. A) The woman should take her time.

   B) They are supposed to leave in twenty minutes.

   C) Alice is arriving in twenty minutes.

   D) They are already late for the appointment.

Section B

Directions: *In this section, you will hear 3 short passages. The passages will be read twice. At the end of each passage, you will hear some questions, which will be read only once. After you hear a question, you must choose the best answer from the four choices marked A), B), C) and D). Then mark the corresponding letter on the Answer Sheet with a single line through the center.*

Passage One

Questions 11 to 13 are based on the passage you have just heard.

11. A) He was a beggar.

   B) He pretended to be a rich man.

   C) He enjoyed helping the poor.

   D) He worked at a train station.

12. A) The artist.   B) The first beggar.

   C) The second beggar.   D) The taxi driver.

13. A) Because the beggar had cheated him.

   B) Because he had missed the train home.

   C) Because the beggar wouldn't go home with him.

   D) Because he had to let the beggar pay for the meal.

Passage Two

Questions 14 to 16 are based on the passage you have just heard.

14. A) Fresh meat.   B) Monkey meat.

   C) Horse meat.   D) Frozen meat.

15. A) Wild horses.   B) Larger monkeys.

   C) Smaller monkeys.   D) Large birds.

16. A) Men's brother—monkeys.   B) Feeding animals in zoos.

   C) Birds, horses and crocodiles.   D) Watching animals in zoos.

Passage Three

Questions 17 to 20 are based on the passage you have just heard.

17. A) 95.   B) 15.

   C) 50.   D) 5.

18. A) 12 months.   B) 24 months.

   C) 18 months.   D) 36 months.

19. A) There are far more right-handed monkeys than left-handed ones.

   B) There are far more left-handed monkeys than right-handed ones.

   C) There are no left-handed monkeys.

   D) There are an equal number of left-handed and right-handed monkeys.

20. A) Left-handed people usually like animals.

   B) Monkeys learn to use their hands from humans.

   C) Human beings are like monkeys in using hands.

   D) Life is not so easy for left-handed people.

Part Ⅱ   Vocabulary

Directions: *There are 20 incomplete sentences in this part. For each sentence there are four choices marked A), B), C) and D). Choose the ONE answer that best completes the sentence. Then mark the corresponding letter on the Answer Sheet with a single line through the center.*

21. Nowadays many young people dream of becoming rich and famous _____.

   A) at one night   B) on one night

   C) overnight   D) by night

22. To be frank, I didn't mean to _____ you during the discussion.

   A) offend   B) object

   C) deliver   D) destroy

23. Jane has learnt the long poem by _____ though she read it only a few times.

   A) mind   B) heart

   C) memory   D) spirit

24. She often takes notes in the _____ when she listens to the teacher in class.

   A) margin   B) border

   C) surface   D) boundary

25. We all believe that he is _____ at swimming and diving.

   A) understanding   B) undergoing

   C) outlooking   D) outstanding

26. This part of our town is heavily _____ by industrial wastes.

   A) populated   B) possessed

   C) polluted   D) processed

27. There are still thousands of people living in _____ in some mountainous areas.

   A) gravity   B) opportunity

   C) responsibility   D) poverty

28. On my last business trip to Dalian the sea was so _____ that many passengers became sick.

   A) shaky   B) tough

   C) rough   D) shivering

29. _____ the city has changed so much that it's beyond recognition.

A) Lastly
B) Lately
C) Late
D) Later

30. The agreement is to take _____ from the beginning of next month.

A) place
B) position
C) charge
D) effect

31. Some *organisms*(有机体) are responsible for _____ food and causing food poisoning.

A) spoiling
B) sparing
C) starving
D) spilling

32. The document should be signed in the _____ of a lawyer.

A) appearance
B) presence
C) reference
D) experience

33. Some old readers are strongly _____ of her newly-published love story.

A) cruel
B) crazy
C) critical
D) crude

34. It is a(n) _____ in this country to go out to pick flowers on the first day of spring.

A) habit
B) custom
C) action
D) movement

35. Her failure to understand the problem _____ too many technical terms.

A) results from
B) results in
C) results by
D) results at

36. Then the doctor _____ my temperature and felt my pulse.

A) examined
B) took
C) held
D) measured

37. I applied for the job but they _____ because I didn't know German.

A) turned me down
B) turned me in
C) turned me on
D) turned me off

38. I am writing _____ my mother to express her thanks for your gift.

A) in memory of
B) with respect to
C) on behalf of
D) on account of

39. A completely new situation will _____ when the new examination system comes into existence.

A) rise
B) raise
C) awake
D) arise

40. Studies indicate that when children are _____ to violence, they may become *aggressive* (好斗的) or nervous.

A) reacted
B) related
C) expanded
D) exposed

Part III Structure

Directions: *There are 20 incomplete sentences in this part. For each sentence there are four choices marked A), B), C) and D). Choose the ONE answer that best completes the sentence. Then mark the corresponding letter on the Answer Sheet with a single line through the center.*

41. Is it true that a relative of yours _____ this weekend?
    A) will be coming to see you   B) will have been coming to see you
    C) would have come to see you   D) would have been come to see you

42. This is the worst time of the year. It _____ every day so far this month.
    A) is raining   B) has rained
    C) rained   D) rains

43. _____ in the countryside means that you have a better environment.
    A) Live   B) Having lived
    C) Living   D) Being lived

44. I think that _____ with the railway, the highway is much better.
    A) comparing   B) compared
    C) to compare   D) compare

45. _____ happens, I'll stick to my position on the issue.
    A) No matter that   B) No matter how
    C) No matter which   D) No matter what

46. It is vital that she _____ a job to support her family.
    A) has   B) have
    C) will have   D) had

47. Every means _____ been tried since then, but the result was failure.
    A) is   B) have
    C) has   D) are

48. It is one thing to speak some English, but it is quite _____ to speak good, natural English.
    A) other   B) another
    C) the other   D) others

49. There _____ in this small bedroom.
    A) are too many furnitures   B) are too much furniture
    C) are too much furnitures   D) is too much furniture

50. This is one of _____ exciting games I've ever watched.
    A) the most   B) most of the
    C) most   D) most of

51. Only by reading extensively _____ you mind.
    A) you will broaden   B) you may broaden
    C) so you broaden   D) can you broaden

52. They had their new house _____ in the earthquake last week.

   A) be destroyed
   B) being destroyed
   C) to be destroyed
   D) destroyed

53. Last year Jack earned _____ his sister, who is a general manager of a joint venture.

   A) as twice much as
   B) twice as many as
   C) twice as much as
   D) as twice many as

54. You _____ your homework last night, but you didn't.

   A) ought to have done
   B) need to have done
   C) must have done
   D) can have done

55. I shall postpone _____ my paper until I get enough information on the subject.

   A) writing
   B) being written
   C) written
   D) to write

56. —What did John think of your decision?

   —He _____ to believe that I really did want to go there alone.

   A) found it impossible
   B) found which impossible
   C) found impossible
   D) found that impossible

57. No one would imagine that this city was just a night's journey from here. It seemed as though _____ in another world.

   A) it to be
   B) it were
   C) it has been
   D) it being

58. Frank is the kind of person whom people like to _____.

   A. make a friend with
   B) make a friend of
   C) make friends with
   D) make friends of

59. In general, the health of older people today is superior to _____ of previous generations.

   A) one
   B) that
   C) some
   D) those

60. We went up to the roof, _____ we had a good view of the parade.

   A) of which
   B) from which
   C) before which
   D) behind which

Part IV Reading Comprehension

Directions: *There are 3 passages in this part. Each passage is followed by some questions or unfinished statements. For each of them there are four choices marked A), B), C) and D). You should decide on the best choice and mark the corresponding letter on the Answer Sheet with a single line through the center.*

Passage One

Questions 61 to 65 are based on the following passage:

On May 29, 1973, Thomas Bradley, a black man, was elected mayor of Los Angeles. Los Angeles is the third largest city in the United States, with a population of three million. About sixteen percent of the city's population are black.

News of this election appeared on the front pages of newspapers everywhere in the United States. Here is how one major newspaper reported the event: Los Angeles Elects Bradley Mayor, Defeating Yorty—Black Win 56% of Votes.

Bradley called his victory "the fulfillment of a dream." During his childhood and youth, people had kept telling him, "You can't do this, you can't go there, because you're a Negro." Nevertheless he had won a decisive victory over a man who had been the city's mayor for three times. Bradley had won 56.3 percent of the votes; Yorty had won 43.7 percent.

Los Angeles voters had many opportunities to judge Thomas Bradley and to form an opinion of him. The son of a poor farmer from Texas, he joined the Los Angeles police force in 1940. During his twenty-one years on the police force he earned a law degree by attending school at night. He was elected to the city council ten years ago. At the time of Los Angeles election three other American cities already had black mayors, but none of those cities had as large a population as Los Angeles. Besides, the percentage of blacks in those other cities was much larger. Cleveland, Ohio, was thirty-six percent black when Carl Stokes was elected mayor of Cleveland in 1967. In the same year Richard Hatcher was elected mayor of Gary, Indiana, which was fifty-five percent black. In Newark, New Jersey, sixty percent of the population were black when Kenneth Glibson was elected in 1970. Thus the election of a black mayor in those cities was not very surprising.

In Los Angeles thousands of white citizens voted for Thomas Bradley because they believe he would be a better mayor than the white candidate. Bradley had spent forty-eight of his fifty-five years in Los Angeles. Four years ago Bradley lost the mayoral election to Yorty. This time Bradley won.

61. Thomas Bradley was elected mayor of Los Angeles because _____.
    A) the black people made up a large percentage of the population in the city
    B) more than half of its citizens, black and white, were in favor of him
    C) he had spent forty-eight of his fifty-five years in the city
    D) he was considered the best candidate in the history of the city

62. Bradley's victory in the mayoral election attracted nationwide attention because _____.
    A) Los Angeles was a major city in the U.S. with a relatively small black population
    B) Los Angeles was the place where most of the major U.S. newspapers were based
    C) 56% of black voters and 44% of white voters in Los Angeles had voted for him
    D) it had fulfilled the dream of the black people throughout the United States

63. Which of the following cities had the largest percentage of black population?
    A) Los Angeles.   B) Cleveland.
    C) Gary.   D) Newark.

64. We may infer from the third paragraph that Los Angeles voters _____.
    A) believed that Thomas Bradley would give them many opportunities to judge him
    B) had been given many opportunities so they have a high opinion of Thomas Bradley

C) had known Thomas Bradley well for his long years of public service in the city

D) had had many opportunities to elect Thomas Bradley mayor of the city

65. Why did the white voters choose Bradley over a white candidate?

A) Because he had proved to be a good policeman.

B) Because they expected him to do a better job.

C) Because he held a law degree from a good university.

D) Because they simply wanted to give him a chance.

Passage Two

Questions 66 to 70 are based on the following passage:

The U.S. generates about four billion tons of solid waste a year. More than 90 percent is composed of agricultural and mining wastes. About 3 percent is from industrial wastes. 250 million tons of garbage comes out from homes, schools, office buildings, stores and hospitals.

This mass of metals, paper, food, plastic, rubber and glass, which is all mixed together, seems of no earthly use to anyone.

Or is it? Many efforts across the country indicate that new technology, properly applied, might some day turn these millions of tons of garbage into an excellent source of raw materials for new uses.

Several new projects are carried out to study the possibility of treating wastes through *pyrolysis*—a system of reducing garbage to basic chemicals, liquids and gases which have commercial value. In Florida, a special tube system provides automatic transport of garbage to a central collection building.

In short, many new ideas are being tested, and many will be needed, since no one method is likely to prove suitable everywhere.

However, many difficult economic and social questions must be answered before real progress can be made. Can recovered materials compete with new materials? What will be needed as encouragement to make resource recovery work? Will citizens pay the cost of changing our waste system?

66. The author suggests that garbage from home and public places _____.

A) makes up the largest portion of solid waste

B) makes up a small portion of solid waste

C) is not really considered as solid waste

D) is considered of no practical value

67. Which of the following is closest in meaning to the question "Or is it?" in Paragraph Three?

A) Or is it true that this mass of solid waste is of no practical use?

B) Or is it right to bury all this mass of solid waste under earth?

C) Or is it wise to mix all this mass of solid waste together?

D) Or is it worthwhile to make so many efforts across the country?

68. *Pyrolysis* (Line 2, Para. 4) is a process which _____.

A) treats a large amount of industrial wastes

B) turns garbage into a new source of raw materials

C) mixes together different kinds of solid waste

D) provides garbage for a collection building

69. Which of the following is true concerning the issue of waste recovery?

A) Many new ideas have been adopted.

B) The present systems have been widely used.

C) Different methods are required in different places.

D) No garbage has been proved useful everywhere.

70. It can be implied from the last paragraph that _____.

A) great progress has already been made in resource recovery

B) recovered materials will be able to compete with new materials

C) working people in the U.S. have been encouraged to recover solid waste

D) citizens may be unwilling to pay the costs of changing the waste system

Passage Three

Questions 71 to 75 are based on the following passage:

Kate, a student in 8th grade, asked lots of questions in math class—until the teacher told her to stop. "He said I was confusing the other kids with my questions," she recalls. "When boys asked questions, he took them a lot more seriously."

You might have thought that such obvious forms of discrimination (歧视) had ended by now. But Esther Greenglass, a psychology professor at York University in Toronto, says many recent studies have found that girls may still be faced with mixed messages about self-confidence and success, which can lower their self-esteem and discourage them from achieving their potential.

The problem worsens at about age 11 or 12, when girls start hitting puberty (青春期) and discovering boys. Many girls' grades drop, and so does their self-esteem. "Girls get the message that, if you're going to be popular, you can't be too smart because the boys won't like you," says Greenglass, who has written extensively on sex roles and discrimination.

Often, girls also sense that boys are considered more capable. In studies in the United States, researchers found that when teachers asked questions, they almost always made eye contact with boys, unless they had attended courses raising their level of awareness. Adding to the problem, according to Greenglass, is the lack of female role models in old textbooks still found in many Canadian schools.

How are girls' attitudes affected? Studies have shown that boys usually attribute their success to their superior ability, while girls attribute their own success to luck. When boys fail at a task, they tend to blame it on external factors; when girls fail, they blame their own lack of ability. Boys are more likely to try a second time to succeed.

71. The first paragraph intends to tell us that _____.

A) girls usually ask more questions than boys in class

B) girls often confuse teachers with many questions

C) teachers tend to give much more attention to boys

D) teachers believe that boys ask more serious questions

72. Findings by Professor Esther Greenglass indicate that _____.

A) sex discrimination in schools has disappeared in Canada

B) Canadian school girls are more self-confident than boys

C) school girls in Canada are confused about their roles

D) in Canada girls and boys achieve equal success at school

73. Researchers in the United States found that when teachers asked questions, _____.

A) they would first turned to boys for answers

B) they wanted to raise the awareness of boys

C) boys responded to them immediately

D) girls avoided eye contact with teachers

74. We can learn from the passage that girls' lack of self-confidence has led to _____.

A) their misjudgment of their own success and failure

B) boys' misunderstanding of their superiority

C) their inability to achieve academic success

D) boys' blaming external factors for their failures

75. What is the best title of the passage?

A) Male and Female Role Models.

B) Puberty and Sex Difference.

C) Girls, Boys, and Success.

D) Sex Roles and Discrimination.

Part Ⅴ   Translation from English into Chinese

Directions: *In this part there is a passage with 5 underlined sections, numbered 76 to 80. After reading the passage carefully, translate the underlined sections into Chinese. Remember to write your translation on the Translation Sheet.*

(76) In many businesses, computers have largely replaced paperwork, because they are fast, flexible, and do not make mistakes. As one banker said, "Unlike humans, computers never have a bad day." And they are honest. Many banks advertise that their transactions(交易) are "untouched by human hands" and therefore safe from human temptation. Obviously, computers have no reason to steal money. But they also have no conscience, and the growing number of computer crimes shows they can be used to steal.

Computer criminals don't use guns. (77) And even if they are caught, it is hard to punish them because there are no witness and often no evidence. A computer cannot remember who used it: it simply does what it is told. The head teller at a Salt Lake City bank used a computer to steal more than one and a half million dollars in just four years. No one noticed this theft because she moved the money from one account to another. (78) <u>Each time a customer she had robbed questioned the balance in his account, the teller claimed a computer error, then replaced the missing money from someone else's account.</u> This person was caught only because she was a drug user. When the police broke up an illegal drug operation, her name was in the records.

Some employees use the computer's power to take revenge (报复) on employers they consider unfair. (79) <u>Recently, a large company fired an employee for reasons that involved his personal rather than his professional life.</u> He was its computer-tape librarian. In his last forty days that he was allowed to work for the company, he erased all the company's computerized records.

Most computer criminals have been minor employees. Now police wonder if this is "the tip of the iceberg." As one official says, "I have the feeling that there is more crime out there than we are catching. What we are seeing now in all so poorly done. (80) <u>I wonder what the real experts are doing—the ones who really know how a computer works.</u>"

Part Ⅵ Translation from Chinese into English

Directions: *In this part there are 5 sentences, numbered 81 to 85, in Chinese. Translate these sentences into English on the Translation Sheet.*

81. 我感到喘不过气来;我开窗你会介意吗?
82. 你们应该理论联系实际,培养应用语言的能力。
83. 他将永远记得家乡解放的那一天。
84. 令人惊讶的是,他竟然放弃升职加薪的机会。
85. 可以肯定的是,奥运会(the Olympics)将为北京带来成千上万的中外游客。

【听力录音文稿】

Section A

1. W: Did you hear the weather forecast?

   M: Yes, they said it would be slightly above freezing tomorrow.

   Q: What kind of weather are they having?

2. M: How long can I keep this book?

   W: Only for a week. You have to return it on time. Otherwise, you'll be fined.

   Q: Where does this conversation most probably take place?

3. W: If I were you, I would take a plane instead of a bus. It will take you forever to get there.

   M: But flying makes me so nervous.

   Q: How does the man prefer to travel?

4. W: Of the two apartments we've just seen, which do you like better?

   M: The single one was cheaper, no doubt, but the two-bedroom one is bigger and it's worth paying the difference.

Q: What does the man mean?

5. M: Excuse me, when will the 9:15 train arrive?

   W: It's been delayed an hour and a half because the bridge was broken.

   Q: What do we learn from the conversation?

6. W: I don't think Joan can have her work finished in less than a week.

   M: Joan has finished it in two days.

   Q: What does the man say about Joan?

7. M: I love autumn, so I take my vacations during that time of year.

   W: Isn't it cold and wet most of the season? I would be bothered by that.

   Q: How does the woman like autumn?

8. W: Why don't you go to the game with me?

   M: I can't stand watching a game I know nothing about.

   Q: What does the man mean?

9. W: I give up! I simply can't learn French.

   M: Why do you say that? I think you're making a lot of progress. Learning any language takes a lot of effort. Why don't you practice those dialogues together?

   Q: What does the man advise the woman to do?

10. W: O.K. I'm almost ready. Just two more minutes...

    M: Come on. Let's get started. We were supposed to have met Alice twenty minutes ago.

    Q: What does the man mean?

Section B

Passage One

Allen was an artist. He didn't have much money, but he was a very kind man. One day, he was coming home by train. He gave his last few coins to a beggar, but then he saw another one, and forgot that he did not have any money. He asked the man if he would like to have lunch with him, and the beggar accepted, so they went into a small restaurant and had a good meal.

At the end, Allen could not pay the bill, of course, so the beggar had to do so.

The artist was very unhappy about this, so he said to the beggar, "Come home with me in a taxi, my friend, and I'll give you back the money for lunch."

"Oh, no!" the beggar answered quickly. "I had to pay for your lunch, but I'm not going to pay for your taxi home!"

Questions 11 to 13 are based on the passage you have just heard.

11. What do we learn about Allen from the story?

12. Who paid for Allen's lunch at the restaurant?

13. Why was the artist very unhappy?

Passage Two

How would you like to have the job of getting the right food for all the different animals in a zoo? If their food is not carefully selected, the animals will refuse to eat or will become sick. As far as possible the food selected is like that which the animal eats when they are wild and free. However, when many special foods agree with the animals, they are usually provided.

Most of the birds and many of the smaller monkeys like mealworms. In many zoos these mealworms are raised in boxes of meal and always kept on hand. Crocodiles eat only two or three times a month, and after a meal they will sleep three or four days. They like horsemeat, but the crocodile likes the meat a few days old before it is served.

The food of the larger monkeys is similar to that of a man. They will eat eggs, potatoes, bread, carrots, and many other foods found on our tables.

Questions 14 to 16 are based on the passage you have just heard.

14. What kind of meat do crocodiles like?

15. Which kind of animal's food is similar to that of a man?

16. What is the story mainly about?

Passage Three

Which of your two hands do you use most? Very few of us can use both of our hands equally well. Most of us are right-handed. Only about five people out of a hundred are left-handed. Newborn babies can grasp objects with either of their hands, but in about two years they usually prefer to use their right hands. Scientists don't know why this happens. They used to think that we inherited this tendency from our animal ancestors, but this may not be true. Monkeys are our closest relatives in the animal world. Scientists have found that monkeys prefer to use one of their hands more than the other—but it can be either hand. There are many bright right-handed monkeys as there are left-handed ones. Next time you visit the zoo, watch the monkeys carefully. You'll see that some of them will prefer to swing from their right hands and others will use their left hands. But most human beings use their right hands better and this makes life difficult for those who prefer to use their left hands. We live in a right-handed world.

Questions 17 to 20 are based on the passage you have just heard.

17. About how many people are right-handed out of 100?

18. At what age can we tell whether a baby is right-handed or left-handed?

19. What have scientists learned about monkeys?

20. Which of the following is true according to the passage?

【试题解析】

第一部分　听力理解

1. 正确答案:D。明天的温度是零上几度,因此很冷。

2. 正确答案:B。对话涉及还书日期,所以是在图书馆。

3. 正确答案:C。男士说:"乘飞机使我紧张。"他宁可坐巴士。

4. 正确答案:B。男士说:"尽管小的那套便宜,但大的那套物有所值。"

5. 正确答案:B。售票员说"火车要晚点一个半小时",而正点是9:15。因此要10:45到。

6. 正确答案:B。录音中提到"她已在两天内完成",即很快就完成了。

7. 正确答案:D。她说秋季大部分时候潮湿又冷,所以她不喜欢它。

8. 正确答案:D。因为他一点都不懂这种比赛,所以他不会去看。can't stand(doing) sth. 指无法忍受(做)某事。

9. 正确答案:B。录音中谈到"为什么你们不一起练习对话"。

10. 正确答案:D。男士说"我们本该在20分钟前就与Alice碰面"。所以他们已迟到。

11. 正确答案:C。Allen是位艺术家。虽然不很富有,但很仁慈,乐于助人。

12. 正确答案:C。他把身上仅剩的一点钱给了第一个乞丐,只好让第二个乞丐替他付账。

13. 正确答案:D。因为他本来想请乞丐吃饭,最后却是乞丐付的钱,因此他很不高兴。

14. 正确答案:C。录音中谈到鳄鱼喜欢吃马肉。

15. 正确答案:B。录音中谈到大猴子的食物跟人差不多。

16. 正确答案:B。全文主要讨论的是对动物园中不同动物的饲养。

17. 正确答案:A。录音中谈到左撇子的人数约为5%,则右撇子的人数为95%。

18. 正确答案:B。2岁,即24个月。

19. 正确答案:D。录音中谈到使用左手与右手的猴子同样多。

20. 正确答案:D。录音中最后一句谈到"我们生活在右手的世界中"。

第二部分　词　汇

21. 正确答案:C。句意为：当今许多年轻人梦想一夜暴富和成名。
overnight 一夜之间。其他三种均无此搭配用法。例:He is nothing overnight. 他一夜之间什么都没有了。

22. 正确答案:A。句意为：坦率地说,在讨论中我不想冒犯你。
offend 冒犯／object 反对(后跟介词 to)／deliver 发送,运送／destroy 摧毁。例:He was afraid of offending anyone. 他怕得罪人。Do you object to my drinking? 你反对我喝酒吗? When shall we deliver the goods? 我们什么时候送货? The house was completely destroyed in the earthquake. 这栋房子在地震中被彻底摧毁了。

23. 正确答案:B。句意为：Jane尽管只读了几遍,就能背诵这首诗了。
learn sth. by heart 是固定用法,意为"记住"。例:You should learn some Tang poems by heart. 你应背诵一些唐诗。

24. 正确答案:A。句意为：她在课堂听课时,常在页边空白处做笔记。
margin 页边空白处 ／border 边界(尤指一国边界)／surface 表面／boundary 边界(主要指某一区域的边界)。例:Start from the margin when you use block-style in writing. 当你用平头式格式写作时,要顶格写。Nobody is allowed to smuggle goods across a border. 任何人不许越境走私。One never gets below the surface with him. 无人能洞察他的内心。Let's mark the boundaries of the football field. 让我们画出足球场的边界。

25. 正确答案:D。句意为：我们都相信他在游泳和跳水上是出类拔萃的。
understanding 理解,理解力／undergoing 经历,遭受(不尽如人意的事)／outlooking (无此词形)／outstanding 出类拔萃的。例:There is an understanding between us that we will not sell to each other's customers. 我们有个协议,不向对方的顾客出售货物。I hope that I

shall never again have to undergo such an unpleasant experience. 我希望我永远不会再遭遇这种不愉快的经历。His war record was outstanding. 他战功卓著。

26. 正确答案:C。句意为：我们镇的这个地方已被工业垃圾深度污染了。
populate 移民于,在……安家落户 / possess 拥有,占有 / pollute 污染 / process 加工。例:Convicts from France were sent to populate the islands. 一些来自法国的罪犯被送到这些岛上居住。The family possess a large amount of wealth. 这户人家拥有大量财富。The city has been polluted. 这个城市已被污染了。They are processing leather to make it softer. 他们加工皮革使之更柔软些。

27. 正确答案:D。句意为：在一些山区,仍有数以千计的居民生活在贫困中。
gravity 严肃,庄重 / responsibility 责任 / opportunity 机会 / poverty 贫困 (前常用介词 in)。

28. 正确答案:C。句意为：在我上次去大连商务旅行时,海浪翻腾,许多乘客都吐了。
shaky 摇晃的,发抖的 / tough 强硬的,棘手的 / rough 粗糙的,(海浪)汹涌的 / shivering 颤抖,(船帆)迎风飘动。例:I was nervous and a bit shaky. 我紧张得有点发抖。She is a tough old lady. 她是位能吃苦耐劳的老妇人。A jeep is ideal for driving over rough terrain. 吉普车是在崎岖不平的地带行驶的理想工具。The child shivered from the cold. 这孩子冷得发抖。

29. 正确答案:B。句意为:这座城市近来发生了如此多的变化,简直就认不出来了。
lastly 最后,终于(副词) / lately 最近,近来(副词) / late 迟到(形容词) / later 以后的,较晚的(形容词)。

30. 正确答案:D。句意为:下个月开始,这个协议就生效了。
take place 发生 / take position(无此搭配用法。但可以说 take a position 摆出一种姿势) / take charge 负责,掌管 / take effect 生效。例:The Great Cultural Revolution took place in 1966. "文化大革命"发生在 1966 年。She was appointed to take charge of the advertising. 她被任命负责广告业务。The contract will take effect next month. 协议下月生效。

31. 正确答案:A。句意为：一些有机体会使食物变质,引起食物中毒。
spoil (使食物)变坏,宠坏(某人) / spare 节省,节俭 / starve 饥饿 / spill 溢出,溅。例:The meat will spoil if we keep it any longer. 这肉再放下去就要坏了。I will spare no efforts to bring about a conciliation with her. 我要不遗余力地争取与她和解。They got lost in the desert and starved to death. 他们在沙漠中迷了路,饿死了。The girl was walking very fast and spilled the milk in her bottle. 姑娘走得太快,把瓶中的牛奶溅了出来。

32. 正确答案:B。句意为:这份文件应在律师到场时签。
appearance 外貌,外观 / presence 出席,在场(in one's presence 某人在场时,当着某人的面) / reference 参考(for your reference 供你参考) / experience 经验。例:In the presence of two witnesses he signed his name. 他当着两个证人的面签了名。

33. 正确答案:C。句意为:一些老读者对她最近发表的爱情小说提出了激烈的批评。
cruel 残酷的 / crazy 疯的 / critical 批评的,挑剔的 / crude 原始的,粗鲁的。例:Don't be so cruel. 不要这样残忍。Don't be so crazy. 不要这样疯。Don't be so critical. 不要一味批评。He is critical of my work. 他对我的工作很挑剔。It was crude of him to say that. 他那样说太粗鲁了。

34. 正确答案:B。句意为:立春那天去室外采鲜花是这个国家的一种习俗。

habit(个人的)习惯／custom(民族的)习俗／action 行动／movement 移动。

35. 正确答案:A。句意为:她无法理解这个问题,原因在于有太多的技术术语。
result from 起因于／result by（无此搭配用法）／result in 导致／result at(无此搭配用法)。
例:It is said that the scar in his face resulted from an accident. 据说他脸上的伤疤是由一场事故造成的。His carelessness resulted in his failure. 他的粗心导致了失败。

36. 正确答案:B。句意为:然后,医生量了量我的体温,并摸了摸我的脉搏。
take ones temperature 量体温(为固定用法)。

37. 正确答案:A。句意为:我申请了这份工作,但他们拒绝了我,因为我不懂德语。
turn sb. down 拒绝某人(为固定用法)。

38. 正确答案:C。句意为:对于您的礼物,我代表我母亲写信向您致谢。
in memory of 为了纪念……／on behalf of 代表／with respect to 关于／on account of 因为,由于。例:The film was shot in memory of the great heroin. 这部电影是为纪念这位女英雄而拍的。I'd like to express my great appreciation to you on behalf of the Chairman of the board. 我谨代表董事长向你表示深深的感谢。I'd like to say a few words with respect to the matter. 关于这件事,我想说几句。On account of his youth he was not allowed to take the advanced course. 他因为年轻,未被批准上高级课程。

39. 正确答案:D。句意为:新的考试制度生效后,会出现崭新的局面。
rise 升起,起身(多用作不及物动词,主语往往是具体的人或事)／raise 举起,养育(多用作及物动词)／awake 醒着的(形容词,多用作表语)／arise 出现,发生(不及物动词,常用于较抽象的主语之后)。

40. 正确答案:D。句意为:研究表明,如果孩子遭受暴力,他们会变得好斗或神经质。
react 反应／relate 相关,相联系／expand 扩张／expose 使暴露,使遭受。例:How did he react to your suggestions. 他对你的建议反应如何? The two events were related to each other. 这两个事件相互联系。The business of the company is expanding to the north part of the country. 这个公司的业务正向国家的北方地区扩展。Don't expose your skin to the sun. 不要让皮肤受太阳曝晒。

第三部分　语法结构

41. 正确答案:A。句意为:你的一位亲戚这个周末就要来看你了,这是真的。
很清楚这句话表达的动作应发生在将来。will be coming 是将来进行时,表示将来某一时间正在进行的动作。这个时态常表示已安排好之事,给人一种期待之感,它一般表示离现在较近的将来,与表示将来的时间状语连用。例:I'll be taking my holidays soon. 我不久将要度假了。The train will be leaving in a second. 火车马上就开。

42. 正确答案:B。句意为:这是一年中最糟糕的时候。这个月迄今为止天天都下雨。
注意:如果句中出现 so far(迄今为止)这样的词组,时态皆要用完成时(或现在完成时或过去完成时)。例:So far, we have not met each other. 到现在为止,我们俩都没见过面。

43. 正确答案:C。句意为:住在农村意味着有一个更好的环境。
句中的谓语动词是 means(意味着),它前面的部分是主语。我们知道,动名词可以作主语,动名词的形态就是动词＋ing。例:Seeing is believing. 百闻不如一见。Saving is having. 节约即是收入。

44. 正确答案:B。句意为:我认为与铁路相比,高速公路要好得多。

compared with 是固定词组,意为"与……比较而言",在句中常用作状语短语。例:Compared with the Western countries, China is only a developing country. 与西方国家相比,中国只是个发展中国家。

45. 正确答案:D。句意为:不管发生什么,在这个问题上我都会坚持自己的立场。

no matter what = whatever 是固定词组,意为"不管什么……"。no matter how = however 意为"不管怎样……"。例:No matter what he said, I didn't believe him. 无论他说什么,我都不信。

46. 正确答案:B。句意为:她能有一份工作以养家是很重要的。

此句为虚拟语气的一种用法。虚拟语气除主要用于条件状语从句外,还可用于主语从句。用于主语从句时,谓语用 should + 动词原形,而 should 可以省略。should 在此是助动词,本身并无实义。这种主语从句由连词 that 引导,常用在 It is (was) important(necessary, desirable, imperative, advisable, vital) that... 句型中。例:It is important that we should speak politely. 我们说话要有礼貌,这是很重要的。It is imperative that we should practice criticism and self-criticism. 应当进行批评与自我批评。

47. 正确答案:C。句意为:自那以后,各种手段都尝试了,但都以失败告终。

means 意为"方式,手段",为可数名词。例:Which is the quickest means of travel? 旅行最快的交通工具是什么?

48. 正确答案:B。句意为:能说点英语是一回事,说一口好英语是另一回事。

it is one thing..., it is another...意为"……是一回事,……是另一回事"。

49. 正确答案:D。句意为:这间小卧室里家具太多了。

furniture 为不可数名词,后面不可加 s,动词也只能用单数。

50. 正确答案:A。句意为:这是我观看过的最令人振奋的球赛之一。

one of...为……之一。注意:在形容词最高级前一般都要用冠词 the。例:This is one of the most attractive novel I have read. 这是我看过的最引人入胜的小说之一。

51. 正确答案:D。句意为:只有博览群书才能拓宽你的思路。

only 位于句首并后跟状语时,全句要倒装。例:Only then did he understand it. 只有那时,他才明白。

52. 正确答案:D。句意为:在上星期那场地震中,他们的那幢新房子毁了。

have sth. done 意为"请别人(或其他因素)完成某件事"。例:I had that door painted only last week. 我上星期才请人将那门油漆过。

53. 正确答案:C。句意为:去年,Jack 比他姐姐挣的钱多两倍。他姐姐是合资公司的总经理。

as many/much(many 修饰可数名词,much 修饰不可数名词) as...与……一样多。例:The boys there are as many as the girls here. 那边的男孩与这儿的女孩一样多。The little boy can eat as much as an adult. 那个小男孩可以跟一个成人吃得一样多。在 as many/much as...前加倍数,如 twice as many/much as...表示多出一倍,three times as many/much as...表示多出两倍等。例:The population in Shanghai is twice as much as that in Hangzhou. 上海的人口比杭州的多一倍。

54. 正确答案:A。句意为:你本该昨晚就完成你的家庭作业,但你却没有。

ought to = should,当它接现在完成时,表示"本来应该已经……,而却没有"。例:You

ought to have done something to help him. 你本应该做些事去帮助他。

55. 正确答案:A。句意为:我将推迟动手写论文的时间,直到我收集了足够的主题信息。

postpone doing sth. 是习惯用法。例:They postponed leaving because of the weather. 由于气候原因,他们推迟了离开的时间。

56. 正确答案:A。句意为:"John 认为你的决定怎样?""我真的想一个人去那儿,他觉得难以置信。"

find it impossible to believe...其中谓语动词是 find, 宾语是 to believe..., impossible 是宾语补足语,但因为宾语太长,放在中间结构失衡,所以用 it 作形式宾语。例:I think it unbelievable for him to buy the house by himself. 我认为他自己买下这栋房子实在不可思议。

57. 正确答案:B。句意为:没人敢想像那座城离这里只一夜路程。它好像是在另外一个世界。

as though = as if 好像(后跟从句,要用虚拟语气)。虚拟语气表示所说的话只是一种主观的愿望、假想和建议等。在 as though/ as if 虚拟语句中,从句的时态是更退一步的,如果与现在事实相反,从句的动词要用过去式。如果与过去事实相反,则从句用过去完成式。例:He looked as if /as though he had not slept. 他看样子好像没睡过觉。You sound as if / as though you were angry. 你这话听来仿佛是生气了。

58. 正确答案:C。句意为:Frank 是那种人们都喜欢与之交朋友的人。

make friends with sb. 同某人交朋友(为固定用法)。

59. 正确答案:B。句意为:大体说来,现在老年人的健康比前面几代要好。

在将两个同样的事物进行比较时,可用 that/those 来代替前面已出现过的被比较的事物。例:The weather of Beijing is colder than that of Shanghai. 北京的天气比上海的冷。The children of this kindergarten are better taken care of than those of that kindergarten. 这个幼儿园的孩子比那个幼儿园的孩子照顾得好。

be superior to... 为固定用法,意为"比……要好"。注意不要再用比较级。

60. 正确答案:B。句意为:我们到了房顶上。从那儿,我们可以很好地观看大游行。

定语从句与先行词(被定语从句修饰的词)或句子用逗号隔开时,这样的定语从句叫作非限制性定语从句,它与先行词或被修饰的句子关系比较松散,只是为了补充说明情况。例:Water, which is a clear liquid, has many uses. 水是一种清澈的液体,有许多用途。有时,定语从句的引导词(即关系代词)还会跟在一个介词的后面,作介词宾语。例:This is the book for which you asked. 这是你所要的书。

第四部分 阅读理解

第一篇短文参考译文及语言注释

1973 年 5 月 29 日,一位名叫 Thomas Bradley 的黑人被选为洛杉矶市市长。洛杉矶是美国的第三大城市,有 300 万人口,其中约 16% 为黑人。

这一选举结果上了美国(所有大小)报纸的头条。以下是一家主要报纸对此事作的报道:黑人 Bradley 击败 Torty 当选洛杉矶市长——他赢得了 56% 的选票。

Bradley 将此次胜利称为"梦想的实现"。在他童年和青年,人们总是这样告诉他,"你做不了这个,你升不上那个位置,因为你是个黑人"。尽管如此,他终于打败了一个已连任三届的市长,取得了决定性的胜利。Bradley 赢得了 56.3% 的选票,Yorty 获得了 43.7% 的选票。

洛杉矶的选民们有很多机会判断 Thomas Bradley,并形成看法。他作为得克萨斯州一位贫穷农民的儿子,在 1940 年成为一名洛杉矶警员。在警察局的 21 年间,他通过上夜校获得了法学学位。10 年前,他被选入市议会。在洛杉矶选举期间,美国其他三个城市已有了黑人市长。但这些城市的人口都比不过洛杉矶。此外,这些城市的黑人比例比洛杉矶大得多。当 Carl Stokes 在 1967 年被选为克里夫兰市市长时,这个地处俄亥俄州的城市里,黑人占 30.6%。同年,Richard Hatcher 被选为印第安纳州加里市市长时,这个市的黑人占总人口的 55%。1970 年,当 Kenneth Glibson 被选为新泽西州纽沃克市市长时,这个市的黑人占总人口的 60%。因此,这些城市的市长由黑人当选并不令人十分惊奇。

在洛杉矶,成千上万的白人选民投了 Thomas Bradley 的票,因为他们相信他会比白人候选人出色。Bradley 在洛杉矶度过了他 55 年生涯中的 48 年。4 年前,Bradley 在市长选举中败给了 Yorty。这次,他赢了。

keep telling him 不断地告诉他。form an opinion of sb. 形成对某人的看法。a law degree 法学学位。city council 市议会。

试题解答

61. 正确答案:B。短文第三段最后一句谈到"Bradley 得了 56.3% 的选票"。

62. 正确答案:A。从短文第一段我们可以了解到,洛杉矶是美国第三大城市,黑人只占该市总人口的 16%。

63. 正确答案:D。从第四段便可知答案。

64. 正确答案:C。从第四段可知,他从事公共服务事业——警察工作已 21 年。公民们应对他比较了解。

65. 正确答案:B。短文最后一段第一句解答了这个问题。

第二篇短文参考译文及语言注释

美国每年要产生 40 亿吨的固体垃圾。90% 以上是农业和矿产垃圾,约 3% 是工业垃圾。2.5 亿吨垃圾来自家庭、学校、写字楼、商店和医院。

这些金属、纸、食物、塑料、橡胶和玻璃的大杂烩,似乎对任何人都没有一点用了。

是这样吗? 国内各地众多的尝试表明:新技术如果使用适当,也许在将来某一天会将成百万吨的垃圾变成具有新用途的绝佳原材料的来源。

人们已着手几个新项目,研究通过 pyrolysis(一种可将垃圾分解成具有经济价值的基本化学物、液体和气体的系统)处理垃圾的可能性。在佛罗里达,有一种特殊的管道系统,可自动将垃圾运输到一个中央采集楼里。

总的说来,人们在尝试很多新想法,但似乎还未找到一个各处都适用的方法,因此这种尝试还是需要的。

但是,在真正取得成果前,还需要解决许多经济与社会难题。再生材料能与新材料相媲美吗? 要推进资源再生工作,还需要有什么激励措施呢? 居民会愿意支付改换垃圾系统的费用吗?

be composed of . . . 由……组成。This mass of metals, paper..., which is all mixed together, seems of no earthly use to anyone. 此句由 which 引导一个非限制性定语从句。recovered materials 再生材料。compete with 与……竞争。

试题解答

66. 正确答案:B。文章第一段解答了这个问题。

67. 正确答案:A。根据上下文判断。因为前面一句谈到"这些金属、纸、食物、塑料、橡胶和玻璃的大杂烩,似乎对任何人都没有一点用了"。

68. 正确答案:B。文章中已对 pyrolysis 的概念作了解释,是一种"可将垃圾分解成具有经济价值的基本化学物、液体和气体的系统"。

69. 正确答案:C。倒数第二段的这句话"人们在尝试很多新想法,但似乎还未找到一个各处都适用的方法,因此这种尝试还是需要的"解答了这个问题。

70. 正确答案:D。文章最后一句"居民会愿意支付改换垃圾系统的费用吗?"说明作者抱怀疑态度。

第三篇短文参考译文及语言注释

Kate 是一位八年级学生。她在数学课上总有许多问题,直到老师打断她。"老师说我总拿我的问题去困扰其他孩子,"Kate 回忆道,"当男孩子问问题时,老师要认真对待得多。"

你也许认为这种明显的歧视现在已不存在了。但是 Esther Greenglass,这位多伦多市约克大学的心理学教授说,近期的许多研究发现,关于自信与成功,女孩们似乎面对的仍是一些混乱的信息。这会打击女孩们的自尊,阻碍她们去开发潜质。

在十一二岁,当女孩子进入青春期并进一步了解男孩子时,这个问题更严重了。许多女孩子的成绩滑坡,她们的自尊也一起失落。"女孩们由此以为,如果你要得人青睐,你不可以太聪明,因为男孩会不喜欢你。"Greenglass 说。他已写作了大量内容涉及性别角色与歧视的著作。

通常的情况是,女孩子也感觉到男孩子被认为更能干。美国的研究表明,除非老师们已进修了有关课程,有了较高的认识水平,否则老师提问时,总用眼光接触那些男孩子。据 Greenglass 说,更糟的是,你可以在许多加拿大学校的旧教科书上发现根本就缺乏具有榜样作用的女性。

女孩子的态度受到了怎样的影响呢?研究表明,男孩子通常把他们的成功归功于自身高超的能力,而女孩子则将成功归结于运气。如果男孩子遇到挫败,他们倾向于将失败归罪于一些外在因素;若女孩子失败了,她们则责怪自己缺乏能力。男孩子更可能去作第二次成功尝试。

by now 到现在为止。句子一般要用完成时。be faced with... 面对……。self-esteem 自尊。sense 感觉,后可跟宾语从句。make eye contact with... 与……目光接触。raise one's level of awareness 提高他们的认识水平。Adding to the problem, according to..., is the lack of female role models in old textbooks still found in many Canadian schools. 此句可以这样改:The lack of female role models in old textbooks <u>still found in many Canadian schools</u> is adding to the problem. 句中划线部分是过去分词短语作定语修饰 the lack of female role models。

试题解答

71. 正确答案:C。文章第一段,那个女孩谈到"当男孩子问问题时,老师要认真对待得多"。

72. 正确答案:C。第四段最后一句谈到"更糟的是,你可以在许多加拿大学校的旧教科书上发现根本就缺乏具有榜样作用的女性"。

73. 正确答案:A。文章第四段有一句谈到"老师们问问题时,总用眼光接触那些男孩子"。

74. 正确答案:A。文章最后一段解答了这个问题。

75. 正确答案:D。根据文章意思,"性别角色与歧视"是最好的标题。

第五部分　英译汉

76. 在许多公司(企业),计算机已在很大程度上取代了日常文书工作,因为它们快速、灵活而准确(且不出错)。

77. 而且即便他们被抓获(发现),也难以惩罚他们;因为没有证人,通常也没有证据。

78. 每当某位被她盗用了款项的客户质疑其账户的余额时,(这位)出纳则谎称(声称)是电脑出了差错,然后用其他客户账户上的钱补足缺额。

79. 最近,一家大公司解雇了一位职员。解聘的理由涉及他的人品(私生活)而非其工作表现。

80. 我在想那些真正的专家——那些真正了解计算机工作原理的人——在做些什么。

第六部分　汉译英

81. I can hardly breathe. Would you mind my(me) opening the windows?

82. You should combine theory with practice and develop the ability to use the language.

83. He will always remember the day (when) his hometown was liberated.

84. To our surprise, he gave up (should give up) the opportunity to get a promotion and a pay raise.

85. It is certain that the Olympics will bring thousands of visitors from home and abroad to Beijing.

2003 年 1 月浙江省大学英语三级考试试卷

Part I　Listening Comprehension

Section A

Directions: *In this section, you will hear 10 short conversations. At the end of each conversation, a question will be asked about what was said. You will hear the conversation and the question only once. After each question there will be a pause. During the pause, you must read the four choices marked A), B), C) and D), and decide which is the best answer. Then mark the corresponding letter on the Answer Sheet with a single line through the center.*

1. A) At the railway station.　　　　B) At the airport.
   C) At a restaurant.　　　　　　　D) At a movie theater.

2. A) He is sick.　　　　　　　　　B) He becomes worse now.
   C) He is stronger than others.　　D) He has not fully recovered.

3. A) She can sew.　　　　　　　　B) She is beautiful.
   C) She can cook.　　　　　　　　D) She is a model.

4. A) It needs more stamps.
   B) It is too heavy to carry.
   C) She should return it to the postman.
   D) She should take it to the post office.

5. A) The bus will not arrive.
   B) The bus will arrive at 12.
   C) The bus will arrive later than expected.
   D) The bridge is being repaired.

6. A) Someone gave it to him.　　　B) He bought it on his birthday.
   C) He got it as a prize.　　　　　D) He doesn't remember where he got it.

7. A) Write an article.　　　　　　B) Take a vacation.
   C) Go on a business trip.　　　　D) Change his plan.

8. A) There are few museums in New York.
   B) Museums in New York are wonderful.
   C) There is a lot to see in New York.
   D) The man studies in New York.

9. A) Singing loudly.　　　　　　　B) Talking to someone.
   C) Doing the washing.　　　　　　D) Playing the music loudly.

10. A) 15.
    C) 35.

    B) 25.
    D) 45.

Section B

Directions: *In this section, you will hear 3 short passages. The passages will be read twice. At the end of each passage, you will hear some questions, which will be read only once. After you hear a question, you must choose the best answer from the four choices marked A), B), C) and D). Then mark the corresponding letter on the Answer Sheet with a single line through the center.*

Passage One

Questions 11 to 13 are based on the passage you have just heard.

11. A) How ice cream was discovered in America.

    B) How ice cream was developed over the years.

    C) How popular ice cream is in Europe.

    D) How ice cream reached England.

12. A) The Roman Emperor Nero.
    C) Some Chinese.

    B) Traveler Marco Polo.
    D) King Charles I.

13. A) Popular.
    C) Disappointing.

    B) Harmful.
    D) Valuable.

Passage Two

Questions 14 to 16 are based on the passage you have just heard.

14. A) Before the First World War.
    C) During the First World War.

    B) After the First World War.
    D) Before the Second World War.

15. A) O and B.
    C) A and B.

    B) O and A.
    D) O and AB.

16. A) How Blood Types Were Discovered.

    B) Different Blood Types.

    C) A Blood Test Is Important for Patients.

    D) What Blood Types Most People Have.

Passage Three

Questions 17 to 20 are based on the passage you have just heard.

17. A) A school teacher.
    C) A college student.

    B) A high school student.
    D) A factory worker.

18. A) The door was locked.
    C) All windows were removed.

    B) All the furniture was taken away.
    D) The police were called in.

19. A) He came from a farmer's family.

    B) He was born and brought up in a city.

C) He liked playing tricks on girls.

D) He was always friendly to others.

20. A) That Ted's friends laughed at her.

B) That she could not talk to Ted.

C) That there was no furniture in the room.

D) That the door of his room had been removed.

Part II   Vocabulary

Directions: *There are 20 incomplete sentences in this part. For each sentence there are four choices marked A), B), C) and D). Choose the ONE answer that best completes the sentence. Then mark the corresponding letter on the Answer Sheet with a single line through the center.*

21. Tired of the city, they _____ the woods and the country.

A) gave up   B) longed for

C) made to   D) looked into

22. All of the visitors were _____ that the little boy could walk on his hands.

A) advanced   B) exhausted

C) supposed   D) amazed

23. Alice is a shy girl. She never gets _____ in quarrels in the class.

A) connected   B) resolved

C) included   D) involved

24. His funny story brought about a _____ of laughter from the audience.

A) burst   B) flood

C) set   D) bunch

25. The fax is arguably the most useful machine to be _____ since the telephone.

A) discovered   B) founded

C) invented   D) recalled

26. They changed the whole _____ of the house just by painting it.

A) appearance   B) figure

C) size   D) surface

27. The plant may grow to a height of several meters, _____ on soil conditions.

A) depending   B) deciding

C) according   D) providing

28. The child looks very much _____ his mother.

A) same   B) like

C) similar   D) alike

29. There was very little we could do _____ the circumstances.

A) on   B) at

C) below   D) under

30. I know this job of mine is not well paid, but, _____, I don't have to work long hours.
    A) of course   B) on the contrary
    C) by the way   D) on the other hand

31. What a terrible experience! _____, you're safe. That's the main thing.
    A) Anyway   B) In general
    C) In short   D) Therefore

32. We are glad that the _____ of the highway was completed ahead of schedule.
    A) instruction   B) institution
    C) construction   D) composition

33. Our main _____ is that the health of the employees will be at risk.
    A) disgust   B) delight
    C) relief   D) concern

34. I have no idea that so many of you were _____ to my proposal.
    A) assumed   B) opposed
    C) regarded   D) trusted

35. In our culture, it's the _____ for the bride's father to pay for the wedding.
    A) condition   B) conduct
    C) custom   D) content

36. That young man was _____ of stealing money from a woman on the bus.
    A) charged   B) scolded
    C) accused   D) blamed

37. John _____ the man through the streets to the railway station.
    A) guided   B) pointed
    C) related   D) acted

38. The detective went from house to house, _____ whether anyone had seen the lost boy.
    A) requiring   B) inquiring
    C) demanding   D) searching

39. That movie is a failure. I found the cinema _____ empty this evening.
    A) practically   B) terribly
    C) probably   D) thoroughly

40. I heard that several students _____ of the course after three weeks.
    A) put out   B) left out
    C) dropped out   D) drove out

Part III Structure

Directions: *There are 20 incomplete sentences in this part. For each sentence there are four choices marked A), B), C) and D). Choose the ONE answer that best completes the sentence. Then mark the corresponding letter on the Answer Sheet with a single line through the center.*

41. Generally, a good lawyer _____ to be fair and sound in his judgment.
    A) is believed   B) believe
    C) is believing   D) believes
42. Only when you see the importance of learning English, _____ work hard at it.
    A) you will   B) you would
    C) would you   D) will you
43. He is often singled out for praise, for his teacher is _____ his homework.
    A) satisfied for   B) satisfying for
    C) satisfying with   D) satisfied with
44. I am not interested in mathematics, for _____ too abstract.
    A) they are   B) what is
    C) it is   D) which is
45. The doctor _____ in the poverty-stricken village was popular with the villagers.
    A) settled down   B) which settled down
    C) who settled down   D) settling down
46. She was _____ that her presence was scarcely noticed.
    A) a so quiet girl   B) so quiet girl
    C) so quiet a girl   D) a such quiet girl
47. Jack failed his chemistry test again. He _____ spent more time in the lab.
    A) must have   B) should be
    C) must be   D) should have
48. The judge thought that Paul, for some reason or other, _____ the truth.
    A) has held back   B) holds back
    C) had held back   D) had been held back
49. He has been to many countries, _____.
    A) including the U.S., the France and Britain
    B) including U.S., the France and Britain
    C) including U.S., France and the Britain
    D) including the U.S., France and Britain
50. Though the electric car is technically possible, _____ not very profitable.
    A) it is   B) but it is
    C) and it is   D) however it is
51. My parents always waited up for me, _____ I got home.
    A) no matter what time   B) however what time
    C) no matter how time   D) whatever how time
52. The teachers all recommended that German _____ the first elective subject in this semester.
    A) be   B) must be
    C) is   D) was
53. It is about time that you _____ down to business.

A) must get   B) got

C) getting   D) will get

54. Maybe I'll _____ the MA program after graduating from college.

   A) consider to take   B) consider to taking

   C) consider taking   D) consider on taking

55. He stayed in Hangzhou for five days, _____ he toured all the major scenic spots.

   A) during which   B) during when

   C) during the time   D) during what

56. At the sad parting she said, "_____."

   A) I hope you to succeed   B) I wish you succeed

   C) I hope you success   D) I wish you success

57. The Japanese cook and dine in much the same way _____ we Chinese do.

   A) as   B) where

   C) like   D) than

58. _____ the secret is known to all, nobody will be interested in him any more.

   A) Before   B) Once

   C) Although   D) Unless

59. Paul never learned a foreign language, _____.

   A) he doesn't think he has to

   B) nor does he think he has to

   C) neither he thinks he has to

   D) he thinks he has not to, either

60. _____, her heart was beating faster and faster.

   A) She listening to the coming footsteps

   B) As she listened to the coming footsteps

   C) When listening to the coming footsteps

   D) To the coming footsteps as she listened

Part IV   Reading Comprehension

Directions: *There are 3 passages in this part. Each passage is followed by some questions or unfinished statements. For each of them there are four choices marked A), B), C) and D). You should decide on the best choice and mark the corresponding letter on the Answer Sheet with a single line through the center.*

Passage One

Questions 61 to 65 are based on the following passage:

In many countries there is a fixed charge for personal services. A certain percentage may be added to the bill at a hotel or restaurant "for the service". In other places the customer may be expected to give a tip, or a small amount of money, as a sign of appreciation whenever services are performed. In the United States there is no consistent practice with regard to tipping. The practice is more common in a large city than in a small town. A Native American may often be in doubt about when and how much to tip when he is in a city that is strange to him. In general, however, a tip is expected by the porter who carries you baggage, by taxi drivers (except, perhaps, in small towns), and by those who serve you in hotels and restaurants.

When you pick up your incoming luggage at an airport, you may tip the man who takes it to the taxi or airport bus. He usually expects 35 cents a bag for his service. In some cities the taxi that takes you to your hotel may have one meter that shows the cost of the trip and another that shows a fixed charge, usually about 20 cents, for "extra". In some cities the taxi driver may expect a tip in addition to the "extra", especially if he carries your suitcase. If no "extra" is charged, a tip is usually given. Hotels usually do not have a service charge, though there are places where *one* is added. It is customary, however, to give something to the porter who carries your suitcases and shows you to your room. If in doubt, 25 cents for each bag he carries is satisfactory. In a restaurant you generally leave about 15 percent of the bill in small change on the table as a tip for the person who has served you. A service charge is generally not included except in some of the larger, more expensive places. If the order is small—a cup of coffee at a lunch counter, or something of the sort—a tip is not usually expected.

61. According to the passage, a tip is _____ for personal services.
   A) a sign of appreciation   B) a fixed charge
   C) the bill at a hotel or restaurant   D) an extra

62. A Native American _____.
   A) knows a lot about tipping
   B) does not often tip a stranger
   C) usually lives in a small town
   D) often works as a porter

63. The word "*one*" in Line 7, Paragraph 2, refers to _____.
   A) service charge   B) extra
   C) hotel   D) room service

64. If a porter carries three pieces of baggage for you, you are expected to give him _____ as a tip.
   A) 50 cents   B) 1 dollar
   C) 1.5 dollars   D) 5 dollars

65. We can learn from the passage that _____.
   A) all American taxi drivers are expected to be tipped
   B) people in small towns know more about tipping
   C) one has to tip a waiter no matter how small the order is
   D) people sometimes do not tip when they are not satisfied

Passage Two

Questions 66 to 70 are based on the following passage:

People are fascinated by robots. Some of them look like mechanical dolls to play with. Most of them look like other machines of today's technology.

One of the advantages of robots is that they can work in situations that are dangerous or harmful for human workers. For example, the continuous smell of paint has a harmful effect on painters, but it doesn't bother a robot. Robots can work in nuclear power plants and in undersea research stations that might be dangerous for humans.

There are robots in the plastics industry and in chemical industry and industrial equipment industries. One of the most common uses of robots is in automobile factories. They can do the heavy, unpleasant, or dangerous work. For example, a computer programmer writes a program that tells how much paint to use, how thick it must be, and the size of the car body. The robot does not waste any time or movements. It never becomes bored. It doesn't need a coffee break. It lasts 20 to 25 years.

Today's robots are simple-minded compared with the ones of the future. Researchers are now working on the sixth generation. These new robots will be able to take information from the environment. They will be able to see, using television camera for eyes. They will be able to touch and hear. Some computers can already understand *a limited vocabulary*. Researchers are trying to develop ones that can understand human speech. They will be able to understand voice commands and then respond.

The new robots will be able to move in more ways. They will have several arms, each will several fingers. The robot will be able to operate these arms and fingers by itself. It will be able to make complex decisions in a working environment.

66. Which of the following is an advantage of robots over human beings?

  A) Robots can be used to entertain people.

  B) Human beings do not smell harmful paints.

  C) Robots are not affected by harmful substances.

  D) Human beings cannot work undersea.

67. Where are robots most widely used in place of human workers?

  A) In a car factory.   B) In a software company.

  C) In a shoe factory.   D) In a big office.

68. Which of the following is true about future robots?

  A) They may be able to control human beings.

  B) They may be able to communicate with human beings.

  C) They will be more simple-minded than today's robots.

  D) They will be able to write computer programs.

69. What does the phrase "*a limited vocabulary*" in Line 4, Paragraph 4, mean?

  A) A fairly large number of words.

  B) A small number of words.

C) Much of human speech.

D) The basic structure of speech.

70. What can we conclude from the passage about the new robots?

A) They will behave more like humans.

B) They will move faster than humans.

C) They will be able to think like humans.

D) They will be more intelligent than humans.

Passage Three

Questions 71 to 75 are based on the following passage:

In some urban centers, workaholism is so common that people do not consider it unusual. They accept the lifestyle as normal. Government workers in Washington D.C., for example, frequently work sixty to seventy hours a week. They don't do this because they have to; they do it because they want to.

Workaholism can be a serious problem. Because true workaholics would rather work than do anything else, they probably don't know how to relax; that is, they might not enjoy movies, sports, or other types of entertainment. Most of all, they hate to sit and do nothing. The lives of workaholics are usually stressful, and this tension and worry can cause health problems such as heart attacks or stomach disorders. In addition, typical workaholics don't pay much attention to their families. They spend little time with their children, and their marriages may end in divorce.

Is workaholism always dangerous? Perhaps not. There are, certainly, people who work well under stress. Some studies show that many workaholics have great energy and interest in life. Their work is so pleasurable that they are actually very happy. For most workaholics, work and entertainment are the same thing. Their jobs provide them with a challenge; this keeps them busy and creative.

Why do workaholics enjoy their jobs so much? There are several advantages to work. Of course, it provides people with paychecks, and this is important. But it offers more than financial security. It provides people with self-confidence; they have a feeling of satisfaction when they've produced a challenging piece of work and are able to say, "I made that." Psychologists claim that work gives people an *identity*, through participation in work, they get a sense of self and individualism. In addition, most jobs provide people with a socially acceptable way to meet others.

71. A workaholic is a person who _____.

A) often behaves in a strange way

B) is often forced to work overtime

C) tends to enjoy working long hours

D) tends to hold higher positions than others

72. The life of a typical workaholic can be described as _____.

A) relaxed   B) healthy

C) serious   D) tense

73. Workaholics regard work as all of the following EXCEPT _____?

    A) a source of happiness   B) a kind of entertainment

    C) a kind of challenge   D) a source of energy

74. The word "*identity*" in Line 5, Paragraph 4, is closest in meaning to _____?

    A) what makes a person feel confident

    B) what makes a person different from others

    C) what makes a person feel satisfied

    D) what makes a person socially acceptable

75. The last paragraph tells us mainly about _____.

    A) the positive side of workaholism

    B) psychological problems of workaholism

    C) the emotional challenge workaholics face

    D) social disapproval of workaholism

Part Ⅴ Translation from English into Chinese

Directions: *In this part there is a passage with 5 underlined sections, numbered 76 to 80. After reading the passage carefully, translate the underlined sections into Chinese. Remember to write your translation on the Translation Sheet.*

Americans' interest in spectator sports seems excessive and even obsessive to many foreign visitors. (76) Not all Americans are interested in sports, of course, but many are. And some seem interested in little else. Television networks spend millions of dollars arranging telecast sports events, and are constantly searching for new ways (for example, using computer graphics and hiring glamorous announcers and commentators) to make their coverage more appealing. Publications about sports sell widely. In the United States, professional athletes can become national heroes. (77) Some sports stars have become more widely recognized than any national leader other than the president. Some of them earn annual salaries in the millions of dollars.

(78) Nowhere else in the world are sports associated with colleges and universities in the way they are in the States. College sports, especially football, are conducted in an atmosphere of intense excitement. Games between teams classified as "major football powers" attract nationwide television audiences that number in the millions. There is a whole industry built on the manufacture and sale of badges, pennants, T-shirts, blankets, hats, and countless other items. Football and basketball coaches at major universities are paid higher salaries than the presidents of their institutions. Athletic department budgets are in the millions of dollars.

Black Americans are heavily overrepresented in the sports of baseball, football, and basketball. While blacks comprise about 12 per cent of the country's total population, they make up well over half of most college and professional football and basketball teams. (79) It is not unusual to see a basketball game in which all the players on the floor are black.

Foreign visitors—especially males—who plan to be in the United States for an extended period of time will enhance their ability to interact constructively with Americans if they take the trouble to learn about sports teams that have followings in the local area. (80) <u>Knowing some-thing about the games and the players improves the foreign visitor's chance of getting to know "average" Americans.</u>

Part Ⅵ Translation from Chinese into English

Directions: *In this part there are 5 sentences, numbered 81 to 85, in Chinese. Translate these sentences into English on the Translation Sheet.*

81. 你不应该让电脑游戏妨碍你的学习。

82. 上星期 Kelly 请我们出席她的婚礼,昨天我们收到了书面邀请。

83. 我不知道他为什么对宇宙会这么好奇。

84. 我们可得出这样的结论:公司的新计划是会取得成功的。

85. 正如这位专家所说的,哪里有水,哪里就有生命。

【听力录音文稿】

Section A

1. M: Good evening. I have a reservation for this evening's flight to Paris.

   W: Can I have your ticket, please?

   Q: What does the conversation most probably take place?

2. W: John, how are you? I heard you were sick.

   M: Yeah. But now I'm feeling better.

   Q: How is John now?

3. M: Your new dresses are beautiful. Where did you find them?

   W: Well, I made them myself.

   Q: What can we conclude about the woman from the conversation?

4. W: This letter was returned to me.

   M: That's because you didn't put enough postage on it.

   Q: What did the man tell the woman about the letter?

5. W: Excuse me. When will the 7:45 bus arrive?

   M: It's been delayed five hours because a bridge was broken.

   Q: What do we learn from this conversation?

6. W: Why are you returning this tie?

   M: I got it for my birthday, but I don't wear ties.

   Q: How did the man get the tie?

7. W: Are you still planning to write the article?

   M: Yes, but only after I get back from my business trip.

   Q: What will the man do first?

8. W: What a wonderful museum.

   M: Yeah, but you should see our museum in New York.

   Q: What do we learn about the man?

9. M: Look, I'm sorry to bother you about this, but that music's really loud.

   W: I didn't realize you could hear it.

   Q: What is the woman probably doing?

10. M: How many people will be coming to the meeting?

    W: We had to cross off fifteen names from our original list of fifty.

    Q: How many people will attend the meeting now?

Section B

Passage One

Most Americans think that ice cream is as American as baseball and apple pie. But ice cream was known long before America was discovered.

The Roman emperor Nero may have made a kind of ice cream. He hired hundreds of men to bring snow and ice from the mountains. He used it to make cold drinks. Traveler Marco Polo brought the methods of making cold and frozen milk from China.

Hundreds of years later, ice cream reached England. It is said that King Charles I enjoyed the food very much. There is a story that he ordered his cook to keep the methods of making ice cream a royal secret.

Today ice cream is known throughout the world. Americans alone eat more than two billion quarts a year.

Questions 11 to 13 are based on the passage you have just heard.

11. What is the main idea of the passage?

12. Who tried to make the way of making ice-cream a secret?

13. What does the passage say about ice cream in America?

Passage Two

It was during World War I that scientists discovered that there were different kinds of blood. They discovered that there were four types of blood. There are only four types of blood for all people in the world. In other words, all people are classed as belonging to one of the four groups. In the United States these blood groups are called type O, type A, type B, and type AB. About one half of all the people in the world belong to the type O blood group. Almost everyone else belongs to the type A group. Blood groups B and AB are quite small. So most people in the world have type O or type A blood.

Today, before a blood transfusion is given, a sample of blood is taken from the patient. This blood sample is sent to the laboratory for a test. This test will tell the doctor whether the patient has O, A, B, or AB blood.

Questions 14 to 16 are based on the passage you have just heard.

14. When did scientists discover the different types of blood?

15. Which blood types do most people have?

16. What is the best title for the passage?

Passage Three

The students at a certain university used to play tricks on each other when one of them was going to receive his first visit from a new girlfriend. Usually the trick was to take all the furniture out of the student's room, so that when his girlfriend arrived, there was nothing to sit on.

Ted Jones was a country boy who had never left his birthplace until his admission to the university. When he arrived there for the first time and heard about this behavior, he disliked it and announced to the other students, "I'm determined that that's not going to happen to me. I'm going to lock my door." His confident words were greeted with laughter by the other students.

When Ted brought his girlfriend to his room for the first time, he was astonished to find that all the furniture was there—but the door of his room was gone.

Questions 17 to 20 are based on the passage you have just heard.

17. Who was Ted Jones?

18. What was the usual trick?

19. What do we learn about Ted Jones?

20. What did Ted's girlfriend find at the end of the story?

【试题解析】

第一部分　听力理解

1. 正确答案：B。乘客说："我已订了今晚飞巴黎的航班。"

2. 正确答案：D。他说："现在感觉好些了。"言外之意还未完全恢复。

3. 正确答案：A。女士说这衣服是她自己做的。

4. 正确答案：A。信退回来了,因为邮资不够。

5. 正确答案：C。录音中说汽车将晚五小时到达。

6. 正确答案：A。他说这领带是有人作为生日礼物送给他的。

7. 正确答案：C。男士说他出差回来后才能写文章。

8. 正确答案：B。女士说："这博物馆真棒!"男士说："是的,但你应该去纽约的博物馆看看。"言外之意它更棒。

9. 正确答案：D。男士说："对不起,这音乐声实在太大了。"

10. 正确答案：C。原先50人,但要从名单中划去15人。现在应是35人。

11. 正确答案：B。整篇内容谈的是冰淇淋的发展史。

12. 正确答案：D。冰淇淋传到英国后,King Charles I 非常喜欢,将它作为宫廷秘方保存。

13. 正确答案：A。美国人一年要消费20亿夸脱的冰淇淋。

14. 正确答案：C。科学家是在第一次世界大战期间发现不同血型的。

15. 正确答案：B。最普遍的血型是O型和A型。

16. 正确答案:B。全文谈的是四种血型的事。

17. 正确答案:C。他是个大学新生。

18. 正确答案:B。恶作剧是,女朋友来时,宿舍的家具空空如也,连个坐的地方也没有。

19. 正确答案:A。他是个乡村孩子,从未离开过家。

20. 正确答案:D。当他第一次带女朋友来时,发现宿舍家具完整无缺,可房门却被人拆走了。

第二部分　词　　汇

21. 正确答案:B。句意为:他们已对城市厌倦,所以向往森林与乡村。
    give up 放弃 / long for 渴望 / made to(无此搭配用法) / look into 调查。

22. 正确答案:D。句意为:所有的客人都感到惊奇,那个小男孩能用手撑着走路。
    advanced 先进的,高级的 / exhausted 精疲力竭的 / supposed 假设的 / amazed 吃惊的。例:
    It is advanced in industrial nations. 在工业国里它领先。I feel exhausted after a day of hard
    working. 一天艰苦工作下来,我精疲力竭。You are supposed to report it to the police as
    soon as possible. 你应该尽快报告警方。I was so amazed to find her here. 看到她在这儿,我
    很吃惊。

23. 正确答案:D。Alice 是个害羞的女孩。她从不卷入班上的矛盾争吵中。
    get connected 接通,联系上 / get resolved 解决掉 / get included(很少这样用) / get involved
    卷入(纷争),陷入(麻烦)。

24. 正确答案:A。句意为:他讲的滑稽故事引来听众一阵笑声。
    a burst of laughter 一阵笑声(固定用法) / a flood of 大量 / a set of 一套 / a bunch of 一束
    (鲜花)。bring about 引来(固定用法)。例:Economic reforms have brought about many
    changes in the country. 改革给这个国家带来了很多变化。

25. 正确答案:C。句意为:毫无疑问传真是自电话以来最有用的发明。
    discover 发现 / found 建立,创建 / invent 发明 / recall 回忆。

26. 正确答案:A。句意为:他们将房子粉刷一新。
    appearance 外观,样子 / figure 体态,人形 / size 大小,尺寸 / surface 表面。

27. 正确答案:A。句意为:这种植物可能会长几米高,这取决于土壤的条件。
    depending on 取决于 / deciding on(就某事)作出决定 / according to 根据(后常跟 to ,不跟
    on) / providing on(无此搭配用法)。

28. 正确答案:B。句意为:这孩子看上去很像他母亲。
    look like. . .看上去像…… / look similar to 看上去与……相似 / be(look) alike 相像(alike
    形容词,只作表语,跟在 be 动词或系动词后面用;不能作介词用)。例:The two girls look
    like twins. 这两个女孩看上去像双胞胎。Gold looks in color similar to brass. 金看上去颜色
    与铜差不多。All music is alike to him because he has no ear for music. 所有音乐对他都一
    样,因为他对音乐没有鉴赏力。

29. 正确答案:D。句意为:在这样的环境下,我们几乎不能做什么。
    under the circumstances 在当时的环境(条件)下,为固定用法。

30. 正确答案:D。句意为:我知道我的这份工作报酬不高,但另一方面,我无需长时间工作。
    of course 当然 / on the contrary 相反地 / by the way 顺便说说 / on the other hand 另一方
    面。例:Does your back feel any better? On the contrary, it feels much worse. 你的背痛好点

了吗？相反,痛得厉害多了。On the one hand, she'd like to finish college; on the other hand, she'd like to get a job and earn some money. 一方面,她很想读完大学,另一方面,她又想去找个工作挣点钱。

31. 正确答案:A。句意为:这段经历真是太可怕了! 不管怎样,你已脱险。这是最主要的。
anyway 无论怎样,不管怎样 / in general 总体说来,一般来说 / in short 简而言之 / therefore 因此。例:Anyway, I'll meet you at the airport. 不管怎样,我还是要去机场接你。In general, the report sounds reasonable. 大体说来,这份报告听上去还合理。In short, we need money very much. Therefore, we shall raise it from every possible source. 简而言之,我们急需钱。因此,我们会通过各种途径筹集。

32. 正确答案:C。句意为:我们很高兴,高速公路的建设提前完工了。
instruction 教导,指导 / institution 机构,研究所 / construction 建设 / composition 写作,作品。例:This book gives instructions for making kites. 这本书教人如何做风筝。Library is a public institution. 图书馆是公益性机构。This road is under construction 这条路在建。Beethoven's compositions are undoubtedly among the world's greatest. 贝多芬的作品毫无疑问是最伟大的。

33. 正确答案:D。句意为:我们最担心的是雇员的健康会有危险。
disgust 讨厌的人(事) / delight 高兴 / relief 解除(痛苦) / concern 担心,关心的事。例:He returned downstairs in disgust. 他厌恶地转身下楼。He delighted the audience with his performance. 他以其表演使观众喜悦。It was a great relief to find that my family were all safe. 看到我的家人安然无恙,我感到极大的宽慰。It's no concern of mine. 此事与我无关。

34. 正确答案:B。句意为:我真没想到你们这么多人反对我的建议。
be opposed to sth. 反对某事。例:The people all over the world are opposed to the war. 全世界人民都反对战争。其余动词搭配上不通。

35. 正确答案:C。句意为:在我们的文化中,新娘的父亲支付婚礼费用是一种习俗。
condition 条件 / conduct 行为,表现 / custom (民族的)习俗 / content 内容。

36. 正确答案:C。句意为:那个年轻人被指控在公共汽车上偷窃妇女钱财。
be charged of (无此搭配用法,习惯用法是:be charged with sth.) / be scolded of 被责备,被责骂 / be accused of 被指控 / be blamed of(无此搭配用法,习惯用法是:blame sb. for sth.)。

37. 正确答案:A。句意为:John 引导那个人穿过马路走向火车站。
guide 为……领路,向导 / point 指点,指向 / relate 相关,相联系 / act 行动。

38. 正确答案:B。句意为:侦探一家家走访,询问是否有人看见失踪的男孩。
require 要求 / inquire 询问 / demand 要求 / search 寻求。例:What do you require of me? 你要求我什么? You can inquire about the price of the product. 你可以作产品询价。This work demands great patience. 这份工作需要很大的耐心。Scientists are still searching for a cure to the common cold. 科学家仍在寻找普通感冒的医治方法。

39. 正确答案:A。句意为:那个电影不受欢迎。我发现今晚电影院里空荡荡的。
practically 实际上的,事实上的 / terribly 十分地,厉害地 / probably 也许 / thoroughly 彻底地,完全地。

40. 正确答案:C。句意为:我听说三周以后一些学生退出了此课程。

put out 灭(火)／leave out 略去,排除／drop out 退出,脱离／drive out 驱逐 出。例:The firemen soon put the fire out. 消防队员很快就扑灭了火。Be sure not to leave out any detail. 不要遗漏任何细节。He had to drop out in his junior year because of his lung trouble. 由于患了肺病,他不得不在大学三年级退学。He was driven out of the country within 24 hours. 他在 24 小时内被驱逐出境。

第三部分 语法结构

41. 正确答案:A。句意为:人们认为大体说来一个好律师在判断上应该是公正合理的。
is believed to be ...认为是……(习惯用法)。例:She is believed to be a good lawyer. 人们认为她是好律师。

42. 正确答案:D。句意为:只有当你看见学习英语的重要性时,你才会刻苦学它。
only 位于句首并后跟状语时,全句需要倒装。例:Only then did he understand it. 只有那时,他才明白。

43. 正确答案:D。句意为:他常被表扬,因为老师对他的家庭作业很满意。
be satisfied with sth. or sb. 满意某事或者某人。be singled out for sth. 选出来作……。

44. 正确答案:C。句意为:我对数学不感兴趣,因为它太抽象了。
mathematics 数学(不可数,尽管词尾有 s)。

45. 正确答案:C。句意为:在贫困山村安家的那位医生受到了村民的喜爱。
settle down 落脚,安家。再则,因定语从句修饰的是人,所以引导词(关系代词)应为 who。be popular with sb. 受到某人喜爱(固定用法)。

46. 正确答案:C。句意为:她是个宁静似水的女孩,人们很少意识到她的存在。
so 的用法是:so+形容词/副词＋a＋名词。such 的用法是:such＋a＋形容词＋名词。

47. 正确答案:D。句意为:Jack 化学考试又不及格。他本来应多花些时间在实验室。
should＋现在完成时,表示"本来应该已经……,而却没有"。例:You should have done something to help him. 你本应该做些事去帮助他。

48. 正确答案:C。句意为:法官认为 Paul 由于种种原因,隐瞒了真相。
hold back 保守秘密,隐瞒。

49. 正确答案:D。句意为:他到过许多国家,包括美国、法国、英国。
除了 U.S. 之前要加冠词 the 外,其余选项中的国名前都不要加冠词。have been to 到过……。

50. 正确答案:A。句意为:尽管电子汽车在技术上是可行的,但它利润不高。
though 尽管……但是……。注意:书面语中用了 though,就不要再用 but。例:Though he hadn't stopped working all day, he wasn't tired. 尽管他整天不停地工作,但他并不感到累。

51. 正确答案:A。句意为:不管我多晚归来,我的父母总等我回来。
no matter what ＝ whatever 是一个固定词组,意为"不管什么……"。no matter how ＝ however,意为"不管怎样……"。例:No matter what he said, I didn't believe him. 无论他说什么,我都不信。wait up for 不上床睡觉以等待……的到来。

52. 正确答案:A。句意为:老师都建议德语为这学期的第一选修课。
此句是虚拟语气用于宾语从句。这类从句的主句谓语动词通常是表示建议、愿望、命令的动词,如 demand, suggest, propose, order, arrange, recommend 等;从句谓语用 should + 动词原形,should 通常省略。例:He suggested that we should leave early. 他建议我们早点动身。

53. 正确答案:B。句意为:是你该做正事的时候了。

   it is about time that ...是……的时候了,该……(固定用法)。这个句型中的 that 从句要用虚拟语气,常常用过去时或过去完成时。time 前可用形容词 high,about 等修饰,起强调语气的作用。例:It's about/ high time that she returned home. 是她该回家的时候了。It's about/high time we went to bed. 该睡觉了。get down to 开始认真着手处理(固定用法)。

54. 正确答案:C。句意为:也许大学毕业后,我会考虑读 MA 课程。

   consider doing sth. 考虑做某事。MA 指的是文科硕士,master of arts.

55. 正确答案:A。句意为:他在杭州逗留了五天。在五天中,他游遍了所有主要的风景点。

   定语从句与先行词(被定语从句修饰的词)或句子用逗号隔开时,这样的定语从句叫非限制性定语从句,它与先行词或被修饰的句子关系比较松散,只是为了补充说明情况。例:Water, which is a clear liquid, has many uses. 水是一种清澈的液体,有许多用途。有时,定语从句的引导词(即关系代词)还会跟在一个介词之后,作介词宾语。例:This is the book for which you asked. 这是你所要的书。注意,非限制性定语从句总是用 which 引导。

56. 正确答案:D。句意为:在伤感的告别会上,她说:"我祝你成功!"

   wish 后如跟宾语从句,从句常用 would + 动词原形。例:I wish you would stay a little longer. 我希望你再待一会儿。wish sb. success. 祝……成功(习惯用法)。

57. 正确答案:A。句意为:日本人在餐饮方面与中国人有很多相同之处。

   the same...as... 与……相同(固定搭配用法)。例:Robbie looked just the same as ever. Robbie 看上去总是那个模样。

58. 正确答案:B。句意为:一旦这个秘密公之于众,没人会对他感兴趣了。

   before 从前 / once 一旦 (后跟从句)/ although 尽管 / unless 除非。

59. 正确答案:B。句意为:Paul 从未学过外语。他也不认为该去学。

   nor, neither 用于否定句后,再引出另一个否定句,后一个否定句均要倒装。例:He didn't go, neither did she. 他没去,她也没去。He can't understand spoken Japanese. Nor can I. 他听不懂日语,我也听不懂。

60. 正确答案:B。句意为:当她听着越来越近的脚步声,她的心也越跳越快。

   注意:如果用过去分词或现在分词短语作状语,则它的真正主语应与主句的主语相一致。比如:如果我们选择 C,则 when listening to the coming footsteps 的真正主语是人(她),但主句的主语却是 her heart. 因而不能选这项。在这种情况下,用完整的状语从句来表达意思会清晰得多。

第四部分　阅读理解

第一篇短文参考译文及语言注释

   在许多国家,个人服务是要收取固定费用的。在酒店或餐馆的账单上,可能还要额外收取一定比例的"服务费"。在其他地方,客户可能要支付小费。小费是指对所接受服务表示谢意的一小笔钱。在美国,关于给小费,没有统一的做法。付小费在大城市比小城市普遍。当美国印第安人来到一座陌生的城市时,他们常常会为何时、该支付多少小费而不知所措。不过,一般说来,小费该付给替你搬运行李的行李工,付给出租车司机(也许小镇上的除外),付给酒店和餐馆为你服务的侍从。

当你在机场领取行李后,你或许应付小费给帮你将行李搬运到出租车或到机场大巴上的服务生。标准常常是每件35美分。在某些城市里,送你去酒店的出租车会有两个计程表,其中一个显示路程的花费,另一个显示固定的价目,通常是20美分,为"附加费"。在某些城市里,出租车除了收取"附加费"外,还应得到小费,特别当你带着大件行李时。如果不收"附加费",则就要付小费。酒店常常不收服务费,尽管也有些酒店收取。不过,通常的做法是,给帮你搬运行李并领路的行李工小费。如果你无法确定怎么付,以每件35美分计,就会令人满意。在餐馆里,你应在桌子上留下账单额的15%作为小费给服务生。除了一些大的、价格昂贵的场所会收取服务费,一般地方都不用服务费。如果你的消费很小,只是在正午的吧台上点了一杯咖啡什么的,则不用付小费了。

no consistent practice 没有统一的做法。with regarding to 关于。A Native American may often be in doubt about <u>when and how much to tip</u> when he is in a city that is strange to him. 句中划线部分为名词从句作介词宾语,由 when 引导,而后面的 when 和 how much 引导的是一个时间状语从句。in general 大体说来。In some cities the taxi <u>that takes you to your hotel</u> may have one meter <u>that shows the cost of the trip</u> and another <u>that shows a fixed charge</u>... 此句中有三个定语从句,分别由 that 引导。in addition to 除此之外。customary 通常的,为形容词。

试题解答

61. 正确答案:A。从文中可知答案。总是在你接受服务后,付给小费。

62. 正确答案:C。文章第一段提到付小费在大城市比小城市普遍。当美国印第安人来到一座陌生的城市时,他们常常会为支付多少小费而不知所措。

63. 正确答案:A。one 是单数代词,指代前面出现过的单数名词,这儿即为 a service charge。

64. 正确答案:B。文章第二段提到"小费标准常常是每件35美分"。如果是3件,则要1美元零5分。

65. 正确答案:D。前面三个选项都明显错误。

第二篇短文参考译文及语言注释

人们对机器人十分热衷。一些机器人看起来像机械玩具娃娃。大多数机器人看起来像现代技术生成的机器。

机器人的优点之一是它们可以在对工人来说危险、有害的环境下工作。比如,长期闻油漆味对油漆工来说会产生有害影响,但机器人则不会。机器人可以在核动力厂工作,在海下实验站工作。这些对人类来说都具有危险性。

在塑料业、化工业和工业设备行业中都有机器人。用机器人最多的一个地方是汽车制造厂。它们可干重活、令人厌烦的或危险的工作。比如,计算机程序员写出一个程序,说明用多少油漆,要多厚及车身的面积大小,机器人干起来不会浪费一点时间或动作。它也不会变得不耐烦。它不需要咖啡小憩,并能工作20至25年。

与未来的机器人比较,当今的机器人头脑简单,研究人员正在着手第六代机器人的研究。这些新机器人能从环境中获取信息。它们会把电视摄影机当作眼睛来看。它们会触摸,能听。一些机算机已经能够理解一定数量的词汇。研究人员正试图开发能理解人类语言的机器人。他们能理解声音指令并作出反应。

新的机器人可以多种方式移动。它们会有几个胳膊,每个胳膊上都有一些手指。机器人能自己操纵胳膊和手指。它们会在工作环境中作出复杂的决定。

compared with...与……相比较,为过去分词短语作状语。be working on ... 正着力于……。make complex decisions 作出复杂的决定。

试题解答

66. 正确答案:C。短文第二、三段解答了这个问题。

67. 正确答案:A。第二段第二句解答了这个问题。

68. 正确答案:B。第四段解答了这个问题。

69. 正确答案:B。a limited vocabulary 意为"有限的词汇量"。

70. 正确答案:A。第四、五段解答了这个问题。

第三篇短文参考译文及语言注释

在一些城市中心,工作狂的现象极其普遍,以致人们对此习以为常。他们视其为正常的生活方式。比如,华盛顿特区的政府人工作人员常常一周工作 60 至 70 小时,他们这样做,并非不得已,而是他们愿意。

不要轻视工作狂的问题。因为真正的工作狂宁肯工作,也不愿做其他事。也许他们不知道怎样休闲,也就是说,他们也许不喜欢看电影、不爱运动或其他类型的娱乐。最重要的是,他们讨厌坐着无所事事。这些工作狂们的生活通常是有压力的,这种压力和焦虑可以引起健康问题。比如心脏病或肠胃紊乱。还有,典型的工作狂家庭观念淡薄。他们很少与孩子在一起,他们的婚姻可能以离婚告终。

工作狂总是这样危险吗?也许不是。当然也有人在压力下也表现良好。一些研究表明,许多工作狂精力充沛,对生活充满兴趣。他们觉得工作其乐无穷,因此他们其实非常快乐。对大多数工作狂来说,工作与娱乐是同样的事。工作富于挑战性,这使他们忙碌并富有创造力。

为什么工作狂如此沉迷于工作?工作有一些好处。当然,它给人们带来薪水,这是重要的。但它给予的远不止经济上的安全感。它给人以自信;当人们完成一件挑战性的工作并能说:"我做成了!"这其实获得了一种满足感。心理学家声称工作给了人们一种身份。通过工作,他们有了自我意识和个体意识。再则,大多数工作都向人们提供了社交的机会。

would rather... than... 宁愿……而非,例:We would rather go boating than climb the mountains.我们宁愿去划船,而不愿去爬山。entertainment 娱乐;most of all 最重要的是。paycheck 薪水。

试题解答

71. 正确答案:C。短文第一段提到"华盛顿的政府工作人员常常一周工作 60 至 70 小时"。

72. 正确答案:D。第二段第五句提到"工作狂们的生活常常是有压力的"。

73. 正确答案:D。第三段提到工作狂们享受工作、工作娱乐不分、工作富有挑战性。工作会消耗精力,不会是精力的来源。

74. 正确答案:B。identity 的原意是"身份",在此应理解为"个性、特性"。

75. 正确答案:A。从短文最后一段可得出正确答案。

第五部分　英译汉

76. 当然,并不是所有的美国人都对体育感兴趣;但是许多(美国)人对此感兴趣。而且有些人似乎对体育以外的东西几乎没有兴趣。

77. 一些体育明星享有比除总统以外的任何国家领导人更广泛的声誉。

78. 体育在世界上任何一个国家都不像在美国那样与大专院校密不可分。

79. 在一场篮球比赛中看到场上球员都是黑人是不足为奇的。

80. 对比赛项目及运动员的一些了解能增加海外来访者对一般美国人的了解机会。

第六部分　汉译英

81. You should not allow computer games to interfere with your study.

82. Kelly invited us to her wedding last week, and we received the written invitation yesterday.

83. I wonder why he is so curious about the universe.

84. We can come to the conclusion that the company's new plan will be successful.

85. As the expert puts it, where there is water, there is life.

2003 年 6 月浙江省大学英语三级考试试卷

Part Ⅰ　Listening Comprehension

Section A

Directions: *In this section, you will hear 10 short conversations. At the end of each conversation, a question will be asked about what was said. You will hear the conversation and the question only once. After each question there will be a pause. During the pause, you must read the four choices marked A), B), C) and D), and decide which is the best answer. Then mark the corresponding letter on the Answer Sheet with a single line through the center.*

1. A) 7:30.　　　　　　　　　　B) 7:45.
   C) 8:00.　　　　　　　　　　D) 8:15.
2. A) At the bookstore.　　　　　B) At home.
   C) At school.　　　　　　　　D) At the library.
3. A) To write another letter.　　 B) To visit her brother.
   C) To post the letter.　　　　　D) To telephone his brother.
4. A) The rain has stopped.　　　 B) The wind has stopped blowing.
   C) It is still raining hard outside.　D) Both the rain and wind have stopped.
5. A) Not exercising in the morning.
   B) Buying a watch for himself.
   C) Exercising right after getting up.
   D) Getting up earlier in the morning.
6. A) She cleaned the house.
   B) She bought a painting for the house.
   C) She painted the house herself.
   D) She hired someone to paint the house.
7. A) He won't go for a walk.
   B) He will take a walk with the woman.
   C) He will go for a walk alone.
   D) He will walk to the park.
8. A) Her son is fat.
   B) She doesn't have enough money.
   C) Her son is still hungry.
   D) She waited for too long.

9. A) In a department store.
   C) At an airport.
   B) On the playground.
   D) At a railway station.
10. A) A newspaperman.
    C) A college student.
    B) A taxi driver.
    D) A school teacher.

Section B

Directions: *In this section, you will hear 3 short passages. The passages will be read twice. At the end of each passage, you will hear some questions, which will be read only once. After you hear a question, you must choose the best answer from the four choices marked A), B), C) and D). Then mark the corresponding letter on the Answer Sheet with a single line through the center.*

Passage One
Questions 11 to 13 are based on the passage you have just heard.

11. A) An eyeglass worker.
    C) An old scientist.
    B) A young doctor.
    D) A news reporter.
12. A) A large book.
    C) A stack of newspapers.
    B) A far-away building.
    D) Stars and planets.
13. A) Large.
    C) Important.
    B) Beautiful.
    D) Simple.

Questions 14 to 16 are based on the passage you have just heard.

14. A) Blue.
    C) Red.
    B) Yellow.
    D) Colorless.
15. A) Because the pilots can't breathe without air.
    B) Because airplanes need air to lift their wings.
    C) Because they need air to see things far ahead.
    D) Because airplanes are moving very fast.
16. A) There is nothing in the sky.
    C) High in the sky the air is thin.
    B) The sky is space.
    D) The sky is all around the world.

Questions 17 to 20 are based on the passage you have just heard.

17. A) A sailor.
    C) A fisherman.
    B) A repairman.
    D) A bus driver.
18. A) In his hometown.
    C) Near a port.
    B) In his wife's town.
    D) Near a garden.
19. A) Late in the evening.
    C) Late in the morning.
    B) Early in the evening.
    D) Early in the morning.
20. A) He had a bad dream.
    C) He saw his ship reaching land.
    B) He found himself among trees.
    D) He thought his ship had hit land.

Part II Vocabulary

Directions: *There are 20 incomplete sentences in this part. For each sentence there are four choices marked A), B), C) and D). Choose the ONE answer that best completes the sentence. Then mark the corresponding letter on the Answer Sheet with a single line through the center.*

21. We should create a _____ environment for learning English.
   A) faithful   B) false
   C) favorite   D) favorable

22. This wild flower is called by _____ names in my hometown.
   A) various   B) variable
   C) separate   D) sensitive

23. Arguing about small details _____ them a lot of time and so some of the people left before the meeting ended.
   A) spent   B) took
   C) charged   D) paid

24. Don't look up in the dictionary every new word that you _____ in reading.
   A) come across   B) come about
   C) come along   D) come up with

25. Because he was fired last week, he has to _____ another job now.
   A) seal   B) seize
   C) seek   D) share

26. You should be careful and stand _____ guard against the same mistake.
   A) up   B) at
   C) with   D) on

27. On American highways the speed _____ is usually 70 miles an hour.
   A) permission   B) limit
   C) control   D) condition

28. In such a case I'd better give up the route I had _____ planned about my traveling.
   A) presently   B) originally
   C) firstly   D) lastly

29. The current _____ is that people all over the world are for peace and against war.
   A) trend   B) tradition
   C) course   D) cause

30. As he is always busy with academic studies, he can hardly find time for his _____ .
   A) habits   B) hobbies
   C) affairs   D) instance

31. I am trying to gather almost all the data that is _____ the topic.
   A) compared to   B) composed of
   C) related to   D) regarded to

32. Hurry up, _____ you'll miss the last train to town.
   A) otherwise   B) so
   C) but   D) and

33. The young teacher _____ her pupil for being lazy.
   A) accused   B) charged
   C) blamed   D) complained

34. He has changed a lot since I saw him last. I can hardly _____ him.
   A) receive   B) recite
   C) realize   D) recognize

35. The meeting started on time. Thirty minutes _____ the chairwoman declared it closed.
   A) after   B) later
   C) late   D) latter

36. The retired worker lives by himself on the state pension but he does not feel _____ .
   A) along   B) alone
   C) lonely   D) lively

37. The problem of widespread unemployment is rather serious, so the local government has taken effective steps to _____ it.
   A) put out   B) set aside
   C) deal with   D) meet with

38. The engineer was under great pressure and eventually he _____ .
   A) broke down   B) broke up
   C) broke off   D) broke away

39. I must say that she is a singer of _____ talent. I like her very much.
   A) scarce   B) general
   C) normal   D) extraordinary

40. She is indeed too tall _____ the fact she is a promising young dancer.
   A) except   B) in spite of
   C) besides   D) except for

Part Ⅲ Structure

Directions: *There are 20 incomplete sentences in this part. For each sentence there are four choices marked A), B), C) and D). Choose the ONE answer that best completes the sentence. Then mark the corresponding letter on the Answer Sheet with a single line through the center.*

41. Please inform me of the time _____ Flight A 45321 takes off from London.
   A) which   B) why
   C) as   D) when

42. The accident is reported _____ at dawn this morning, killing about ten people.
   A) to have occurred   B) to have been occurred

C) occurred   D) occurring

43. He has a large collection of novels, _____ are in English.

A) many in which   B) many books of which

C) many of which   D) many one of which

44. This composition is indeed very good. I'm afraid that he _____ it himself within 25 minutes.

A) won't have written   B) can't have written

C) mustn't have written   D) shouldn't have written

45. _____ smart you may be, you are expected to be modest.

A) No matter what   B) No matter when

C) No matter how   D) No matter why

46. As a member, he tried hard to make his voice _____ in the committee.

A) heard   B) hear

C) hearing   D) be heard

47. Only after he was sent to prison _____ how serious his crime was.

A) he came to know   B) has he come to know

C) he has come to know   D) did he come to know

48. _____ his homework, the school boy dashed to the playground to join his friends in the game.

A) Finished   B) With finishing

C) Finishing   D) To finish

49. All the employees in the company know _____ the boss says is always right.

A) what   B) why

C) how   D) that

50. As we felt the ground _____ to shake, we all hurried out and stood in the open.

A) to begin   B) begun

C) has begun   D) begin

51. He considers _____ an MA program after graduation in two years.

A) taking   B) to take

C) took   D) taken

52. As a rule Mr. Smith went for a walk after supper, _____ by a white lapdog.

A) following   B) followed

C) to follow   D) having followed

53. We _____ the final of the National Cup on TV when power failure came.

A) are watching   B) watched

C) were watching   D) watch

54. The old gentleman seemed _____ in reading the newspaper on the wall of the library.

A) to absorb   B) being absorbed

C) absorbing   D) to be absorbed

55. _____ has something to do with his odd character.

A) That she does not like him   B) She does not like him

C) What she does not like him   D) She did not like him

56. The burglary (盗窃) _____ before I arrived at the office; all I could do was to call the police.

     A) has occurred   B) had occurred

     C) was occurring   D) would occur

57. It was the powerful mine _____ killed a group of the enemy.

     A) which   B) who

     C) what   D) that

58. The hostess insisted that everyone present _____ a short speech of congratulation.

     A) would give   B) must give

     C) give   D) gave

59. She devoted her life to helping _____ .

     A) poor   B) the poor

     C) the poors   D) poors

60. I think it is about time we _____ our journey to the sea shore.

     A) should start   B) started

     C) start   D) are starting

Part IV   Reading Comprehension

Directions: *There are 3 passages in this part. Each passage is followed by some questions or unfinished statements. For each of them there are four choices marked A), B), C) and D). You should decide on the best choice and mark the corresponding letter on the Answer Sheet with a single line through the center.*

Passage One

Questions 61 to 65 are based on the following passage:

Today television is one of the most popular forms of entertainment in the home. Some people in places where television reception is good may think that television has taken the place of radio. Television, however, is actually a kind of radio. It uses special equipment for sending and receiving the picture. The television sound system uses the same type of equipment that is used in other forms of radio.

Exchanging messages with ships at sea was one of the first uses of radio. Modern radio is still used for *this purpose* and for communication across oceans. On land radio provides a means of instant communication even with moving vehicles such as taxicabs or service trucks.

Police forces use two-way radio to get information to and from officers in squad cars (警备车) and on motorcycles. Small portable sets make it possible to communicate with a central exchange while walking or riding in a city or over a rural area. Observers in airplanes can report traffic accidents, and traffic jams by radio to police officers on the ground.

Radiotelephones are used in many places. Connection with the regular telephone service can be provided for boats, trains and cars. *Isolated* places in deserts, forests, and mountainous regions are linked by radiotelephone in many parts of the world. Thus by means of radio people can communicate with others wherever service is provided.

61. According to the passage, television _____ .
    A) has taken the place of radio
    B) is no longer popular in the home
    C) can be regarded as a kind of radio
    D) has nothing in common with radio

62. In paragraph two, "*this purpose*" refers to _____ .
    A) exchanging messages with ships at sea
    B) communicating across oceans
    C) sending and receiving the picture
    D) instant communication with moving vehicles

63. According to the passage, radio is used in the following ways EXCEPT _____ .
    A) at sea
    B) on land
    C) in the air
    D) underground

64. The word "*Isolated*" in the last paragraph means _____ .
    A) sandy and mountainous
    B) clean and not polluted
    C) without any living things
    D) separated or distant

65. The best title for the passage is _____ .
    A) Television and Radio
    B) Radio and Its Uses
    C) Radio and Radiotelephones
    D) Modern Communication

Passage Two

Questions 66 to 70 are based on the following passage:

The dog, called Prince, was an intelligent animal and a slave to Williams. From morning till night, when Williams was at home, Prince never left his sight, practically ignoring all other members of the family. The dog had a number of clearly defined duties, for which Williams had patiently trained him and, like the good pupil he was, Prince lived for the chance to demonstrate his abilities. When Williams wanted to put on his boots, he would murmur "Boots" and within seconds the dog would drop them at his feet. At nine every morning Prince ran off to the general store in the village, returning shortly not only with Williams's daily paper but with a half-ounce packet of Williams's favorite tobacco, John Rhiney's Mixed. A gun-dog(猎狗)by breed, Prince possessed a large soft mouth specially evolved(进化)for the safe carrying of hunted creature, so the paper and the tobacco came to no harm, never even showing a tooth mark.

Williams was a railway man, an engine driver, and he wore a blue uniform which smelled of oil fuel. He had no work at odd times—"days", "late days" or "nights". Over the years Prince got to know these periods of work and rest, knew when his master would leave the house and return, and the dog did not waste this knowledge. If Williams overslept, as he often did, Prince barked at the bedroom door until he woke, much to the annoyance of the family. On his return,

Williams's slippers were brought to him, the paper and tobacco too if previously undelivered.

A curious thing happened to Williams during the snow and the ice of last winter. One evening he slipped and fell on the icy pavement somewhere between the village and his home. He was so badly shaken that he stayed in bed for three days and not until he got up and dressed again did he discover that he had lost his wallet containing over fifty pounds.

The house was turned upside down in the search, but the wallet was not found. However, two days later—that was five days after the fall—Prince dropped the wallet into Williams's hand. Very muddy, dirty and wet through, the little case still contained fifty-three pounds, Williams's driving license and a few other papers. Where the dog had found it no one could tell, but found that he had recognized it probably by the faint oil smell on the worn leather.

66. What does the passage tell us about gun-dogs?
   A) They are the fastest runners of all dogs.
   B) Their teeth are removed when they are young.
   C) They can carry birds, etc. without hurting them.
   D) They can produce many young dogs.

67. It annoyed Williams's family when _____ .
   A) Williams had to go to work at night
   B) the dog made loud sounds in the house
   C) the dog was used to traveling by train
   D) the dog was confused about the time of the day

68. The dog eventually found Williams's wallet because _____ .
   A) he knew where Williams had fallen
   B) he had seen it there and recognized it
   C) it contained over fifty pounds
   D) it had the smell familiar to him

69. Which of the following is true of Williams according to the passage?
   A) He often did not get enough sleep.
   B) He often slept later than he should.
   C) He did not drink heavily.
   D) He liked saving money.

70. Which of the following is the best description of Prince?
   A) He was clever and loyal to Williams.
   B) He liked the sight of his owner.
   C) He understood human language.
   D) He was the best friend with William's family.

Passage Three

Questions 71 to 75 are based on the following passage:

The failed Skylab(空间站) will come screaming home to earth in disappointment sometime next month, but it will fall we know not where.

That precise information is beyond even the calculations of scientists and their computers.

The best they can tell us is that the space station, weighing 77 tons and as high as a 12-story building, will break into hundreds of pieces that will be scattered across a track 100 miles wide and 4000 miles long.

We are again exposed to one of those unexpected adventures, or misadventures, of science that attracts our attention from the boring routines of daily existence and encourages us to think a lot about man's future.

What worries Richard Smith, the Skylab's director, is the "big pieces" that will come through the atmosphere. Two lumps, weighing 2 tons each, and ten weighing at least 1,000 pounds each, will come in at speeds of hundreds of miles an hour, and if they crash on land they will dig holes up to 100 feet deep.

What worries us, with our lack of scientific knowledge and our quick imagination, is both the big and small pieces, although project officials say there is very little chance that anyone will be injured by them.

That is good to know, but it does not remove the doubts of the millions who still remember the nuclear accident at Three Mile Island. That accident took place in 1979 in spite of what scientists had assured us as to the safety of the nuclear reactor.

71. Where the Skylab will fall _____ .
    A) cannot be predicted even by computers
    B) is kept secret from the whole world
    C) is made public to all countries
    D) is predicted by the scientists involved in the program

72. The broken Skylab will _____ .
    A) be in two lumps—one weighing 2 tons and the other weighing 10 tons
    B) fall with the force of a 12-story building
    C) cover a large round area
    D) break into 12 big pieces and hundreds of smaller ones

73. In the fourth paragraph, we are told that _____ .
    A) people usually do not pay attention to the environment
    B) people expect to be exposed to dangers in their daily existence
    C) the accident makes people worry about our safety on the earth
    D) most people consider their life boring

74. The author refers to the accident of Three Mile Island _____ .
    A) to express his doubts about scientists' assurance
    B) because he fears that a piece of the Skylab may strike a nuclear reactor
    C) to remind the reader of the terrible accident
    D) because the nuclear reactor there and the Skylab were built by the same company

75. What does the author mainly try to tell us in the passage?

A) Science and technology need improving.

B) Science may bring disasters to the human race.

C) People should not readily believe experts.

D) Ordinary people are more imaginative than scientists.

Part V Translation from English into Chinese

Directions: *In this part there is a passage with 5 underlined sections, numbered 76 to 80. After reading the passage carefully, translate the underlined sections into Chinese. Remember to write your translation on the Translation Sheet.*

English is not only used as a foreign language, it also has some kind of special status (地位) in those countries where it has been chosen as an official language. This is the case in Ghana and Nigeria, for example, where the governments have chosen English as the main language to carry on the affairs of government, education, commerce, the media, and the legal system. (76) In such cases, people have to learn English if they want to get success in life. (77) They have their mother-tongue to begin with and they start learning English, in school or in the street, at an early age. For them, in due course, English will become a language to fall back on—when their mother-tongue proves to be inadequate for communication—talking to people from a different background, for example, or to people from outside the country. For them, English becomes their "second" language.

In 1985, the population of India was estimated to be 768 million. English is an official language here, alongside Hindi. (78) Several other languages have special status in their own regions, but English is the language of the legal system; it is a major language in Parliament; and it is a preferred language in the universities and in the all-India competitive exams for senior posts in such fields as the civil service and engineering. Some 3,000 English newspapers are published throughout the country. There is thus great reason to learn to use the language well. In real terms, (79) the English speakers of India may only number 70 million—a small amount compared with the total population. On the other hand, this figure is well in excess of the population in Britain.

When all the estimates for second-language use around the world are added up, we reach a figure of around 300 million speakers—about as many as the total of mother-tongue users. But we have to remember that most of these countries are in parts of the world (Africa, South America) where the population increase is four times as great as that found in mother-tongue countries. (80) If present trends continue, within a generation mother-tongue English use will have been left far behind.

Part VI Translation from Chinese into English

Directions: *In this part there are five Chinese sentences, numbered 81 to 85. Translate these sentences into English and write them on the Translation Sheet.*

81. 为了保护环境,我们必须减少各种污染。

82. 请多穿些衣服,因为恐怕天气会变冷。

83. 一个大学生应该知道如何关闭计算机。

84. 你什么时候来这里的? 其实你不必亲自来看望我。

85. 连接两个港口城市的高速公路是上个月建成的。

【听力录音文稿】

Section A

1. W: Are you leaving? It's 7:15, now.

   M: No, I'm going to wait another half an hour.

   Q: When will the man leave?

2. W: Bill, after I finish here at school, I'm going to the library.

   M: Ok. I'm just going to stay home.

   Q: Where is the woman now?

3. M: Have you written to your brother yet?

   W: Yes, but I haven't mailed the letter yet.

   Q: What is the woman going to do?

4. M: Is it still raining outside?

   W: No, but the wind is still blowing.

   Q: What can we conclude from this conversation?

5. M: I want to take exercise, but never seem to find the time.

   W: Why not do it first thing in the morning?

   Q: What does the woman suggest?

6. M: Your house looks nice. What did you do to it?

   W: I had it painted.

   Q: What does the woman do?

7. W: Hullo, Jim. Do you feel like coming for a walk?

   M: Go for a walk? I wouldn't mind.

   Q: What will the man do?

8. M: I'm still hungry, mother. I want the chocolate cake that I saw on the menu.

   W: But your weight is already a problem. Eat something that won't make you fatter.

   Q: What is the mother worried about?

9. M: Kate, Look! The passengers are coming off the plane, and there is Susan.

   W: Which one? The tall one with the blue suitcase or the one with the package under her arm?

   Q: Where does this conversation most probably take place?

10. M: I wonder when Mr. Carson can finish marking our papers.

W: Very soon, I think. He is leaving for San Francisco. He has to finish his grading by then.

Q: Who is Mr. Carson?

Section B

Passage One

Hundreds of years ago a Dutch eyeglass maker named Lippershey held two different glass lenses in a straight line. Lippershey looked at a far-away church through the lenses. He was surprised to notice that the church looked larger through the glasses. The Dutch eyeglass maker wrote about his discovery. Some time later the great Italian scientist Galileo read about Lippershey's discovery. Afterwards, he made his own telescope. Galileo used this telescope to study the stars and planets. Galileo made many important discoveries about the stars and planets using his simple telescope.

Questions 11 to 13 are based on the passage you have just heard.

11. What was Lippershey?

12. What did Lippershey see through his glasses?

13. How does the passage describe Galileo's telescope?

Passage Two

What is the sky? Where is it? How high is it? What lies above the sky? I am sure that you have asked these questions. They are very difficult to answer, aren't they?

If someone asked you: "What color is the sky?" I expect that you would answer: "Blue." I am afraid that you would be wrong. The sky has no color. When we see blue, we are looking at blue sunlight. The sunlight is shining on little bits of dust in the air.

Is the sky full of air? I am sure you have asked this question, too. We know that there is air all around the world. We could not breathe without air. Airplanes could not fly without air. They need air to lift their wings. Airplanes cannot fly very high because as they go higher, the air gets thinner. If we go far enough away from the earth, we find there is no air.

Perhaps we can answer some of our questions now. What is the sky? Nothing. Where is it? It is all around the world. The sky is space. In this space there is nothing except the sun, the moon, and all the stars.

Questions 14 to 16 are based on the passage you have just heard.

14. What color is the sky according to the passage?

15. Why can't airplanes fly without air?

16. Which of the following is NOT true according to the passage?

Passage Three

Dick was a sailor on a big shop. It went to Japan and Australia, so Dick was often on the ship for several months at a time. When he woke up in the morning and looked out, he only saw the sea, or sometimes a port.

When he was twenty-three, Dick got married and bought a small house with a garden in his wife's town. It was far away from the sea. Then he had to go back to his ship, and he did not come home for two months. He went from the port to the town by bus, and was very happy to see his wife again.

The next morning he slept until 9 o'clock. Then he woke up suddenly and looked out of the window. There were trees a few feet away. He was very frightened and jumped out of bed, shouting, "We've hit land!"

Questions 17 to 20 are based on the passage you have just heard.

17. What kind of work did Dick do?

18. Where did he buy a house?

19. When did Dick wake up?

20. Why did Dick get frightened when he woke up?

【试题解析】

第一部分　听力理解

1. 正确答案：B。现在是 7:15,男士欲再等 30 分钟,故他将在 7:45 离开。
2. 正确答案：C。女士告诉 Bill,学校这里的事情办完后她打算去图书馆。可见此时这位女士是在学校。
3. 正确答案：C。女士回答男士信已经写完但还没寄出。显然这位女士要准备去寄信了。
4. 正确答案：A。女士告诉男士雨已经停了,但风还很大。
5. 正确答案：C。女士提议要想找到锻炼身体的时间,不妨将其安排为早晨要做的第一件事情,即起床后立即去锻炼。
6. 正确答案：D。女士告诉男士,房屋之所以显得特别漂亮是因为她请人对其进行了粉刷。请注意这个结构:have something done "请人做某事"。
7. 正确答案：B。这位男士不介意女士对他提出一起散步的邀请。
8. 正确答案：A。孩子借口没吃饱,想吃巧克力糕点。对此母亲指出,体重已经超常的孩子应该吃些别的不易发胖的食品。
9. 正确答案：C。此题的开头信息"乘客下飞机了"便明示了对话发生的场所是机场。
10. 正确答案：D。"完成阅卷"的时间是此题谈论的核心信息。由此可以确认 Mr. Carson 是教师。
11. 正确答案：A。短文一开始就说明了 Lippershey 的身份"a Dutch eyeglass maker"。
12. 正确答案：B。从两块前后成直线的镜片中 Lippershey 看到了远处被放大了的教堂。
13. 正确答案：D。最后,短文对 Galileo 通过这一简单望远镜所获的发现作了概括性的描述。
14. 正确答案：D。文中提到,天空是无色的。它看似蓝色,那是因为空气中的微尘折射了阳光所造成。
15. 正确答案：B。文中提到,飞机需要有空气对其机翼产生提升力才能飞行。
16. 正确答案：A。文中提到,天空中不仅有悬浮的微尘,在太空中还存在着各种星体。

17. 正确答案:A。短文一开始便介绍了"Dick was a sailor on a big shop"。培养正确把握开篇信息的能力在听力训练中是十分重要的。

18. 正确答案:B。23 岁时 Dick 结了婚并在他妻子居住的城市购买了一个带花园的小居所。此题为细节题,检查考生对重要信息的注意品质。

19. 正确答案:C。见到久别的妻子,Dick 美美地睡到早晨九点才醒来。

20. 正确答案:D。长期在海上工作,难得见到陆地;看到窗外的树木使 Dick 习惯性地误认为轮船触礁了。

第二部分 词 汇

21. 正确答案:D。句意为:我们应该创造一个有利于英语学习的环境。
faithful 忠实可靠的 / false 错误的,虚假的 / favorite 宠爱的 / favorable 有利的,起促进作用的。例:We can sail there in an hour, if the wind is favorable to us. 如果顺风(风向对我们有利),一小时的航程就可以到达那儿。

22. 正确答案:A。句意为:这种野花在我的家乡有着各种不同的名字。
various 各种各样的,不同的 / variable 可变的,不定的 / separate 分离的,个别的 / sensitive 敏感的,灵敏的。例:There are various colors to choose from. 有各种各样的颜色可供选择。There are various ways of getting to the station. 从这儿去车站有各种不同的走法。

23. 正确答案:B。句意为:在小细节上的争论花费了他们大量的时间,于是一些人提前退出了会议。
spend 花费,消耗 / take 花费,占用 / charge 要价,收费 / pay 支付。注意下列搭配:spend some time in doing something; spend money on something / take sb. some time to do something / charge (sb.) some money for sth. / pay sb. to do sth. / 例:The work took us a week to finish. 我们花了一个星期完成这项工作。It takes (us) an hour to go there. (我们)到那里需要一个钟头。

24. 正确答案:A。句意为:在阅读中不要一遇见生词就查词典。
come across 偶然遇见 / come about 发生,产生 / come along 进展,陪伴 / come up with 赶上,提出。例:I've just come across a beautiful poem in this book. 无意间我在这本书中读到了一首优美的诗歌。I came across my old college roommate in Shanghai last month. 上个月在上海我遇到了大学时代同寝室的老同学。

25. 正确答案:C。句意为:上周他被炒了鱿鱼,所以他不得不重新再找个工作。
seal 封条,印记 / seize 抓住,夺取 / seek 寻找,图谋求得 / share 共享。例:We sought an answer to the question, but couldn't find one. 我们寻求这个问题的答案,可是没能找到。They are seeking the most reasonable diet which will do good to their health. 他们在寻找有益于他们健康的最合理的饮食。

26. 正确答案:D。句意为:你应该仔细,谨防再犯同样的错误。
stand / be on (one's) guard 是固定短语,意为"警戒,提防"。例:Be on your guard against pickpockets. 谨防扒手。

27. 正确答案:B。句意为:美国高速公路的时速限制通常为每小时 70 英里。
permission 许可,允许 / limit 限制,限定 / control 支配,管理 / condition 条件,情形。例:The speed limit is the fastest speed you are allowed to drive a car at. 限速是指允许驾车

的最快速度。speed limit 是固定词组,意为"限速"。

28. 正确答案:B。句意为:情况既然如此,我还是放弃原定的旅游线路吧。
presently 目前 / originally(事件发生时间上的)最初,原先 / firstly 首先,(按逻辑顺序排列上的)最初 / lastly 最后,终于。例:This is not what I had originally expected. 这不是我事先期盼的。The novel originally came from a true love affair. 这本小说源自于一个真实的爱情故事。Who was the original owner of this house? 谁是这座房子最早的主人?

29. 正确答案:A。句意为:当前的趋势是全世界人民热爱和平,反对战争。
trend 倾向,趋势 / tradition 传统,惯例 / course 过程,进程,路线 / cause 原因,理由,事业。例:The trend of wages is still upwards. 劳动所得的工资报酬总在不断地提升。

30. 正确答案:B。句意为:他一直忙于学术研究,几乎没有时间用于业余爱好。
habit 习惯,习性 / hobby 业余爱好 / affairs 事务 / instance 事例,例证。例:Any personal hobbies such as sports, music and collecting stamps never had a place in his life. 任何一种个人的业余爱好,如体育活动、音乐、集邮等等,在他的生活中从未有过地位。

31. 正确答案:C。句意为:我设法收集几乎所有与此主题有关的数据。
compared to 被比作 / composed of 由……组成 / related to 与……有关,涉及。例:These occurrences seem to be related to each other. 所发生的这些事件之间似乎有着某种联系。

32. 正确答案:A。句意为:赶快,否则就要误了去省城的最后一班火车了。
otherwise 否则 / so 那么,这样看来 / but 但是 / and 但,却。例:We'll go early, otherwise we may not get a seat. 我们得早一点去,不然就没有座位了。I've got one more page to write; otherwise I've finished. 我又多写了一页,不然的话已经完成了。

33. 正确答案:C。句意为:那位年轻教师责备她的学生学习懒散。
accuse sb. of... 指控某人…… / charge sb. with ... 控告某人…… / blame sb. for sth. 因某事责备某人。/ complain about (of)... 抱怨……。

34. 正确答案:D。句意为:自从上次见过他之后,他变化很大,我几乎认不出他了。
receive 收到,接到 / recite 背诵,朗读 / realize 了解,实现 / recognize 认知,看出。例:I recognized Peter although I hadn't seen him for 10 years. 虽然我有 10 年没看到彼得了,但我认出了他。I don't recognize this word——what does it mean? 我不认识这个单词,它的意思是什么?

35. 正确答案:B。句意为:会议准时举行。半小时后女主席宣布会议结束。
after 在后面 / later 过后,稍后 / late 晚,迟 / latter(两者中)后者的。例:But some time later it began to rain. 但过了些时候开始下雨了。

36. 正确答案:C。句意为:这位退休工人靠政府的养老金独自生活,不过他并不感到寂寞。
along 共同,一起 / alone 单独的 / lonely 孤独的,寂寞的 / lively 活泼的,生动的。例:When his wife and two little children left him, he was very lonely. 妻子和两个孩子离他而去后,他很孤独。Working as a writer can be a very lonely existence. 当作家会是一种很寂寞的生涯。

37. 正确答案:C。句意为:广泛存在的失业现象是一个颇为棘手的问题。对此,当地政府采取了一些有效措施。
put out 熄灭 / set aside 留出,拨出 / deal with 应付,处理 / meet with 偶遇,碰到。例:The book deals with this problem. 这本书论述了这个问题。The teacher deals fairly with his

pupils. 这个教师公平地对待他的学生。

38. 正确答案:A。句意为:这个工程师承受了巨大的压力,但最终他还是垮掉了。

break down 毁掉,倒塌,垮掉 / break up 分裂 / break off 中断,突然停止 / break away 突然离开,脱离。例:By helpful kindness the teacher broke down the new boy's shyness. 老师的爱心消除了孩子的羞怯。

39. 正确答案:D。句意为:她是个非凡的歌唱家,我十分喜爱她。

scarce 缺乏的,稀有的 / general 一般的,普通的 / normal 正常的,标准的 / extraordinary 特别的,非凡的。例:Perhaps the most extraordinary building of the nineteenth century was the Crystal Palace. 也许 19 世纪最不寻常的建筑物要算"水晶宫"了。

40. 正确答案:B。句意为:尽管她是个很有潜力的舞蹈演员,但她的个子太高。

except 除……之外 / in spite of 虽然,尽管…… 仍 / besides 除……之外 / except for 除……以外。例:I went out in spite of the rain. 尽管下雨,我还是出去了。In spite of great efforts, we failed to carry our plans through. 尽管我们做出了巨大努力,我们还是没能完成计划。

第三部分 语法结构

41. 正确答案:D。句意为:请告诉我 A 45321 航班从伦敦起飞的时间。

when 引导的定语从句修饰 time,在定语从句中作时间状语。which 是关系代词,不能在引导的定语从句中作状语。why 是关系副词,在定语从句中作原因状语。as 作为关系副词用时,在定语从句中作方式状语。

42. 正确答案:A。句意为:据报道,这起事故发生在今天清晨,有 10 人在事故中丧生。

不定式的完成式表示该动作发生在句子谓语动词之前。

43. 正确答案:C。句意为:他收藏了大量小说,其中不少是英文版的。

which 引导的非限制性定语从句作介词 of 的宾语。关系代词 which 指代"他所收藏的大量小说"。选项 A 之所以不正确,是因为介词 in 的意义为"在……内部"。此题看似简单,但不少考生在这里往往举棋不定,时常出错。分析其原因主要在于对基本表达方法掌握得不够扎实。其中之一(一些 / 许多 /……)的英文表达方法为:one / some / many /……of the…。掌握了英文关于"在……当中"的正确表达方法,自然就知道选项 B 和 D 错在哪儿了。

44. 正确答案:B。句意为:这篇作文写得的确很好。恐怕这不可能是他自己在 25 分钟之内写出来的。

情态动词 will 表示"意愿";can 表示逻辑上的"可能性";must 表示肯定的"推测";should 表示"责任或义务"。当 can 用于否定句中且后面跟动词的完成式时,表示对过去所发生事件的"怀疑"或"不肯定"。例:Surly she can't have taken all the heavy suitcases to the room by herself. 她一个人是不可能把所有这些沉重的箱子都搬进屋里的。

45. 正确答案:C。句意为:不论你多么聪明,你都应该戒骄戒躁。

参见 2003 年 1 月试卷第 51 题的试题解析。

46. 正确答案:A。句意为:作为委员会的一名成员,他积极发表自己的意见。

在复合宾语中,当动词的过去分词作宾语补足语时,宾语具有受动含义。例:He acknowledged himself defeated. 他承认自己失败了。They found the room crowded with people. 他

们发现屋里挤满了人。

47. 正确答案:D。句意为:他是在被送进牢狱后,才意识到自己所犯罪行的严重性。
only 引起的状语位于句首时,句子的主谓结构须倒装。

48. 正确答案:C。句意为:完成作业后,那男孩奔向操场与同学们一起做游戏去了。
当分词或者分词短语作时间状语时,现在分词表示与谓语动词的动作同时发生;过去分词的完成式表示其动作在谓语动词之前发生。但在非正式文体或口语中,一般式常常代替完成式。动词不定式的一般式表示将要发生的动作。

49. 正确答案:A。句意为:公司的所有员工都认为老板说的话始终是正确的。
what 在它所引导的主语从句中作动词 say 的宾语,说明 say 的内容。

50. 正确答案:D。句意为:当感到地面震动时,我们所有的人都跑了出来,呆在空旷的地方。
感觉动词 see, hear, watch, listen to, feel 等后面不能接动词的谓语形式,须接不带 to 的动词不定式或现在分词。接动词不定式时强调动作本身;接现在分词时强调该动词动作发生时的情形。

51. 正确答案:A。句意为:他考虑过两年毕业后,去攻读文学硕士。
consider 后面要求接动词的 ing 形式。

52. 正确答案:B。句意为:晚饭后 Mr. Smith 通常带着他的小狗去外面散散步。
过去分词短语作伴随状语。

53. 正确答案:C。句意为:当我们正在观看电视上的国家杯决赛时突然停电了。
句式"... be doing... when... ",意为"正在……突然……"。

54. 正确答案:D。句意为:这位老先生似乎正聚精会神地在阅览图书馆墙报栏中的报纸。
动词 seem 后面接带 to 的不定式动词。当表示"全神贯注地做……"时,须使用"to be absorbed in doing..."结构。

55. 正确答案:A。句意为:她不喜欢他是与他的怪脾气有关。
英文中,句子作主语时必须有关联词引导。that 在引导主语从句时本身没有意义,也不担任从句中的句子成分,仅起连接作用。例:That he will come to the discussion is certain.
(或者 It is certain that he will come to the discussion.)

56. 正确答案:B。句意为:到办公室时盗窃已经发生。我只好报警。
"盗窃"行为发生在"我到办公室"之前,故应该使用过去完成式。

57. 正确答案:D。句意为:正是这个威力强大的地雷消灭了一群敌人。
这是一个强调句。本句强调主语部分。强调句句型为:It is... that (who)...。除谓语动词外,被强调的部分放在 It is (was) 与 that (who) 之间。当被强调的部分为人时,可用 who 连接,其余使用须用 that 连接。例:It was a group of the enemy who were killed by the powerful mine.

58. 正确答案:C。句意为:女主人坚持要每个在场的人讲几句简短的贺辞。
在表示请求、建议、命令的动词:ask(请求), demand(要求), request(请求), insist(坚持), prefer(宁愿), suggest(建议), propose(建议), order(命令), command(命令)等后接宾语从句时,其宾语从句谓语动词使用"should + 动词原形"的形式。

59. 正确答案:B。句意为:她将自己的一生奉献给了帮助穷人的事业。
定冠词与某些形容词连用,使形容词名词化,代表某一类人。例:the sick 病人,the wounded 伤员,the aged 老人。

60. 正确答案:B。句意为:我想,我们该出发去海滨了吧。

在 It is (about) time (that)... 句型中,从句的谓语动词用过去式表示将来。意为"是该做某事的时候了"。例:It is time we went to the library. 我们该去图书馆了。

第四部分 阅读理解

第一篇短文参考译文及语言注释

如今看电视是家庭中最喜爱的娱乐消遣方式之一。生活在电视接收情况良好地方的人们,可能认为电视已经取代了收音机。然而,电视机实际上就是一种无线电接收器。它使用独特的装置来传送和接收图片。电视机的声音播放系统使用的仍旧是与其他收音机相同类型的装置。

无线电通讯最早的应用之一是与在海上的船只互递消息。现代无线电设备的发展仍然是为了这一目的,并且实现了横跨大洋的通讯目的。在陆地,收音机是一种快捷的消息传递工具,即使是在运动中的车辆,如出租车、货运车,都能及时收听消息。

警察使用双通道无线电接收装置,使警车与摩托车上的干警之间建立起通讯联系。小型便携式通讯机使你在城市或乡间任何地方散步、乘车时都能与中央交换机及时沟通。飞机上的监测人员可以通过无线电设备向在地面上的值勤警官报告交通事故和交通拥挤情况。

无线电话得到了广泛的应用。它可以为轮船、火车和汽车提供与固定电话的连接业务。它可以使沙漠、森林和山区这些与外界隔离的地方同世界的许多地方建立联系。为此,只要处在提供无线电业务服务的范围内,人人都能用无线电话与他人进行实时通讯。

take the place of... 代替……。equipment 设备,器材,装置,不可数名词。例:laboratory equipment 实验室设备;equipment and parts 器材;Our school has been given some new equipment. 我们学校有了一些赠送的新设备。exchange A with B 与 B 交换 A。例:May I exchange seats with you? 我和你调一个座位好吗? central exchange 中央信息交换设备。by means of 依靠。

试题解答

61. 正确答案:C。可从第一段的第三句中找到答案。

62. 正确答案:A。可从第二段中找到答案。

63. 正确答案:D。选项 D 的内容文中没有提到。

64. 正确答案:D。可从第四段中找到答案。

65. 正确答案:B。本篇讲述的是无线电在海陆空方面的应用。

第二篇短文参考译文及语言注释

一条名叫 Prince 的猎犬非常聪明,是 Williams 的仆人。从早到晚,只要 Williams 在家,它总是跟随其后,几乎无视家里的其他成员。Prince 每天都要做一些明确属于它职责范围内的事。这是 Williams 耐心教出来的。Prince 就像个听话的小学生,随时准备向其主人展示自己的职责。Williams 要穿靴子时就会喃喃低语"靴子呢",几秒钟后 Prince 便把靴子放在了 Williams 的跟前。每天早上九点钟 Prince 便直奔村里的综合商店,一会儿工夫,不仅替 Williams 买回了当天的报纸,还为 Williams 买回了他最喜爱的一小包半盎司重的 John Rhiney's Mixed 烟叶。Prince 是一条猎犬,那张独特的由进化而来的宽厚大嘴专用于稳当地衔叼猎物而不伤它。它甚至于在报纸和烟叶上从不留下任何牙印。

Williams 是铁路工人,一个火车司机。身着一套满是机油味的蓝色制服。他的工作时间时常变动,有时白天不上班,有时是下午,而有时则是晚上休息在家。多年来 Prince 熟悉了主人的作息时间。知道主人何时要去上班了,何时就要下班回家了,从没有弄错过。如果 Williams 睡过了头,他经常这样,Prince 就会对着他的卧室门"汪汪"地叫,直到把他叫醒。家里人对此颇感烦恼。当 Williams 下班进门时,如果拖鞋、报纸和香烟事先没有准备好,Prince 就会马上为他取来。

去年,在冰天雪地的冬天发生了一件稀罕事。一天晚上,Williams 滑倒在村子与他家之间冰冷的路边上。这一跤摔得很厉害,Williams 在床上躺了三天。当他起床穿衣时,发现他那装有五十几英镑的皮夹不见了。

翻遍了家里所有的地方,没有找着那只皮夹。可是两天后——自他摔跤后已经五天过去了——Prince 把那只沾满泥浆,又脏又湿的皮夹放在了 Williams 手中。皮夹里的五十三英镑还在,Williams 的驾驶执照和一些其他证件也都在。谁也说不清究竟 Prince 是在哪儿找到这只皮夹的,但发现它可能是通过皮夹上淡淡的机油味认出来的。

lived for 为……而活着。例:He lived for adventure. 他平生喜欢冒险。句子 He had no work at odd times—"days","late days" or "nights". 说明 Williams 工作时间的不固定性,"—"之后的内容进一步指明其可能的闲暇时间,at odd times 偶尔。

试题解答

66. 正确答案:C。可从第一段的最后一句中找到答案。

67. 正确答案:B。可从第二段的第四句中找到答案。

68. 正确答案:D。可从第四段的最后一句中找到答案。

69. 正确答案:B。可从第二段的第四句中找到答案。

70. 正确答案:A。全文贯穿了这一思想。

第三篇短文参考译文及语言注释

下月某个时间,一个已经失效的空间站将带着沮丧呼啸地飞回地球。我们只知道它会掉下来但不知道它会落在哪里。

甚至科学家和他们的计算机都无法作出精确的计算。

他们所能够告诉我们的只是,这个重 77 吨,高达 12 层楼的空间站将分裂成数百块残片,散落在 100 英里宽 4000 英里长的范围内。

我们将再一次面临使我们摆脱枯燥琐碎的日常生活,激励我们为人类未来进行更多思考的科学所带给我们的其中一些预料不到的危险或灾难。

令空间站主任 Richard Smith 担心的是那些将穿越大气层的"大块头们"。其中有两块残片各重 2 吨,有十块残片至少各重 1000 磅,它们以每小时数百英里的速度进入大气层。如果落在地面上,将会砸出一个 100 英尺的深坑。

尽管负责空间站管理的官员们说,几乎不会有人受到它们的伤害。而我们,藉于贫乏的科学知识和快速的想象力,所担心的却是所有的那些大小残片。

官员们的话自然是个好消息。可是却不能消除几百万人至今还记忆犹新的,对三里岛核意外的疑虑。那次意外事件发生在 1979 年。尽管当时科学家就安全问题作出过保证,核反应堆不会对我们的生命安全产生任何影响。

第一段第一个句子中的谓语动词 come 带了三个状语,screaming 和 in disappointment 作伴随状语,home to earth 作地点状语。连词 but 在 but it will fall we know not where 句中作"尽管……还是"解。在第四段的这个长句中,介词短语"of science... about man's future"是"those unexpected adventures, or misadventures"的定语,这个短语中的 science 又被一个 that 引导的长长的定语从句"that attracts our attention from the boring routines of daily existence and encourages us to think a lot about man's future"所修饰,说明科学在给我们带来舒适和憧憬的同时也给我们带来了威胁和忧虑。介词短语 with our lack of scientific knowledge and our quick imagination 带着讽刺和批评的口吻。assure sb. of... 向某人保证……。例:I can assure you of the reliability of the news. 我可以向你保证这消息是可靠的。as to 关于。

试题解答

71. 正确答案:A。可从第二段中找到答案。

72. 正确答案:D。可从第五段中找到答案。

73. 正确答案:C。可从第四段中找到答案。

74. 正确答案:A。可从文章的最后一段中找到答案。

75. 正确答案:B。文章的第四段和最后一段说明了这个问题。

第五部分　英译汉

76. 在这种情况下,如果人们想在生活中获得成功,就必须学习英语。

77. 他们首先开始学习母语,并且从小就开始在学校或街头学英语。

78. 在他们自己的地区,好几种其他的语言拥有其特殊的地位,但是英语是法律系统的语言。

79. 在印度讲英语的人数可能只有七千万,这与印度的总人口相比较是个小数字。

80. 如果目前的趋势继续下去,在一代人的时间之内以英语为母语的使用就会被远远地抛在后面/大大落后。

第六部分　汉译英

81. In order to protect the environment, we must reduce various kinds of pollution.

82. Please put on more clothes, because I'm afraid it will get cold.

83. A college student should know how to turn off a computer.

84. When did you come here? In fact you needn't have come to see me in person.

85. The highway that links/connects the two port cities was built last month.

2004 年 1 月浙江省大学英语三级考试试卷

Part I Listening Comprehension

Section A

Directions: *In this section, you will hear 10 short conversations. At the end of each conversation, a question will be asked about what was said. You will hear the conversation and the question only once. After each question there will be a pause. During the pause, you must read the four choices marked A), B), C) and D), and decide which is the best answer. Then mark the corresponding letter on the Answer Sheet with a single line through the center.*

1. A) At a theater.   B) At a railway station.
   C) At an airport.   D) At a travel agency.

2. A) Tea.   B) Coffee.
   C) Both tea and coffee.   D) Something cold.

3. A) Twenty.   B) Twenty one.
   C) Twenty four.   D) Twenty five.

4. A) She will come over later.   B) She will prepare for her exam.
   C) She will stay with her parents.   D) She will do some exercise.

5. A) Weekend weather.   B) Holiday plan.
   C) Bill's promise.   D) Sunday school.

6. A) Buy a gift for the woman's father.
   B) Buy a gift for his father.
   C) Get the woman's father to buy her a watch.
   D) Get his father to buy him a watch.

7. A) Richard's.   B) Lucy's.
   C) Karen's.   D) Karl's.

8. A) Go on a vacation.   B) Rent a house.
   C) Find a job.   D) Get back home.

9. A) Tom will be late.   B) Tom will surely be on time.
   C) Tom can't come.   D) Tom is not welcome.

10. A) She is married to an Arabian.
    B) She can do the translation.
    C) She is the person who wrote the letter.
    D) She knows who can do the translation.

Section B

Directions: *In this section, you will hear 3 short passages. The passages will be read twice. At the end of each passage, you will hear some questions, which will be read only once. After you hear a question, you must choose the best answer from the four choices marked A), B), C) and D). Then mark the corresponding letter on the Answer Sheet with a single line through the center.*

Passage One

Questions 11 to 13 are based on the passage you have just heard.

11. A) He prefers planes to trains for traveling.

    B) He prefers trains to planes for traveling.

    C) He prefers living in a city to the country.

    D) He prefers living in the country to a city.

12. A) They are always crowded.

    B) The seats there are uncomfortable.

    C) There aren't enough toilets.

    D) They are far away from the city.

13. A) Planes are safer, faster and more convenient.

    B) Trains are cheaper, faster and more convenient.

    C) Trains are cheaper, safer and more comfortable.

    D) Planes are safer, cheaper and more comfortable.

Passage Two

Questions 14 to 16 are based on the passage you have just heard.

14. A) Underground buildings.   B) Ancient civilizations.

    C) Climate changes.   D) Energy crisis.

15. A) In China.   B) In Turkey.

    C) In Spain.   D) In Canada.

16. A) Hot.   B) Warm.

    C) Cold.   D) Comfortable.

Passage Three

Questions 17 to 20 are based on the dialog you have just heard.

17. A) Get his calculator repaired.

    B) Return his calculator and get a new one.

    C) Buy a calculator with new features.

    D) Return his calculator and buy a cheaper one.

18. A) One of its buttons doesn't work.   B) It is too expensive.

C) It doesn't have any new features.   D) The figures cannot be removed.

19. A) $ 49.99.   B) $ 37.99.
    C) $ 27.99.   D) $ 39.99.

20. A) A new calculator.   B) A new receipt.
    C) The money he paid.   D) Some records.

Part II   Vocabulary

Directions: *There are 20 incomplete sentences in this part. For each sentence there are four choices marked A), B), C) and D). Choose the ONE answer that best completes the sentence. Then mark the corresponding letter on the Answer Sheet with a single line through the center.*

21. They need the additional help to get the work done as _____.
    A) scheduled   B) involved
    C) referred   D) represented

22. Tension has been _____ between the employers and the workers on strike.
    A) grown up   B) pulled up
    C) built up   D) put up

23. Can you describe the _____ by which paper is made from wood?
    A) measure   B) process
    C) origin   D) source

24. He didn't want to retire at an early age and lead a (n) _____ life.
    A) lazy   B) blank
    C) empty   D) bare

25. The old couple _____ a hard living by selling vegetables every day on the roadside.
    A) lived   B) earned
    C) passed   D) saved

26. The situation was _____ delicate between the two countries in the early 90's.
    A) extraordinary   B) extremely
    C) eventually   D) hopefully

27. The story of Lei Feng _____ millions of people to give help to those in need.
    A) struggled   B) inspired
    C) discouraged   D) created

28. They gave each member a number, but they _____ No.13 as no one wanted to have it.
    A) pointed out   B) made out
    C) let out   D) left out

29. The company _____ him a very high salary, but he still wasn't content with it.
    A) afforded   B) offered
    C) provided   D) supplied

30. Every man or woman in China over the age of 18 is _____ to the right to vote.

A) engaged

B) enjoyed

C) protected

D) entitled

31. However bad the situation is, the facts should not be _____ the people who are concerned about public affairs.

A) kept from

B) kept away

C) kept up

D) kept out

32. As a young boy, he only received three years of _____ education, but he loved reading and later became a famous writer.

A) formal

B) normal

C) constant

D) former

33. I'm leaving for the airport in 15 minutes; so just give me the news _____.

A) in time

B) in brief

C) in line

D) in detail

34. As the managing director can't go to the reception, I'm representing the company _____.

A) in his consideration

B) for his part

C) on his behalf

D) from his point of view

35. After long talks, they managed to _____ an agreement on rates of pay.

A) arrive

B) reach

C) come

D) signal

36. He is a very kind man, _____ to his family and friends.

A) loyal

B) royal

C) confident

D) proper

37. An advanced public transportation system is _____ to the development of a big city.

A) initial

B) partial

C) essential

D) proper

38. The headmaster had been trying to _____ money for a new science project.

A) arise

B) rise

C) raise

D) arouse

39. Although I spoke to him many times, he never took any _____ of what I said.

A) notice

B) remark

C) observation

D) attention

40. _____ the terrible flood of bad novels and poor works, there are good novelists.

A) For

B) Since

C) Though

D) Despite

Part Ⅲ　Structure

Directions: *There are 20 incomplete sentences in this part. For each sentence there are four choices marked A), B), C) and D). Choose the ONE answer that best completes* *the sentence. Then mark the corresponding letter on the Answer Sheet with a single line through the center.*

41. "Why didn't you use that printer?"
    "Because it wasn't _____ to fit it."
    A) as enough good.   B) good enough
    C) enough good   D) good as enough

42. The boy looked at the stranger carefully, _____ who he could be.
    A) to wonder   B) wondered
    C) wondering   D) having wondered

43. The boss won't give the workers pay unless they _____ their work today.
    A) finish   B) finished
    C) will finish   D) had finished

44. The city has now over ten five-star hotels, almost _____ there were six years ago.
    A) as many as three times   B) three times as many as
    C) as three more times as   D) as three times many as

45. The culture and customs of America are more like _____ of Great Britain and some other European nations.
    A) that   B) which
    C) what   D) those

46. The wounded soldier had the message _____ straight to the army commander.
    A) sent   B) to send
    C) to be sent   D) being sent

47. _____ people say about him, I'm sure that he is innocent.
    A) Whoever   B) Whatever
    C) However   D) Whenever

48. He spoke English confidently and fluently, _____ impressed me most.
    A) so that   B) it
    C) that   D) which

49. There are five Chinese restaurants in the downtown area; and this is by far _____.
    A) better   B) the better
    C) best   D) the best

50. I didn't mean _____ anything, but those apples looked so nice that I couldn't resist _____ one.
    A) to eat; trying   B) to eat; to try
    C) eating; to try   D) eating; trying

51. Mr. Green is not the same person _____ four years ago in college.
    A) who was   B) what he was
    C) as he was   D) that he was

52. He showed me a photo of the fancy hotel on the seashore _____ he stayed for a week.

A) there
B) where

C) which
D) that

53. It was with great joy _____ we got the news that China had successfully launched its first manned spacecraft.

A) which
B) because

C) as
D) that

54. Try to imagine _____ the Pacific Ocean in a small sailing boat.

A) crossing
B) to cross

C) to be crossed
D) on crossing

55. Dream of the Red Chamber is said to _____ into several foreign languages in the last decade.

A) be translated
B) translate

C) have been translated
D) have translated

56. We warned the children time and again _____ the electric lamp.

A) not to touch
B) not touch

C) not touching
D) should not touch

57. It was vital that we _____ every measure to protect the beautiful scenery around the lake.

A) must take
B) will take

C) have to take
D) take

58. You promised her a letter; and you ought to _____ to her days ago.

A) write
B) have written

C) be writing
D) be written

59. _____ is now the northern Sahara Desert fed much of the civilized world 2500 years ago.

A) This
B) That

C) What
D) It

60. I want to leave my car around here. Can you tell me if _____ a parking lot near here?

A) there is
B) is there

C) there has been
D) there it is

Part IV Reading Comprehension

Directions: *There are 3 passages in this part. Each passage is followed by some questions or unfinished statements. For each of them there are four choices marked A), B), C) and D). You should decide on the best choice and mark the corresponding letter on the Answer Sheet with a single line through the center.*

Passage One

Questions 61 to 65 are based on the following passage:

Many people who are rich are also well-known. Ted Sweeney was an exception to this rule. His family moved to San Francisco from Los Angeles when he was one month old. That's where he grew up. At the age of seventeen he was hit by a train. Although he was not seriously hurt, the railroad paid him $25,000. Instead of going to college he bought a small store. Six months later the government bought his land to build a new highway. He sold it for $95,000.

With this money he moved to Detroit. He started a small company that made parts for the car manufacturers. It was very successful and by the time he was 23 he was a millionaire. When he was 24 he got married. He and his wife had three daughters in the next five years. By the time he was 30 he had over ten million dollars.

Then tragedy struck. He was involved in a traffic accident. He did not die but his wife and daughters did. Six months later he sold everything he owned and put his money in stocks. Ted then moved to New York. He lived for the next forty years in a one-room apartment.

He spent most of his days wandering through the city looking in garbage cans for food. He never worked. He rarely talked to anyone except himself. Most people were afraid of him. His clothes were always old and dirty.

Shortly before he died he moved back to Los Angeles. After spending two weeks there he was put in jail because he had no money and no job. City workers tried to help him. They offered him work but he would not work. Towards the end he would not talk to anyone at all.

When he died, he was a lonely man. But someone remembered his name. They knew he had lived in Detroit and had been successful. It was learned that he had put his stocks in a box at a Detroit bank. After they were sold and all the taxes paid, there was still over a hundred million dollars left.

61. Where did Sweeney grow up?
   A) Los Angeles.   B) Detroit.
   C) San Francisco.   D) New York.

62. Sweeney became successful in business by _____.
   A) making car parts
   B) selling his land to the government
   C) putting his money in stocks
   D) depositing money at a bank

63. Which of the following statements about Sweeney's life in New York is implied in the passage?
   A) He led a poor life there.
   B) He made many friends there.
   C) He was not allowed to work there.
   D) He stayed in jail for some time there.

64. How old probably was Sweeney when he died?
   A) Over 50.   B) Over 60.
   C) Over 70.   D) Over 80.

65. What can we conclude from the passage?
   A) People may not be aware of their wealth.
   B) Sweeney became rich by selling garage cans.

C) Sweeney lost all his money in the stock market.

D) People may be rich but not well-known.

Passage Two

Questions 66 to 70 are based on the following passage:

If it were only necessary to decide whether to teach elementary science to everyone on a mass basis or to find the gifted few and take them as far as they can go, our task would be fairly simple. The public school system, however, has no such choice, for the jobs must be carried on at the same time. Because we depend so heavily upon science and technology for our progress, we produce specialists in many fields. Because we live in a democratic nation, whose citizens make the policies for the nation, large numbers of us must be educated to understand, to support, and when necessary, to judge the work of experts. The public school must educate both producers and users of scientific services.

In education, there should be a balance among the branches of knowledge that contribute to effective thinking and wise judgment. Such balance is defeated by too much emphasis on any one field. This question of balance involves not only the relation of the natural sciences, the social sciences, and the arts, but also relative emphasis among the natural sciences themselves.

Similarly, we must have a balance between current and classical knowledge. The attention of the public is continually drawn to new possibilities in scientific fields and the discovery of new knowledge; these should not be allowed to turn our attention away from the sound, established materials that form the basis of courses for beginners.

66. According to the passage, the task for the public school system is _____.

   A) easy   B) unnecessary

   C) complicated   D) simple

67. Whom must the public school educate according to the writer?

   A) Specialists only.   B) Both common people and specialists.

   C) Common people only.   D) Both experts and officials.

68. The writer believes that the public school education must take care of _____.

   A) the natural sciences only   B) the social sciences only

   C) the arts only   D) all useful fields

69. Which of the following does the writer think most important to students?

   A) Both newly-found and well-established knowledge.

   B) The basis of courses for beginners.

   C) The latest developments in science and technology.

   D) The work of experts.

70. Which of the following is the best title for the passage?

   A) Judging the Work of Experts.

   B) Education and Knowledge.

   C) Subjects in Public School System.

D) Balance in Education.

Passage Three

Questions 71 to 75 are based on the following letter:

Dear Mr. Paul,

Well, I've just signed the lease(租约) and I'm opening my own radio and TV repair shop. Even though I haven't finished half the course yet, the practical experience I had before I started and what I've learned from you folks so far makes me feel I can *make a go of it*.

I guess that gives you some idea why I've gotten a little behind in my payments. I think I owe you for three months right now. It takes a lot of money to start a shop, fix it up and get all the tools and equipment.

Everybody's been very nice to me. The companies I approached have all agreed to give me credit even though I'm new and never did any business with them before. Well, you folks have known me for nearly six months now and until recently I've always paid on time. You know what can be made in this business and from the good grades and reports I've had on my assignments I think you know I have what it takes to make this business a success.

So I'm asking you to do what the people who don't know me have done. I want to complete the course just as fast as I can. The more I know the better I can do, but I want you to give me credit. I want to finish the course and pay you when the shop starts earning money.

Maybe six months from now, I'll have an easy time paying. In the meantime keep me going and you can count on getting your money when I'm through. I've got to hold on to all my money for working capital.

I'll appreciate your cooperation.

Very truly yours,

John Johnson

71. This letter was written to ask for permission _____.

   A) to delay paying the money   B) to open a repair shop

   C) to borrow some money   D) to complete the course

72. How does the writer describe himself?

   A) He is a friendly person.   B) He is good at doing business.

   C) He is a good student.   D) He is an experienced repairman.

73. How does the writer feel about his new business?

   A) Uncertain.   B) Amazed.

   C) Satisfied.   D) Confident.

74. The letter writer promises that he will _____.

   A) try hard to earn money

   B) eventually pay for the course

   C) thank everyone who helped him

   D) take more courses from the school

75. Most likely, "**make a go of it**" (Line 3, Para. 1) means _____.

A) "cause the business to succeed"

B) "make the business expensive"

C) "open the repair shop"

D) "gain more knowledge from the business"

Part Ⅴ Translation from English into Chinese

Directions: *In this part there is a passage with 5 underlined sections, numbered 76 to 80. After reading the passage carefully, translate the underlined sections into Chinese. Remember to write your translation on the Translation Sheet.*

Nearly every day, giant tankers carry 8 million barrels of oil from Saudi Arabia(沙特阿拉伯)to refineries(炼油厂) around the world.

But after the recent bombing in Riyadh, energy analysts(分析家) are nervously reassessing (重新评估) the stability of supplies of crude from the oil kingdom.

Since oil prices are relatively high entering winter, Americans will notice any further problems in Saudi Arabia as they fill up their gas tank or pay for home heating oil. (76) The price for West Texas crude closed above $32 a barrel last week, the highest point since the beginning of October and up from about $25 a barrel last year at this time.

The higher price of crude is already reflected in steeper costs than last season: home heating oil is up some 19 cents a gallon, and gasoline is 9 cents a gallon higher.

"The only thing keeping prices above $25 a barrel is fear of terrorist(恐怖分子) activity," says Dennis Gartman, publisher of the Gartman Letter, an influential political and economic newsletter. (77) "All things being equal and if there are no terrorist attacks, these are very high prices."

The US depends heavily on Saudi Arabia for oil. In terms of that arrangement, (78) one key concern, says Mr. Gartman, is the long distance that Saudi Arabia moves its oil to terminals(终点). "The pipelines are long and exposed as they move across the desert," he says. "I don't care how vigilant(警觉) you are, there are places that you are not defending."

So far, however, there have been no attacks on the pipelines, producing areas, or terminals. The most recent attack was on a housing complex. But energy analysts are taking seriously such a target—more political than economic—particularly since (79) Saudi Arabia is the second-largest supplier of oil to the United States and represents one-third of all oil produced by OPEC(石油输出国组织).

(80) "The problems should remind us how dependent we are on Saudi oil production," says Robert Hormats, vice chairman of Goldman Sachs International in New York. "We have an interest in a stable Saudi Arabia."

Part VI Translation from Chinese into English

Directions: *In this part there are five sentences, numbered 81 to 85, in Chinese. Translate these sentences into English on the Translation Sheet.*

81. 他渴望早日康复，回到校园继续他的教学和科研工作。

82. 当地经济的四大特点可以归纳如下。

83. 玛丽考虑结婚后辞掉工作，在家照顾丈夫和孩子。

84. 一个小孩是否能健康成长取决于他生活的环境。

85. 他宁可住在宁静的乡村，而不愿迁往喧闹的城市。

【听力录音文稿】

Section A

1. M: I am traveling to Rome on Flight BA 762. Do I check in here?

   W: That's right. Can I see your ticket and passport, please?

   Q: Where are the speakers?

2. W: Would you like some hot coffee or tea?

   M: I do like them both, but I'd rather have something cold.

   Q: What would the man like to drink now?

3. W: Anne must be over twenty now?

   M: Yes, when Tom left London ten years ago, Anne was already fifteen.

   Q: How old is Anne now?

4. W: Good evening, John. I'm so glad that you could come to join us. But where is Sally?

   M: She sends her apologies. She has a big exam tomorrow and she must be sure to be ready for it.

   Q: What is Sally going to do tonight?

5. M: Did Bill say it will clear up Sunday?

   W: I don't think he said it but it probably will.

   Q: What are the speakers talking about?

6. M: What do you think I can get for your father?

   W: Why don't you get him a watch?

   Q: What is the man trying to do?

7. W: Richard, is this your dictionary?

   M: No, Lucy. It's Karen's. Mine was sent to Karl.

   Q: Whose dictionary is it?

8. M: Are you still planning to rent a house?

   W: Yes, but not until I get back from my winter vacation.

   Q: What will the woman do first?

9. M: Do you think Tom will get here on time?

   W: If Tom doesn't, nobody will.

   Q: What does the woman mean?

10. W: The letter is written in Arabic. Do you know who can translate it for me?

    M: How about Janet?

    Q: What can we learn about Janet?

Section B

Passage One

How can anyone like flying? It's a crazy thing to do. Birds fly; people don't. I hate flying. You wait for hours for the plane to take off, and it's often late. The plane's always crowded. You can't walk around and there's nothing to do. You can't open the windows and you can't get off. The seats are uncomfortable, there's no choice of food and there are never enough toilets. Then after the plane lands, it's even worse. It takes hours to get out of the airport and into the city.

I prefer traveling by train. Trains are much better than planes; they're cheaper, safer, and more comfortable. You can walk around in a train and open the windows. Stations are more convenient than airports, because you can get on and off in the middle of cities. If you miss a train, you can always catch another one later. Yes, trains are slower, but speed isn't everything. Staying alive and enjoying yourself is more important.

Questions 11 to 13 are based on the passage you have just heard.

11. What can we say about the speaker?

12. What does the speaker say about airports?

13. How does the speaker compare trains and planes?

Passage Two

The idea of underground houses is very old. People in the past lived in underground houses and underground cites in China, Spain, and Turkey. Today there are large underground shopping centers in Japan, Korea(R.O.), and Canada. Some countries also build underground factories and warehouses.

In the United States more people are beginning to build underground house. Underground houses save open land. When houses are underground, there is more land for parks, tennis courts, and gardens. Underground houses also save energy. They use only a little energy to stay warm or cool.

Joyce Rinker has an underground house in Michigan. One day in February, the outside temperature was cold, but the temperature inside the house was warm. The next year, in July, the outside temperature was hot, but the temperature inside the house was comfortable.

Questions 14 to 16 are based on the passage you have just heard.

14. What does the speaker mainly talk about?

15. Where are underground shopping centers found?

16. What's the temperature like in Joyce Rinker's underground house in July?

Passage Three

M: Excuse me.

W: Yes?

M: I bought this calculator here yesterday but it doesn't work.

W: Oh, let's see what's wrong.

M: This button doesn't work. When I push it, nothing happens.

W: You're right. I'll give another one. Do you have the receipt?

M: Yes. Here you are.

W: All right. Let's see if I can find you another one. Oh, here's one. It's almost the same but it has this new feature too.

M: How much is this one?

W: It's $49.99.

M: That's more than I paid for the other calculator.

W: Yes, it's more expensive but you can just pay the difference. For $12.00 more you get the new feature.

M: No, thanks. I just want another calculator like the one I bought.

W: I'm sorry, but we don't have another one like that. This is all we have right now.

M: Do you have a cheaper one?

W: No. The one for $49.99 is our cheapest.

M: All right. I'll get my money back then.

W: OK. Sorry we can't give you the right one. Would you sign here for the return? We have to keep these records. Thanks. Here's your money.

M: Thank you. Bye-bye.

W: Bye now.

Questions 17 to 20 are based on the dialog you have just heard.

17. What does the man want to do?

18. What's wrong with the calculator?

19. How much did the man pay for his calculator?

20. What does the man get in the end?

【试题解析】

第一部分　听力理解

1. 正确答案:C。男士询问的是前往罗马的 BA762 航班是否在此办理行李托运,所以应该是在机场。

2. 正确答案:D。男士此刻想喝点冷的饮料。

3. 正确答案:D。男士说到 Anne 十年前十五岁,所以她现在应该是二十五岁。

4. 正确答案:B。Sally 明天有个重要的考试,由此推断出她今晚得准备。

5. 正确答案:A。it will clear up 是指天要放晴。

6. 正确答案:A。男士问女士该给她父亲买个什么礼物。

7. 正确答案:C。此题要求能听辨出人名加所有格。

8. 正确答案:A。此题要求判断事件发生的时间先后。关键要掌握 not until 的用法。

9. 正确答案:B。女士用条件句强调 Tom 不会迟到。

10. 正确答案:B。How about ...? 常引出委婉的建议、推荐、看法等。

11. 正确答案:B。谈话显然在强调乘火车优于坐飞机。

12. 正确答案:D。做此题时不要混淆飞机和飞机场。机场远离市区是一个不便之处。

13. 正确答案:C。解答此题只需结合主题加以概括。

14. 正确答案:A。本文主要介绍地下建筑。

15. 正确答案:D。文中说到日本、韩国和加拿大有地下购物中心。

16. 正确答案:D。地下室夏天凉爽,故选 comfortable.

17. 正确答案:B。顾客本想调换一个价格相同的计算器。

18. 正确答案:A。顾客拿回来的计算器的质量问题是有个按键坏了。

19. 正确答案:B。营业员推荐一款 49.99 美元的计算器,比原先那个贵 12 美元。

20. 正确答案:C。最后顾客只好退货,并获得全额退款。

第二部分 词 汇

21. 正确答案:A。句意为:要按时完成工作,他们需要额外的帮助。
as scheduled 按预先安排/ involve 使卷入,常用在 be involved in 这一结构中/refer 指,常用搭配是 refer to（指,参考）和 be referred to as(叫做,被称为)/represent 代表。例:Four cars were involved in the accident. 这起事故有四辆车卷入其中。The disease was referred to as SARS. 这种疾病被称作 SARS.

22. 正确答案:C。句意为:雇主和罢工工人之间的关系越来越紧张。
grow up 成长/pull up (车辆)减速并停下来 /build up 积累、逐步形成和发展/ put up 提出。解此题时要注意句首的被动语态。

23. 正确答案:B。句意为:你能描述一下用木材造纸的过程吗?
measure 措施/ process (加工)过程 /origin 起源 /source 来源。

24. 正确答案:C。句意为:他不愿意年纪轻轻就退休,从而过着空虚的生活。
lazy 懒惰/blank 空白/ empty 空虚/ bare 光秃秃。这题主要测试形容词与名词间的习惯搭配。

25. 正确答案:B。句意为:那对老夫妻靠每天在路边卖蔬菜艰难度日。
这里主要要求掌握 earn a living(谋生)这一固定搭配。

26. 正确答案:B。句意为:90 年代初期,两国间的形势十分微妙。
此题首先要求用副词,故排除 extraordinary（非凡的）。用 extremely(极为)强调微妙的程度。

27. 正确答案:B。句意为:雷锋的故事激励了数百万人去帮助那些需要帮助的人。
struggle 奋斗,斗争/inspire 激励,鼓舞/ discourage 使泄气/create 创造。此题关键是读懂

题意及掌握 inspire 的词义。

28. 正确答案:D。句意为:他们发给每个成员一个号码,但空出 13 号,因为没人愿意要这个号。

point out 指出 / make out 弄清楚 / let out 释放,放掉 / leave out 遗漏,略去。西方文化中常把 13 当作不吉利数字而刻意回避,所以发号码时不设 13 号,即跳过、略去。

29. 正确答案:B。句意为:公司给他开出很高的薪水,但他仍不满意。

这里四个选项中只有 offer 常带双宾语。provide/supply sb. 后面常接 with sth.,意为“向某人提供某物”。

30. 正确答案:D。句意为:在中国,18 周岁以上者,不论男女,都有选举权。

注意题干中空格后的介词 to,它与 entitle 构成固定搭配 be entitled to,意为“拥有(被赋予)权利、资格等”。例:The old man is entitled to free medical treatment. 老人可以享受免费医疗。

31. 正确答案:A。句意为:无论形势多坏,都不能向关心公共事务的人们隐瞒事实。

keep from 不让……知道 / keep away 离开 / keep up 保持 / keep out 不进入。例:You can't keep the matter from others. 你不可能不让其他人知道这件事。Children should be kept away from fire. 不要让小孩接近火。Close the door and windows to keep the cold out. 关上门窗别让寒气进来。

32. 正确答案:A。句意为:他小时候只接受过三年的正规教育,可他爱读书,后来成了知名作家。

formal 正式的 / normal 正常的 / constant 持续的 / former 以前的。

33. 正确答案:B。句意为:15 分钟后我要动身去机场,就告诉我简要新闻吧。

解题关键在于理解题干中的上下文:时间不多了,简明扼要报一下新闻。

34. 正确答案:C。句意为:因为总经理无法出席招待会,我替他代表公司参加。

句中动词 represent 和词组 on one's behalf 都有“代表”之意。

35. 正确答案:B。句意为:经过漫长的会谈,他们就付款标准达成了协议。

可以用在 agreement 前与之搭配的常见动词或动词词组有 reach, sign, arrive at, come to 等。

36. 正确答案:A。句意为:他人挺好,对家人和朋友都很忠诚。

此题要求能辨别音、形相近的词:royal 王室的,皇家的 / loyal 忠诚的,忠实的。

37. 正确答案:C。句意为:对一个大城市的发展来说,发达的交通系统是至关重要的。

initial 最初的 / partial 部分的,偏心的 / essential 必不可少的 / proper 恰当的。

38. 正确答案:C。句意为:校长一直在为一个新的科学项目筹款。

这是几个因词形接近而易混淆的词。arise *vi.* 出现 / rise *vi.* 上升 / raise *vt.* 提升,筹集 / arouse *vt.* 唤起,唤醒。

39. 正确答案:A。句意为:虽然我找他谈过好多次,但他从不以为然。

四个选项中的词作名词时搭配各不相同。例:take notice, make a remark, make an observation, pay attention.

40. 正确答案:D。句意为:尽管劣质小说和平庸作品比比皆是,优秀的小说家仍大有人在。

句子的前半部分虽然在语意上类似于让步状语从句,但结构上只是一个名词词组,所以要选介词 despite。

第三部分 语法结构

41. 正确答案:B。句意为:"你为什么不用那个打印机?""因为它不够好,不匹配。"
此题考的语法点是 enough 的用法。基本规则是 enough 在充当形容词时出现在被修饰的名词前,在充当副词时出现在被修饰的形容词或副词之后。

42. 正确答案:C。句意为:男孩仔细地看着陌生人,心想他到底是谁。
该句中前一个是主句,逗号后非谓语从句中的动词与主句是主谓关系,时间上又和主句谓语动词是同时的,故用现在分词。

43. 正确答案:A。句意为:老板不会付工钱给工人们,除非他们今天完成工作。
当主句谓语是将来时态时,从句中的将来时常用一般现在时表示。

44. 正确答案:B。市内现有十多家五星级宾馆,是六年前的三倍。
要记住"数字 + times + as many/much as ..."这一结构。

45. 正确答案:D。句意为:美国的文化和习俗更接近于英国和一些其他欧洲国家。
这里用 those 指代前文中提到的"文化和习俗"。

46. 正确答案:A。伤员请人把信直接交给陆军指挥官。
此题主要考 have something done 这一用法,与之相对应的是 have someone do something。其中动词"do"的执行者都不是 have 的主语。

47. 正确答案:B。句意为:无论别人说他什么,我都坚信他是清白的。
Whatever people say about him 可理解为 No matter what is said about him。

48. 正确答案:D。句意为:他说英语既自信又流利,这给我留下深刻印象。
空格前加了逗号,表明要用非限定性定语从句,先行词要用 which。

49. 正确答案:D。句意为:市区共有五家中国餐馆,而这家比其他几家要好得多。
by far 放在比较级或最高级前强调程度高出许多。这里是比较两个以上,故用最高级,并加定冠词。

50. 正确答案:A。句意为:我本来不想吃东西,可这些苹果看上去太诱人了,我忍不住要尝一个。
mean 表示"打算"时,后接动词不定式;resist 后常接名词或动名词。

51. 正确答案:C。句意为:格林先生与四年前在大学相比已判若两人了。
解此题只需记住 the same as 这一固定搭配。

52. 正确答案:B。句意为:他给我看了一张摄于一家豪华海滨酒店的照片,他在那里住了一星期。
where 在从句中充当状语,所对应的先行词是 hotel。

53. 正确答案:D。句意为:听到中国第一艘载人飞船发射成功的消息,我们欣喜若狂。
这是一个强调句,套用的是 it is ...that...结构。

54. 正确答案:A。句意为:想像一下乘坐一艘小帆船横渡太平洋的情形。
这是一个祈使句,imagine 是句中的谓语动词,它后面接动名词 crossing。

55. 正确答案:C。句意为:据说,在过去十年间,《红楼梦》已被译成多种外语。
此题测试要点是时态语态。

56. 正确答案:A。句意为:我们警告过孩子们好几次,不要去摸电灯。
此题考查要点是 warn 后面常接否定词,再加不定式,即:warn someone not to do some-

thing。

57. 正确答案:D。句意为:至关重要的是:我们必须采取一切措施保护沿湖一带的美丽风景。由 it is + vital, necessary, essential, important, etc. + that 引导的从句中动词要用原形,相当于动词前省略了 should。

58. 正确答案:B。句意为:你许诺给他写信,你几天前就该写了。此题要注意的重点是 ought to 后面的动词时态,因为是几天前该做的事,所以用完成时。

59. 正确答案:C。句意为:现在的撒哈拉沙漠北部在 2500 多年前哺育了文明世界的大部分人口。此题的结构比较复杂。它的谓语动词是 fed,之前的部分是一个名词性从句,充当整句的主语,故要用 what 引导。

60. 正确答案:A。句意为:我想把车停在这里。你能告诉我附近有停车场吗?这里考查的是基本的存在句。

第四部分　阅读理解

第一篇短文参考译文及语言注释

多数富人往往同时名声显赫。Ted Sweeney 却是这个规律中的一个例外。在他才一个月大时,他全家从旧金山搬到了洛杉矶。他在那里长大。17 岁那年他被火车撞了一下。虽然他没受重伤,铁路公司赔付了他 25000 美元。他没有去上大学,而是买下了一家小店铺。六个月后政府因修建铁路买下了他的地。他卖地得了 95000 美元。

带着这笔钱他搬到了底特律。他开了一家小公司,为汽车生产商制造零部件。公司生意很成功,他 23 岁就成了百万富翁。他 24 岁结了婚。在接下来的五年里他和他妻子生了三个女儿。30 岁时,他的财富已超过了一千万。

悲剧随之向他袭来。他遭遇了一场车祸。他死里逃生,但他的妻子和女儿们无一幸免。六个月后他卖掉了公司,用这笔钱买了股票。之后 Ted 搬到了纽约,在一个单间公寓里一住就是 40 年。

他大多数时间在市内流浪,从垃圾筒里找吃的。他不工作,也极少与别人攀谈,只是自言自语。大家都怕他。他的衣服总是又旧又脏。

在他去世前不久,他搬回了洛杉矶。两周后他被送进了监狱,因为他没钱,也没工作。市政工人们想要帮他。他们给他活干可他不愿意干。最后他不愿意跟任何人说话。

他孤独地死了。但是有人记起了他的名字。他们知道他在底特律住过,而且很成功。听说他把他的股票放在底特律一家银行的一个盒子里。这些股票卖掉并完税后,仍有一亿多美元。

第一段 an exception to this rule 中 this rule 指的是有钱人往往会有名这一规律。

试题解答

61. 正确答案:C。第一段中有交代。

62. 正确答案:A。他经营的是汽车零配件。

63. 正确答案:A。他在纽约以捡垃圾为生。

64. 正确答案:C。家庭悲剧发生时他至少 30 岁,此后他在纽约 40 年,回洛杉矶后不久就去世了。

65. 正确答案:D。从文中最后一段第一句可找到答案。

如果只需决定是面向大众讲授基础科学或是找出少数天才教得越深越好,我们的任务就会十分简单。然而,公立学校系统没有这样的选择余地。因为上述两个任务必须同时完成。由于我们的进步极大地依赖科学技术,我们要培养各个领域的专门人才;由于我们生活在一个民主国家,公民决定国家政策,大量的人必须接受教育,从而去理解、支持,并在必要时评判专家们的工作。公立学校必须同时培养科技服务的提供者和使用者。

教育必须求得不同知识领域间的平衡以获得有效的思想和明智的判断。过于强调任何一个领域都会打破这种平衡。这个平衡问题不但牵涉到自然科学、社会科学和人文科学,它还涉及自然科学本身之内各学科间的侧重。

依此类推,我们必须获得现代知识和古典知识间的平衡。公众的注意力永远会关注科学领域新的可能性和新知识的发现。但是我们不能因此而忽略构成针对初学者基础课程的那些扎实、完善的材料。

the gifted few 少数天资聪慧的学生。

试题解答

本文整体较抽象,句子也较长。理解全文和回答问题的关键是读懂作者的主要意图,即公共教育要照顾到精英与大众的平衡、社科与人文的平衡、新旧知识的平衡。所有问题都是围绕这一主题的。

66. 正确答案:C。作者强调公立学校担负双重任务。

67. 正确答案:B。第一段中阐明了公立学校既要培养专门人才,又要面向大众。

68. 正确答案:D。第二段中强调了各学科间的平衡。

69. 正确答案:A。最后一段回答了这个问题。

70. 正确答案:D。综观全文,平衡是关键。

第三篇短文参考译文及语言注释

保罗先生,

我刚签了租约准备开一家自己的无线电修理店。虽然我还没有学完课程的一半,但凭我原有的实践经验和从你们那里学到的本领,我觉得我会干得很出色的。

我想这样说会让你们渐渐明白我为什么拖欠了这些款项。我大概欠你们三个月的账。开张一间店铺、装修门面,并购置所有的工具设备要花一大笔钱。

大家都对我很帮忙。我接触的公司都同意让我赊账,虽然我是新手,以前从未跟他们有过生意往来。你们认识我已有近六个月了,直到最近我都是按时付款的。你们了解这个行当能赚多少钱;而且从我的良好成绩和作业反馈中,我想你们也知道我有把生意做好的能力。所以我想请求你们做一件那些不太认识我的人已经做了的事。我想尽快学完课程。学得越多,我就能做得越好。不过我想要你们给我赊账。我想先学完课程,等我的店赚钱后再付钱给你们。

大概从现在算起六个月后,我的日子能好过些,可以还钱了。在此期间,让我继续修课。相信我,等我过了这一关我会还钱的。目前我手头的钱都得作运作资本。

感谢你们的合作。

非常真挚的
约翰·约翰逊

文中 you folks 是对对方较亲近、随便的称呼,其作用相当于我们说的套近乎;approach 作动词,有找人联系、洽谈业务之意;第四段中 the people who don't know me 指的就是第三段提到的公司。

试题解答

71. 正确答案:A。写信者拖欠了学费,要求缓交。信中讲述了提这个要求的理由。

72. 正确答案:C。信的第三段提到了这一点。

73. 正确答案:D。全文都显得很自信,尤其开头和结尾说得较明确。

74. 正确答案:B。结尾的第五段他作了保证。

75. 正确答案:A。他既有以前的经验,又从朋友那学到了许多有益的东西,为此从上下文可判断 A 是正确答案。

第五部分　英译汉

76. 上周西得克萨斯原油的收盘价高于每桶 32 美元,是自 10 月初以来的最高价。

77. 即便所有因素相同,也没有恐怖袭击,这些也是非常高的价格。

78. 令人担心的一个关键是从沙特阿拉伯把原油运到目的地的遥远距离。

79. 沙特阿拉伯是对美国的第二大石油供应国,它的石油产量占石油输出国组织石油产量的三分之一。

80. 这些问题应该让我们清醒地认识到我们对沙特石油产品的依赖程度。

第六部分　汉译英

81. He hopes to recover soon and return to the campus for teaching and research.

82. The four characteristics of the local economy can be summed up as follows.

83. Mary is thinking of quitting her job after she gets married, so that she can look after her husband and children.

84. Whether a child can grow healthily or not depends on the environment he lives in.

85. He would rather live in the peaceful countryside than move to the noisy city.

2004年6月浙江省大学英语三级考试试卷

Part I   Listening Comprehension

Section A

Directions: *In this section, you will hear 10 short conversations. At the end of each conversation, a question will be asked about what was said. You will hear the conversation and the question only once. After each question there will be a pause. During the pause, you must read the four choices marked A), B), C) and D), and decide which is the best answer. Then mark the corresponding letter on the Answer Sheet with a single line through the center.*

1. A) The woman is joking.
   C) He's leaving in three weeks.
   B) The refrigerator doesn't work well.
   D) It's not surprising the milk went bad.

2. A) Study math with John.
   C) Discuss the problem with John.
   B) Take John to a teacher.
   D) Grade John's math test.

3. A) He will not eat the food.
   C) He will make a wish.
   B) He will take a bite of the cake.
   D) He will cook a great cake.

4. A) Take a walk in the rain.
   C) Go on a picnic.
   B) Delay their picnic.
   D) Call their uncle.

5. A) Secretary.
   C) Boss.
   B) Student.
   D) Customer.

6. A) At 8:30.
   C) At 9:00.
   B) At 9:30.
   D) At 10:00.

7. A) The man is too careful.
   B) The man shouldn't have locked the back door.
   C) The woman would lock the back door herself.
   D) The man should be more careful.

8. A) Starting her vacation.
   B) Looking for a new job.
   C) Complaining to her friend.
   D) Helping her friend to find Mr. Martin.

9. A) He is an excellent dancer.
   B) He doesn't dance very often.
   C) He doesn't talk about dancing very often.
   D) He goes dancing four times a week.

10. A) To the post office.　　　　　B) To a meeting.
　　　C) To the club.　　　　　　　　D) To Chris' house.

Section B

Directions: *In this section, you will hear 3 short passages or conversations. At the end of each passage or conversation, you will hear some questions. The passage or the conversation will be read twice. After you heart a passage or a conversation, you must choose the best answer from the four choices marked A), B), C) and D). Then mark the corresponding letter on the Answer Sheet with a single line through the center.*

Passage One

Questions 11 to 13 are based on the passage you have just heard.

11. A) To find out who is more intelligent, man or animals.
　　B) To find out which animal is more intelligent than man.
　　C) To find out which animal is the most intelligent.
　　D) To find out the IQs of different animals.

12. A) To hide the food lest it be eaten by the monkey.
　　B) To see how the monkey manages to find the food.
　　C) To see how fast the monkey finds the food.
　　D) To see whether monkeys have similar taste to man's.

13. A) The monkey was busy looking for the food.
　　B) The monkey was looking at the professor through the keyhole.
　　C) The monkey was moving directly to the box with the food.
　　D) The monkey was looking around in the room.

Passage Two

Questions 14 to 16 are based on the passage you have just heard.

14. A) Attractive scenery.　　　　　B) Nice weather.
　　C) Friendly people.　　　　　　D) Beautiful mountains.

15. A) Take a walk.　　　　　　　　B) Go swimming.
　　C) Go to a concert.　　　　　　D) Go for a lake tour.

16. A) People looking for business partners.
　　B) People looking for a place for holiday.
　　C) People interested in music.
　　D) People interested in outdoor sports.

Passage Three

Questions 17 to 20 are based on the passage you have just heard.

17. A) Ask for another gift that is useful.

    B) Exchange it for something useful.

    C) Return it to the person giving her the gift.

    D) Keep it for as long as possible.

18. A) To make the marriage legal.　　　B) To make the couple richer.

    C) To honor the couple.　　　D) To express good wishes.

19. A) The marriage will not be legal.

    B) The couple will lead an unhappy life.

    C) Others will look down upon the couple.

    D) The marriage will break up soon.

20. A) Because he has to work for his three children.

    B) Because he has to make enough money for his wife's family.

    C) Because it is a necessary ceremony at marriage.

    D) Because it is a necessary gift to exchange for his marriage.

Part II Vocabulary

Directions: *There are* 20 *incomplete sentences in this part. For each sentence there are four choices marked A), B), C) and D). Choose the ONE answer that best completes the sentence. Then mark the corresponding letter on the Answer Sheet with a single line through the center.*

21. We should _____ primary importance to the psychological health of the students.

    A) pay　　　　　　　　　　B) place

    C) attach　　　　　　　　　D) provide

22. The best students are _____ special scholarship.

    A) rewarded　　　　　　　　B) awarded

    C) presented　　　　　　　　D) represented

23. Yesterday the parties concerned sat together _____ several solutions to the problem.

    A) exposing　　　　　　　　B) exploring

    C) expressing　　　　　　　D) exploding

24. Experts from all parts of the world meet yearly in Hiroshima to _____ a conference on atomic war threats.

    A) present　　　　　　　　　B) attend

    C) join　　　　　　　　　　D) participate

25. The application of the new technology enables the factory to _____ twice as many machines as it did last year.

    A) turn down　　　　　　　　B) turn off

    C) turn to　　　　　　　　　D) turn out

26. The car was repaired but not quite to the owner's _____.
    A) pleasure
    B) satisfaction
    C) joy
    D) delight
27. They had a(n) _____ argument for several hours without reaching an agreement.
    A) bored
    B) excited
    C) heated
    D) interested
28. It was not Tom's _____ that he was late for school, because he was delayed by a traffic accident.
    A) fault
    B) error
    C) mistake
    D) failure
29. The students are eager to know what the weather will be like tomorrow because it will _____ their picnic directly.
    A) effect
    B) affect
    C) infect
    D) influence
30. She has been _____ twice since joining the company one year ago because of her excellent work.
    A) improved
    B) advanced
    C) promoted
    D) developed
31. The sports meeting had to be _____ because of the stormy weather.
    A) called on
    B) called for
    C) called up
    D) called off
32. Even David, the best student in the class, could not solve this problem, _____ other students.
    A) let alone
    B) let out
    C) let off
    D) let down
33. It was reported that only a five-year-old child _____ the serious traffic accident yesterday.
    A) endured
    B) survived
    C) lived
    D) passed
34. If you take this medicine twice a day it should _____ your illness very soon.
    A) treat
    B) recover
    C) cure
    D) restore
35. I don't think I know the girl in blue, although she _____ me of someone I know.
    A) recalls
    B) reminds
    C) suggests
    D) recognizes
36. There is no _____ in applying for the job since you don't have a BA degree.
    A) idea
    B) point
    C) example
    D) cause
37. On _____ men smoke more cigarettes than women.
    A) usual
    B) general
    C) average
    D) common

38. In order to improve our writing, we must _____ this plan.

    A) admit   B) advise

    C) correct   D) adopt

39. Tom could not _____ his mother that he had told the truth.

    A) convince   B) confine

    C) convert   D) confess

40. I'm afraid that your car won't be _____ until tomorrow. We have to replace the engine.

    A) finished   B) present

    C) prepared   D) ready

Part III Structure

Directions: *There are 20 incomplete sentences in this part. For each sentence there are four choices marked A), B), C) and D). Choose the ONE answer that best completes the sentence. Then mark the corresponding letter on the Answer Sheet with a single line through the center.*

41. The fellow I spoke to gave no answer, _____ puzzled me.

    A) that   B) which

    C) what   D) who

42. He was very busy yesterday, otherwise he _____ to the meeting.

    A) had come   B) came

    C) would come   D) would have come

43. I will go home for a vacation as soon as I _____ my exams.

    A) am finished   B) finish

    C) will finish   D) finished

44. _____ from space, our earth, with water covering 70% of its surface, appears as a "blue planet".

    A) Seen   B) Seeing

    C) Having seen   D) To see

45. She is the only one among the girls who _____ to experiment with snakes.

    A) are courage enough   B) is courage enough

    C) have enough courage   D) has enough courage

46. Would you mind _____ quiet for a moment, I'm trying _____ my composition in time.

    A) keeping; finishing   B) to keep; to finish

    C) keeping; to finish   D) to keep; finishing

47. _____ the boy had said turned out to be true.

    A) That   B) What

    C) Which   D) As

48. This is the very topic _____ at the meeting tomorrow.

A) discussed   B) having discussed

C) to be discussed   D) discussing

49. "What do you think of Mary's work, Bob?"

"Well, her work is _____."

A) good, if not better than, ours

B) as good as, if not better than, ours

C) as good, if not better, than ours

D) good, if not better, like ours

50. _____ difficulties we might meet with, we will carry out our plan.

A) Whatever   B) Whichever

C) Whenever   D) Wherever

51. "I wish we could meet each other again before long."

"_____."

A) So I could   B) So could I

C) So I do   D) So do I

52. It is impossible for me to finish so many exercises in _____.

A) such a short time   B) so a short time

C) such short a time   D) a so short time

53. It was noisy outside and he tried to make himself _____, but he couldn't.

A) hear   B) heard

C) hearing   D) be heard

54. It was because of his laziness _____ he failed the final exam.

A) so   B) that

C) so that   D) therefore

55. A cold is nothing to you _____ it is merely a cold; but it sometimes becomes a danger.

A) so long as   B) even though

C) no matter when   D) unless

56. You can find _____ in the book *on baby care*.

A) many advice   B) some advices

C) a lot of advices   D) lots of advice

57. He _____ on the essay for an hour but so far has written only a hundred words.

A) worked   B) has been working

C) works   D) is working

58. I would have come sooner, but I _____ that you were waiting.

A) did know   B) had known

C) don't know   D) didn't know

59. They will fail, because I think they _____ a general understanding of the situation.

A) are lacking   B) lack

C) lack of   D) have lacked

60. The boy was very frightened _____ he gave his watch to the robbers.

A) that   B) and

C) but   D) if

Part IV   Reading Comprehension

Directions: *There are 3 passages in this part. Each passage is followed by some questions or unfinished statements. For each of them there are four choices marked A), B), C) and D). You should decide on the best choice and mark the corresponding letter on the Answer Sheet with a single line through the center.*

Questions 61 to 65 are based on the following passage:

One of the best-known proverbs must be "early to bed and early to rise make a man healthy, wealthy, and wise." The promise of health, wealth, and wisdom to those who join the ranks of the *early* retirees and *risers* must be particularly appealing to many people in our contemporary society. There is no doubt that one of the greatest concerns of modern man is his health. It is estimated that in the United States $200 billion are spent on health care each year. The medical field has grown into such a big business that it employs 4.8 million people.

Much more interest has been shown in preventive medicine in recent years. This is probably due to the increasing costs of medical treatment, but the writings of such people as Dr. Kenneth Cooper have also played an important role. In his book *Aerobics*, Dr. Cooper communicated his message of the benefits of exercise so effectively that many other authors have followed in his trail, and literally millions of readers have put on their sports shoes and taken to the highways and byways of America. A recent survey showed that over 17 million people are jogging. Many of these are so serious that they trained themselves to run the 26 miles and 385 yards of the hard and tiring marathons(马拉松) that are organized all over the country. The last time I was in Honolulu, I was amazed to see hundreds of people, young and old, running for their lives. And I discovered many of them have run in the Hawaiian Marathon. Exercise has also become a major part of conversation. At a dinner party recently, the president of a bank asked me, "You look like a runner; how far do you run each day?" A few days later when I appeared on a national television show, the host suddenly asked me if I was a regular runner. On both occasions the conversation turned to the subject of exercise and I found that this is a subject on many people's minds.

61. The "*early risers*" mentioned in Paragraph 1 are _____.

   A) people who go to bed early   B) people who have a lot of money

   C) people who get up early   D) people who give up their work early

62. What does the writer think of the $200 billion spent on health care each year?

   A) It's a big sum of money.

   B) It's a huge waste of money.

   C) Most people can't afford the expensive medical treatment.

   D) The medical field provides a lot of job opportunities.

63. According to the passage, nowadays what people are most interested in is _____.

A) how to be a millionaire

B) how to keep fit

C) how to win the Hawaiian Marathon

D) how to develop aerobics in America

64. Why are the examples of conversation in the second paragraph used?

A) To show a usual way of starting a conversation.

B) To show the change in people's conversation topics.

C) To show the importance of running.

D) To show people's interest in exercise.

65. *Aerobics* is a book about _____.

A) marathon   B) preventive medicine

C) traveling   D) exercise

Questions 66 to 70 are based on the following passage:

Teacher evaluations(评价) have been carried out in a lot of schools in recent years. Every term the students are given the opportunity to evaluate their teachers. The students are supposed to judge their teachers' lectures, interests in students' problems, methods of exercise, and general ability to conduct a class. Then, when the teacher has left the classroom, they must write their evaluation on the forms provided. They are not supposed to exchange views or discuss their responses. After everyone has completed the forms, one student collects and puts them in envelopes.

It is very difficult to evaluate another person's performance fairly. For example, Santa recently wrote irresponsible remarks about her teacher because she was failing the course. Her friend Sam wrote a marvelous description of the same teacher because he was receiving an A in the course. Both Santa and Sam were not fairly evaluating the teacher. They were influenced by the grades they were earning and were unfair in their judgments.

Another irresponsible form of evaluation occurred when James rated his teacher excellent because the teacher is "*easy*". He gives few tests and only assigns(分配) one paper during the entire term. His lectures are often filled with jokes and endless stories about his family. On the other hand, James rated Professor Jones poor because he assigns homework daily, gives pretest previews and post-test reviews, and packs his lectures with information.

Santa, Sam, and James have not thought about their teachers' teaching abilities. They have written unfair evaluations and have not given thought to their evaluations. They have not made fair judgments, but instead have been influenced by their own personality and have equated (使等同) little work with excellence in teaching.

66. Santa and Sam judged their teacher by _____.

A) his teaching ability   B) his humorous stories

C) the grades that they were earning   D) his marvelous remarks

67. James' evaluation was influenced by _____.

A) the amount of coursework   B) his own performance
C) the teacher's ability   D) the teacher's family background

68. The word "*easy*"(Line 2, para.3) most probably means _____.
    A) not difficult   B) not proud
    C) not strict   D) not serious

69. The students didn't evaluate their teachers fairly because _____.
    A) it was difficult for them to do so
    B) they didn't know how to make judgments
    C) their personality affected them a lot
    D) they received unfair treatment

70. The best title for this passage is _____.
    A) Teacher Evaluations   B) Student Judgment
    C) Easy and Tough teachers   D) How to be Fair

Questions 71 to 75 are based on the following passages:

There is probably no sphere of human activity in which our values and life styles are reflected more vividly than they are in the clothes that we choose to wear. The dress of an individual is a kind of "sign language" that communicates a complex set of information and is usually the basis on which immediate impressions are formed. Traditionally, women cared much about their clothes, while men took pride in the fact that they were completely lacking in clothes consciousness.

This type of American culture is gradually changing as men's dress takes on greater variety and color. Even as early as 1995, a research in Michigan revealed that men attached rather high importance to the value of clothing in daily life. White-collar workers in particular viewed dress as a symbol of control, which could be used to impress or influence others, especially in the work situation. The white-collar worker was described as extremely concerned about the impression his clothing made on his superiors. Although blue-collar workers were less aware that they might be judged on the basis of their clothing, they recognized that they would be laughed at by their fellow workers if they were any different from the accepted pattern of dress.

Since that time, of course, the patterns have changed: the typical office worker may now be wearing the blue shirt, and laborer a white shirt; but the importance of dress has not decreased. Other investigators in recent years have helped to establish its significance in the lives of individuals at various age levels in different social and economic groups.

71. Our values and lifestyles are probably reflected most vividly in _____.
    A) any sphere of human activity   B) the clothes that we wear
    C) the sign language people use   D) complex set of information

72. In a world of changes, men's clothes have become _____.
    A) various and colorful   B) traditional and formal
    C) fashionable and colorful   D) reasonable and formal

73. Traditionally, people thought that _____.

A) men were proud of the clothes they wore

B) women were concerned greatly with their clothes

C) both men and women paid great attention to their clothes

D) neither men nor women showed great interest in clothes

74. Blue-collar workers were aware of their clothes because _____ .

A) they were extremely concerned about their impression on their superiors

B) they knew clearly that people would judge them by their clothes

C) they wanted to impress and influence their fellow workers

D) they didn't want to be laughed at by their fellow workers

75. The passage mainly suggests that _____ .

A) women pay more attention to their clothes than men do

B) women always like beautiful dresses

C) people have attached more importance to dress

D) American culture is changing greatly

Part Ⅴ Translation from English into Chinese

Directions: *In this part there is a passage with 5 underlined parts, numbered 76 to 80. After reading the passage carefully, you should translate the numbered parts into Chinese. Remember to write your translation on the Translation Sheet.*

It has been found that less than one shopper in five makes a complete shopping list before going to the store. (76) The reason for this is that seven out of ten of today's purchases are decided in the store, where the shoppers tend toward impulse (冲动) buying. (77) Buying groceries on impulse has risen for the past forty years, and this rise has coincided (重合) with the growth of self-service shopping. However, in grocery stores where clerks wait on customers there is much less impulse buying. (78) It is hard for people to buy on impulse if they have to address a clerk.

Psychologists have joined forces with merchandising experts. It is their job to persuade people to buy products which they may not need or even want until they see them attractively presented. It was discovered by the psychologists that shoppers want help in their purchases. (79) Having so many choices confuses them, and they prefer the package that attracts them. Therefore, it is now more usual for food packers to pay attention to their package design. (80) Attraction depends heavily on the position of the product on the shelf, however. Thus, persuading the shopper to buy is easier if the product is located at eye-level.

Part Ⅵ Translation from Chinese into English

Directions: *Translate the following sentences into English. Remember to write your translation on the Translation Sheet.*

81. 我喜欢旅游,但我又不愿花钱。

82. 尽管下雨,昨天的足球赛还是按计划举行了。

83. 他还没来,但我记得告诉过他上课的时间。

84. 从我朋友那儿借来的这台计算机的工作性能不太好。

85. 抱歉,因为生病,明天的会我去不了。

【听力录音文稿】

Section A

1. W: The milk in the refrigerator is sour.

   M: No joke. It's been there for three weeks.

   Q: What does the man imply?

2. M: John's grades in math are low. Maybe he needs some help.

   W: I think that we should talk to him first.

   Q: What are these people probably going to do?

3. W: This cake is great. Why don't you try some?

   M: I wish I could but I cannot eat anymore.

   Q: What will the man probably do?

4. M: It's really rainy today.

   W: How about putting off the picnic until tomorrow.

   Q: What does the woman suggest they do?

5. M: Make thirty copies for me and twenty copies for Mr. Brown.

   W: Sure, sir. As soon as I make the final correction on the original.

   Q: What is the woman's job?

6. M: Don't you have to go to work at 9:00?

   W: No, I start half an hour later today and half an hour early tomorrow.

   Q: What time does the woman start work today?

7. W: If I were you, I'd be more careful about locking the back door at night.

   M: Don't worry. No one will break in.

   Q: What does the woman mean?

8. M: Are you going to tell Mr. Martin that you are looking for another job?

   W: No, not yet. Besides, if I don't find one, I can probably stay here a while longer.

   Q: What is the woman doing?

9. M: Martin always talks about how he loves to dance.

   W: Yes, but you don't see him out on the floor very often, do you?

   Q: What does the woman say about Martin?

10. W: Ted, could you mail these letters on your way to the club?

    M: The club's closed. I'm meeting Chris at his house.

    Q: Where is Ted going now?

Section B

Directions: *In this section, you will hear 3 short passages or conversations. At the end of each passage or conversation, you will hear some questions. The passage or the conversation will be read twice. After you hear a passage or a conversation, you must choose the best answer from the four choices marked A), B), C) and D). Then mark the corresponding letter on the Answer Sheet with a single line through the center.*

Passage One

A university professor recently made several experiments with different animals to find out which was the most intelligent. He found out that monkey was more intelligent than other animals.

In one experiment the professor put a monkey in a room where there were several small boxes. Some boxes were inside other boxes. One small box had some food inside of it. The professor wanted to watch the monkey and to find out how long it would take the monkey to find the food. The professor left the room. He waited a few minutes outside the door. Then he knelt down and put his eye to the keyhole. What did he see? To his surprise he found himself looking directly into the eye of the monkey. The monkey was looking at the professor through the other side of the door.

Questions 11 to 13 are based on the passage you have just heard.

11. What was the purpose of the professor's experiments?

12. Why did the professor put the food in a small box?

13. What did the professor see through the keyhole?

Passage Two

No matter what type of holiday you are looking for you will find the answer in Switzerland. There is really no other country quite like it, for here you have some of the finest and most beautiful scenery in the whole of Europe together with an attractive climate, hotels and the friendliest people you could wish to meet.

Think of the variety of attractions. You may seek outdoor sporting activities. Walking, swimming, riding, sailing and fishing are just a few variety of outdoor activities by coach or railway, free afternoons on a lake steamer, visits to historic cities—these are just a few more of the variety of interests for your holiday in Switzerland. In the evening music fills the air, whether it is the local village band or an all-star variety show.

Questions 14 to 16 are based on the passage you have just heard.

14. Which of the following is NOT mentioned as an attraction of Switzerland?

15. What do Swiss people like to do in the evening?

16. Who do you think would be interested in this advertisement?

Passage Three

In the United States, couples usually receive gifts from their relatives and friends when they get married. Sometimes a bride will exchange a gift for something else if she doesn't find it useful. We give gifts to express our good wishes for the marriage, but gifts aren't necessary for the marriage itself. However, in some societies gifts are very important, and the marriage isn't legal without them. One type of this gift is called bride service. A young husband must work for his wife's family. He may work for as long as fifteen years or until the third child is born. Bride service may seem strange to us, but it is necessary in societies where people don't have money or material things to exchange at marriage.

Questions 17 to 20 are based on the passage you have just heard.

17. What can a bride do if she finds her marriage gift useless?

18. Why do people give gifts to a newly married couple?

19. What will happen in some societies if there are no gifts at a marriage?

20. Why does a husband have to work for his wife's family in some societies?

【试题解析】

第一部分　听力理解

1. 正确答案:D。牛奶已在冰箱放了3周,难怪要酸。

2. 正确答案:C。女士觉得John数学很差,需要帮助,男士建议先和他谈谈。

3. 正确答案:A。女士请男士品尝蛋糕,但男士已吃饱了。

4. 正确答案:B。因为下雨,女士建议把郊游推迟到明天。

5. 正确答案:A。男士请女士为他和Brown先生分别准备30份和20份的复印件,女士回答完成最后的文稿修改后就去做。可见她是做文秘工作的。

6. 正确答案:B。9点上班。但是今天要迟半小时,明天要提前半小时。

7. 正确答案:D。女士对男士说:"假如我是你,晚上就把后门锁上。"可见她觉得男士应该谨慎一点。

8. 正确答案:B。男士问女士是否要把她正在找工作的事情告诉Martin先生。

9. 正确答案:B。Martin常说自己爱跳舞,而女士却说很少在舞池里看到他。

10. 正确答案:D。女士让Ted把信寄给俱乐部,Ted回答俱乐部已关门,他要到Chris家去。

11. 正确答案:C。录音开头第一句就提到,教授用不同动物做实验是为了搞清哪种动物最聪明。

12. 正确答案:C。录音提到,教授为了观察猴子多久才能找到食物。

13. 正确答案:B。录音最后一句提到,猴子正从门的另一面通过锁眼观察教授。

14. 正确答案:D。录音开头提到,瑞士有美丽的景色、宜人的气候和友好的人们,没有提到山脉。

15. 正确答案:C。录音中提到,晚上到处是各种各样的音乐演出,而"散步、游泳、湖上泛舟"则是白天的活动。

16. 正确答案:B。从第一句可知,这个广告的对象是有意度假者。

17. 正确答案:B。录音开头提到,有时新娘可用不称心的结婚礼物交换其他的物品。

18. 正确答案:D。录音提到,人们送礼物是为了表达对新人的祝福。

19. 正确答案:A。录音提到,在有的地方,没有礼物的婚姻是非法的。

20. 正确答案:D。录音最后一句提到,对于贫穷无钱购买结婚礼物的丈夫来说,为他妻子的家庭干活,可作为他交换婚姻的礼物。

第二部分　词　汇

21. 正确答案:C。句意为:我们应十分重视学生的心理健康。

pay attention to 注意／ place 放置／attach... to 把(重点等)……放在／provide sb. with sth.,或 provide sth. for sb. 为某人提供某物。例:The farms provide the city with fresh eggs and milk.农庄为城市提供新鲜鸡蛋和牛奶。

22. 正确答案:B。句意为:最佳学生被授予特别奖学金。

reward 酬劳,奖赏／ award 授予(一般指政府部门或有关组织授予)／present 赠送,呈现／ represent 代表。

23. 正确答案:B。句意为:昨天有关方面坐在一起,寻找解决问题的方法。

expose 使暴露,使曝光／explore 探测,探究 ／ express 表达 ／explode 使爆炸。

24. 正确答案:B。句意为:来自世界各地的专家们一年一度相聚广岛,参加关于核战争威胁的会议。

present 出席,提出,呈现／ attend 参加／join in 参加,加入／participate in 参加。

25. 正确答案:D。句意为:新技术的应用能使工厂生产出的机器产量比去年翻一番。

turn down 关小(音量),拒绝／turn off 关掉／turn to 转向,变成,求助于／turn out 生产,制造。例:We have to turn to the expert for help.我们不得不请求专家的帮助。

26. 正确答案:B。句意为:车子修好了,但车主不十分满意。

pleasure 愉快,乐事／satisfaction 满意,令人满意的事物／joy 欢乐,喜悦／delight 快乐,高兴。

27. 正确答案:C。句意为:他们热烈讨论了好几个小时,但没有达成协议。

bored 乏味的／ excited 激动的／ heated 热烈的／ interested 对……感兴趣的。

28. 正确答案:A。上课迟到不是 Tom 的过错,因为他被交通事故耽搁了。

fault (性格和习惯上的)弱点或行为上的过失,也指违反某一规定所造成的错误。例:He is still a good boy with all his faults. 他尽管有这样那样的过错,但还是一个好孩子。／mistake 错误,过失,误会,指因认识不足或判断失误而无意中犯下的错误。例:Since a lot of people make mistakes in life, I'll give you a change.因为很多人在一生中都会犯错误,所以我会给你一个机会。／error 同 mistake,也可指道德上的错误。／failure 失败。

29. 正确答案:B。句意为:学生们很想知道明天天气如何,因为这会直接影响到他们的郊游。

effect 结果,效果,影响／affect (指消极、负面的)影响／infect 传染,感染／ influence (on) (指积极、正面的)影响。

30. 正确答案:C。句意为:由于工作出色,她自一年前进入公司后已被提升两次了。

improve 改善,改进／ advance 前进 ／ promote 提升,升职／ develop 发展。

31. 正确答案:D。句意为:运动会因暴风雨不得不取消。

call on 号召，呼吁；访问 call on sb. 拜访某人 call at some place 访问某地 / call for 要求，提倡，为……叫喊 / call up 召唤，打电话给…… / call off 取消 = cancel。

32. 正确答案：A。句意为：班里最好的学生 David 也解不出这个题目，更别提其他人了。
   let alone 更不用说 / let out 放掉，泄露 / let off 放出，饶恕 / let down 放下，使失望。

33. 正确答案：B。句意为：据报道，昨天的交通事故中，只有一个 5 岁的孩子幸存。
   endure 耐久，忍耐 / survive 幸免于，幸存，生还 / live 生活，居住 / pass 通过。

34. 正确答案：C。句意为：如果你每天两次服该药，就能马上治好病。
   treat 对待，治疗 / recover 痊愈，复原 / cure 治愈，痊愈，cure sb. of a desease... 治愈某人的病 / restore 恢复，修复，重建。例：His health is entirely restored. 他已完全恢复健康了。

35. 正确答案：B。句意为：我认为我不认识那个穿蓝衣服的女孩，尽管她让我想起了我的某个熟人。
   recall 回想 / remind sb. of / about sth. 提醒某人某事，使某人想起某事 / suggest 建议 / recognize 认出。

36. 正确答案：B。句意为：你没有硕士学位，所以你去应聘这个工作没什么意义。
   idea 想法，主意 / point 意义 / example 例子 / cause 原因，事业。例：There is no point in doing sth. 做某件事情没有意义。

37. 正确答案：C。句意为：一般来说，男人抽烟比女人多。
   as usual 照常，照例 / in general 一般地，大体上 / on average 平均，一般说来 / in common 共同。

38. 正确答案：D。句意为：为了提高写作能力，我们必须采纳该计划。
   admit 承认 / advise 建议 / correct 改正 / adopt 采用，收养。

39. 正确答案：A。句意为：Tom 不能让他的母亲相信他说了真话。
   convince sb. of sth. 使某人确信……，使某人信服…… / confine 限制，禁闭 / convert... into 使……转变成，转换 / confess 承认，坦白。

40. 正确答案：D。句意为：你的车恐怕明天才能修好，因为我们必须更换发动机。
   finish 完成 / present 给，提出，呈现 / prepare for 为……做好准备 / be ready 准备好。

第三部分　语法结构

41. 正确答案：B。句意为：我同他讲话的那人不作答，这让我很困惑。
   非限制性定语从句，which 指代前面整个句子。

42. 正确答案：D。句意为：昨天他很忙，要不他就来开会了。
   虚拟语气。此句表示与过去事实相反。

43. 正确答案：B。句意为：考试一结束我就要回家度假了。
   在时间和条件状语从句中，用一般现在时代替将来时。

44. 正确答案：A。句意为：我们的地球表面 70％ 被水覆盖，从太空中看，就像一个蓝色的星球。
   此句的主语是 our earth，所以应用 see 的过去分词 seen，表示被动。例：Followed by the students, the teacher entered the room. 后面跟着学生，老师走进了教室。试比较：Following the students, the teacher entered the classroom. 老师跟着学生，走进了教室。

45. 正确答案：D。句意为：她是这些女孩中唯一有勇气用蛇做实验的。
   当"one"的前面加了"this, the , the only"等词，定语从句的关系词 who 指代 one，作从句主语时,后接单数谓语。比较:She is one of the five girls who have enough courage to experiment with snakes. 她是敢用蛇做实验的五个女孩之一。who 指代 the five girls。

46. 正确答案:C。句意为:你安静一会儿可以吗?我想及时完成作文。

mind + 动名词。有些动词后面只能跟动名词,不能跟动词不定式。这些词包括:mind, enjoy, practice, risk, appreciate, finish, admit, allow, resist, stand, consider, delay, deny, fancy, favor, imagine, miss, postpone, recommend, suggest, look forward to, object to 等。try to do sth. 尽量做某事,try doing sth. 尝试做某事。例:She tried opening the door with the ID card. 她尝试用身份证开门。

47. 正确答案:B。句意为:那个男孩说的话最后被证实是真的。

what 引导的主语从句。也可以说:All(that) the boy had said turned out to be true.

48. 正确答案:C。句意为:这就是明天会上要讨论的话题。

动词不定式作定语表示还没有发生的事。试比较:This is the very topic discussed at the meeting yesterday. 这就是昨天会上讨论的话题。过去分词表示动作已经完成。This is the very topic being discussed now. 这就是正在讨论的话题。现在分词表示动作正在进行。

49. 正确答案:B。句意为:"Bob,你觉得 Mary 干得任何?""哦,她的工作,如果不比我们做得更好,至少也和我们一样好。"

as good as 和……一样……。如果补全省略部分,则是:Well, her work is as good as ours, if her work is not better than ours. 所以短语 as good as 应同时符合主句和从句。选项 A 中,从句进行比较,但主句没有;选项 C 中,主句用原级比较,而从句是用比较级进行比较。

50. 正确答案:A。句意为:不论我们遇到什么困难,我们也要实施我们的计划。

whatever = no matter what。例:No matter what you say, I'll never give up. 不论你说什么,我决不让步。

51. 正确答案:D。句意为:"希望不久我们能再次相会。""我也希望如此。"

so 引导的倒装句。其他如 neither, nor 引导否定意义的倒装句。例:I don't eat meat and neither does Tom. 我不吃肉,汤姆也不吃肉。"I haven't seen that film." "Neither/Nor have I. "我没看过那部电影。""我也没有。"

52. 正确答案:A。句意为:对我来说,在如此短的时间内做完这么多的练习,是不可能的。

such + a + 名词性短语。例:such a beautiful flower。比较:so + *adj*. 例:so beautiful a flower。

53. 正确答案:B。句意为:外面很吵,他努力想让大家听到,但做不到。

过去分词作宾补,表示被动。

54. 正确答案:B。句意为:正是由于他的懒惰使得他期末考不及格。

强调句。it is + 被强调部分 + that...。例:It was in this classroom that we saw the famous scholar. 就是在这个教室里我们见到了那位著名的学者。

55. 正确答案:A。句意为:如果只是感冒,没什么了不起;但有时感冒会成为危险。

so long as 引导的条件状语从句。例:I don't mind your knowing anything so long as it goes no further. 你知道什么我都不介意,只要你不告诉别人。/even though 即使/no matter when 无论何时/unless 如果不,除非。

56. 正确答案:D。句意为:你会在照料婴儿一书中找到好多建议。

advice 是不可数名词,其他还有:furniture, information, news 等。如要表示"一件、几件"这类概念,前面须加定语,如:a set of furniture 一套家具, some information 一些信息, a piece of news 一条新闻。

57. 正确答案:B。句意为:他已写了一个小时的文章,但到目前为止只写了一百个字。

现在完成进行时表示一个持续到现在的动作。so far 到目前为止。

58. 正确答案:D。句意为:我不知道你在等我,要不早就来了。

本句是一句错综句,主句用的是虚拟语气,表示与过去事实相反。but 从句是对过去事实的真实描写,所以用一般过去时。

59. 正确答案:B。句意为:他们会失败,因为我觉得他们对形势缺少整体的了解。

一般现在时表示现在的情况或现状。如:They enjoy skating. 他们喜欢溜冰。

60. 正确答案:B。句意为:男孩十分害怕,就把手表给了劫匪。

and 连接两个并列句。

第四部分　阅读理解

第一篇短文参考译文及语言注释

"早睡早起,使人健康、富有和聪慧。"这一定是最有名的谚语之一。对加入早睡早起行列的人们承诺健康、财富和聪慧,这对当代社会的许多人尤其有吸引力。毫无疑问,健康是当代人最为关注的事情之一。据估计,美国每年花在保健上的费用高达 2000 亿美元。医药业已成为雇员达 480 万的庞大行业。

近年来,人们对保健药品越来越感兴趣,这可能是由于医疗费用的持续增长。但是 Kenneth Cooper 博士等人的大作也起了很大的作用。在他的《有氧运动》一书中,Cooper 博士把锻炼的好处阐述得如此娓娓动听,许多其他作家也纷纷步其后尘。确切地说,有成千上万的美国读者穿上了运动鞋,来到全国的大街小巷。最近的一次调查显示,超过 1700 万的人们在慢跑,其中很多人十分认真地自觉锻炼,参加全国各地组织的长达 26 英里 385 码的艰苦乏味的马拉松比赛。上次我在火奴鲁鲁时,很惊讶地看见老老少少成百上千的人们在为他们的生命而奔跑。我发现其中很多人参加了夏威夷马拉松比赛。锻炼也已成为聊天的重要内容。在最近的一次宴会上,一位银行总裁问我:"你看起来像个跑步运动员,每天跑多少?"几天后我参加一个全国性的电视秀,主持人突然问我是否经常跑步。在这两个场合中,谈话都转向了锻炼这个话题。我发现这是很多人心目中的热门话题。

The promise of ... to those who ... must be particularly appealing to many people in our contemporary society. who 引导的定语从句,修饰 those。that 引导的从句作真正的主语,it 是形式主语。Many of these are so serious that they... marathons (马拉松) that are organized all over the country. so...that 引导一个结果状语从句,that 引导定语从句,修饰 marathons。

试题解答

61. 正确答案:C。可从第一段第一句的"early to bed and early to rise"猜出其意。

62. 正确答案:A。可从第一段的第三句和第四句找到答案。

63. 正确答案:B。综观全文,尤其是第二段作者举的几个例子,可知人们对保持健康的关注。

64. 正确答案:D。第二段的最后一句点明题义。

65. 正确答案:D。可从第二段的"... his message of the benefits of exercises"找到答案。

第二篇短文参考译文及语言注释

近几年,很多学校实施了教师评价制。每学期学生都有机会评价他们的老师,他们可以就老师的授课、对学生问题的关心、练习方法以及驾驭课堂的总体能力作出评判。当授课教师离开教室,学生们必须在发给他们的表格上填写他们对老师的评价,他们不可以交换或讨论各自的观点和看法。每个学生都完成填表后,一个学生收集所有表格并放入信封。

要公正地评价别人的表现是相当难的。比如 Santa 最近很不负责地给她的老师写了评语,因为她这门功课不及格。而她的朋友 Sam 则给同一位老师很高的评价,因为这门课他得了 A。他们都受到了成绩的影响,没有做到公正评价。

James 则因为老师很"松"而给予他很高的评价。这就产生了另一种不负责任的评价。那位老师很少考试,整个学期只布置一篇论文,课堂上经常讲笑话或者滔滔不绝地闲话家长里短。另一方面,James 给 Jones 教授的分打得很低,因为他每天布置家庭作业,要求考前预习和考后复习,上课时信息量很大。

Santa、Sam 和 James 都没有考虑老师们的教学能力,写下了不公正的评价,毫不顾及他们的评语所带来的结果。他们没有作出公正的评判,相反地,他们受到了自己个性的影响,把老师少布置作业和教学优秀等同起来。

carry out 执行,履行。例:The government has decided to carry out the new policy. 政府已决定执行新的政策。It is very difficult to evaluate... it 是形式主语,而不定式 to evaluate... 才是真正的主语。例:It's impossible to learn English well within two weeks. 要在两周内学好英语是不可能的。pack 挤满,塞满。例:The bus was packed with people. 公共汽车里挤满了人。instead 代替,顶替。表示和前面相反的情况和状态。例:The naughty boy didn't go to school that day, instead, he went to a net bar. 那天这个顽皮的男孩没有去上学,而是去了网吧。

试题解答

66. 正确答案:C。可从第二段的最后一句找到答案。

67. 正确答案:A。从第三段中两位老师的行为对比,可得出答案。

68. 正确答案:C。可从第三段的第二句和第三句找到答案。

69. 正确答案:C。可从最后一段的"but instead..."一句中找到答案。

70. 正确答案:A。综观全文,"教师评价制"是最好的答案。

第三篇短文参考译文及语言注释

可能没有任何人类活动领域能比我们选择所穿的衣服更生动地反映我们的价值观和生活方式。一个人的衣着犹如一种"手势语",它传递出一组复杂的信息,并常常是他人形成即时印象的基础。从传统上来讲,女性非常关心自身的衣着,而男性则对他们完全缺乏对衣服的了解这一事实引以为豪。

随着男性衣服出现了更多的款式和颜色,这种美国文化正在逐渐改变。早在 1995 年,密歇根州的一份研究就显示男性对着装在日常生活中的重要性相当重视,特别是白领工作者,他们将着装视为控制力的象征,它可以给别人留下印象或影响别人,尤其是在工作环境中,白领工作者被描述成极其在意自身着装给上司留下印象的一类人。虽然蓝领工作者较少意识到人们对他们的判断也许建立在他们着装的基础上,但他们也认识到了如果自己与普通认可的穿衣模式有任何不同的话,他们就会受到工友的嘲笑。

当然,从那时起,穿衣模式已发生了变化,典型的办公室工作者现在也许身穿蓝色衬衫,体力工作者也许身穿白色衬衫,但衣服的重要性并未降低。近年来,其他的调查者也帮助证实了着装在属于不同社会经济群体的各种年龄阶段的人生活中所起的重要作用。

There is probably no sphere of human activity in which our values and life styles are... in which 引导定语从句,which 指代 sphere of human activity,这里不能用 that 代替 which。这句可改写为:Only the clothes that we wear can most vividly reflect our values and lifestyles. take pride in 对……引以为豪。view... as... 把……视为…… the impression his clothes made on his superiors,画线部分是定语从句,修饰 the impression,省略了引导词 that。make an impression on 给……留下印象。例:The West Lake has made a deep impression on the visitors from all parts of the world. 西湖给来自世界各地的游客们留下了深刻的印象。...and a laborer a white shirt. a white shirt 前省略了 may now be wearing。

试题解答

71. 正确答案:B。从开篇第一句中可以找到答案。

72. 正确答案:A。从第二段的第一句中可以找到答案。

73. 正确答案:B。从第一段的第三句中可以找到答案。

74. 正确答案:D。从第二段的最后一句中可以找到答案。

75. 正确答案:C。从开篇第一句的主题句以及第三段的最后两句,可以得出结论:人们越来越关注衣着了。

第五部分　英译汉

76. 这一现象的理由是如今十起购物决定中有七起是在店内作出的。

77. 冲动性购买日用品在最近四十年来呈上升趋势,而这种趋势与自助购物的增长相重合。

78. 如果人们必须同商店职员交涉,他们就不会冲动性地去购物。

79. 可选择的很多,令人们困惑,因此他们首选包装上吸引人的物品。

80. 然而,物品的吸引力在很大程度上取决于它们在货架上的位置。

第六部分　汉译英

81. I like traveling but I hate spending money.

82. Despite the rain, the football match was held as planned yesterday.

83. He hasn't come yet. But I remember telling him when to go to class.

84. The computer I borrowed from my friend doesn't work well.

85. Sorry, I can't go to the meeting tomorrow, because I am ill.

2005年1月浙江省大学英语三级考试试卷

Part Ⅰ   Listening Comprehension

Section A

Directions: *In this section you will hear 10 short conversations. At the end of each conversa-tion, a question will be asked about what was said. The conversation and the ques-tion will be spoken only once. After each question there will be a pause. During the pause, you must read the four choices marked A), B), C) and D), and decide which is the best answer. Then mark the corresponding letter on the Answer Sheet with a single line through the center.*

1. A) At home.   B) In a restaurant.
   C) In a department store.   D) In a factory.

2. A) Because she isn't interested in the class.
   B) Because she is afraid of the teacher.
   C) Because she prefers reading outside.
   D) Because she doesn't want to interrupt the class.

3. A) She is seriously ill.   B) She doesn't feel well.
   C) She is afraid of car driving.   D) She wouldn't like any drinks.

4. A) A clerk.   B) An assistant.
   C) A customer.   D) A passenger.

5. A) It's windy.   B) It's cold.
   C) It's warm.   D) It's rainy.

6. A) As a friend.   B) As her daughter.
   C) As a wild cat.   D) As her mother.

7. A) The man should ask someone else.   B) She doesn't have time to help him.
   C) The man should try to do it on his own. D) She's afraid she can't be of much help.

8. A) To wait for her turn.   B) To fill in an application form.
   C) To make a phone call.   D) To change her number.

9. A) A speech on television.   B) An article in the newspaper.
   C) A meeting with the president.   D) A conversation on the phone.

10. A) His house needs painting.   B) He broke his ladder.
    C) He spilled some paint.   D) His window is broken.

Section B

Directions: *In this section, you will hear 3 short passages or conversations. At the end of each passage or conversation, you will hear some questions. The passage or the conversation will be read twice. After you hear a passage or a conversation, you must choose the best answer from the four choices marked A), B), C) and D). Then mark the corresponding letter on the Answer Sheet with a single line through the center.*

Passage One

Questions 11 to 13 are based on the passage you have just heard.

11. A) They are all very successful.
    C) Their popularity lasts for many years.
    B) They only perform at night.
    D) They appear and disappear very soon.

12. A) Because he looks after their money.
    C) Because he is important to them.
    B) Because he pays for their clothes.
    D) Because he writes all the songs.

13. A) Pop-stars are rather poor.
    C) Pop-stars are all very rich.
    B) Pop-stars have quite a hard life.
    D) Pop-stars spend a lot of money on clothes.

Passage Two

Questions 14 to 16 are based on the passage you have just heard.

14. A) It is the largest state in the US.
    B) It is the coldest state in the US.
    C) It is the northernmost state in the US.
    D) It is the state with the least sunshine in the US.

15. A) To give free land.
    C) To offer generous reward.
    B) To provide free housing.
    D) To give financial aid.

16. A) May and June.
    C) July and August.
    B) June and July.
    D) January and June.

Passage Three

Questions 17 to 20 are based on the passage you have just heard.

17. A) Middle school students.
    C) Elderly people living alone.
    B) University students.
    D) The middle-aged.

18. A) It's not normal.
    C) It's understandable.
    B) It's nothing serious.
    D) It's permanent.

19. A) They could not adapt themselves to the new environment.
    B) They missed their parents and old friends very much.
    C) They were afraid of their teachers and classmates.
    D) They were too proud to make friends with others.

20. A) More than 13 percent.
    C) More than 25 percent.
    B) More than 18 percent.
    D) More than 50 percent.

Part II Vocabulary

Directions: *There are 20 incomplete sentences in this part. For each sentence there are four choices marked A), B), C) and D). Choose the ONE answer that best completes the sentence. Then mark the corresponding letter on the Answer Sheet with a single line through the center.*

21. The teacher lost his _____ when the monitor told him that six students were absent.
    A) mind
    B) temptation
    C) sense
    D) temper

22. I've been so busy recently that I don't know who has been _____ the US president.
    A) elected
    B) singled out
    C) chosen
    D) picked up

23. What a pity! There are no tickets _____ for the coming concert.
    A) approachable
    B) advisable
    C) accessible
    D) available

24. She was so _____ in reading the novel that she didn't hear the bell ringing.
    A) concentrated
    B) absorbed
    C) attracted
    D) drawn

25. When I saw these old photos, I couldn't help _____ what had happened ten years before.
    A) reminding
    B) recalling
    C) recognizing
    D) reserving

26. The company has promised to _____ no efforts on the cooperation with us.
    A) spare
    B) save
    C) share
    D) make

27. _____, it looked simple. But, in fact, it was rather complicated.
    A) Firstly
    B) At first sight
    C) To begin with
    D) From the beginning

28. It was not a grand occasion, so we were allowed to wear _____ clothes.
    A) formal
    B) casual
    C) simple
    D) plain

29. Movies, sports and music are forms of _____. They help us relax.
    A) entertainment
    B) advertisement
    C) commitment
    D) agreement

30. It was the technician's carelessness that _____ the accident.
    A) put off
    B) brought in
    C) led into
    D) resulted in

31. Yesterday I bought a new tie to _____ this green shirt.
    A) go after
    B) go with
    C) go on
    D) go by

32. The cat was playing with a(n) _____ mouse.

  A) alive   B) live

  C) living   D) lively

33. It is _____ of Jane to often forget where she puts her things.

  A) typical   B) individual

  C) peculiar   D) particular

34. Mum took _____ of the fine weather to do washing on Saturday morning.

  A) chance   B) advantage

  C) effect   D) interest

35. The patient felt much! better, so the doctor _____ him to take a holiday by the sea.

  A) suggested   B) considered

  C) advised   D) accepted

36. Try some of the cake. I _____ it especially for you.

  A) baked   B) cooked

  C) fried   D) boiled

37. The teacher told the students that they should review their lessons at _____ intervals.

  A) proper   B) regular

  C) adequate   D) moderate

38. Be _____ . You can't expect such a small child to do all the work on his own.

  A) honest   B) serious

  C) logical   D) reasonable

39. You have to buy some new shoes as these are _____ .

  A) worn out   B) broken down

  C) used up   D) sold out

40. Because this picture is not genuine, it is completely _____ .

  A) priceless   B) worthless

  C) valuable   D) invaluable

Part Ⅲ   Structure

Directions: *There are 20 incomplete sentences in this part. For each sentence there are four choices marked A), B), C) and D). Choose the ONE answer that best completes the sentence. Then mark the corresponding letter on the Answer Sheet with a single line through the center.*

41. By no means _____ possible for me to attend the party tonight.

  A) it is   B) is it

  C) should it   D) it should

42. Mary's handbag with three credit cards and two thousand dollars _____ when she was on the train.

  A) was stolen   B) were stolen

C) has stolen   D) have been stolen

43. Human beings are superior to animals _____ they can use language as a tool to communi-
    cate.

    A) in which   B) in that
    C) for which   D) for that

44. Your mobile phone needs _____ . You'd better have it done tomorrow.

    A) repaired   B) to repair
    C) repairing   D) being repaired

45. By the end of this term, we surely _____ the first eight units.

    A) have finished   B) had finished
    C) will be finishing   D) will have finished

46. How many hours you spend in learning English _____ how well you can learn it.

    A) decide   B) decides
    C) deciding   D) to decide

47. It's raining heavily. I'd rather you _____ to meet me.

    A) don't come   B) did not come
    C) won't come   D) not come

48. They were all very tired, but _____ of them would stop to take a rest.

    A) any   B) none
    C) some   D) neither

49. Television is another major means of communication, _____ us to see as well as _____
    the performers.

    A) permitting; to hear   B) permitting; hearing
    C) to permit; to hear   D) to permit; hearing

50. The heavy rain _____ , the students went on planting trees.

    A) had stopped   B) stopped
    C) having stopped   D) being stopped

51. _____ yesterday _____ I learned that the famous scholar would give a lecture on IT
    industry.

    A) It was not until; when   B) It was until; that
    C) It was not until; that   D) It was until; then

52. Whenever a pupil makes a mistake, teachers should show him how to correct it _____
    punish him.

    A) other than   B) rather than
    C) sooner than   D) or rather

53. They said I shouldn't have done that to help him. But I don't regret _____ what I
    thought was right.

    A) to do   B) to have done
    C) having done   D) being done

54. The local government accepted the proposal put forward at the conference _____ the pub-

lic transportation be improved.

    A) for　　　　　　　　　　　　　B) which

    C) that　　　　　　　　　　　　　D) how

55. _____ the introduction to the film, I had no desire to go to the cinema.

    A) Reading　　　　　　　　　　　B) Having read

    C) Read　　　　　　　　　　　　　D) To have read

56. Would you be _____ close the window for me, please?

    A) so kind to　　　　　　　　　　B) kind as to

    C) so kind as to　　　　　　　　　D) kind enough

57. _____ side of the street is lined with all kinds of flowers.

    A) Both　　　　　　　　　　　　　B) Neither

    C) Each　　　　　　　　　　　　　D) Either

58. Sorry, Mr. Brown is out, and I have no idea _____ .

    A) where he has been　　　　　　B) where he has gone

    C) he has been where　　　　　　D) he has gone where

59. When _____ why he was absent last time, he just stared at me and said nothing.

    A) asked　　　　　　　　　　　　B) to be asked

    C) asking　　　　　　　　　　　　D) was asked

60. We had to wait for a long time to get our visas, _____ ?

    A) didn't we　　　　　　　　　　B) did we

    C) hadn't we　　　　　　　　　　D) shouldn't we

Part Ⅳ　Reading Comprehension

Directions: *There are 3 passages in this part. Each passage is followed by some questions or unfinished statements. For each of them there are four choices marked A), B), C) and D). You should decide on the best choice and mark the corresponding letter on the Answer Sheet with a single line through the center.*

Passage One

Questions 61 to 65 are based on the following passage:

    In some countries as many as nine out of ten adults read at least one newspaper a day. Seen in purely business terms, few products can ever have been so successful in reaching as much of their market. Why do so many people read newspapers?

    There are five basic functions of a newspaper: to inform, to comment, to persuade, to instruct and to entertain. You may well think that this list of functions is in order of importance but, if so, you would not be in agreement with the majority of the reading public. Of the two broad *categories* of newspaper, the popular and the quality, the former has a readership of millions, while the latter, only hundreds of thousands. Yet the popular papers seem largely designed for entertainment. They contain a lot of comment and persuasive language. The quality newspapers put a much higher value on information and a much lower one on entertainment.

It is not only in content that the two kinds of paper differ. There is a difference, too, in the style in which the articles are written. The popular papers generally use more dramatic language with a lot of word-play. Their reporters tend to use shorter sentences and avoid less well-known vocabulary. This means that popular newspapers are easier for a native speaker to understand, though probably not for a non-native speaker.

In order to decide whether a newspaper is a quality or a popular one it is not even necessary to read it, since you can tell simply by the way it looks. Popular papers are generally smaller with fewer and shorter articles. But they have bigger headlines and more photographs.

61. Out of 500, _____ adults read a newspaper every day according to the passage.

    A) 400   B) 425

    C) 450   D) 475

62. How does the writer describe a popular newspaper?

    A) It carries many articles and few photographs.

    B) It is intended to educate people.

    C) It contains a lot of information.

    D) It aims at entertaining people.

63. Which of the following words could be used in place of "*categories*" in Paragraph 2?

    A) forms.   B) types.

    C) texts.   D) parts.

64. Who tend to read a quality newspaper more often?

    A) Politicians.   B) Foreign visitors.

    C) Sports fans.   D) Housewives.

65. What does the last paragraph tell us about the two kinds of newspaper?

    A) Their difference in appearance and volume.

    B) Their difference in the information given.

    C) Their difference in readership and price.

    D) Their difference in the language used.

Passage Two

Questions 66 to 70 are based on the following passage:

"It hurts me more than you", and "This is for your own good." These are the statements my mother used to make years ago when I had to learn Latin, clean my room, stay home and do homework.

That was before we entered the permissive period in education in which we decided it was all right not to push our children to achieve their best in school. The schools and educators made it easy on us. They taught that it was all right to be parents who take a let-alone policy. We stopped making our children do homework. We gave them calculators, turned on the television, left the teaching to teachers and went on vacation.

Now, teachers, faced with children who have been developing at their own pace for the past

15 years, are realizing we've made a terrible mistake. One such teacher is Sharon Klompus, who says of her students—"so passive"—and wonders what happened. Nothing was demanded of them, she believes. Television, says Klompus, contributes to children's passivity. "We're not training kids to work any more," says Klompus. "We're talking about a generation of kids who've never been hurt or hungry. They have learned somebody will always do it for them. Instead of saying 'go look it up', you tell them the answer. It takes greater energy to say no to a kid."

Yes, it does. It takes energy and it takes work. It's time for parents to end their vacation and come back to work. It's time to take the car away, to turn the TV off, to tell them it hurts you more than them, but it's for their own good. It's time to start telling them no again.

66. In the permissive period, parents were told _____ .
   A) to leave their children alone
   B) to go on vacation without their children
   C) to encourage their children to work hard
   D) to help their children with their schoolwork

67. How does Sharon Klompus describe her students?
   A) They like to work out problems themselves.
   B) It is easy for them to get hurt and angry.
   C) They often make silly mistakes.
   D) They are lazy and spoiled.

68. Which of the following is NOT true of the situation in the past 15 years?
   A) Children have been allowed to watch television as they like.
   B) Children have been forbidden to develop themselves.
   C) Children have been allowed to use cars.
   D) Children may or may not do homework.

69. What does the writer want to tell parents?
   A) They should set a good example for their kids.
   B) Kids should have more activities at school.
   C) They should be stricter with their kids.
   D) Kids should be pleased at home.

70. What would the writer say now about her mother?
   A) She was hard-working and devoted.
   B) She was not nice and kind.
   C) She was lazy and careless.
   D) She was right and wise.

Passage Three

Questions 71 to 75 are based on the following passage:

During her childhood, Rachel showed an interest in nature and in writing. After high school, she entered Pennsylvania State College for Women, aiming at becoming a writer. She switched to biology, however, thus setting the course of her life. Rachel went to Johns Hopkins University for further study and became a member of the zoology (动物学) staff at the University of Maryland.

For fifteen years, Rachel worked for the United States Fish and Wildlife Service, writing and editing publications. Fortunately, her employer encouraged her to reach a larger audience. Rachel's poetic style of writing in three books about the ocean caught the imagination of the general reader. Her rare talent as both a physical scientist and a gifted writer earned her the National Book Award for the *Sea Around Us*.

Rachel's next book marked her as a leading fighter for the preservation of the natural environment. She began writing *Silent Spring*, knowing that she would be personally attacked and *ridiculed*. She continued writing despite the ill health that slowed her progress. Upon completing the book, she wrote to a close friend, "I have felt obliged to do what I could—if I didn't at least try I could never again be happy in nature. But now I believe I have at least helped a little."

Rachel Carson did more than help a little. Although both government and industry opposed her, specialists in public health, the press, and the public itself all supported her fight against the irresponsible use of insecticides (杀虫剂). Her book eventually led the government to ban DDT.

71. The passage describes Rachel as _____.

A) a writer and an editor

B) a scientist and a writer

C) an employer and animal lover

D) a professor and a poet

72. We know from the passage that Rachel was the author of at least _____.

A) 3 books

B) 4 books

C) 5 books

D) 6 books

73. Which of the following is true about the book *Silent Spring*?

A) The book gained great support from both the government and industry.

B) The book was written when Rachel was in good health.

C) The book is concerned with the oceans in the world.

D) The book deals with environmental protection.

74. The word "*ridiculed*" in Paragraph 3 most likely means _____.

A) counted on

B) praised

C) laughed at

D) employed

75. What does the writer IMPLY about banning DDT?

A) The public thought it was wrong to do so.

B) The industry was opposed to doing so.

C) The government was forced to do so.

D) The press did not care about it.

Part V Translation from English into Chinese

Directions: *In this part there is a passage with 5 underlined parts, numbered 76 to 80. After reading the passage carefully, you should translate the numbered parts into Chi-*

It is difficult to imagine what life would be like without memory. The meanings of thousands of everyday perceptions (感觉,知觉), the bases for the decisions we make, and the roots of our habits and skills are to be found in our past experiences, which are brought into the present by memory.

(76) Memory can be defined as the capacity to keep information available for later use. It includes not only "remembering" things like arithmetic or historical facts, but also involves any change in the way an animal typically behaves. (77) Memory is involved when a rat gives up eating grain because he has smelled something wrong in the grain pile. Memory is also involved when a six-year-old child learns to swing a baseball bat.

(78) Memory exists not only in humans and animals but also in some physical objects and machines. Computers, for example, contain devices for storing data for later use. It is interesting to compare the memory-storage capacity of a computer with that of a human being. The instant-access memory of a large computer may hold up to 100,000 "words"—ready for instant use. An average U. S. teenager probably recognizes the meaning of about 100,000 words of English. (79) However, this is only a very small part of the total amount of information which the teenager has stored. Consider, for example, the number of faces and places that the teenager can recognize on sight.

(80) The use of words is the basis of the advanced problem-solving intelligence of human beings. A large part of a person's memory is in terms of words and combinations of words.

Part VI Translation from Chinese into English

Directions: *Translate the following sentences into English. Remember to write your translation on the Translation Sheet.*

81. 我们昨天看电影的那家影院是镇上最好的。
82. 这个实验表明,世上一切事物都在运动。
83. 这个月中旬爸爸送给我一台电脑作为生日礼物。
84. 今日的西湖已非几年前的西湖了。
85. 前几天我病了,否则我早就来看你了。

【听力录音文稿】

Section A

Directions: *In this section you will hear 10 short conversations. At the end of each conversation, a question will be asked about what was said. The conversation and the question will be spoken only once. After each question there will be a pause. During the*

1. M: Who puts the chocolate into the boxes?

   W: That's done by a machine which is able to count them automatically. Please, this way. I'll show you now.

   Q: Where are the two speakers?

2. M: Why are you one hour late for class?

   W: I was seven minutes late. Since the class had begun, I just sat outside reading.

   Q: Why did the woman sit outside?

3. M: Let's go and have something to drink. There's a nice bar near the theatre.

   W: Thank you very much, but I'm still car-sick.

   Q: What's the woman's problem?

4. M: Did you get lost in the supermarket?

   W: I'm afraid so. An assistant working on the first floor gave me the wrong directions.

   Q: What is the woman?

5. M: Look at the lake. I'm glad we'll be able to go skating this weekend.

   W: Not if it's windy. Come on, I'm freezing.

   Q: What is the weather like?

6. M: Mary, why are you so upset about your cat playing with that black one?

   W: Suppose you've got a daughter. Don't you mind who she is making friends with?

   Q: What does Mary look upon her cat as?

7. M: Can you show me how to operate this machine?

   W: I doubt I know more than you, but I'll try.

   Q: What does the woman mean?

8. W: Here is my application form.

   M: Would you please wait until your number is called?

   Q: What does the man ask the woman to do?

9. M: How do you like the President's speech yesterday evening?

   W: Unfortunately I got home too late to watch it.

   Q: What are the two people talking about?

10. M: Gordon, what happened to your window?

    W: When I was painting the house last week, I hit it with the ladder.

    Q: What problem does Gordon probably have?

Section B

Directions: *In this section, you will hear 3 short passages or conversations. At the end of each passage or conversation, you will hear some questions. The passage or the conversation will be read twice. After you hear a passage or a conversation, you must choose* *the best answer from the four choices marked A), B), C) and D). Then mark the corresponding letter on the Answer Sheet with a single line through the center.*

Passage One

Many young people want to become pop-stars. It is their dream in life. They think that pop-stars earn a lot of money, that they lead interesting and exciting lives, and that thousands of fans admire them. And, of course, they are famous!

Yes, but first they must become stars. Most performers start life with a group. This is the pattern nowadays. But there are many groups and competition is sharp. Groups appear and disappear almost overnight. Only a small number survive. Almost without exception they work tremendously hard before they reach the top.

And very few reach the top-and stay there. In England there are perhaps 30 or so groups at the top. Most of these do not earn very much money; perhaps 500 pounds each time they perform. What is more, they have quite a lot of expenses. They have to pay a manager, for example. He is the key person in their lives and he takes about 20% of their earnings—perhaps more. Then there are their clothes, their instruments and their vehicle. Sometimes they are still paying for the last two items!

And don't forget, they have to travel a great deal-sometimes 2000 miles in one week. At times they even sleep in their vehicle instead of a hotel, just to save money.

So now, what do you think? Are pop-stars so well off? And do they have such wonderful lives?

Questions 11 to 13 are based on the passage you have just heard.

11. What is true about pop groups in Britain?

12. Why is a pop group's manager well paid?

13. What is the general idea expressed by the speaker?

Passage Two

There are still places in the world that need settlers. One of these places is Alaska, the largest state in America. To help settlers, the government will give each pioneer a huge piece of land free. Settlers can build a wooden house from their own trees.

But to make a living from the land takes hard work. Because Alaska is so far north, its crops have a short growing season. Only a few weeks separate the frosts of spring and autumn. Corn, tomatoes and apples need more time to become ripe. Another problem for the settler is that much of Alaska has a layer of soil under the ground that is always frozen.

However, during June and July, the sun shines both night and day, and some crops grow rapidly. Cabbages weigh as much as 45 pounds. Alaska grows some of the world's finest vegetables.

For those who are willing to work hard Alaska offers a chance for a rewarding life.

Questions 14 to 16 are based on the passage you have just heard.

14. What does the passage say about Alaska?

15. What does the government do to encourage settlement in Alaska?

16. When do crops grow rapidly in Alaska?

Passage Three

Many people feel lonely sometimes, but it usually only lasts between a few minutes and a few hours. This kind of loneliness is not serious. In fact, it is quite normal. However, for some people, loneliness can last for years. Psychologists are studying this complex phenomenon in an attempt to better understand long-term loneliness.

Most researchers agree that the loneliest people are between the ages of 18 and 25, so a group of psychologists decided to study a group of college freshmen. They found that more than 50% of the freshmen were lonely at the beginning of the semester as a result of their new circumstances, but had adjusted after a few months. 13% were still lonely after seven months due to shyness and fear. They felt very uncomfortable meeting new people, even though they understood that their fear was not reasonable. They remained unhappy because they were afraid to make new friends and they thought that there was little or nothing they could do to improve their condition.

Questions 17 to 20 are based on the passage you have just heard.

17. Who are the loneliest among these people?

18. What do psychologists think of long-term loneliness?

19. Why did the students in the research feel lonely?

20. According to the study, how many students recovered from loneliness after a few months?

【试题解析】

第一部分 听力理解

1. 正确答案:D。女士问的是巧克力如何装到盒子里的,男士回答:"是由机器自动记数的",然后提出要带女士参观。从两个人的对话可以判断是在工厂里。

2. 正确答案:D。女士说:"我只迟到了7分钟,但因为课已开始,我就坐在外面看书了。"所以她是不想打断正在进行中的课。

3. 正确答案:B。女士说:"非常感谢,但我还有点晕车。"因此她是感到身体不适。

4. 正确答案:C。女士说:"一层的服务员给我指错了方向。"

5. 正确答案:B。女士说:"我冻死了。"可见天气很冷。

6. 正确答案:B。女士说:"设想你有一个女儿,你在乎她与谁交友吗?"可以看出这位女士把她的猫看成是自己的女儿。

7. 正确答案:D。女士说:"我想我不会比你知道得多,但我会尽力的。"说明她觉得自己恐怕帮不了什么忙。

8. 正确答案:A。男士说:"请等一等,我们会叫你的号的。"

9. 正确答案:A。女士说:"可惜我回家太晚了,没有赶上看。"她用的是动词 watch,所以是指电视。

10. 正确答案:D。女士说:"我上周在给房子粉刷时,梯子把它(窗)给碰了。"

11. 正确答案:D。文章中有这么一句:"But there are many groups and competition is sharp. Groups appear and disappear almost overnight."(但是这样的团体很多,竞争也很激烈。这样的团体会在一夜之间出现和消失。)

12. 正确答案:C。文章中有这么一句:"They have to pay a manager, for example. He is the key person in their lives and he takes about 20% of their earnings——perhaps more."(如他们得付钱给他们的经理。他是他们生活中的关键人物,拿走他们20%的收入——或许更多。)

13. 正确答案:B。这是一个有关全文的问题,需要从文章中的许多细节中概括。文章中讲到他们面临激烈的竞争,成名得快,衰败得也快,还得支付经理高额的费用,等等。从这些细节来看歌星的生活是很艰难的。

14. 正确答案:A。文章第一段中有这么一句:"One of these places is Alaska, the largest state in America."明确说明Alaska是美国最大的州。对这一题的解答提示考生:答题一定要根据所听到的内容,不能凭常识。

15. 正确答案:A。文章第一段中有这么一句话:"To help settlers, the government will give each pioneer a huge piece of land free."(为了帮助定居者,政府无偿提供给每一个开拓者一大块地。)

16. 正确答案:B。文章第三段中有这么一句话:"However, during June and July, the sun shines both night and day, and some crops grow rapidly."(然而,六七月间,太阳日夜照射,一些作物长得很快。)

17. 正确答案:B。文章第二段中有这么一句话:"Most researchers agree that the loneliest people are between the ages of 18 and 25, so a group of psychologists decided to study a group of college freshmen."(大部分研究人员认为最感孤独的人是那些18岁到25岁之间的,因此一些心理学家决定将一群大学新生作为研究对象。)

18. 正确答案:A。文章第一段就说:"Many people feel lonely sometimes, but it usually only lasts between a few minutes and a few hours. This kind of loneliness is not serious. In fact, it is quite normal. However, for some people, loneliness can last for years."(许多人有时都会感到孤独,但这种孤独通常只延续几分钟或几个小时。这种孤独感并无大碍,实际上,这是很正常的。然而,有些人的孤独感会持续几年。)说明持续几分钟或几个小时的孤独感是正常的,隐含的意思是:持续几年的孤独感就不正常了。

19. 正确答案:A。文章第二段中说道:"They found that more than 50% of the freshmen were lonely at the beginning of the semester as a result of their new circumstances, but had adjusted after a few months."(他们发现50%的大学新生由于不适应新的环境在学期之初感到孤独……)

20. 正确答案:D。"They found that more than 50% of the freshmen were lonely at the beginning of the semester as a result of their new circumstances, but had adjusted after a few months."(他们发现50%的新生由于不适应新的环境在学期之初感到孤独,但几个月后就好了。)

21. 正确答案:D。句意为:班长告诉老师有6名学生缺席时,老师发脾气了。

动词 lose 与 temptation 和 sense 不搭配。lose one's temper 的意思是 become angry(生气),lose one's mind 的意思是 become crazy(发疯)。从句子意思来看,老师是生气,而不是发疯。

22. 正确答案:A。句意为:我最近很忙,不知道谁当选美国总统了。

美国实行的是选举制,该选举用 election,而不用 choose 或 single out(挑选,选出)。短语 pick up 的意思是"拣起"。

23. 正确答案:D。句意为:真可惜,音乐会的票已经没有了。

approachable 的意思是"可接近的,可通达的";advisable 的意思是"可取的,适当的";accessible 的意思是"可进入的";available 的意思是"可获得的"。句中讲的是音乐会的票,因此应该用 available。

24. 正确答案:B。句意为:她小说读得那么入神,以至于没有听到铃声。

concentrate 与介词 on 搭配,表示"专心,专注";attract 常用于短语 attract somebody to something 或 be attracted to somebody 中;draw 在表示"吸引"这一意思时,常用于下列一些短语:draw (somebody's) attention 或 to draw attention to oneself。absorb 的用法是 be absorbed in something,因此从搭配来看应该用 absorb。

25. 正确答案:B。句意为:我看到这些老照片时,禁不住回忆起十年前发生的事。

remind 的意思是"提醒,使想起",指的是某个人或某样东西使人想起;recognize 的意思是"认出,识别";reserve 的意思是"保留,留出";recall 的意思是"回忆起,回想起",符合本句的意思。

26. 正确答案:A。句意为:公司承诺不遗余力与我们合作。

spare no efforts 是一个成语,意为"不遗余力"。save 和 share 都不能有这样的用法。make 可以与 efforts 搭配,但用在这里意思不对。

27. 正确答案:B。句意为:乍一看,这很简单。但实际上很复杂。

firstly 的意思是"首先",表示先后顺序;to begin with 的意思是"首先,第一",也表示先后顺序;from the beginning 的意思是"从一开始",不符合本句意思。at first sight 的意思是"乍一看,一见之下",符合本句意思。

28. 正确答案:B。句意为:这不是一个盛大的场合,所以我们可以穿得随意些。

formal 的意思是"正式的,正规的",意思恰好与句意相反;simple 只是表示"简单,朴素",不表示正式与否;plain 表示便服,与制服(uniform)相对;casual 的意思是"非正式的,不拘礼节的",符合本句意思。

29. 正确答案:A。句意为:电影、体育运动和音乐是不同形式的娱乐,有助于我们放松。

四个词的意思分别为:"娱乐","广告","承诺,许诺","协定,协议",所以选择 A。

30. 正确答案:D。句意为:技术人员的粗心导致了这场事故。

put off 的意思是"推迟"等;bring in 的意思是"引入,带进"等;lead into 的意思是"通向某个地方";result in 的意思是"导致"。因此选项 D 符合句子意思。

31. 正确答案:B。句意为:昨天我买了一条新领带来配这件绿色的衬衣。

go after 的意思是"追求,追逐";go with 的意思是"相配,协调"或"伴随"等;go on 的意思是

"发生,进行等";go by 的意思是"经过"或"依照,遵循"。

32．正确答案:B。句意为:老鼠正在与一只活的猫玩耍。
alive 的意思是"活着的,活生生的";live 可用作动词,也可用作形容词,作动词用的意思是"活着,生存",作形容词的意思是"活的,有生命的"或"(广播等)现场直播的,实况转播的";living 可用作名词,也可用作形容词,作名词用的意思是"生计",用于 make a living、earn a living 等短语中,作形容词的意思是"活(着)的",如 living relatives 等;lively 的意思是"灵敏的,活跃的"或"现存的,在使用中的",如 living language。

33．正确答案:A。句意为:简老是忘了她把东西放哪了。
typical 的意思是"典型的,有代表性的"或"表现出个性特征的,一向如此的";individual 可用作名词或形容词,用作名词的意思是"个人,个体",用作形容词的意思是"个别的,个人的"或"独特的";peculiar 的意思是"奇怪的,古怪的"或"特有的,独特的";particular 的意思是"特定的,某一的","特殊的,特别的"或"挑剔的"等,也可以作为名词,意思是"详情,细目",作名词时通常用复数。

34．正确答案:B。句意为:星期天上午妈妈乘着天好洗东西。
该句的考点是动词 take 与名词搭配所构成的短语,take 与 chance 不搭配;take 可与 effect 搭配,意思是"生效,起作用";take 可与 interest 搭配,构成短语 take interest in something,意思是"对……感兴趣";take 与 advantage 搭配,构成短语 take advantage of,意思是"利用,占……的便宜",符合本句意思。

35．正确答案:C。句意为:病人感到好多了,所以医生建议他去海边度假。
suggest 的意思是"建议",要用虚拟语气,即 suggest (that) somebody (should) do something,也可表示"暗示,使人想起";consider 的意思是"考虑";advise 的意思是"建议",用法是 advise somebody to do something;accept 的意思是"接受","承认,同意"等。

36．正确答案:A。句意为:尝尝我特地为你做的蛋糕。
bake 的意思是"烘,烤",cook 的意思是"煮,烧",或作为名词,意思是"厨师";fry 的意思是"油炸,油煎",boil 的意思是"煮沸,烹煮"。烤蛋糕要用 bake。

37．正确答案:B。句意为:老师告诉学生要定期复习功课。
proper 的意思是"适合的,恰当的","合乎体统的,正当的"等;regular 的意思是"规则的,有规律的"或"定期的,固定的"等;adequate 的意思是"充足的,足够的"或"胜任的";moderate 的意思是"中等的,一般的"或"温和的,稳健的"等。

38．正确答案:D。句意为:讲点道理,你不能指望这么小的孩子自己去完成所有这一切。
honest 的意思是"诚实的";serious 的意思是"认真的"或"严肃的"等;logical 的意思是"符合逻辑的,合乎常理的";reasonable 的意思是"合理的,有道理的"或"通情达理的,讲道理的"等。

39．正确答案:A。句意为:你得买双新鞋了,这双已经破了。
wear out 的意思是"穿破,用坏"或"(使)疲乏,(使)厌倦"等;break down 的意思是"垮掉,崩溃"等;use up 的意思是"用光";sell out 的意思是"卖光"。

40．正确答案:B。句意为:这幅画不是真的,所以一文不值。
priceless 的意思是"贵重的,无法估价的";worthless 的意思是"无价值的,无用的";valuable 的意思是"贵重的,有价值的";invaluable 的意思是"极为有用的,价值高得无法估量的"。四个词中只有一个是表示没有价值的,即 worthless。

41. 正确答案:B。句意为:我今天晚上绝对不可能出席晚会。

    本题的一个考点是 by no means 这个短语后面需要用倒装,另一个考点是句型 it is + adj. + to do sth.。C 选项中没有动词 be,A、D 选项都没有倒装。因此选 B。

42. 正确答案:A。句意为:玛丽在火车上时,她那装有三张信用卡和 2000 美元的手提包被偷了。

    该题所考的语法点有两个:一个是 Mary's handbag with three credit cards and two thousand dollars 中的主干部分是 handbag,是一个单数概念,three credit cards and two thousand dollars 是包中的内容,因此后面还是要用单数;另一个考点是时态,句子讲述的是一个过去某一时间(即在火车上)发生的某一个行为,因此用一般过去式就可以了,因此选 A。

43. 正确答案:B。句意为:人类之所以优于动物是因为人类能够用语言这个工具进行交际。

    该题的考点是句子之间的逻辑关系。句子前半部分说 human beings are superior to animals(人类优于动物),后半部分是解释原因。A、C 选项后面所跟的均是定语从句,用来修饰前面的先行词,不符合本句意思。选项 D 在本句中无法解释,短语 in that 意为"因为,原因在于",符合本题意思。例:I've been lucky in that I have never had to worry about money.

44. 正确答案:C。句意为:你的手机该修了,你最好明天就去修。

    该题的考点是动词 need 的用法。need 用作动词表示"需要"时,后接名词(如:The soup needs more salt.)或用于以下表达:sth. needs doing / sth. needs to be done(如:The house needs painting. / The house needs to be painted.)手机需要修可以是 needs repairing 或 needs to be repaired,因此选 C。

45. 正确答案:D。句意为:到学期结束时我们肯定能学完 8 个单元。

    本题的考点是将来完成时。在 by 后接将来的某一个特定时间(如:by the end of this year, by the end of this month)时要用将来完成时。

46. 正确答案:B。句意为:你花在英语学习上的时间决定你能学到什么程度。

    该题的考点是主谓一致。本句的主语是 How many hours you spend in learning English,这要作为一个整体来看,所有后面应该用单数,据此可以排除选项 A。另外这个主语后面应该用一个谓语动词,因此 C、D 选项不对。

47. 正确答案:B。句意为:雨下得很大,我倒希望你没有来接我。

    该题的考点是虚拟语气在从句中的用法。在 would rather, had rather 之后的从句中,谓语动词要用虚拟语气,而这种虚拟语气须用动词的过去式表示。因此,选项 B,did not come 是答案。例:He would rather you came on Friday. 他更希望你星期五来。

48. 正确答案:B。句意为:他们都很累了,但是没有一个人愿意停下来休息。

    该题的考点是代词的用法。any 和 some 都表示肯定,不符合本句意思。Neither 只能用于"(两者之中)无一个",因此选 B。

49. 正确答案:A。句意为:电视是另一种主要的交际手段,使我们能够看到并听到表演者所说的。

    该题的考点有两个:一个是表示伴随的独立结构,另一个是 as well as 前后应该用同样的结构,即 to see 和 to hear,因此选 A。

50. 正确答案:C。句意为:大雨停了,学生们继续植树。

该题的考点是独立结构。句子前半部分是独立结构,是后半部分的原因,即因为雨停了,所以学生们可以继续植树。

51. 正确答案:C。句意为:直到昨天我才知道这位著名的学者将要作一个 IT 产业方面的讲座。

该题的考点是 it is not until...that 的用法。这是一个固定用法,为加强语势结构,强调的是 until 后面的部分,意为"直到……才……"。例:It was not until I met her at the cafeteria that I learned about John's leaving. 直到我在餐厅碰到她我才知道约翰走的事。

52. 正确答案:B。句意为:学生犯错误时,老师应该告诉他如何改正,而不是惩罚他。

other than 的意思是"不同于"或"除了";rather than 的意思是"不是……而是";sooner than 是比较级;or rather 的意思是"或者"。选项 B 表示"不是……而是",符合本句意思。

53. 正确答案:C。句意为:他们说我不应该帮助他,但是我并不为自己做了我认为该做的事而后悔。

该题的考点是动词 regret 的用法。该词用作动词时的用法是:regret (doing) sth.（如:I now regret leaving school so young. 我现在后悔那么年轻就放弃了学业。）或 regret that（如:He was beginning to regret that he'd come along. 他开始后悔他来了。）或 regret to say/inform/tell（如:I regret to inform you that your contract will not be renewed. 我抱歉地告诉你,你的合同不再续了）。

54. 正确答案:C。句意为:当地政府接受了会议提出的改善公共交通的建议。

该题的考点是英语中表示建议的词的用法。动词 propose 及其相应的名词 proposal(建议)都要求从句中用虚拟语气。如:I propose that we discuss this at the next meeting. 我建议我们下一次会议讨论这个问题。又如:The proposal that the President should be directly elected was welcomed by everyone present. 需要直选总统的建议受到了与会者的一致欢迎。类似的词还有 suggest 及其相应的名词 suggestion。

55. 正确答案:B。句意为:看了该片的介绍后,我就不想去看电影了。

该题的考点是独立结构。这里的 having read the introduction to the film 是独立结构,是后半部分的原因,即我不想去看电影了。

56. 正确答案:C。句意为:能不能请你把窗子关上?

该题的考点是 so...as to 结构(如此……以致)。例:The particles are so small as to be almost invisible. 这些粒子小到几乎看不见。如果用 kind enough,后面应该用 to。例:Surely no one would be foolish enough to lend him the money? 当然,没有人会那么蠢,借钱给他。

57. 正确答案:D。句意为:街道的两边摆满了各种各样的花。

该题的考点是代词的用法。both 后面应跟复数,neither 表示"(两者之中)无一个",each 的意思是"两个以上中的各个",而 either 是表示"(两者之中)任一的,每一的"。Either 可用于 either side/end/hand 等,意思是 both sides, ends, hands 等。例:He sat in the back of the car with a policeman on either side. 他坐在车的后面,两边都有警察。

58. 正确答案:B。句意为:对不起,布朗先生出去了,我不知道他去哪里了。

该题的考点是宾语从句中的语序问题,即在宾语从句中用正常语序。例:I don't know why he came. 我不知道他为什么来。Do you know what time it is? 你知道现在几点了吗?

59. 正确答案:A。句意为:问到他上次为什么缺席时,他只是盯着我,什么也没说。

该题的考点是被动语态以及状语从句的用法。该句的状语从句完整的应该是:When he was asked why he was absent last time,这里 he was 省略了。

60. 正确答案:A。句意为:我们得等很久才能拿到签证,是吗?

该题的考点是反意疑问句。反意疑问句附着在陈述句之后,对陈述句所说的事实或观点提出疑问。这种疑问句由助动词或情态动词加主语(常与陈述句的主语相同)构成,陈述句部分如果用肯定,则疑问句部分用否定,反之亦然。本题的陈述句中用的是动词 have,即 do 的过去式,而且是肯定,所以疑问句部分用 do 的过去式,并用否定。

第四部分　阅读理解

第一篇短文参考译文及语言注释

在一些国家,90%的成年人每天至少读一份报纸。纯粹从商业的角度来看,很少有产品能够像报纸那样占领市场。为什么有那么多人读报纸呢?

报纸的基本功能有五个:提供信息、发表评论、说服读者、引导读者、给读者带来娱乐。你完全有理由认为所列的五种功能是以其重要性来排序的,但是,如果真是那样的话,你会与大多数读者的意见相左。在两大类报纸——通俗报纸和优质报纸——中,前者有成百万上千万的读者,而后者只有成千上万。而通俗的报纸似乎主要是娱乐性的,其中有大量的评论性和具有说服力的语言。优质报纸则非常重视其所提供的信息,娱乐的成分要少些。

两种报纸的差别不仅仅在内容上,文章的风格也有所不同。通俗报纸通常用更多的戏剧性的语言,有许多的语言妙用。这些报纸的记者往往使用简短的句子,避免不常用的词汇。这意味着通俗报纸更容易被本族语读者所理解,当然,非本族语者可能还是会看不懂。

要确定一份报纸是优质的还是通俗的,你甚至不用去读,因为你可以简单地从报纸的外观来判断。通俗报纸通常小一些,文章量少而短,但是它们的标题较大,且有较多的图片。

试题解答

61. 正确答案:C。文章第一段第一句是这样的:In some countries as many as nine out of ten adults read at least one newspaper a day. 十个人中有九个人每天至少读一份报纸。

62. 正确答案:D。文章第二段讲到报纸的五大功能之一就是给读者带来娱乐,这是点题之句。用排除法也可以答对这道题。选项 A 说的是通俗报纸刊载文章多,图片少,与文章最后一句话不符。选项 B 说通俗报纸的意图是教育读者,文章中找不到依据。文章第二段最后一句描述优质报纸的特点时提到:优质报纸则非常重视其所提供的信息,娱乐的成分要少些。由此可以排除 C。

63. 正确答案:B。这是一道考查考生从上下文猜测词义的题。在短语 of the two broad categories of newspaper 后面文章紧接着提到两类报纸,即通俗的和优质的,因此可以推断 category 的意思是类别。所以选 B。

64. 正确答案:A。这道题问的是优质报纸的读者群。鉴于优质报纸的特点,即"优质报纸非常重视其所提供的信息,娱乐的成分要少些",外国游客、体育迷、家庭妇女是不太会感兴趣的。因此选 A。

65. 正确答案:A。文章最后一段主要说两种报纸的差别,即在外观、厚薄及风格方面。因此选 A。

第二篇短文参考译文及语言注释

"这对我的伤害超过对你的伤害","这是为你好,"这些是多年前我不得不学拉丁文、打扫自己的房间和做家庭作业时我妈妈常说的话。

那是在我们进入教育的宽容放任阶段之前。在教育的宽容放任阶段,我们认为不逼迫我们孩子在学校竭尽全力是对的。学校以及教育者们都对我们很宽容,他们教育我们:作为父母采取放任自流的政策就行了。我们不再要我们孩子做家庭作业,我们给他们计算器,打开电视机,把教育的任务交给老师,而我们去度我们的假。

现在,面对这些在过去的15年以其自身的节奏在发展的孩子们,老师们意识到我们犯了一个可怕的错误。持这种观点的老师之一是莎伦·克伦普斯,她说她的学生是"那么被动",她不知道是怎么回事。她认为是由于对学生太宽容了。克伦普斯说电视造成了孩子的被动。她说:"我们不再训练我们的孩子工作,我们所谈论的是一代没有受过伤害、没有挨过饿的孩子。他们知道总有人会帮他们做的。你不是告诉他们'去查一查',而是直接把答案给了他们。对孩子说'不'是要花精力的。"

没错,这需要花精力,还需要努力。该是父母们结束度假回到教育孩子的工作上来的时候了。是拿走他们的汽车、关掉电视、告诉他们这对你的伤害超过对他们的伤害、是为他们自己好的时候了。是开始对他们说"不"的时候了。

试题解答

66. 正确答案:A。文章第二段中讲到教育的宽容放任阶段的特点时有这么一句话:They taught that it was all right to be parents who take a let-alone policy. 选项A就是对这句话的解释。

67. 正确答案:D。文章第三段讲到克伦普斯对她学生的评价时提到她的学生"很被动……我们不再训练我们的孩子工作……他们知道总有人会帮他们做的……"这一切都说明这些孩子懒惰,而且被宠坏了。

68. 正确答案:B。该题可以用排除法来得到答案,把正确的排除就可以了。选项A说的是孩子们可以看电视,选项C说的是孩子有汽车,选项D说的是孩子们可以做家庭作业,也可以不做,根据文章的最后一段我们可以看出这些都是事实,是作者呼吁要改变的因此选择B。而且文章中第三段中也明确提到在过去的15年中孩子们以其自身的节奏在发展。

69. 正确答案:C。这一题考查的是对全文的理解。文章中指出对孩子宽容、溺爱的危害,从而指出家长应该对孩子严格,也就是文章最后一段的意思。

70. 正确答案:D。对这个问题的回答需要考生理解全文。第一段中讲到作者的母亲曾经对他说的话,最后一段作者发出呼吁,要父母们对孩子严格些,并说该是对孩子们说第一段中作者的母亲曾对他说过的那些话的时候了。这说明作者认为他母亲的教育方法是可取的、明智的。

第三篇短文参考译文及语言注释

在她孩提时代,雷切尔对自然和写作表现出了兴趣。中学毕业后她进入了宾夕法尼亚州立女子学院,希望成为一名作家。然而,她转学了生物,因此也就设定了她的生活轨迹。(后来)雷切尔进入约翰·霍普金斯大学继续学习,并成了马里兰大学的动物学教师。

十五年来,雷切尔任职于美国渔业和野生动物中心,同时还写作、编辑出版物。所幸的是她的老板鼓励她写作。雷切尔所写的关于海洋的三本书中诗一般的写作风格捕捉到了普通读者的想象力。她那集自然科学家与天才作家于一身的罕见的才能使她的作品《我们周围的海》获得了全国图书奖。

雷切尔的下一本书使她成了保护自然环境的领军人物。她开始写《静静的春天》,尽管她知道这会招致人们对她的攻击,她会被人们嘲弄。她虚弱的身体减缓了她的写作进程,但她还是坚持写作。该书完成后,她在给她朋友的信中写道:"我感到有一种义务要做我能做的,如果我连试都不试一下,那在我身处自然界时我再也不会感到幸福。但现在我相信我至少做了一点。"

雷切尔·卡森所做的不只是一点。尽管政府和产业界都反对她,公共健康方面的专家、媒体以及公众都支持她为反对不负责任地使用杀虫剂所做的努力。她的书最终导致政府对DDT发出禁令。

试题解答

71. 正确答案:B。文章第二段最后一句话中提到她是一位自然科学家,又是一位天才作家,因此选择 B。

72. 正确答案:B。文章中提到她写了三本有关海洋的书,在第三段中又提到了她的下一本书,即《静静的春天》。因此可以判断她至少写了四本书。

73. 正确答案:B。文章第三段描述的是她的作品《静静的春天》。文章中提到政府和产业界的反对,因此选项 A 可以排除。第二段中提到她写的三本关于海洋的书,由此可以排除选项 C。她的书《静静的春天》使她成了保护自然环境的领军人物,但没有说这本书是涉及环境保护的。而在第三段中提到写《静静的春天》时她身体虚弱,因此减缓了写作进程。因此选择 B。

74. 正确答案:D。这是一道考查考生从上下文猜测词义的题。从上下文来看《静静的春天》带给她的是诸如攻击那样的负面影响,因此选项 A、B、D 均可以排除,所以选择 C。

75. 正确答案:C。文章最后一段开始说政府和产业界都反对她,文章最后一句话说道:她的书最终导致政府对 DDT 发出禁令。因此可以得出结论:政府是被迫对 DDT 发出禁令的。

第五部分　英译汉

76. 记忆可以被定义为一种储存日后可用信息的能力。

77. 老鼠由于在一堆粮食中嗅到了某种可疑的东西而不去吃那粮食时,那就是记忆在起作用。

78. 不仅人类与动物有记忆,一些物体和机器也有记忆。

79. 然而,这只是一个十几岁孩子所储存的所有信息中的很小一部分。

80. 语言的使用是人类高级的解决问题能力的基础。

第六部分　汉译英

81. The cinema where we saw the film yesterday is the best one in town.

82. The experiment showed/shows that everything in the world is in motion.

83. In the middle of the month, Dad sent/gave me a computer for my birthday/as my birthday gift.

84. The West Lake today is no longer what it used to be some years ago.

85. I was ill several days ago, otherwise I would have come to see you earlier/sooner.

试 卷 答 案

2002 年 1 月试卷答案

1.C 2.A 3.C 4.B 5.C 6.C 7.C 8.B 9.B 10.A
11.B 12.B 13.A 14.D 15.B 16.A 17.A 18.D 19.A 20.C
21.A 22.D 23.C 24.B 25.B 26.A 27.D 28.A 29.D 30.A
31.C 32.B 33.A 34.B 35.A 36.C 37.B 38.C 39.A 40.A
41.D 42.C 43.A 44.C 45.B 46.B 47.C 48.A 49.A 50.B
51.B 52.C 53.D 54.D 55.A 56.C 57.C 58.D 59.D 60.A
61.D 62.C 63.B 64.A 65.A 66.D 67.B 68.B 69.B 70.C
71.C 72.C 73.B 74.D 75.A

2002 年 6 月试卷答案

1.D 2.B 3.C 4.B 5.B 6.B 7.D 8.D 9.B 10.D
11.C 12.C 13.D 14.C 15.B 16.B 17.A 18.B 19.D 20.D
21.C 22.A 23.B 24.A 25.D 26.C 27.D 28.C 29.B 30.D
31.A 32.B 33.C 34.B 35.A 36.B 37.D 38.C 39.D 40.D
41.A 42.B 43.C 44.B 45.D 46.B 47.C 48.B 49.D 50.A
51.D 52.D 53.C 54.A 55.A 56.A 57.B 58.C 59.B 60.B
61.B 62.A 63.D 64.C 65.B 66.B 67.A 68.B 69.C 70.D
71.C 72.C 73.A 74.A 75.D

2003 年 1 月试卷答案

1.B 2.D 3.A 4.A 5.C 6.A 7.C 8.B 9.D 10.C
11.B 12.D 13.A 14.C 15.B 16.B 17.C 18.B 19.A 20.D
21.B 22.D 23.D 24.A 25.C 26.A 27.A 28.B 29.D 30.D
31.A 32.C 33.D 34.B 35.C 36.C 37.A 38.B 39.A 40.C
41.A 42.D 43.D 44.C 45.C 46.C 47.D 48.C 49.D 50.A
51.A 52.A 53.B 54.C 55.A 56.D 57.B 58.C 59.B 60.B
61.A 62.C 63.A 64.B 65.D 66.C 67.A 68.B 69.B 70.A
71.C 72.D 73.D 74.B 75.A

2003 年 6 月试卷答案

1.B 2.C 3.C 4.A 5.C 6.D 7.B 8.A 9.C 10.D
11.A 12.B 13.D 14.D 15.B 16.A 17.A 18.B 19.C 20.D
21.D 22.A 23.B 24.A 25.C 26.D 27.B 28.B 29.A 30.B

31.C　32.A　33.C　34.D　35.B　36.C　37.C　38.A　39.D　40.B

41.D　42.A　43.C　44.B　45.C　46.A　47.D　48.C　49.A　50.D

51.A　52.B　53.C　54.D　55.A　56.B　57.D　58.C　59.B　60.B

61.C　62.A　63.D　64.D　65.B　66.C　67.B　68.D　69.B　70.A

71.A　72.D　73.C　74.A　75.B

2004年1月试卷答案

1.C　2.D　3.D　4.B　5.A　6.A　7.C　8.A　9.B　10.B

11.B　12.D　13.C　14.A　15.D　16.D　17.B　18.A　19.B　20.C

21.A　22.C　23.B　24.C　25.B　26.B　27.B　28.D　29.B　30.D

31.A　32.A　33.B　34.C　35.B　36.A　37.C　38.C　39.A　40.D

41.B　42.C　43.A　44.B　45.D　46.A　47.B　48.D　49.D　50.A

51.C　52.B　53.D　54.A　55.C　56.A　57.D　58.B　59.C　60.A

61.C　62.A　63.A　64.C　65.D　66.C　67.B　68.D　69.A　70.D

71.A　72.C　73.D　74.B　75.A

2004年6月试卷答案

1.D　2.C　3.A　4.B　5.A　6.B　7.D　8.B　9.B　10.D

11.C　12.C　13.B　14.D　15.C　16.B　17.B　18.D　19.A　20.D

21.C　22.B　23.B　24.B　25.D　26.B　27.C　28.A　29.B　30.C

31.D　32.A　33.B　34.C　35.B　36.B　37.C　38.D　39.A　40.D

41.B　42.D　43.B　44.A　45.D　46.C　47.B　48.C　49.B　50.A

51.D　52.A　53.B　54.B　55.A　56.D　57.B　58.D　59.B　60.B

61.C　62.A　63.B　64.D　65.D　66.C　67.A　68.C　69.C　70.A

71.B　72.A　73.B　74.D　75.C

2005年1月试卷答案

1.D　2.D　3.B　4.C　5.B　6.B　7.D　8.A　9.A　10.D

11.D　12.C　13.B　14.A　15.A　16.B　17.B　18.A　19.A　20.D

21.D　22.A　23.D　24.B　25.B　26.A　27.B　28.B　29.A　30.D

31.B　32.B　33.A　34.B　35.C　36.A　37.B　38.D　39.A　40.B

41.B　42.A　43.B　44.C　45.D　46.B　47.B　48.B　49.A　50.C

51.C　52.B　53.C　54.C　55.B　56.C　57.D　58.B　59.A　60.A

61.C　62.D　63.B　64.A　65.A　66.A　67.D　68.B　69.C　70.D

71.B　72.B　73.B　74.D　75.C